MARCEL HOLT

The Dawn Age Blight

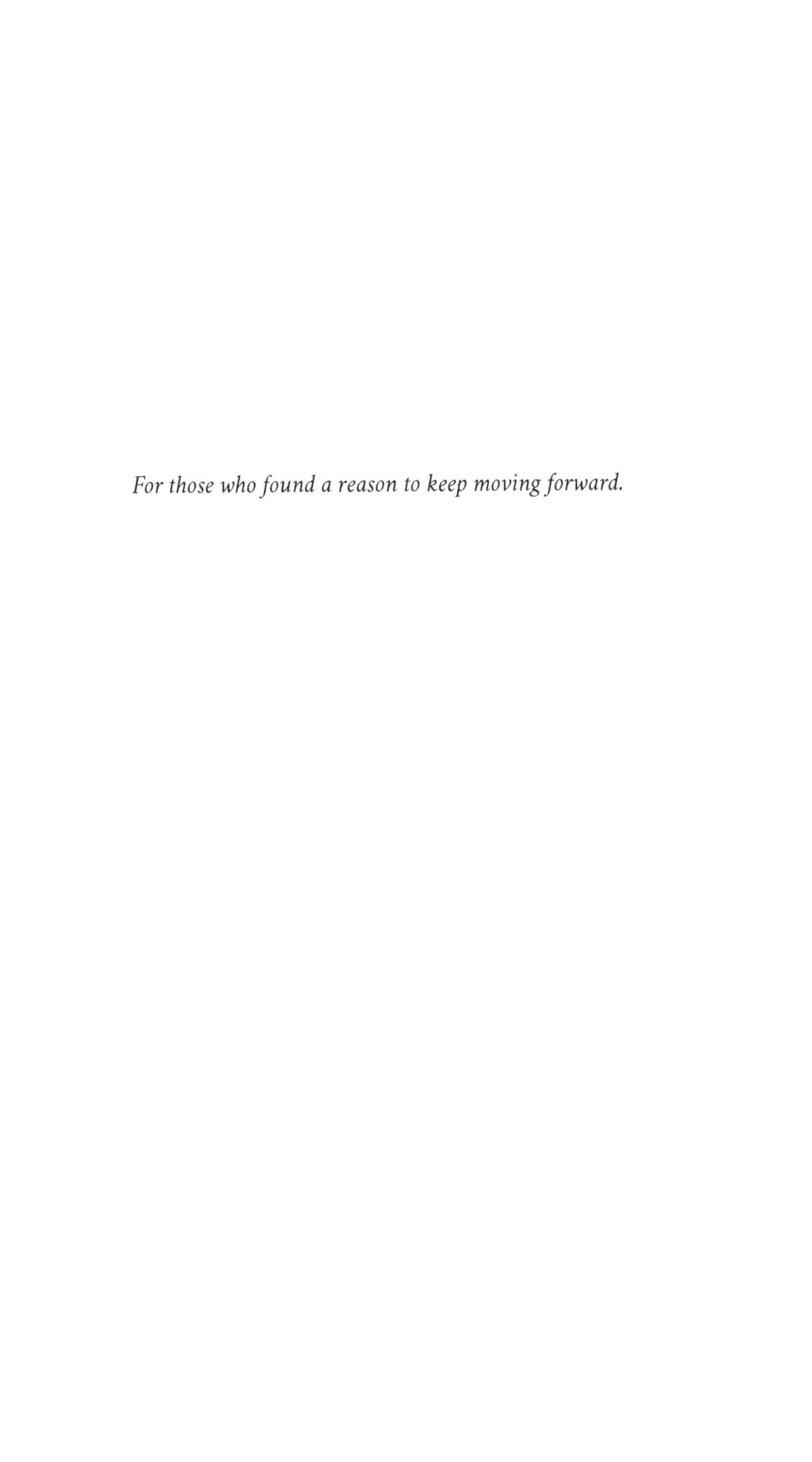

For those who found a reason to keep moving forward.

Content Warning

Though this book is a work of fiction, it addresses some very real topics that may be disturbing to some readers. I've done countless hours of research and reflection on my own personal experiences to deliver these sensitive themes with the respect and accuracy they deserve. The following subjects in this work include but are not limited to:

- Generalized violence
- Two instances of transphobic comments
- Mentioned child neglect
- Mild body horror
- Body dysmorphia through a fantasy lens (not to be confused with gender dysphoria)
- Implication of suicidal ideation
- Mentions of human trafficking through a fantasy lens
- Generalized creepy comments from men
- Xenophobia

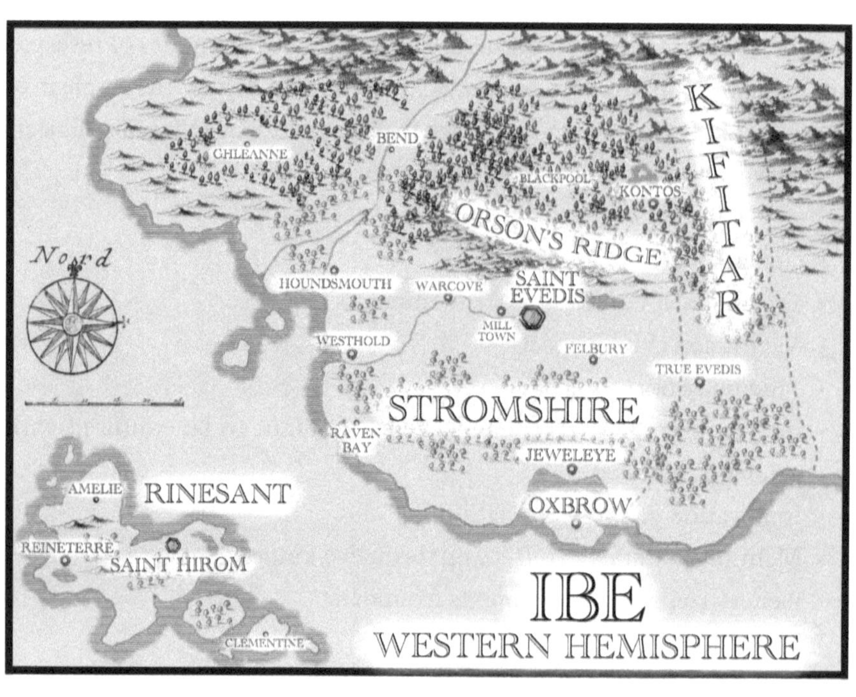

Nord
CHLEANNE
BEND
BLACKPOOL
KONTOS
KIFITAR
ORSON'S RIDGE
HOUNDSMOUTH
WARCOVE
SAINT EVEDIS
MILL TOWN
FELBURY
WESTHOLD
TRUE EVEDIS
STROMSHIRE
RAVEN BAY
JEWELEYE
AMELIE
RINESANT
OXBROW
REINETERRE
SAINT HIROM
IBE
WESTERN HEMISPHERE
CLEMENTINE

Prologue

Asaph made the journey many times before, but it never got any easier. He hid under his hood until he passed city limits, traveling deep into the woods.

He was taught from childhood to always watch his back for followers. In this business, one could never be too careful. To his fortune, folklore deemed these woods 'cursed,' since the era of the exalted Saint Evedis. His time in believing in curses had long since passed, and found it helpful for deep-seeded fear to keep prying eyes away.

Mist began to gather– he was getting close. Each step he took required extra effort to pull his feet from the muck. He purchased tall, thick boots just for this part of the job. Even still he felt as the cold seeped into his bones.

The air grew heavy, but he tread on until he could not anymore— not from exhaustion, but instead a physical barrier. An impenetrable, opaque wall of fog loomed before him.

Asaph pulled a stone from his pocket. When he was given the stone at the start of the job, he figured it to be the brunt of an inside joke. Now understanding the token, he marveled at its power and otherworldly appearance. The solid black stone fit in the palm of his hand. Like an uncut gem it held uneven faces and edges. No matter how the light hit the stone, no reflection could be seen.

Asaph presented the stone to the fog, and the wall gave in.

The change was instant. The world around him rearranged, as if mirrored but something felt fundamentally *off.*

Asaph considered the phenomenon before him could be seen as a piece of myth or legend, and technically it was. But legends held no scientific reason. Legends were not a place of business deals.

It did not take much longer for Asaph to reach the laboratory. It was part of his contract as the Collector to bring in rare materials for the laboratory staff, most namely Professor Mila Bastel.

Asaph was grateful to work closest to Bastel– She was not one for riveting conversation beyond alchemical processes. But when she spoke, she was genuine. A rarity in Asaph's line of work.

Most often Asaph arrived at a vacant laboratory. No one worked as many hours as Bastel did.

Professor Bastel heard Asaph as his heavy steps ascended into her wing of the laboratory.

"You should know better than to bring those filthy boots in here, Collector," Bastel said, "I've half a mind to set my dogs on you."

"Is that what you're calling them now?" Asaph asked.

"I'm open to other suggestions," She answered, "I assume you have my samples?"

"No other reason why I'd be here."

"Really? Not even to see me?"

"Seems an awfully long commute for a 'hello' and to watch you clean beakers."

Asaph pulled a secured case onto one of her worktables and unlatched the locks. He opened the case to reveal little glass vials full of opaque liquid. He ran a hand over the vials. They emitted a soft glow in a spectrum of colors, reddish violets, blues, and greens.

"Stunning variety…." Bastel mused.

"There's certainly more where that came from, if your boss remembers to pay me."

"Don't shoot the messenger, but I'd expect another delay in payment. He's currently dealing with some internal disputes."

Asaph sighed, fiddling with a stray pipette, "I heard. One of his acolytes conspired against him, correct?"

Bastel faltered for a moment, "I wouldn't so confidently gab about such a secretive topic around here if I were you."

"If I heard about it from the other side of the veil, it's not much of a secretive topic, is it?" Bastel said nothing. "Your silence speaks volumes."

"The people from Ibe seem to be far too bold for their own good..." Bastel noted, half to herself, "If I show you my newest project will it get you to shut up?"

"Certainly."

Professor Bastel led Asaph to the innermost part of the laboratory, a large, vaulted room with no windows. She showed him to a cage, one of many made of Ebian steel.

The only light came from lanterns along the hallway. The cage before Asaph remained very dark. A pair of glowing eyes met his own, then more illuminated.

Asaph took a step back, reaching for his blade as he was met with a writhing, white body lashing at the cage with needle-sharp teeth and claws. The monster's shriek was unlike anything Asaph had ever heard. Bastel appeared unphased, as she reviewed a chart adjacent to the monster's gaping maw.

"What... *is* that thing?" Asaph asked.

"Its genetic makeup is classified, even for you," Bastel answered, "But I invite you to take a guess."

"I've a few ideas..."

Bastel stepped even closer to the cage. She gave the beast a set of commands. Come. Sit. Watch. At ease. Asaph watched in awe as the monster followed each one perfectly.

"How did you get it to do that?" Asaph asked.

"The same way you train any other animal– though some physiological alterations helped with a few of the kinks."

The laboratory was quiet, save for the monster's heavy breaths.

"... Collector? Is something the matter?"

Asaph felt a smile creep along his face.

"No. It's *perfect*. When will the others be ready?"

1

Chapter 1

Ber carved another line in the wall as the day crept to an end. The fog appeared about the same regardless of the hour, but he grew perceptive to the subtlest of changes. What sparse vegetation that survived here rotated its shriveled leaves at the little light that trickled in. Most notably, different beasts would come out at every 'dawn' and 'dusk.'

During his time here– two months, three weeks, and five days, to be exact– Ber learned how to best avoid them. He learned the paths to take, the best methods to mask his scent, and how to silence each step.

But with each day, he would deviate from one of his set paths. He added his findings to a map. He expanded his findings, little by little, in hopes to escape his prison.

He had found the barriers of the fog a few times before, but each location was the same. The barriers appeared from the blinding mist as a stark, white wall that extended out to the heavens. He tried everything to get past those walls. He cringed as he remembered passing out from exhaustion, wailing on the first barrier he came across. Ber learned the hard way by waking up below a beast's jagged, hungry maw, how to be methodical. When he found a new piece of the barrier, he walked along it to find weaknesses, abnormalities, anything he could exploit.

Today was no different. He returned to his 'home' to record his findings, an abandoned cottage that hugged the bend of a creek. It consisted of wood panels stained by age and moisture. He entered through what was left of the door.

He set his gear aside. The hunger pains were setting in. He steeled himself to focus on adding to the map, while his memory was still fresh. Once he finished, he took a step back from the large parchment. The walls of the fog still held no definitive shape, and there were no signs of escape.

Not yet, Ber kept telling himself, *Gods help me, I'll leave this place or die trying.*

Ber sighed, resigning himself to prepare a meal. He was fortunate enough to come across a house with so many supplies, but he refrained from eating into the nonperishables. He pulled a sizable catfish from his bag and made quick work of cleaning it.

Most standard animals did not enter the fog. Nearly all that did did not last long.

Before he could eat, he heard a knocking at the window.

"Like clockwork…" Ber said, "I wonder what you could be here for?"

He opened the window to lone, soggy crow. An odd exclusion to the rule, crows tended to come and go from the fog as they pleased. The bird shook off the rain and cawed at him. Ber offered the innards to the bird.

"I shouldn't be feeding you. A lone crow's bad luck."

The crow ignored him as it shoveled down bits of catfish. Ber enjoyed its company. Bad luck or not, it was one of the few creatures in the fog that did not try to kill him.

The bird stopped. It tilted its head, eyeing past Ber and towards the door. The bird called louder than before, the tone Ber recognized as a warning call. He launched himself from his chair turning to the doorway to find a new visitor.

Another monster... Ber was used to fog's beasts preying upon him, and learned how to put them out of their miserable existence. But this one was alone, and beasts this small never challenged him alone.

Ber wasted no time. He threw a dagger at the beast's skull. It dodged the blade but found itself cornered. It bared its teeth and snarled low. Ber approached, readying another dagger.

Before Ber could dispatch the monster, his other visitor made a surprise appearance. The crow swooped down between the monster's front legs. For a moment, Ber could have *sworn* the monster looked just as puzzled as he was.

The monster examined the bird curiously. It no longer snarled, but it returned to watching Ber's every move with glowing, amber eyes.

This was new. Most abominations trapped with him in this fog showed a cold and calculating kind of intelligence, but this one showed something starkly different.

Could this be one of Ibe's beast? Or maybe...? Ber took a chance. He sheathed his dagger.

"Well hello, beastie," He said, trying his hand at Ibean tongue.

It snarled in response. Ber backed away.

"Come now," He continued, "No need to be snappy. You look mean, but that must not be all true with that little bird hanging around you."

Ber backed away further, being sure not to turn his back to the creature.

"Come here, beast. I know you're cold and hungry."

Slowly he sat back in his chair. The crow perched beside Ber again. The creature hesitantly drew closer.

"How many more mouths will I have to feed around here?" Ber mused.

He gave a sizable piece of catfish to the creature. It spent no time devouring the piece whole. *Maybe this thing is just an animal,* Ber considered.

The fog proved to be a desolate and lonely place. Whatever it was, it was nice to have someone to talk to. Even if this someone could rip his face off in a moment's notice.

"I may have been a bit ill-tempered with you," Ber continued to the beast, "I'm sorry. Being in the fog for so long does things to you– though I'm sure I don't need to tell *you* that."

The beast sat and appeared to listen. Ber examined it in detail in the fire's light. It stood at the height of a large dog, and was covered in black fur and scales. It's head held a mouthful of sharp teeth and a pair of piercing eyes that glowed like embers. The body did not seem complete, as parts of it were gaseous, drifting in and out of its solid form.

Ber caught a glint of light from the creature's neck. He leaned just a bit closer, and the creature snarled again. It looked to be a delicately woven trinket with an odd charm obscured from the fur.

"No monster would have something pretty like that hanging around its neck. Were you someone's pet...?" Ber chuckled at a horrid, discomforting thought, "Who even knows, perhaps at one point you might have been a person."

The creature stiffened. Its eyes met his. He felt his stomach drop– a shiver ran down his spine as he wondered just how much intelligence, how much memory this beast retained. How much humanity did the others have?

The necklace caught his attention again.

"That... thing around your neck, may I see it for a minute?"

The creature appeared to consider the favor for a moment. With a huff it struggled to remove the necklace before clumsily sliding it to Ber.

Ber marveled at the necklace, lifting it delicately. He paid special attention to the stone at its center. No matter what angle he held it at, the stone showed no refraction of light. The stone emitted a smoke-like aura. It encased Ber's arm like a sleeve. His eyes widened as he recognized what he now held in his possession, and flashed a wide, toothy grin. Relief rushed through his body so fast, he fell into a laughter that erred on the side of maniacal. The beast's ears pinned back in response.

"How did you...! Y'know what? I won't question a *very* good thing. I'm not sure how you got hold of something like this, but this is how I get out of here!" Ber kneeled to his guest, "If you allow me to part with this necklace, I can lead you out as well. Have we got a deal, beastie?"

The creature proved difficult to read. Ber wondered what it was thinking behind those glowing eyes. After a pause the creature nodded hesitantly, a gesture that ran a shiver down Ber's spine.

"...We'd best be on our way then, yeah?"

Together the pair set off to the barrier. The creature followed behind Ber in complete silence. The two stayed in the shadows as they trekked, their heads on a swivel for what might be lurking.

The beast stopped. Ber could feel its stillness and followed suit. For a moment, he wondered if this was the beast's ploy to get the drop on him, then he saw what it saw. From the brush emerged a large, pale beast. Its antlers were twisted, no longer a crown but a cage around its head and shoulders. Ber and the beast lay deathly still until it passed, praying it did not pick up their scent.

After a few excruciating minutes, it moved on. The two continued on their path and up the hill.

Ber halted to catch his breath. Just ahead stood the barrier. Dim beams of light from the other side were just barely visible, like peering through a filthy window.

"Alright," Ber said steadily, "You're going to have to trust me on this: I need to go in first so I can lead you through. Is that okay?"

The beast took the thread from between his fingers. It held on and stepped forward, standing beside him.

"Oh, you want to go through together? I guess we can try it that way…"

Holding the necklace together, they passed through the barrier and out of the fog.

2

Chapter 2

Nora emerged just outside the fog's barrier. The sun's gentle light weaved through the trees and danced on her body. She sat up, realizing she was human once more.

She looked at her slender hands. They changed to an ashen black up to the wrist. Regardless, she relished feeling the day's warmth in her returned form.

She took a brief moment to look around for the odd man that accompanied her. The place she emerged into wasn't at all like the place she entered the fog from. Far off lay the unconscious man she met in the fog. He had fallen face down onto the pale earth.

Nora sighed. She figured she would do him one more favor before taking her leave and roll him out of the dirt. She used the heel of her worn boot to flip over his body. The man jolted up, causing a layer of dust to float from his clothes.

"Just making sure you're awake so you don't get mugged out here." Nora said.

The man remained drowsed in confusion before taking in the stranger before him. Dark locks of disheveled curls drooped from Nora's shoulder. Intimidation pierced through him with her bitter, awfully familiar gaze.

"Wha—oh, thank you." The man paused, "Have we… Are you…?"

"Yes. That was me. I'd appreciate it if we don't bring it up again."

The man nodded. He picked himself up. He dusted himself off with his magic, a form of gust and clouds.

Nora stood back; even in absolute privacy, how could anyone be so carefree about magic? Aside from the already unusual situation, something about this man seemed especially strange. She assumed that the fog had impaired his judgment.

"Gods, it's gorgeous here…" He said, marveling at the environment outside the fog. The fog diluted the bordering land considerably, but it was still much more vibrant and beautiful than inside its walls.

"… How long were you in there?" Nora asked.

"Long enough," The man shrugged off the question. He gave into a wide grin, "Thank you so much for your help, you have my sincerest gratitude! Honestly, I'm not sure how much longer I could have stayed in there…" the man proceeded to ramble, and Nora failed to decipher what he was saying under such a strange accent. She wondered how difficult it would be to sneak away while he was talking. "…Oh, my name's Ber, by the way!" He smiled warmly and offered his hand.

Dark brown eyes matched the shade of his *atrocious* hair and thick, angled brows. His face was sunken, but there lay a subtle softness to it. Paired with his wide grin, his youth became much more obvious.

"Are you saying 'Bear?' Like a bear?"

"What's a bear?"

Oh boy.

"Nevermind. I'm Nora." She shook his hand with an err of caution. Her focus shifted the fog, its presence barricading her route as far as her eyes could see. Its grey and gaseous composition churned steadily. She could have sworn that it crept closer since she awoke. Ber turned to match her view.

"It's been… interesting, but I have to find my horse and leave." Nora said as she paced off.

"Your 'horse' wouldn't happen to be a dragon, would it?" Ber asked.

Nora turned and froze. She sensed that the man was just as suspicious as he was long winded. Her assumptions of something sinister in Ber grew.

"I saw a little one weaving in and out, searching for something, or someone. I can help you find 'em!"

"I appreciate it, but I'd rather find her on my own."

"It might not be that easy." He warned, "The fog can displace you very far off. Your beast's senses are compromised by the fog, so she's just as lost as we are. But, I have some ideas as to where she may be."

"Ber, was it?" Nora started, "To be blunt, why in the *hell* should I ever trust some forest cretin like you?"

"If I'm a forest cretin, what does that make you?" Ber sounded more curious than annoyed. It pissed Nora off even more.

"I'm not playing this game. You give me a reason or I'm walking."

Ber sighed. "… You're right. I can't give you any credible reason. Not anything you'd believe, anyway," He took a moment to think of an alternative. "Maybe instead, I can give you a bit of advantage over this situation."

Nora listened, despite her best judgment.

"… You're probably wondering why I was still human in the fog," He tugged at his worn collared shirt to reveal part of his shoulder. He revealed a thin patch of dark feathers protruding from his skin, "and you're probably wondering what this is. *This* is why I needed your necklace. If ya really want to know, you can snatch it from me any time, and you can run into town to fetch a pretty price for my head." He paused and took a deep breath, "I would really, *really* rather not have that happen."

Nora processed this man and his argument. The world she stumbled upon was a shady fairytale that she wanted no part in. Nora considered, however, that she was just as involved as Ber was, as much as she would hate to admit. She gave Ber some grace, for his attitude on the situation seemed far too foolish to be a legitimate threat, even if he was only showing a façade.

"… What do you want in return?" Nora asked, "Surely you wouldn't help me for free."

"If you wouldn't mind, could you help me to this city here? I believe it's not too far, so it wouldn't be a big hassle after we find your dragon."

Ber pulled out a map. The map was warped and *very* old, but the place Ber gestured to was undoubtedly Saint Evedis. *Of course.* Nora sighed.

"I suppose that's fine. I'm headed that way anyway," Nora said, immediately regretting the words leaving her mouth.

"Thank you! I won't let ya down, we'll find your dragon very soon, I'm sure." Ber said. He gathered his things and began to walk against the wind. "Let's get going!"

A sense of dread nested deep within Nora. A journey in solitude was one ordeal. But to her, she would rather be trampled by mammoth rams multiple times over than share this journey with a strange, talkative man. She immediately began to plot how to ditch Ber. She considered that it would not be too difficult once she found Lotte.

3

Chapter 3

Nora and Ber began to trek west, despite their final destination lying in the southeast. Ber spouted something about the area's wind patterns and beast behavior, but Nora couldn't understand much of what he was saying. As a result, she spaced out. A bitter taste lingered on her tongue from this nuisance hanging around, but she put aside her dissatisfaction to focus on the task at hand.

She considered that her accommodations could be worse. *He is offering to help me, after all,* Nora considered. Regardless, she found herself toying with the dagger hitched to her leg, making Ber visibly wary.

She realized that Ber had stopped talking, and enjoyed the peace. She took to observing her surroundings as she walked. Towering pines began to thin, giving way to open patches of bleached meadow grass. Ber too took in the landscape, appreciating the sun's dull warmth. The fog, not too far off, served an aching reminder to the two as to what may become of this land.

Just as Nora started to relax in the silence, Ber spoke up once again. She could feel her very life drain from her body.

"So, I'm guessing you knew the fog was dangerous before you entered. Why did you go in?" He asked, "Are you, like, a nomad? Homeless?"

Nora glared at him from the side of her eye, "I could ask you the same question."

Ber laughed it off, "'Guess you're right!" He glanced over to her. "You know, the entire time I was in there, you were the only human I came in contact with. I mean, eh," He chuckled, "The hell beasts in there kept me occupied, I suppose."

Ber pondered for a quiet moment. He stopped and turned to Nora.

"… You *were* one of those things. How is it that you held onto your— your humanity like that?"

"I don't want to talk about it unless you have an answer for me."

"Not an answer, but maybe a theory," Ber said, "Nora, may I see your hand?"

Nora offered her hand with reluctance. Ber grasped her wrist.

"What are you-" before she could hesitate, Nora realized that Ber's hand was giving off a dim, silver-blue glow. The faint scars in her skin flooded with black. Moments later, her dark, smoke-like magic was released from her palms.

It was a sight she feared for as long as she could remember. She gathered that Ber came from somewhere entirely different, but she also knew the consequences of showing aura far too well. It was not something she wished to remember nor relive. Red in the face, she jerked her arm back.

"Interesting," Ber said, "I've never seen shadow magic in person. 'Guess it's no wonder you were able to stay sane in the fog."

"First, don't touch me ever again. Second, what does that even mean?!"

"It means that you're very lucky. Most people wouldn't even make it walking as far as you did through the fog. Still…" He said as he glanced at the necklace she traded to him. "You're also very unfortunate. It's a very rare and distinct magic. Many people would kill for that kind of power."

"… Listen," Nora said, "I have no idea where you come from, but people here do not simply flaunt their magic like you do. In the wrong parts you can be *killed* if someone sees you."

Ber's face turned dismal. "Really?"

"Yes, really. So if you wouldn't mind, could you keep yours to a minimum?" She asked as she continued on her path, and Ber followed.

"Sure, but what about your beast? She's a magic beast, no doubt."

"Yeah," Nora rubbed her neck, "that's just as big of a problem, but giving her refuge in Saint Evedis is the least I can do. I owe the poor thing, if that makes sense."

"It does."

Together Nora and Ber weaved between tree patches for their search. As they walked, Ber ran his fingers through the pines and brush. He looked up to Nora, taking in the sternness painted on her face. He wondered if it was her default expression.

Ber spoke up, "Nora, I'm sorry I made aura from your hands… If I knew—"

Nora cut him off, "Don't worry about it. Let's just keep moving."

They gained higher ground, treading up an eroding hill. From the top Nora could scan the treetops, but not by much. She whistled for Lotte, but to no avail. Bitter wind brushed through her, still directioned towards the fog. Its veil obscured a good portion of the landscape. Its inescapable presence sent her chills.

Day was already coming to an end. It felt silly to mourn a daily occurrence, but Nora could not help how she felt. Until today, she had taken daylight for granted.

"Nora, look here."

Ber brought her attention to an object protruding from the gravel and handed it to her. It was a dark, lightweight scale that covered her palm. Its teardrop shape was perfectly divided by a smooth ridge. Nora brushed the side of the scale and tucked it in her pouch.

"We're getting close, I hope," Nora said.

Ber studied the wind and watched the area. "Your dragon probably is, or was, resting deeper in these woods. I say we check there."

"Good plan." She started to descend from the mound, when she realized Ber was not following. Instead, he leapt from the steep side of the hill, sliding down with grace with the help of his magic. He landed a ways ahead of her. She paced up to him, not sure whether to be impressed or begrudged.

"Cute. But you really shouldn't be doing that," She urged.

"C'mon, no one's out here! Besides, if anyone did see they would just think I had fancy feet," He bumped her shoulder, "and they'd be jealous like you are."

"Please..." Nora huffed as she made a brisk walk ahead.

As she walked, Nora couldn't help but pull out the scale from her pouch. She brushed its edges, longing to find her friend. She almost wished that her abilities acquired in the fog stayed for a time like this. Almost. All of this would be over and done with if she could trace the dragon's scent from the scale. She could even cover more ground on four legs.

Nora considered how she reformed, luckily to her normal self. *How did my stuff stay on me, anyway?*

As Nora kept her eyes on the scale, lost in thought, Ber looked about. From the corner of his eye he spotted movement and the dim glow of a lantern.

"Get down."

"Wha-" Ber shoved her into a maple tree. She wanted to protest, but she peered beyond the tree to see what he hid her from. A man was collecting firewood under the light of his dim lantern in the distance.

"What should we do? Maybe he can help us..?" Ber whispered.

"The grizzly with an axe? Absolutely not, we have to leave!" Nora said.

"What're you kids doing out 'ere?" The man scolded, making them jump, "If yer out here catchin' monsters, I'll make sure you don't come back!"

"Eh, hello!" Ber exclaimed, giving in to nervous cheerfulness. The man furrowed his brow at Ber, who was now shaking. Nora realized that she would have to do the talking. Not exactly her strong suit.

"Yes, hi... We're so sorry, we're just lost and..."

"Just lost, eh?" The man's voice lowered. He pulled out from his torn coat a tarnished pocket watch to check the time. He sighed and slung his axe over his shoulder.

"Guess you two don't really look like the harmful type. Come now, I'll have you rest at my home for the night," He sighed.

Ber and Nora looked at each other, unsure about the stranger's offer. But the two were *tired*. Nora decided to go with it. Against her better judgment, she craved a bed to sleep in.

"Th-thank you, sir," Nora said.

She helped Ber up and followed the mysterious man through the woods. She looked around at the impeding darkness of the woods to plan an emergency runaway, or maybe a tree to climb. She then glanced at Bers hand, which was readily grasped on the dagger attached to his belt. She felt almost relieved that he was taking something seriously, for once.

When they entered the man's house, he stopped and spoke, "It isn't much, but the space will make do for the night." The interior was drenched in orange light. The main room was small, but felt warm and almost safe.

"Papa?" A voice peeped. From a pile of blankets emerged a young girl. She rubbed the sleep from her eyes and embraced her father. Weary eyes met with Nora's.

"Brita, these two are travelers. They are staying just for the night."

Ber crouched to her height, "Hello Brita, my name is Ber!"

"And I'm Nora, it's nice to meet you."

"Hi…" She murmured.

The man set his gear down at the doorway.

"So," The man said, "Where're you folks from?"

"I came from northern Stromshire, but I visited the outposts out here often. Or, I used to," Nora answered. The man's brows raised. He wanted to speak, but held himself back.

"The outposts? Brother sells pelts there all the time! You haven't seen my brother around, have you?" Brita asked.

Nora was unsure how to answer.

The father spoke up, "He left weeks ago to trade but hasn't returned, yet."

Nora swallowed. "I haven't been in a long while. And I haven't seen any young salesmen on my way here, either. Sorry."

"What about you, kid?" The man directed at Ber, "You don't look like you're from around here. Have ye seen any fur traders down south?"

"Pa, don't assume!" Brita interjected.

"No, you're right, I'm not from around here… But no, I haven't seen your brother, sorry to say," Ber said. He prayed that he had not seen what was left of the brother in the fog.

The old man caught himself upon his desperation. "I, eh, just thought I shoulda asked… You two looked starved, I'll make some dinner." Brita followed behind, and Nora and Ber offered to help.

The evening crept along. Few words were exchanged, excluding some small talk, trying to keep things light. After a filling meal of a mild stew, Ber had the idea to teach Brita a card game. Admittedly, Nora was glad he could break the quiet. She dismissed the chance to play the first round and observed the game.

He pulled the cards from his heavy luggage— How he carried that pack, she had no idea. Each card in the deck bore strange markings and illustrations. The figures included animal skulls, bushels of coral, and floating hands with a piercing eye at the center of the palm.

To begin the game, Ber shuffled the cards, using more fancy wind magic to show off. She couldn't say anything with the awestruck child present, but she exchanged a look to Ber. Now she knew he was doing this just to piss her off.

Nora watched as the game progressed. It seemed easy enough, but it was so fast paced that she could not keep up with the card's hierarchies and abilities of each one.

After a while, she realized the man was no longer in the room. She followed after him, gently interrupting.

"Need help with the dishes, sir?"

"Ah, please."

The man moved aside so Nora could dry the dishes after he cleaned them. The stranger was quiet, but Nora respected and appreciated his similar mannerisms to her. Boisterous laughter rang out from the other room to break their comfortable silence.

"I can get Ber in here to help if you want," Nora suggested.

"No need," The man said, "Brita needs the fun."

The man tried to pull his attention back, but found his gaze on Nora's ashen palms. "I'm sorry to ask, but what happened to your hands?"

Nora frowned as she looked to her darkened hands. Like a persistent ink, the marks stained her hands after her escape from the fog. She suspected it was from her magic, but the reason why was uncertain.

"Something I came in contact with in the woods, I believe," Nora said, "though I'm glad to see it fading."

Not technically lies.

The man nodded, "Awful lot of dangerous things in these woods lately. You need to make sure no poachers see a mark like that on ya, understand?"

"If it were up to me, I'd rather not run into them at all."

The man chuckled, "You've got a point. Just know they might get the wrong idea. A lot of the survivors from Stormfire got harassed for marks like those. Myself included."

Nora forced her attention to the dishes at hand. She resisted prying further.

"My family's been through enough. We can only pray for further protection."

"Of course," Nora said. "But like you said, these woods are now more dangerous than ever. Why not leave?"

"You talkin' about the fog?"

"… Yes. When it comes, leaving your home will be the only option."

"I've accepted this—I'm trying to, anyway." The man looked distant. "It's hard moving away from everything you have, and someone you love."

Nora solemnly nodded. She knew his feeling well. "I best be gathering my things for bed. Thank you again, sir, for opening your home to us."

"Calum is fine. I know good folk when I see 'em. We're a dying breed, so we gotta help each other out when we can."

Nora smiled as she dismissed herself. For tonight, it was nice to be considered 'good folk.'

Nora was greeted with the sight of a defeated Ber and a boisterous Brita, yielding all the cards.

"I won three times in a *row!*" The girl announced.

Calum's face brightened, "I should've told you, the kid's a shark. I hope you didn't wager anything important!"

"Ah, not that kind of game, sir!" Ber assured, "I may have just lost some pride, is all. I should call it a night, before I lose any more."

"How 'bout one more game?" Brita asked.

"Brita, let the man rest. I'm sure our guests have much traveling to do tomorrow," Calum said.

The girl wanted to protest, but she agreed to retire for the night. As she left, Ber gave a sheepish 'goodnight' to Brita.

Nora and Ber's host, though quiet, gave the two a smile hidden under the thick beard. He returned to his own room for the night, leaving Nora and Ber in the main room. Under dim lantern light the two prepared for bed.

"Ber," Nora spoke. Her voice breaking the silence for once almost made Ber jump.

"Y-yes?"

"I don't believe I ever thanked you for helping me out of the fog, so… Thanks."

"Of course!" Ber said. "Anything else you'd like to talk about?"

"No. I wanted to thank you is all."

"You sure?"

"Yes. We're leaving early. I recommend you let me sleep before I get ugly again."

Ber agreed to her condition. The two slept through the night, something they both seemed unfamiliar with recently, on threadbare sheets and spare pillows.

4

Chapter 4

-Months earlier-

Suryc flipped the pocket watch in his palm until it grew warm. He spent the better half of the ball alone, forced to linger in his thoughts.

Golden lights and laughter illuminated the ballroom. Stromshire's balls did not occur often, especially with rising tensions between common folk and city authorities. This did make for these events to become much more extravagant, however. Sweet wine, sweeter women, and enchanting music would have made for a pleasant night, he considered.

Suryc lifted another drink from a platter, adding to his collection, and leaned deep into his seat. What dampened his usual upbeat mood was the fact that it was likely the last ball he would ever be invited to.

"Mind if I sit with you?"

Suryc was caught off guard by a tall man standing before him. He appeared well-dressed, even for the occasion. He sported a cordial, genuine smile. Suryc used to play a center role at these gatherings, but that time had waned. With curbed enthusiasm, he gestured to the stranger to come sit with him.

The man looked terribly familiar. Suryc considered the possibility of interacting with him in one of his few, but notable drunken stupors.

"You must be Mr. Harland, correct?"

Harland. A tainted name. Suryc was tempted to lie for the sake of his pride, but he knew it would not get him anywhere. He swallowed.

"Yessir, but you may call me Suryc. To whom do I owe this pleasure?"

The man leaned into the him. The gold lining his ears danced in the soft light. "You can call me Asaph. I have a proposition for you."

The connection clicked.

"Asaph, the 'King of Thieves?' I thought I recognized you." Suryc took a drink, "Surely you know you're a wanted man in these parts, even amongst the nobility."

The man before him was a walking urban legend. Suryc heard numerous stories of Asaph, of how he frequented parties such as these. He considered it all baseless gossip.

"I appreciate your concern, but most of these folk have been clients at one point or another."

To that, Suryc hummed in disbelief.

"I'll get right to the point," Asaph continued, "I am the head of a set of very exceptional trades, and I am currently searching for talent to sponsor my work."

Suryc leaned more on the side of amused than intrigued by the offer. He hid a smirk behind the rim of his glass.

"I'm afraid I don't understand."

"I am in the business of what is usually considered 'unobtainable.' I've been in this business for well over fifteen years, and now I'm being commissioned to fetch some big prizes."

"So, you're trying to hire me to be, what, some kind of bounty hunter?" Suryc asked.

Before he could go in for another drink, Asaph weighed down his hand. "It's much bigger than that, Suryc. I was in a position much like yours when I was your age. I had a taste of power, and I had it ripped away from me. I was wronged, and things were taken from me that were rightfully mine. I am offering you an opportunity that I did not have."

"You're being awfully vague, Master Asaph," Suryc jabbed.

His words did not phase Asaph. The man instead directed his attention to a gathering of nobles across the ballroom.

"I'm certain you know of the Lane family— A household name, pockets so deep they practically own the country."

"I imagine they would, if the remaining Irvings weren't still around."

"You mean *Irving*."

Suryc hummed, "I'm sure the other brat is out there somewhere."

Asaph continued, "Fair point. Now, the head of the house is Marc, there. He took something from me, so it was only fair that I took *everything* from him."

Suryc looked to him, awaiting an explanation. Mr. Lane was born in wealth, certain to die in wealth. Surely Suryc would have heard of such a claim.

"That whole dispute is over now, of course. And Mr. Lane there, he bought his 'everything' back."

He finally returned his gaze to Suryc. Two silver eyes met his own. They resembled the constellation of tiny jewels sewn into his coat.

"Marc there, is living proof of how I dislike insecurities in a deal… Come with me. I will prove this all to you."

This was something Suryc wanted to see. Whether or not this man was telling the truth, Asaph's confrontation with Marc Lane would prove to be the highlight of the evening. With a quick nod, he followed Asaph across the ballroom.

The crowd parted for Asaph with Suryc in tow. The Lanes chatted among the other nobles until they spotted Asaph. Knowing better than to stick around, most of the party left Marc upon his arrival.

"Good evening, Mr. Lane," Asaph said.

"Ah, Asaph…! Enjoying the festivities this evening?"

"As always, sir," Asaph answered, "I assume you have met Master Suryc?"

Marc's eyes lit up, "Of course! You're the heir to Harland Ports, I take it?"

"Yes, sir! We have been busier than ever," Suryc lied, "But business is good! I should give you my thanks, for being such a long standing customer."

"I should be thanking you for your service, son. Couldn't do my own business without you!"

The enthusiasm was overplayed, sure. Suryc did not care. For the first time in a long spell, Suryc was genuinely acknowledged by someone who was not the wait staff. His presence felt no longer like a stale formality.

Asaph nodded to the man beside Marc.

"Good evening to you as well, Blanche. How are you feeling? I recall our last encounter, you seemed under the weather."

The young man eyed Asaph, "… Better."

"That's great to hear! Now, Marc— I'd like to ask a small favor, from my family to yours. I've noticed the interest on our transaction has not been paid in a while…"

"Consider it done. Come to my office later, you may look at my other wares as well."

"Excellent! I appreciate your business, as always," Asaph bowed, "Until later, Mr. Lane, Mr. Blanche."

Suryc excused himself as well. As they left the Lanes, Suryc pulled him aside.

"How did you do that?"

"Like I said, Marc and I had a deal. If you are interested in my proposal, I could show you more."

"It is admittedly tempting."

"Suryc," Asaph began, "I am not offering employment for some trivial scheme. I am asking for your partnership."

"What are you asking from me, exactly?"

"I am asking you to be the public figure for me, the flagship of a movement."

Suryc frowned. He double-checked his surroundings before whispering.

"Do you know what I am to these people? I'm a *joke,* Asaph. I refuse to squander what is left of my resources on a *chance.*"

Asaph thought on his words for a moment. The man before him may have carried himself proudly, but there were cracks in the façade. "You are already taking a chance. I'm sure you've heard the echoes of revolution, Mr. Harland. Not just in your county, but throughout the nation. It is very likely that the same blood your family used to get where it is today will rip everything away from you. The least you can do is take initiative, and keep the power in capable hands."

Suryc swallowed. "What do you suggest I do, then?"

"Put some money aside to hire for a campaign. Insist to these folk that you are on *their* side. Instill some fear for the monsters outside their walls, the dangers of magic, and you will soon have a following."

"I still don't understand," Suryc said, "How can I be sure that this will not be a waste of time and money? How do you tie into all this?"

"Think of me as your campaign manager," Asaph said, "You're a smart man and I'm certain you are the perfect choice. When it's all said and done, money will not be a concern ever again. Who knows, perhaps you may be able to restore the family name as well."

"A fine agreement, I must admit," Suryc said, "Where do we begin?"

5

Chapter 5

"… And even with magic blood, your people still choose to do things the hard way?"

"You mean start a fire with a flint? Yes, what's so hard to understand about that?"

Nora and Ber had left early that morning, and had been on the road since. The day was already coming to an end, so they set up for camp.

"I mean— your fingers are *right there,*" Ber argued.

"And tons of people understand that, but following the laws of the land is what keeps us safe." The words left a sour note on Nora's tongue. *I sound like my old lady.*

Ber snorted, "Well that's just stupid."

"I know."

What was a gentle breeze picked up, lifting smoke and ash from their fire into Nora's face. Nora swiftly moved away, hacking up smoke.

Ber came over to check on her. "I'm sorry…"

"Don't be, it's not like you control the wind—" Nora had a realization, and coughed again, "—Well, I suppose you can."

"Well, I promise that wasn't me," Ber chuckled, awkwardly patting her shoulder.

When Nora could finally catch her breath, she relieved herself on the fresh cold air rolling in. Ber eyed her, sensing something still was not right.

Nora took in a couple more deep breaths, as she too tried to pinpoint her feeling. She struggled to identify what smelled so familiar in the wind, the smallest hints teasing her nose. Then it came to her. *That's my jerky.*

"Nora, what's wrong?"

Nora forced her aching feet back into her boots, "Lotte's not far. I know it."

Ber noticed the sides of her neck sprouted dark veins, the same dark color of her hands when they exited the fog. There was an unknown intensity that ran through Ber when she looked at him.

"Are you coming?"

"Of course," Ber said.

Nora led Ber through the brush in a dead straight line. Ber dared not to slow her down, but tried to speak between hurdles.

"I do not question your certainty. Actually yes I will. How can you be so sure it's her?"

Though Nora's pace stayed quick and steady, she started to pant, "The damn thing— took my meat. I can smell it. Either it's her— or her droppings," she paused, "But what matters is that she's close."

Intimidation aside, Ber knew better than to question her further. He tried not to dwell on his time in the fog, but he recalled what she was feeling vividly— Like chasing a high that she could never reach. When she could take it no longer, she threw her hands in the air with a curse, grazing a tree in the process.

"It's *right here*— So why is nothing here?!"

For once, Ber's silence frustrated her to her very core. *How could he be so clueless?!* She spun around to meet his eyes, and his face read utter *fear.*

His eyes shifted from the tree, and back to her. Nora glanced over to find that she scalped the bark from where she slashed. *No...* She looked to her hands, now armed with black claws and fur. Nora yelped, stumbling back before falling to the ground.

"Wh-what's happening to me...? Why is this happening again?!"

"Let me help you—"

"*No*— Stay away from me!"

A single creak of the trees was their only warning, as the tree's limbs fell from above, separating Nora and Ber. From below Nora's feet the earth shifted. A passage opened. With it, the scent grew two-fold.

No other thought occupied Nora's panicked mind; she needed to know what awaited her at the end of the passage. Ber felt the tremor, too. He refused to let Nora go in her frenzied state alone and followed suit.

Through the large hole, he dodged the fibrous roots overhead. He shielded his mouth and nose from the churned dust of the tunnel as he trudged on. He turned a corner, then another, when he saw gentle light at the end of the passage.

This was not what Nora saw. She practically stumbled into the passage, trying to ignore the throbbing aches in her body urging to transform. She paced on, ignoring the chill permeating her body. She took a turn, then another, until her body felt numb, and all she could see was an opaque, solid grey.

This felt similar to the fog, yet the air remained light. Nora lost track of how far she had walked, or if she was walking at all. Once again, she was alone, and surrounded in grey.

From the other side emerged a grey mass. The mass looked upon their indefinite shape, unsure what to make of themself.

Her and the creature were one. Nora's essence melted away, until she did not know who she was anymore.

The surrounding area was just as perplexing. The creature looked about the new landscape in awe. Gigantic, spiraling clouds suspended the creature in the starry sky and swarmed around the creature. The clouds were smoky and so dense, the mass could only see what was above. The sky seemed like nothing but void.

From the clouds emerged a dark mass, disturbing its vapors with its massive wings. It opened its white eyes; they were as shining and brilliant as the stars above. A colossal raven presented itself before the creature. The bird was clearly visible, but did not seem like a physical being.

"Hello, what brings you here?" The bird asked.

Hesitant, the creature said, "I... I am not sure. I do not know what any of this is, or what I am. Perhaps you could help me?"

The raven gave the creature a steady gaze, as if trying to peer into their soul. With a swipe of the raven's wing, the creature reformed. The creature's identity returned as Nora. All of her memories surged back to her in an instant. Her form regained some solidity as well.

She looked to her palms. They returned to their beastial, taloned form. She dreaded what the rest of herself looked like.

Nora felt something within her, like a tight knot in her stomach unravel. Tears flowed from her face, drifting away into the clouds. Emotions pushed back, and a voice long suppressed, rose within her.

"Why, why is this happening to me? I am stripped to nothing, but the world is somehow kicking me down even more!" She startled herself with the power behind her voice. She continued, "… Where do I even go from here? If I keep turning into- into *this*, and if all I can do is dig a deeper hole for myself and then—then…" Her words drifted off, and were replaced by a wave of sobs.

The spirit came closer, still peering with wide, almost curious eyes.

"I cannot tell what lies in the future. No being does. But my child, you are indispensable. Every creature has purpose, and you are no different. Inside of you, I see a spirit unlike any I have seen in a long time."

The spirit raised one clawed foot. It clenched its talons. Nora's human form returned. Slow and weak, she got to her feet.

"These forms you possess, they are equally stitched to your spirit. Like yourself, they have a purpose."

Nora, keeping its gaze, swallowed.

"You must learn to view situations from a different angle. There is no existing thing that is exactly as it appears," The spirit spoke.

The spirit opened its left wing, pulling from it a large, nearly transparent feather and gave it to Nora. The moment it fell upon her palms, it turned ink black and radiated with Nora's aura.

Before her eyes, the feather morphed into a flawless black sword with a faint shine and iridescent sheen. She held it upright and marveled at the weapon's beauty and utter flawlessness, then at her disheveled self in the reflection of the blade.

"This blade will guide you. It has bonded with you and fused with your aura of shadow. The blade will obey you and only you. Do you understand?"

Nora nodded. The bird craned its head skyward, listening to something troublesome that Nora couldn't hear. The feathers along the neck of the bird rose and stuck out like quills.

"I must go, but you shan't forget my words. I wish you well, *Ulvendottir.*"

With a powerful beat of wings and a storm of blinding feathers, the spirit vanished and the strange place was no more.

-

When Nora came to, she lay flat by the lakebed, too dazed to stand just yet. From afar she heard Ber calling out to her. Gradually, she lifted herself to sit upright.

"Nora...!" Ber ran to her side and panted, "Man, I thought I lost ya for a minute. What happened? Are you alright?"

Nora rubbed her temples, "I'm not sure."

Ber kneeled, "Are you hurt?"

"No."

"Good! Let me help ya up." Ber smiled, lending a hand. "So, eh... What about your dragon? Any luck?"

The strange wave of calm Nora found herself in receded with the thought of Lotte. The scent was gone but the air held something else.

"The track is gone. But she's close, I can feel it," Nora said, "I hate to say it but for now, we need to recoup back at camp."

"Agreed, you look terrib— tired."

Nora hummed, wiping the excess mud from her backside, "You sure know how to dish out compliments, Ber."

"Well, I *was* gonna say terrible... I think I'm making it worse."

"Don't fret. I don't care." Nora's voice was deadpan.

The lakebed Nora and Ber found themselves in was in a small divot of a quarry. They trekked up and back into the woods, while Nora made the futile attempt to rid herself of filth.

"... I should thank you." Nora said.

"What for?"

"Most people wouldn't try to help someone like me— and in that state…" She glanced at her hands. They returned to normal, save for the traces of black veins branched up her wrists. She made a quiet sigh.

"It wouldn't be right to leave you in the state you were in. Besides," Ber said, "I know first-hand what you just went through."

"Really?"

Nora's eyes glanced to the stone laced around his neck. She could not help but wonder what he would look like in her state. Nora caught his eyes glancing back.

"What?"

"I think there's something stuck in your hair," Ber said, "a twig, maybe?."

Nora felt around her mop of hair, her coils cementing together from the drying mud. Something pricked her finger. She paused, carefully pinching and pulling the foreign object from her hair.

She inspected it for just a moment, a straight, ink-black feather. *It's just a feather, but why is it familiar?*

The feather answered immediately. It doused itself in shadows before growing, transforming into a solid black blade.

That mist, the huge bird, that... this feather— Nora's hazy memory of her dream-like state flooded back. She dropped the blade and backed away.

"The hell— That was all real?!"

Seconds later, the blade reverted back into a feather. Ber, just as shocked from seeing Nora pull a sword out of her hair, marveled at the little thing. He hesitated, then lifted the feather by the quill.

Nora waited with baited breath to see it transform again, to confirm that what she saw was true. Nothing happened. But Ber saw it, too.

"I wish *my* feathers did that!" Ber tried to laugh off his confusion, "So… where did you find this thing?"

"I'm not sure you'll believe it. I hardly can."

"I think we are well past the point of rational explanation for… anything, really."

Nora sighed, "When I was in that craze, I entered a mist. My body and brain went haywire until a big bird showed up, shared some wisdom, gave me a sword, and left."

"… Oh."

"Yeah," Nora said, "Does *any* of that sound familiar to you, from wherever you came from?"

"Nope."

"Of course. How silly of me to think any of this would make a lick of sense."

Ber went quiet. Crunching leaves filled the silence as he thought of a response.

"This is not my native language, Nora. And your… expressions are not the ones I grew up with, so communication is hard."

Nora listened.

"But, maybe if you say what you know, and I say what *I* know, maybe we can piece some of this together."

Nora gave into a slight smile.

"I'd like that— After I get cleaned up, of course."

"Of course," Ber repeated, "You look like shit."

Like sobering from a high, Nora felt utterly drained from her crazed state. *If this is my new normal I hope I can get used to this.* Even as her senses dulled to their normal state, she could still feel that something was not right. Her senses did not fail her when she heard human footsteps, and movement past the brush.

Her realization came too late. Before she could alert Ber, a pair of leather clad hunters made eye contact with her. A voice rang out and more appeared. Each hunter was adorned with colorful parcels from their trade- fine silks and fabrics, iridescent scale armor, and embellishments made of exotic furs and feathers.

Nora and Ber backed away in tandem. Ber's hand reached for his bag.

"I reckon these are the hunters you talked about?" Ber muttered to Nora.

"Poachers, yes…" A dread ran through Nora, "… Ber, what if they have *her?*"

Ber swallowed as one poacher, one he and Nora could only assume was the troop's leader, walked straight to them. He seemed unbothered by their weapons.

"Good evening, ladies. What brings you two out to the middle of nowhere?"

Nora felt something change in Ber. Like a twitch, Ber held a flash of utter resentment, and turned to something completely unexpected to Nora. With a cordial smile, he walked up to the man.

"Oh, thank the *Gods* you're here!" Ber began. The other man could not help but tilt his head as he approached, "Me and my merchant partner here are *hopelessly* lost! If you could direct us to the closest main road we'd be forever grateful, and we can be out of your hunting grounds in a heartbeat!"

Ber's performance made Nora's stomach sink. *Is he serious?*

"We found your fire, but where's all your stuff?" The man asked.

"Ransacked. Everything was either stolen or destroyed by these damned beasts," Ber sighed, clenching a fist, "Honestly, what you lot are doing is such an honorable service, to wipe these foul creatures out!"

The man's eyes narrowed, "Alright… Listen, we're after a high value beast in these parts. If you have any insight on a dragon in the area, I *might* just forget that I saw you here."

"Yes—*yes*, actually! The terrible thing was flying north. It scared the life out of us, practically!" Ber said.

Another poacher snuck up behind Nora, prodding her back with a spear. "This one here's awfully quiet…"

"A-aye, everything he said is true," Nora managed to say.

The poacher unhitched the pouch at Nora's side with the end of his spear. With a quick swipe he flung it over to himself, spilling the pouch's contents. He looked almost bored as he searched through the contents, until his eyes widened. He pulled a map, and Lotte's scale from the pile.

"Well, they're not lying about seeing the dragon, but they're definitely no merchants."

The leader shook his head, expression hidden beneath the brim of his hat. "A damn shame, you two. Looks like we're taking you, after all."

"Wait! I can trade you something *better*," Ber said.

"Like what, pretty boy?"

"Let's see…" He mulled, digging through his bag, "…Perhaps something like this?"

Without even reaching back, he sent a fist out of the bag, flying towards his face. Icy knuckles struck the man's skin with an echo of thunder. The man hit the ground with a thud.

Ber's other hand reached for Nora's. Before she could take it and run away, he was seized by more poachers and struck at the base of his head. In an instant the light left his eyes, as he went limp.

"Ber!" Nora cried out.

But she too was knocked out when something was brought to her nose, and her vision once again went grey.

6

Chapter 6

"Miss Alice, do you happen to know where we are?"

"Precisely."

"… Precisely what?"

Alice gestured Viviane over. She peered over Alice's shoulder— not a hard feat, given her short stature. The map was upside down, but Viviane knew better than to question her methods.

With surefire accuracy, Alice pinpointed their location. "We're right here— which is a problem. We visited the towns directly north *and* directly south, and I *know* those damned poachers must be stationed around here. I wouldn't be surprised if the place is swimming with 'em…" Alice began muttering to herself.

Viviane listened— rather, she tried to, as she scoped the land. She checked her pocket book over and over again. *No, this couldn't be right… Or was it?*

"No," Viviane said, "I suppose I mean where are we in regards to topography? Makes a difference with the sediment, you know."

Alice blinked. "*What.*"

Alice watched as Viviane knelt to a patch of bare earth, "I mean… this must be sandy loam, right? Or is it loamy sand…?"

"Saints, Viv, how should *I* know that?"

"Goodness, you're right. It's not like we shared the same science classes," Viv teased. She flicked her companion square on the forehead.

35

"Fine, fine, let me have a look…" Alice looked at the tattered pocketbook, then back to the dirt, "Yep, that's sandy loam. Looks like I might have to find you a new dirt book."

Viviane hummed, "Good luck with that. I'm pretty sure it was a Saint Evedis library exclusive."

"We'll see about that."

Before Alice could return to her scouting, Viviane gasped.

"There it is!" Viviane ran over to what Alice thought was the most unassuming shrub she had ever seen. "Nobilis *vopos,* the Fox's Fists."

Alice crouched with Viviane to prod the little plant. Viviane swatted her hand away.

"It's poisonous."

Alice cringed, "Of course it is…" She struggled to lift herself back up, "… And this plant's gonna help my nonproblem how, exactly?"

"Chemistry, my dear. This is a crucial ingredient to the final product, just like baking!"

"Just like baking," Alice echoed.

"You know, you didn't have to join me if you didn't want to. I can fend for myself."

"It's not that. It's just–" *What was it, exactly? 'I needed an excuse to spend time with you' definitely would scare her off… I was doing something out here other than watching her fawn over shrubs, wasn't I?*

A voice called from behind Alice and Viviane.

"Captain!"

Saints, what now? Alice turned to find a shipmate running to her from her ship.

Alice stood straight and squared herself, "Keene. Yes, what is it?" Alice asked.

"I–we…" Keene paused, flinging sun bleached braids away from her sweaty face. She gathered herself. "… We went back to the ship with supplies and th-there's something in the crow's nest."

"A beast?"

"Unlike any I'd ever seen, Captain. We're gonna need you for this one."

"And the Bachelor, any sign of him?" Alice asked.

"Nay, not a hide nor hair."

Alice's smile grew wide.

"Excellent. Grab your plant, Viv. It's our lucky day."

—

The beast was easy to spot, even from onshore. It crammed its body into the crow's nest, its finned tail drooping off the side. One eye peered out from behind the rails, wild and blue.

Alice clasped her hands together, not bothering to curb her excitement.

"Crew, you know the drill! Everyone off the ship if you want to keep your limbs."

They did just that. Viviane watched from the sidelines. Vials in hand and jaw clenched, she readied herself to bolt in her direction if things went wrong.

Alice held a dagger between her teeth as she made the tedious climb to the beast in the crow's nest. When Alice was close enough, the beast landed a precise slap to her face with its tail. Alice spat out her dagger, scowling as she watched it plummet down into the sea.

"That was one of my favorites, you git," She grumbled, "It's a good thing you're cute– at least I think you are...?"

The beast above her snarled. Alice linked her strong arm to a step in the ladder, allowing the other to search through her bag. She fumbled for a while until she took hold of its contents— sausages.

With a less-than-graceful toss, Alice tossed a chunk of meat upwards. With a snap the beast lunged its neck towards the scraps. Alice tossed another, then one more, when her grip became slick with fat.

Alice looked again into the beast's eye, interested, but still wary. She knew the beast was not leaving its spot, so she descended the ladder. In her mind, she prepared to face her crew empty-handed.

It's the boarcat situation all over again, Alice dreaded, *Robbie's gonna shoot the damn thing if I don't think of something.*

Alice took one more glance up at the beast to find it vanished. Alice turned to find the beast right on top of her. With its wings and glossy scales on full display, Alice knew without a doubt it was a dragon, and an uncommon one at that. It was on the smaller end, but no doubt it could dispatch her on the spot if it wanted to. Oddly enough, it did not. Alice chose her actions carefully.

Its eyes were trained on her, then the bag. She tossed a morsel to the beast, then another. She was reaching the bottom of the bag. The dragon sensed hesitation and closed the gap between them. It was far too close for comfort, but Alice was no longer in control of the situation. She let the beast sieve through her bag.

Is it... purring?

Alice wondered if the thing could possibly be someone's beast. *Surely not the Bachelor's,* Alice considered. Its face was right there— so close, she could pet it. A bad idea, of course, but she did it anyway.

On shore, the crew watched in disbelief as their captain fed and pet a beast into submission. Again.

"She's joking..." Abigail said.

Viviane grew tired of waiting. She began to walk back on board, and the rest of the crew followed.

"Thank you all for being so patient. Just give us a minute before we onboard..."

The crew obeyed and stayed put. She approached slowly, careful not to startle the dragon. Alice ushered her closer.

"Have you completely lost it?!" Viviane whispered.

"Yeah, I thought that was obvious. Got any more pastries?" Alice asked, "It's food driven."

The beast eyed Viviane now, slitted pupils blown wide. Viviane sighed. Searching through her belongings, she handed what was left of her snacks to Alice to feed to the beast.

"Your not going to have a crew if you keep behaving like this," Viviane reminded.

"They can deal. I keep my rates low, and this is the tradeoff. Honestly, I'd think of it as a win-win."

"Just what are you planning to do with that thing?"

The dragon swallowed a pastry whole. *What a waste, it didn't even taste it...* Alice scritched its cheek as finished its snack. It bellowed contentedly.

"Easy. It's gonna be our new mascot."

7

Chapter 7

Ber drifted in and out of consciousness. With the strike to his head, he could not collect a coherent thought. He tried to curse himself for his uselessness, but the only thing present on his mind were the consistent waves of pain rolling over his skull.

His eyelids flitted, bringing attention to one of his captors.

"I got word there were some valuable beasts in these parts. I didn't realize that I'd luck out with *you!*" The man smiled.

"'Guess we over packed for the occasion," Said another.

"The boss just might give us a promotion!"

"Good. I'm sick of being in the wastes."

The two, and perhaps a few other voices, were celebrating. When Ber's eyes focused, he saw the odd one out, his face sour as he drug Nora along. The ice-burnt welt against his cheek seemed to stop bleeding, but there was no doubt it still burned.

Looking to his side, Ber noticed Nora was waking up, too.

Drug through the dirt, Nora and Ber arrived at a rather lavish tent. All around them stood hunters of equal opulence. From behind a set of curtains emerged a tall and clean-cut man. He took immediate interest in Nora and Ber. He addressed their keepers.

"Magic folk?" He asked.

"Aye," The burnt man said, "But not an ounce of riches on them, Mr.

Suryc."

"Obviously… At least you will bring a good sum of profit, I suppose." The boss said, "A shame, really. We could have worked out a trade, but no matter. Get a caravan ready."

"You can at least talk to us like people. Just what in hell are you planning to do with us?" Ber asked.

The man turned to Ber, flushed with anger. He exhaled and smiled, "You like to talk, don't you?" his eyes turned to Nora, who admitted the faintest nod, "… I will humor you, while my men prepare your depart—"

From outside the tent trouble stirred. The noise escalated to crashes and shouts. The boss rested his head in his hand, relieving the creases in his face.

"Starke. Jansen. Go stop whatever the hell is going on out there."

A couple of burly hunters responded in salutes. They marched out in unison, only to be thrown back in along with a few small, metal canisters. The canisters bursted with smoke and sparks, blinding everyone in the room.

"Take those bandits down, *now!*" The boss demanded.

A force drug Nora and Ber out of the tent. Still bound, the two were ushered to a large, ornate ship. They kept their heads down to avoid both magic and bolts flying through the air. Nora was able to catch a glimpse of the chaos. Each caravan and tent was overturned, destroyed, and decorated with fire.

Nora and Ber boarded the ship along with their new set of captors. The pirates threw the two into the a storage room in the hull.

—

Suryc emerged from the chaos of the camp, his dapper attire disheveled and eyes red and teary from smoke. He looked upon his enemy's fleeting ship in disbelief. His eyes met with a single rogue, perched upon the ropes of the *Coral Fang*. He had wanted to face down with their infamous Captain for months now. But not like this.

The look in this rogue's eyes was something he would not soon forget. Green and almost feral, they watched him. Pairing with a wide, wicked smile, he knew she would show no mercy.

That girl... Is she *the Captain?* Suryc could not shake that she seemed terribly familiar.

The thought escaped him when the Captain signaled with a raise of her arm. A round of blasts pierced the air. Cannons blew off chunks of the Suryc's main ship. In a rain of splintered wood, it began to sink lopsided into the bay's shallow waters.

Suryc's mouth went agape.

"MY SHIP!"

"Eat it, git!" The rogue called out. To add insult to injury, she landed a series of 'warning shots' around the man's feet, forcing the man to scatter.

In a moment's notice, the *Coral Fang* sped off, vanishing off to sea. Suryc unloaded numerous rounds at them but to no avail. By the time their heavier blasters were loaded, the ship was already gone.

Starke limped back to his boss.

"S-sir?"

"It looks like we'll have to lick our wounds from this one. But no matter," Suryc said, "Get my horse, Starke. I've some research to do about our little pirate."

His hunter knew that scowl. Any further bad news would be a dangerous idea. Perhaps now was not the best time to tell the Bachelor that every one of their beasts were released. And that their gunpowder was stolen. Against better judgment, he told him anyway.

The Bachelor inhaled, gripping his pistol.

"Were the beasts released or taken?"

"R-released, actually... I don't think I saw them try to grab one."

"A foolish thing to do," Suryc said, "but I suppose this gives us our first hint."

8

Chapter 8

"… Would now be a good time to apologize?" Ber asked.

"I might be slightly concussed. You're going to have to be more specific," Nora said.

"I got us kidnapped, twice, and I probably made it worse by punching a guy."

Nora shrugged, or tried to through the ropes.

"You gave us the best shot for getting outta there," She said, "Besides, I should be the one apologizing. We probably wouldn't be here if I didn't run off into the woods."

Ber hummed, "So it's decided, we're both awful."

"Indeed."

Nora chuckled, shaking the chairs they were tied to. Like her voice it was raspy. If they made it off this ship in one piece, Ber would make the effort to hear the sound again.

"You know, with this being my second– no, third kidnapping, you'd think I'd know how to avoid these situations."

"Is that right?" Nora asked, blowing the hair out of her face, the feather still stubbornly clung in the curls, "Maybe with your experience, you can hatch an idea on how to get out of here."

"But why would you leave?" A voice chimed.

A copper-haired woman appeared. The strange woman wore a long, black leather coat and a pair of luxurious black boots. Short, messy hair and a soft face betrayed how young she really was.

"Listening to the two of you bicker has been rather entertaining!" She laughed as she waltzed in, taking a swig from her flask.

The girl's accent was equal parts peculiar and proper, and much unlike the rest of the crew Nora and Ber encountered.

"I'm Alice, a pleasure to meet the two of you. I'm the manager of this fine establishment."

"... *You* are the captain?" Nora asked.

"Mhm!" Alice affirmed, "Crazy, I know. It's also a crazy story of how I came to be in charge of these brutes, but I'll save the story telling for another time. Satya!"

A slender, red stoat trotted over to Alice.

"Could you untie their bonds for me, please?" Alice asked the stoat. The creature huffed and obeyed. "I apologize for the crew treating you like this, I'm attempting to teach them some manners but it's just not working..."

"Why would you untie us?" Ber asked.

"I can tell that you two aren't ones to put up a *real* fight. We're also far offshore, so I hope a daring escape wasn't in the books for you."

"I'm sorry if I come off as a little rude, but you don't seem much like a captain..." Ber spit out.

"Well excuse me, princess, for not matching the stereotype." Alice teased.

"...'*Princess?*'" Ber muttered to himself.

"Now that pleasantries have been taken care of, let me give you a little tour of this lovely vessel!" Alice announced, "Wait, I messed up somewhere... I think I forgot to ask for your names."

"I'm Nora, and this is Ber," Nora said, "But I still have one question. I'm sure you've already looked through our belongings and found nothing of monetary value. So, what exactly do you want from us?"

"We can get to business later, I assure you. For the time being, I *must* show you around!"

Captain Alice scooped up the stoat. The little thing scurried into her breast pocket before Alice trotted ahead. Nora and Ber exchanged concerned looks before deciding to follow along.

When they stepped out onto the main deck, the sun had already set. Small, scattered lanterns gave off a warm glow that danced with the sway of the sea.

"You'll find life aboard the *Coral Fang* to be quite pleasant, most of the time. You'll just have to deal with standard sailor shenanigans," Alice explained.

As they passed some of the crew members, Nora and Ber were given mixed looks. Some were friendly, some gave off glares. For the most part, they were far too busy celebrating the day's plunders, or far too drunk, to care.

One tall, blonde woman acknowledged the two with a nod. Nora was tall, but this woman dwarfed her. Nora did not know what was more intimidating, the woman, or the black, winged beast perched on her shoulder. Nora recognized it as a raptor, what species, she was not sure. Its red eyes, hooked beak, and talons on both its wings and feet all looked sharp.

Alice led them into the Captain's quarters near the front of the ship. Its warm lighting and elegant furnishings top to bottom made Nora feel like she was in a palace somewhere, instead of a boat.

Lounging in a chair in the entryway sat a dark skinned woman. Her hair was tied back with a ribbon to make a tidy ponytail. Shorter, delicate waves of hair were neatly tucked behind her unpointed ears. Completely intrigued with her book, she paid no attention to the company.

"Ah, here you are!" Alice exclaimed, "Viv, meet Nora and Ber, the new meat!"

Bright hazel eyes peered over the book.

"They do *seem* fit for the job," The woman set the book aside and greeted Nora and Ber, "I'm Viviane, how do you do?" Her accent too was peculiar, soothing and elegant.

"We're doing well, thank you," Ber grinned. He looked over to Nora, which reminded him to do more than exchange pleasantries. He continued, "So, eh, why did you take us onto your ship, again?"

Alice turned pinker at the second mention of their business.

"Well, there is a logical reason. You see—"

"Our Captain here doesn't think things through, this is why," Viviane interrupted.

"Will you shut up?" Alice huffed, but there was no venom behind her words. "… We're a tad short-staffed, and we—*I* assumed that you two wouldn't mind too much, given we saved you from Mister 'Bachelor.'"

Ber and Nora glanced at each other.

"I'm flattered… I think," Nora said, "If you asked me just a few days ago, I would have taken your offer gladly. But Ber and I have unfinished business. We have issues to attend to in Saint Evedis."

Alice sighed, "We may be pirates, but I can't make you work for us. But of course out of all places, you two need to go to the Capital. Fortunately for you, we're headed south anyway."

"What's wrong with Saint Evedis?" Ber asked.

"Oh, I can name a million things wrong with that place. But let's just say I'm wanted there–I'm wanted most places, really, but especially there," Alice spread out a map on the tea table, "We can take you to the mouth of the Evedis River, but no further. Needless to say, but the ship doesn't maneuver too well near the fog patches."

Nora reviewed the map. It was of much higher quality than hers. The canvas was meticulously amended with new patches of fog. She tried to memorize the patterns.

"Now if you will excuse me, it's getting late. Let me make sure that the guest cabin is prepared for you."

Alice left the two alone with Viviane.

"Do you and Alice cocaptain the ship, Miss Viviane?" Ber asked.

"You flatter me! No, I am just the cook— but a damn good one," Viviane winked.

Nora figured she told the truth, but something did not add up. Rather, Nora needed the full story. The woman was clad in fine clothing— too fine for a standard cook. *And why is she allowed in the Captain's quarters, if she is just a member of the crew?*

"This room is beautiful. The whole ship is, really. I've never seen anything like it," Nora said.

Viviane chuckled, "Thank you. When Alice looks for a score, she aims big! As you could probably glean from her, she doesn't have a typical… business model. But it works."

There was a pause.

"… May I ask you two an odd favor—"

Before Viviane could continue, Alice waltzed back into the room.

"So, I've a change of heart! You lot will be working off your debt to me! I feel it's fair, two days of work for two days of travel. Think of it as… a working interview, maybe?"

Ber smiled, "I can take on those terms."

Nora nodded in agreement. Alice showed them to the 'guest suite.' For such a lavish ship, Nora expected a bit more than a repurposed broom closet. But that was not the reason for her irritation.

"Captain," Nora tried, "I don't want to come off as ungrateful, but… Why is there just the one bed?"

"Oh! Are you saying you two aren't—"

"*No.*"

"Huh, you could have fooled me. You two can figure it out. 'Night!"

Alice turned on her heel to take her leave. Nora could tell the captain was smirking as she left. Ber looked away, toying with the collar of his shirt.

"… She's just trying to get under your skin, Nor."

"It's a good thing we're only here for a couple of days, otherwise I'd be committing mutiny. Let's just rotate who gets the bed. I'll take one of the hammocks for tonight."

"You sure?"

"Yes… Good night, Ber."

Nora shuffled to a vacant hammock. She set aside her things, save for her dagger (something she grew accustomed to since the start of her travels). Once she found a comfortable position, it did not take long for the sea to rock her to sleep. That night, she dreamt the sound of Lotte's soft snores, as if she were right beside her.

9

Chapter 9

"Who, exactly, was that man you took us away from?"

Captain Alice set down her tea. Nora and Ber found their first day of labor aboard *Coral Fang* to be quite easy, so they had ample time for lunch. Which, of course, Alice invited herself to.

With a handful of skilled sailors and a Captain who could direct the water herself (much to Ber's excitement), there was not much dire work to do. However, the *Fang* was a *massive* ship. Other members of the crew had enlisted the two on a lengthy list of chores that had gone long overdue.

"You haven't heard of ol' Bachelor?!" Alice asked.

"You mentioned him briefly last night. Otherwise, no," Nora said.

"Really? He's the new bastard on the poaching scene. He shimmied his way up the ranks pretty quick, I heard. I reckon it's because he comes from old money."

"What does his business have to do with yours?" Nora asked, "Surely you didn't rescue us out of the goodness of your heart."

"You'd be correct. I'm not out here trying to make a name for myself as some martyr," Alice turned to face the porthole, "I'm out here for cash, among a few other things. But what he's doing to beasts– and people too… There are some things that should never be cargo."

"What are they doing to them…?" Ber asked, his voice too small for his liking.

Alice eyed him for a moment, "You're not from around here, are you, Ber?"

Ber laughed nervously, "Is it that obvious?"

"They traffic to the highest bidder, mate. For folk it's your standard labor, sometimes they're held for ransom. For the beasts, most of them are sold for parts and blood. I hear the demand for aura is so steep, they're switching to people now."

"Aura?"

"It's another word for magic blood, Ber," Nora said.

Alice took a drink, taking the edge off such a sobering topic, "I've half a mind to sell my own blood at this point! The rate for strong blood I hear is *insane.*"

Nora tried to move her thoughts from where Lotte could be. She might be a dragon, but she was still so young. Nora loathed the thought of her dragon caged somewhere, awaiting an ill fate.

"All those new cartels are run by the Bachelor. A shame, really. I knew of him before he became a major, royal dick. His fleet's gotten so big it's become a common name in these parts," Alice said, "That is why he is my white whale."

Ber's brows furrowed, "Your what?"

"It's an Evedan term for something you vow to pursue at all costs," Nora explained.

"Speaking of, I've got to show you my newest haul. If the Bachelor saw this, he'd be shitting bricks!" Alice said, her smile beaming.

—

Alice led the two down several locked doors and flights of stairs. To Nora, it was almost dizzying to think they were still aboard a ship.

At the bottom of the stairs was a jail cell, holding a dark, spiny mass.

The beast was unmistakable.

"Lotte!"

The beast flipped around in whip-like speed. She met Nora's eyes through the bars, howling impatiently for their reunion.

"Crikey, you already know each other?!" Alice asked, "Guess it's no wonder Bachelor was hot on your trail."

Nora turned to Alice, "Why is she locked in the cage?"

"Well, I certainly couldn't have her flying around the ship. Not until I taught her some spacial awareness, anyway," Alice gestured to the room, an utter wreck.

"No," Nora said, her temper rising, "I mean why is she down here in the first place?"

"She was weak and hungry. She needed a place to rest while she gained her strength. You know what people like the Bachelor do to vulnerable beasts like her."

Nora cursed. *She had a point. But is this a point I should really take from another thief?*

"Let's just– take a moment to breathe and explain ourselves," Ber advised, daring to move between Alice and Nora as the two inched closer.

But Alice went on, "I should really be asking you why you separated from your dragon in the first place."

Nora felt a pang of guilt run through her. *Maybe she* did *care for her cargo.*

"We… we had an argument," Nora said.

Whatever Alice was expecting, it was not that. "With the dragon. Of course," Alice said, "Listen, mate. I don't want to keep her locked up just as much as you, but I certainly can't have her scaring the crew. 'Crew's already on my case about her… Is she safe to let out below deck? Maybe I could keep her in the cargo room, for now."

Nora thought for a moment, before Lotte started purring and gently attempting to preen Nora's still-filthy hair through the cage. Either she forgave Nora, or she was an excellent liar.

"I don't think she'll hold a grudge," Nora said, "I, on the other hand, might still need a moment."

Alice nodded, taking keys in hand. Nora watched her carefully, as Alice stepped toward the cage. She used slow, but clear movements as she unfastened the lock. Ber claimed to have experience with dragons. Now, he was noticeably *tense*. He was allotted a utility knife by the crew, which he clenched tightly.

It was quiet for a moment, as Alice unlocked the cage, expressionless. *If she was afraid, she's good at hiding it,* Nora thought. She wondered just how many times the captain managed beasts like these on her ship.

With a distinct *clink*, the door was open. Lotte wasted no time bursting out of the cage and unfurling herself as much as the chamber would allow. She practically wrapped herself around Nora, and Nora received a face full of prickled scales.

Nora had to pat her scales down to see that Lotte's eyes were fixed. She was looking through Alice and directly at Ber. Ber unsheathed the knife.

"I thought she was safe to let out!" Alice said in a harsh whisper above Lotte's growling.

"I forgot she hates strangers, especially men," Nora admitted, "Ber, put the knife down. Now."

Ber hesitated, but did just that. He paused a moment, before bowing his head to Lotte. Slowly, Lotte unraveled herself from Nora. Nora and Alice watched, mouths agape as Lotte nudged her horned head into Ber's hands.

"You all owe me explanations. But first," Nora turned her attention to Alice, "Thank you, Alice, for keeping Lotte safe."

10

Chapter 10

That night, Alice, Viviane, Nora, and Ber reconvened. Nora walked in to Alice petting Satya in her hands.

"'Had a little parley with the crew. I think it's in our best interest that I know who I'm dealing with…" Alice said, "I'm inviting you over for a little chat with me and Viv– I'll see you in the meeting room."

Nora and Ber obeyed. The air was tense. Looking at the Captain, Alice almost seemed apologetic— A good sign, at least. Maybe Nora would not be cast overboard.

"Y'know what I've learned with a life at sea?" Alice asked, setting down her stoat. "There's an odd comfort, a camaraderie among thieves– there really is no need to keep up the act of law-abiding citizens."

In a demonstration, Alice held up her hand. With no effort, she accumulated the dew from her glass upright to her fingertips. The dew froze into little darts. With a flick of her fingers, Alice shot the darts at Nora and Ber. Ber was quick enough to swipe the little dart from the air, using his aura without thinking. Nora was not so lucky, as the small shard of ice hit her squarely on the forehead. It was enough to leave a little red mark.

Alice's eyes lit up at Ber, "You control water, too?"

"Vapors and wind, technically. Though ice is light enough for me to handle, too."

"I bet you're a fine fighter, Ber. You should show me some pointers sometime."

"I'd love to! I'd like to train Miss Nora, too."

"*You* have magic, too?" Alice asked.

Nora felt as Alice and Viviane's eyes scanned her. "Yes, but I'm not very good at this kind of thing."

"Despite Alice's flaunting, we're not all gifted magicians, dear," Viviane said to Nora, "I can make plants grow a bit, but otherwise I'm quite ordinary."

Alice leaned into the table, "Here's what I *really* want to know: How do you tame a beast like a dragon? That's almost unheard of!"

At first, Nora did not know how to answer. She could tell the truth, had the truth not been a long story.

"I didn't 'tame' Lotte. I saved her, and she saved me," Nora said simply, "Since then, we have had a mutual understanding. Mostly. What about you, Ber? How on Ibe did you know how to do that?"

Ber shook his head, "It's, eh, a long story."

"How can someone talk so much and yet be so secretive?" Nora asked pointedly.

Viviane and Alice chuckled.

"I can't say that I blame you, Ber. We all have business we prefer to keep private," Viviane said.

"Lastly, I have to ask— what in the Saint's names has possessed you two to go to Saint Evedis?"

"I told you before, we have matters to attend to. It's urgent business the Queen needs to hear."

"The Queen. Right," Alice said, "Is that *really* the reason you're going? That seems like a lot of trouble, to go halfway across the country just for some rich folks hired by the richer to tell you 'no.' I'd add, too, meeting with the Queen of all people is near-impossible."

"You pry too much, Alice," Viviane chided, "But still, I'm curious– are you doing it for the heroism? The money? Because odds are, neither of those things will come of it."

Nora sighed. She found her frustration not with the thieves before her, but rather herself for really not thinking her plans through.

"Let's just say I'm a concerned citizen. Because above all else, I have the misfortune of living here," Nora said.

"On top of that, we have undeniable proof of what's inside the fog. They'll have to listen," Ber added.

Viviane drunk on his words, "... Then perhaps they will, if you are blessed with the right audience. I hope, for everyone's sake, that they listen."

Alice leaned in, "You were in the fog...? What was it like?"

"I thought that was the last question..." Nora said.

"Horrendous," Ber said, "Monsters run rampant, and the air is hardly breathable. There's a reason why people don't come back out."

"And yet, you did...?"

"Not without Nora's help," Ber explained, "We both held onto our sanity long enough to help each other out of there."

Nora looked to Ber. They exchanged a brief look, uncertain of how to explain further. Nora broke the moment of silence.

"Captain, Miss Viviane– something in us both changed when we entered the fog." She pulled back her sleeve, revealing her black veins, "Not just mentally, but physically. I must warn you of the undesirable... side effects, and pray you don't make the same mistakes as I did."

"... We take a lot of risks out here, mate," Alice said, "but rest assured, I don't plan to risk my life with a battle I know I can't win."

Nora breathed a sigh of relief from her words. If she could save a handful of not-terrible thieves from an excruciating existence in the fog, perhaps all of her trouble will be worth something.

As Alice turned her attention, speaking again to Viviane and Ber, Nora noticed something in her. The reddish hair Alice styled in perfect, short waves framed her face in such a way that Nora felt a sense of familiarity in her.

Alice's green eyes glinted back over to her. She smirked.

"See somethin' you like, Nora?"

Nora looked away, embarrassed for staring. "N-no, sorry. It's just that you look awfully familiar."

"I get that a lot. Probably on the account of all my wanted posters. I have a tendency for theatrics, but the drawback is every town wants my head."

"Every town wants your head because you like to set off explosives…" Viviane pointed.

"So there you go. Everyone's a critic, but I will not apologize for art."

11

Chapter 11

"I don't think you're ready for this, Ber!"

"One way to find out. Unless you're *scared*, Cap'n!"

Ber and Captain Alice found each other in a standoff. Craving the need to exert some energy, the two agreed on a duel— no weapons, just one water magician, and the other wind and vapor.

Ber said his folks called it 'storm magic.' Nora never realized one could wield two auras at once.

"That's because I can't," Ber had said, "Not technically. If the material is similar in composition, some magicians like myself can wield both as one."

A wide space on the main deck was cleared out for the duel. The work on the *Coral Fang* was completed for the day, so everyone onboard gathered to see the show. Nora would be lying to herself if she said she wasn't interested as well. Both Ber and Alice talked big game, so she was curious to see who would end up on top.

Alice made the first move. She summoned water from the sea and cast it around herself like a belt. She did not hold back. She lashed out as Ber took the defensive. Ber did not appear worried, however— He grinned, like he was anticipating something. The wind around the two picked up.

He met her power by deflecting the water, transforming it into ice and mist. Alice took advantage of this, for she too could control the ice.

Alice collected the ice and directed it back to Ber. It hit him square in the chest, causing him to stumble back and fall to the floor.

The spray and ice doused the main deck as they fought. The crew cheered on for their Captain, roaring in delight as Alice raised a fist in the air.

Something struck Nora when it came to the Captain's movements. She was fluid, *fast* in her movements. But the act obscured something Nora noticed in a quick glimpse— Alice relied heavily on her right arm. Nora wondered if Ber had clocked it too.

Ber got back to his feet in one swift movement. Alice seemed so occupied and the water fight she had with Ber, she neglected to realize the winds building around the two until it was too late. Ber directed all his energy towards Alice. The hurricane winds uprooted her and sent her flying to the floor. After a moment, the Captain raised her shaky hand in an OK gesture.

Ber expected some backlash, but the crew still cheered— a good match is a good match, after all. Viviane came to Alice's side to help her up. She asked to see to her wounds, to which Alice declined.

"I'm alright, Viv, 'just got thrown minorly!"

"Yes, so 'thrown' is my concern, dear..."

Ber approached Alice and Viviane.

"I'm sorry if I went a little too hard. I've been told I can be a bit rough..." Ber said.

"Please, that was the most fun I've had in a long while! Besides, you've given me a a new goal— Next time, I'll demolish you!" Alice said with a smirk.

—

The day crept to an end. Having some spare time to herself, Nora found a private corner and went fishing. She pulled the flyfishing hook from her ear, its lure fashioned out of one of Lotte's shed scales, and got to work. She did not expect to catch anything, and her prediction came true when Ber joined her.

Like the night before, Nora and Ber waited for Viviane to complete her kitchen duties so they could reconvene. Enough time had passed for the remainder of the crew to clear out.

"You didn't have to wait for me to have dinner, dears."

"Oh, I was going to. But Ber had to stop me," Nora said, "Sorry to say, I'm not waiting around for the Miss Captain to show up."

Viviane chuckled. She took her seat at the bench. Even if the food was lukewarm, it was still damn good, Nora thought. She wondered how Viviane managed to make the simplest of roasts taste this good.

"Speaking of, where is she?" Viviane asked.

"The night winds picked up a bit. I think she's still rearranging the sails," Ber answered.

"… Can I ask you two an odd favor?"

"I guess it fits, given the odd circumstances," Nora responded.

"Just like you have your reasons to be traveling, we have our own reasons to not be sticking around Stromshire," Viviane said, "However, I'm in shortage of some herbs only found in this province."

Viviane began sketching out a list of herbs on a small parchment, then handed it to Nora. Nora studied the list.

"I suppose it shouldn't be too hard. I've heard of most of these."

Viviane leaned in, nearly toppling her glass.

"Really?"

"Sure. My old lady had a bunch of these in her garden, back in the day."

Ber peered over Nora's shoulder.

"What's an infini-cabbage?" He asked.

"Oh, you should probably get that from a professional," Viviane pointed, "If you could, even finding a few would really help. I'll send our raptor to Saint Evedis Post to retrieve whatever you can find. Would, say, two weeks be sufficient?"

Nora nodded, "That should be plenty of time."

"Thank you so, so much."

Nora never considered herself good at reading others, but there was something about Viviane she could not help but notice. Perhaps it was her tone, the way she carried herself. Nora knew it well, an air of sorrow.

Nora chose not to read further, for she had been wrong about people before. This was a ship of oddballs, after all.

Alice came in not long after.

"Sorry for the hold up, did I miss anything?"

"No, dear! We were just talking about how we should keep in touch, once Nora and Ber reach the city."

Alice hummed, "That's not a bad idea! I'll have Ian send you both the job offer to join the crew. I'm sure you'll change your minds once you get there!"

"…You named that little nightmare with hooks for feet 'Ian?'" Nora asked.

"He needed a strong name for a strong young man," Alice nodded, "Anyway, I wanted to discuss with you the plans for dumping you tomorrow morning."

The four discussed over dinner their dropoff point. Alice proposed stopping at the mouth of the Evedis Delta. Nora knew it would be hell walking through that marsh. But even with her and Ber's detour, their travel time would be cut significantly from her original route.

Gross jobs and obnoxious pirates aside, Nora found herself actually enjoying the company around her. A small part of her wondered if a life on the high seas could work for her and her dragon. Lotte liked Alice well enough, after all. Nora then took into account how much time had passed with the three, and the glasses of rum she had since since demolished could be clouding her judgment.

Nora got some clarity when her eyes focused on Viviane, raising her glass and the others followed.

"To free labor—!" Alice started.

"To *new friends*," Viviane corrected, "I do hope our paths cross again."

"Here here!"

Nora smiled. She too raised her glass, bringing it to the other three in a melodious *clink*.

12

Chapter 12

Nora and Ber awoke to a loud bang that shook the entire ship. They rushed to the main deck. The air was heavy with cannon smoke. Nora noticed Alice's red hair through the smoke. She grabbed Ber and rushed towards her.

"Alice, what the hell is going on?"

"What's it look like?! We're under fucking siege by the Bachelor! You need to grab your dragon and get out of here!"

"We're not leaving you to fend for yourself. But either way, we're going to need the keys," Ber said.

Alice swore. She ran below deck, and Nora and Ber followed behind. They ran by the cannons as they were lit and blasted in succession.

"I get why he hates you, but he must *really* hate you," Ber said.

"Well, it probably is because I shagged him, and I didn't stick around to cuddle."

"Really?!"

"No, It's probably because I BLEW UP HIS BLOODY SHIP!"

Alice quickly unlocked Lotte's room.

"I hope for your sakes, she's strong enough to fly again—"

Lotte answered that question immediately. In the span of a few seconds, the dragon burst through the door, grabbed Nora, and barreled out from below deck towards the sunlight. It all felt familiar to Nora, as it was how she made her escape just the month before.

When Nora got her bearings, she clambered out from Lotte's grasp and onto her back. She found herself airborne, her dragon's dark wings spread across the sea and the chaos below. She caught a glimpse of the scene below her. Ber and Alice were back on deck, watching what might happen next. The Bachelor's crew was shouting and firing more rounds at the *Coral Fang*, others began aiming weapons at her and Lotte.

Nora thought about leaving, to stick to her original plan. It would take one command. But Nora found herself in stasis.

Damn it.

Nora pulled Lotte back towards the ship. She had her scoop up Ber in her front claws. The man screamed until Nora pulled him up to the dragon's back.

"Stop screaming, you're stressing me and Lotte out. You got a plan to help or not?"

"I do, actually!"

The Bachelor's crew worked fast, but Lotte was faster. Lotte zipped by the mast while Ber cut a gash straight through the sail. In the second fly-by, Lotte went lower. Nora timed between the cannon fire to fly between the ships. Ber worked his magic on the portholes. It was not enough to freeze them over, but it was a start.

Alice caught onto the plan. She stood on the railing and rose her arms. The waves turned to ice on the port side of the enemy ship. It was not enough to stop them entirely, but it was enough to escape.

Nora smiled to herself. She flew by once more to wave off her former captors. She was glad she did when she saw Viviane.

"Get your shit, or we're selling it!"

Nora obliged, having Lotte snatch their belongings. Unceremoniously they split ways. As much as Alice wanted to end the Bachelor, she knew his reinforcements would soon come. The *Coral Fang* sped off to the open seas, and Lotte, Nora, and Ber made an emergency landing in the marsh.

13

Chapter 13

Hours passed since their escape. The moment they reached the shore Lotte's wings gave out and they began the walk deep into the marsh. The second hour in, Nora figured they gathered enough space from their original captors. She finally felt herself relax.

Usually Nora welcomed the silence, but now she could not help but feel down after departing the *Coral Fang*. The leaders of the ship may have been insufferable at times (mainly Alice), but she could not deny those two days held the more laughter than she could remember in her recent memory. She stepped on with Ber behind her, wading through the bulrushes and onto an old path.

Ber followed Nora's footsteps as they tread through extra soft earth, taking care to not trip. A glint kept catching his eye, as the feather in Nora's hair glinted in the moonlight.

"Nora," Ber spoke.

"Yes, Ber?"

"Do you remember what I said, before we were kidnapped?"

"No," Nora admitted.

"We agreed to piece this… *Whatever* is going on, together," Ber said, "I figure since we got a bit more intel from Miss Alice and Viviane, now would be a good time."

"Oh, sure," Nora spotted Lotte, awaiting them at the top of a hill, "Let's get out of this muck first. We can jot down some things when we make camp."

Nora and Ber pried the wet boots from their feet, praying the warm night breeze would be enough to dry them overnight. Ber managed to scrounge a small fire, as Nora flipped open a well-worn book of field notes.

"You like writing?" Ber asked.

Nora shrugged.

"Most of these are old mercantile transactions. But I found that keeping my thoughts on track is easier if I write things down… Let's start from the start with the fog– what do you know?"

Ber frowned. For once, it seemed he did not want to talk. He turned away from Nora before he spoke.

"How to put this…" Ber began, "… I'm from a nation very far away. My nation— much to our misfortune, is responsible for the fog's creation."

Nora studied Ber's words. *Certainly no nation could have made this, could it?* Nora grew up being told Stromshire was the most powerful nation in the world, after all. But no mage, not even from Saint Evedis, could conjure something like what she witnessed. She considered, however, that it was possible Ber and the fog hailed from the uncharted frontiers in the east. How the two got here, however, remained a mystery.

"How is that possible?"

"It was a massive feat of magic, though I'm still not fully sure how he did it…"

"'He?' It was just one man?"

"Oh, he had help. It has a two-fold purpose; to fragment your nation, and to serve as a holding place for his weapons. I suppose, too, he used it for the dumping site for his undesirables."

Before Nora could say anything, Ber turned back to her with a plastered smile.

"But I don't want to dampen the mood with all that! What is the story behind the feather? What do you remember?"

Ber's behavior worried Nora, but she figured he would talk when he was ready. Nora remembered back to that day in the quarry. While her other dreams faded quickly after waking, this one stayed clear in her mind. But this was not a dream. She absently brushed her hair, finding the quill still there, tied to her with an invisible thread.

"I believe a spirit spoke to me. It looked like a raven, and said things aren't what they seem– something like that. It gave me this sword that's bonded to me, saying it would help me."

"That explains why it turned back into a feather when *I* touched it."

"There was one more thing," Nora said, "She said what's happening to my body... It said those forms are equal parts of myself."

The condition did not feel real. But saying it aloud made Nora feel exponentially worse. If she dwelled too long on the feeling she would surely crumble. She pushed the feeling aside and pressed on with her notes.

"Then, your condition has much deeper roots than just the fog?"

"I guess so. I mean... there's children's stories of spirits turning people to animals, but there was never any substance or explanations behind it."

Ber nodded. Perhaps he grew up with similar stories.

"Mom would know more about this kind of stuff than I do. I kinda regret not listening to her!" He chuckled.

Nora felt a twinge of unease with his tone. She knew she should not care, but part of her wondered what Ber's life was like before the fog, and what he left behind.

They found themselves still full from their last meal aboard the *Coral Fang*, deciding instead to snack on Viviane's pastries. Nora considered it a blessing, as they could save heartier food for later. Nora's eyes trained on the campfire. Her mind wandered, as she thought about the road ahead. Alice and Viviane took them closer to Saint Evedis, but Nora knew their journey was far from over.

Nora looked down from the hill at the swampland below. Fireflies danced on the warm summer air between the grasses, moving in little waves. The sea beyond it was dark and calm. What was left of the crescent moon reflected off the waves with the faintest glow. Nora watched what was left of the *Coral Fang* sail away, its amber lights creeping down into the horizon.

Ber looked almost surprised when Nora spoke. He too seemed lost in thought

"I think we reached a good stopping point, for now. Thank you, Ber."

Ber nodded, "So, what do we have so far in that book of yours?"

Nora handed him the notebook. He stared for a moment before humming to himself.

"What," Nora said, "Is my handwriting really that bad?"

"It's not that! It's just... What does this say?"

"Which part?"

Ber hesitated.

"... All of it."

14

Chapter 14

The members of the *Coral Fang* escaped with little injury from the Bachelor's skeleton crew. Save for some damage on the starboard side, they remained unscathed for another day. The Captain did what she did best after a successful day— throw a rager on the high seas.

Fortunately for Alice, there were plenty of offshore "ports" she could choose from once she hit international waters. These floating cities were ideal for both rowdy pirates and repairs from not-so-legal activities.

The crew already left for the evening, leaving Alice and Viviane to get ready on their own.

"Alice?" Viviane peeked into their chamber.

"Yes, Viv?" Alice called as she applied rouge to her cheeks.

"Do you think those two will be alright on their own?"

"Ber and the other one? I mean, probably. You didn't get attached to them, did ya?"

Unable to colour in her brows without her hand shaking, Alice pulled out a small dagger to aid in the shaping. It made a somewhat successful attempt, for she had to redo the other brow to match.

"No, but I was thinking… Maybe it would be fun to pester them for a while," Viviane suggested.

"Hm. Seems boring. Besides, they were headed east, weren't they? That is, like, the opposite of what our plan was."

Viv's brow furrowed from agitation to Alice's remark.

"*Your* plan…"

Alice looked into her vanity's mirror to catch Viviane's disapproving glance, and rolled her eyes. Alice huffed, continuing to powder her face.

Viviane did not want a fight. But there were topics— numerous, that they had yet to discuss on their separate goals. She tried to lighten her tone.

"… Anyway, we don't exactly have any missions at the moment, so why not? Find a port *not* owned by Harland, and decommission the *Fang* for a week or two…"

"I don't know, Viv… We've lost some momentum, sure, but we would have to put our whole expedition on hold," Alice turned around from the mirror, "And besides, this ship's not insured, what if someone takes her from under us?"

"Dear, you worry too much. It would still be an adventure."

Viviane leaned in and picked up a brush to blend a missed spot near Alice's nose. Alice felt her own breath hitch.

Viviane smirked, "Besides, you forget our raid from… three camps ago, I think? I snagged that hex for the ship, so no one's taking her unless they want to be impaled by the floorboards."

Alice gave a toothy grin and laughed, "You know me so well!"

15

Chapter 15

At dawn, Nora rolled from her blankets. She groggily gathered her things, uncaring for how loud her stumbling was. Lotte was not hard to spot in the tall grass, as she lumbered over something. As Nora waded through the grass, she picked up the stench of decay.

Ber rolled to his side, opening his eyes to find Nora having an argument with a dragon. Though he could pick up just one side of the conversation (hardly), he had a sense the dragon was winning.

"Fine, either leave it or eat it quick. I'm not flying with that stench– *NO*, I don't want it…!"

"Everything all right?" Ber asked.

"Just peachy. Saints, why couldn't I just have a horse like a normal person? Or at least a drake…"

Preparing for her flight, Lotte's wings stretched out, much further than Ber anticipated, as she blotted out the early morning sun. The beast seemed in much better condition, having ample rest, open air, and various marsh creatures to snack on. Nora folded her blankets in a way to craft a makeshift saddle. She took a moment to clean the dirt from between Lotte's scales before looking back to Ber.

"Are you nervous? You're not talking my ears off."

"A bit," Ber admitted, "Mostly, I'm just excited. I worked with beasts before, but never like this."

"If we plan to arrive in Saint Evedis next week, it's something you will get used to."

Nora checked her map one more time before hopping on Lotte. She grabbed Lotte's attention, pointing east and skyward.

"You ready? It will be just like yesterday... But longer and less chaotic, I hope."

Ber nodded. He gingerly shuffled onto Lotte, careful to leave Nora some space. When Lotte took off, her wings beating on the wind, Ber's efforts were for nothing. He clung to Lotte's scales, to Nora, praying for the pummeling wind to subside.

"Stay still, and keep your mouth shut. You might choke on dust, or a bug," Nora instructed, raising her voice above the howling wind, "We'll land again in a few hours."

Shakily, Ber removed a sweaty hand from his grip on the dragon.

"Let me try something..."

He held out his hand, then curled it in. In a moment, the wind around them ceased, leaving Ber and Nora in a quiet bubble. Nora marveled at Ber's creation, as the gusts turned to a light breeze.

"I'll admit, I'm impressed!" Nora said.

With the gusts gone, Ber took the opportunity to look at the land below. The wetlands reflected the colors of the morning sky like little mirrors. He spied down on a large colony of marsh rabbits, and back up to a flock of shorebirds soaring beside them. The sunrise was beautiful and radiant, in a way Ber had never seen before. He began to laugh.

"Saints, are you freaking out again?" Nora asked.

"No, this is beautiful!" Ber cheered, confident enough to run his fingers on the wind. "Do you really do this all the time?"

"As of recent, yes," Nora said. *I really do take this view for granted...*

—

"So, where do you think we are?"

"Not sure. But were headed eastward, so it's progress."

After a few hours Lotte grew tired, queuing Nora to land and finish their day's travel on foot.

Peeking out from the scrub sat a storage shed. Most of the surrounding trees were blighted, but a handful from the old grove still bore apples. No other buildings were anywhere in sight, but it still seemed like it could still be in use.

"What luck, we found camp!"

"Hold it, Ber. We were lucky enough last time to be invited to someone's house. We can't just walk in."

"Why not?" He asked, "Doubt this place gets much traffic. Besides, would you rather sleep in there, or in the woods?"

He made a valid point.

"… If we die, that's on you. I've heard enough horror stories that start out like this."

The two peered through age-stained glass into the large shed. Hay piled up to the shed's ceiling, but otherwise it remained vacant. Reluctantly, Nora lifted Ber up to squeeze through the window. The two were about the same height and frame, but Nora felt her muscles cry out when for a moment she held all his weight in her hands.

"Saints, what do they feed you wherever you come from…?"

Ber got leverage and entered. He made his way to the main door. Nora could hear his nervous laughter from the other side. *Oh boy.* The door clicked and opened.

"… Was the door unlocked the whole time?"

Ber laughed even harder. He made the mistake of turning his back, and Nora kicked him.

The two entered, and began to settle in for the evening. Lotte followed them in not long after. The beast made the best of it, rolling in the hay pile until dust flooded the room. She too settled and began shoveling the hay into a neat roost.

Nora loathed the idea of being chased by some livid farmers, or worse. She considered, however, that it was a welcome change from traveling late into the night.

Ber followed Lotte's idea, rearranging the loose hay into a makeshift bed.

"Much better than facing monsters and poachers out there, yeah?"

"I suppose."

"So… how do we fight them off next time? The poachers, that is."

Nora's tilted her head, unsure if she heard him right. "There's no *fighting* them off, Ber. If you see any delinquents out here, you *leave.*"

"Of course," Ber hesitated but he continued, "Have you ever had to fight someone, or something?"

"Aside from livestock, not really," Nora realized after that was not entirely true. "… But I suppose learning some self-defense wouldn't be a bad idea. We are in the middle of nowhere, after all."

Ber sat up, neglecting to hide his excitement, "D-do you want me to give you some pointers?"

"Ber, it is *so* late. Get some rest before I go ballistic."

"Tomorrow morning?"

Nora hesitated, "First thing tomorrow morning. We have to leave before anyone finds out we're here."

"It's a deal!"

Ber reached over his side of the hay pile, shaking her hand. Nora's lips curved slightly.

"Even if you're not from here, you're still awfully strange, Ber."

"Funny, I was thinking the same thing about you."

She rolled her eyes. "It's getting late, we should get some sleep."

Ber obeyed, bidding her goodnight.

—

That morning, Ber snagged an apple for breakfast and found Nora outside, already dressed. She paused her stretching to tie up her hair.

"Haven't seen anyone around, so we're safe for now," Nora turned to Ber, "Ready for practice?"

"Sure. You are… excited about this?"

"Not 'excited,' really… It's just nice to look forward to something that's not traveling, you know?"

"Of course."

He led the way, careful not to show her his blatant disbelief.

"Alright let's get started," Ber said, still rubbing the sleep from his eyes, "But first, how much experience do you have with a blade?"

"Well, I've cut ropes and gutted fish," Nora answered honestly.

Ber nodded. "Good enough." he replied, taking a bite from his apple.

"Do you want to use your, eh, hair thing?"

Nora had almost forgotten about it. She gingerly pulled the feather from her hair. In an instant its blade form returned.

"The first thing you need to remember is to never be afraid of your own weapon. If you have any fear with what you are fighting with, then you won't be able to protect yourself. Or others," Ber said.

Nora examined her blade. If she was honest with herself, she was afraid of the thing. She had no idea what it could do, or why it bound itself to her. But she took Ber's words to heart; she willed herself to not be afraid, or at least pretended to.

"My advice is to get used to the sword and its weight. What also helps me is to imagine the blade as an extension of your arm." Ber said.

Ber produced an old machete he found in the shed. He swung the blade swiftly in figure eights. Nora copied him and slowly swung the sword back and forth.

"Good! Why don't you try this?"

Nora practiced for a long while by swinging the blade in various ways. She copied Ber in new movements and positions. Ber enjoyed the attention. He decided to treat Nora to a show, adding finesse to his movements and spinning the blade front to back.

Nora jumped when she heard Ber yelp. Ber nicked his own arm. It seemed superficial, but but blood had already started to fill the wound and spill down his arm.

"I… meant to do that," Ber said, his face pink, "One last thing before we take a—a more than necessary break; don't get too cocky. Otherwise, *this* happens."

Ber gestured to the arm that he was now clutching to stop the bleeding.

Nora helped Ber back into the shed to rest and to help bandage up his wound. She cleaned his arm as best as she could. She took a clean shirt from her bag and tore it to make a bandage. She made a mental note to get a medicine kit on her next visit to town.

"Sorry about your shirt," Ber said.

Nora shrugged, "The bandage needed to be clean. Besides, that just means *you're* out one shirt until you buy me a new one."

Ber laughed at that.

"To be honest Nora, I'm not too skilled with swords. I just wanted to teach you what I know so we can protect each other and…" His words trailed off.

"You? 'Not too skilled?' No way." Nora teased, finishing her work on the bandage, "So, what weapon *can* you use well?"

"I'll show ya!"

—

Ber opened his large case crammed with random possessions and clutter. He dug through the case to reveal a massive axe.

How was that thing hiding under all that junk?

Ber lifted the large weapon with ease. The axe appeared worn, but still very formidable. Dull and frayed bands were tied to the handle and dangled off. A very unusual yet beautiful weapon. Ber took a moment to brush over the axe.

"It may look bulky, but she's super reliable! This thing's been with me everywhere," Ber said, bringing the axe up to rest it on his shoulder.

"Wait a minute, you just hurt yourself. You're not planning on flailing that axe around outside, are you?"

Ber hummed thoughtfully, "*Outside!* That's a better idea than what I had in mind."

Ber paced out the door. Nora sighed and followed.

As they walked towards an adequate opening, the wind picked up. What Nora thought was a natural occurrence turned out to be from Ber. His grip tightened around the axe handle. He sliced through the air with equal parts grace and power, while the wind turned to gusts. Nora realized that what she thought was frivolous tricks with his axe was actually used to gather power. He made sure Nora was looking while he swung the weapon in an arc, well over his head, and struck back down to the earth.

A burst of white clouds and wind left the axe in a thunderous rumble. Nora failed to brace herself, and could not help but watch in shock and awe of Ber's strike. When the clouds dissipated, Nora approached. She stepped over the thin layer of frost radiating from the strike. She eyed where the blade cleaved the earth, leaving a significant divot in the ground.

"Ber," Nora said, careful with her words, "where… *exactly,* are you from?"

Ber's smile vanished. For someone so talkative, Nora found it unsettling that he was at a loss for words.

"… If I told you, I don't think you would believe me."

"Maybe so, if you had told me a couple days ago. But since then, I turned into a monster and a bird gave me a sword," Nora said, "So try me."

Ber ran a hand through his hair. Nora noticed a pair of black earrings in his pointed ears she had not noticed before.

"There is an ancient legend that this world is tied to another. It is not a twin, rather a sister— the same in many ways, but also vastly different. I believe your kind call it the 'Shadow Veil.'"

Nora knew of this legend. It served as a fable for why daylight weans in at the end of the year. She tried to wrack her brain for what that other world was called.

"… Are you saying you are from Ebi?"

Ber nodded.

Nora decided to entertain his claim, at least for now. She had a million other questions. *Curiosity has a price, Nora,* a familiar voice rang inside her.

"Is that why you're going to Saint Evedis?" Nora said simply.

"That's right. I reckon someone in that big city might know how to stop the fog"

Finally the man started making some sense. Of course, Nora still had pressing questions, the curiosity she urged to press down. Mostly it had to do with the origin of the feathers that prickled along Ber's neck. From her angle she could see small plumes just beneath his shirt collar.

She remembered his words to her just outside the fog.

This is why I needed your necklace. If ya really want to know, you can snatch it from me any time, and you can run into town to fetch a pretty price for my head.

Nora glimpsed to her hands, her own remnants of what she was in the fog. What once were claws and hair returned to normal, save for the color of her hands and forearms, stained a hueless dark grey.

For the sake of Nora's peace of mind, she assumed his predicament was like her own. What happened in the fog should stay in the fog, after all.

Ber clasped his hands together. It brought Nora out of her thoughts.

"Well! Sorry to make us have a late start. Let's hit the road, shall we?"

16

Chapter 16

The two set off again towards Saint Evedis. They traveled for what Ber thought felt like weeks, but Nora tracked was a few days. Nora made sure to keep in tune with Lotte, sensing when she grew weary from travel. At dusk, they set up camp, finding shelter in abandoned buildings and caves when they could.

As Ber and Nora expected, avoiding the patches of fog delayed their straight shot to Saint Evedis. Most of the patches were avoidable, covering only acres at a time. But some strips stretched out in a seemingly never ending expanse. In those cases, Nora had no choice but to pick a side, and pray she could reach the edge before nightfall.

What Nora did not foresee was Ber's adoration for her dragon. She was surprised to see just how playful Lotte could get with him, without breaking any of his bones.

Nora considered Ber was not the worst company she could have kept on her travels. She could admit the man kept her entertained on the days she used to spend alone. Ber would trail on all day– about what Nora could hardly recall. He was talented in talking about nothing for hours.

"So," Ber said, getting comfortable on the dragon's back, "where's our next stop?"

Nora turned, sitting sidesaddle to review their map.

"We'll stop somewhere in this patch of wilderness. If we pass civilization,

I'll find as much cloud cover as possible."

"So… are we not visiting *any* towns?"

"We'll go into town for food and shelter, when the weather is rough. We really can't afford to be tourists, Ber. Not out here…" Nora said, "… Besides, there's far more exciting things to see once we're in Saint Evedis."

Ber took her words to heart. As exciting as it all was to explore this new land to him, he kept his focus on the crown jewel of Ibe. Even in his lessons back home, they emphasized the sheer size and power of the Capital– lofty towers, gold lined streets, and social elites among a country of wasteland. His instructors may have been wrong about the wasteland bit, but Ber was intrigued by whatever was to come with Saint Evedis.

They soared for hours. Nora guided Lotte to keep her on track, while Ber kept himself busy by enjoying their view, as well as the occasional snack.

Of course eventually, Ber got bored.

"You don't talk much, do ya?" Ber spoke after a while.

To this Nora stayed silent and continued to gaze ahead.

"C'mon, there has to be something we can talk about." Ber looked around at the endless sky around them. "Hey, we're soaring across the sky on a *dragon*, and you do this all the time!"

"… Mhm."

"I mean, how amazing is that?"

"I won't deny that this is great– I'm very grateful for Miss Lotte here," Nora said, patting the beast, "But why must you destroy every peaceful moment?"

"Come on, I give you *plenty* of peaceful moments–"

"Sleep does not count."

"—But I can't help that you're fun to talk to," Ber said, "Fun to tease, too."

Nora huffed and turned around. "I'd almost be flattered if I wasn't irritated with you. Now shut your mouth before I kick you off."

Before Ber could make a rebuttal, something below caught his eye.

"Eh, Nora?"

"For Saint's sake, what?!"

Nora followed his gaze down to the clearing below. A pack of large animals cornered what Nora thought might be a horse. Upon closer inspection, it appeared to be poachers honing in on a target on horseback.

For once, Ber said nothing, as he watched the scene took place. He wanted to throw himself off and intervene, but he knew this was Nora's call.

"We barely survived our scrape with poachers last time…" Nora considered aloud.

Nora preferred to not give herself a gruesome death, to pursue a better life. She owed Lotte that, too. But, she could not watch as someone suffered the same way she had.

"… Damn it all. Lotte, let's go."

Nora leaned into her beast as Lotte took a steep dive, causing Ber to nearly lose his lunch. When Lotte was close enough she spread her wings again, stalling their flight as they swept by the hunters.

With her sheer size and speed, Lotte warded the hunters from their target. The target sped off into the woods, and the poachers turned their attention to their larger prize.

A poacher sounded their whistle. Approaching down the hills came more poachers, all fully clad in leather armor.

"They sure work fast," Nora muttered as she unsheathed her blade.

Their rapturous mounts drove away Lotte and kept her occupied, leaving Nora and Ber to fend for themselves. Cooperating as one, the poachers formed a tight circle to take them down.

Nora and Ber faced apart, weapons held high as a way to make some space between them and the poachers, but they all stood together, caging them in. They toyed with their ropes and spears, all watching to see their next move.

"Where are you lot in a hurry to?"

"Why don'tcha stick around with us for a while?"

Nora cocked her head. She signaled to Ber, who swirled his axe and struck the ground with a hurricane force. While most of the poachers successfully braved the winds, a few flew back. In the dust, she disarmed the man with her blade. Catching him off guard, she kicked the man down and held him under the heel of her boot.

"Tempting, but we best be going," Nora answered.

Ber backed towards her. The dust began to settle, and she realized how quick the poachers regained their ground. They wove together into a smaller, tighter circle.

From behind their original target returned, pulling on the reigns for the horse to rear back. The man atop the horse aimed his bow and shot several poachers, one after another.

The straggling enemies finally turned away, falling back into the woods. The stranger unraveled, giving a sigh of relief.

He approached Nora and Ber. His stocky horse towered over the two, and nearly rivaled Lotte's size.

"Are either of you hurt?"

"I don't think so," Ber managed.

"Good, good..." The man said, swiping stray hairs from his face. He caught his breath and reached down to shake Nora and Ber's hand, "The name's Arvo, sorry we had to meet like this."

The man seemed a bit older than Nora and Ber. His long, reddish-brown hair had a few streaks of grey peeking through. It was pinned back behind his pointed ears.

Ber smiled, "The pleasure's mine, I'm Ber."

"Nora."

Arvo dismounted his horse, "I want to thank you for your help. I bit off more than I could chew, I suppose," Arvo chuckled, "At the very least, I'd like to treat my fellow travelers with dinner. I don't think I have anything suitable for your scaled friend here, however."

"You're not... terrified of her?" Nora gestured to Lotte.

Arvo held out his hand for a moment. He pinched the base of a fallen leaf, bringing forth the smallest hint of smoke and a perfect ember circle through the leaf.

"I'm a friend to fellow targets," Arvo said simply.

Ber and Nora looked at each other. Both of them missed a few too many meals to deny such an offer.

—

Where Nora and Ber landed was not far from the local hub of Houndsmouth. Arvo led Ber and Nora through the cramped streets and into a narrow, brick alley. The alleyways forked multiple times to the point where they couldn't remember the direction out. Then he unlocked a dark, weathered door and down a set of stairs. Nora considered the likelihood of their acquaintance planning an ambush– she could not help it, given her track record. But she also considered how the man witnessed her and Ber fight back poachers just an hour before. She pushed her anxieties aside for the promise of food.

"I don't think Ed's back, yet…" Arvo said to himself, "Let me drop off some things, then we can get something to eat."

He gestured to worn but rather comfortable looking armchairs beside the fire before he left. The main room was dark, and it was obvious that no one until recently lived in the tenement. What puzzled the duo most was the dim warmth from the fire. The flames were so mild, Nora felt that she could stick her hand in and not get burned. She avoided the temptation, in case she was wrong.

"Do you think this place is a cult?" Ber asked suddenly.

"Why would you say that?"

Ber ticked his fingers as he brought up his points, "A *very* handsome man pretends to need rescuing. He shows us this… house-thing. Perhaps when he comes back, he'll tell us his prophecies and force us to join his legion."

"Are you making absurd comments just to get a reaction out of me?"

"Maybe," Ber grinned, "But I *am* serious, we should be careful with whoever we're dealing with."

Arvo stepped back into the room.

"We're not a cult. If you'd like to leave, the door's always open. Except at night, I guess…" He mulled, "But that's besides the point. I apologize if I came off a bit vague. Do you still want dinner?"

As promised, Arvo bought Nora and Ber food from one of the many merchants on the sunnier side of the tenements. Ber was delighted at the sight of flaky dough spread over a hot, metal surface and loaded with cheese and fruits. It won Nora over when she saw the same dough loaded with meat. They unceremoniously filled their stomachs to relieve their stressful meeting.

Arvo wiped the corner of his mouth from his own meal, some spiced meat skewer Nora was quite jealous of.

"… So, me and my partner run an organization called 'Hearth,'" Arvo began, but was distracted by the blatant disbelief on Ber's face, "It's *not* a cult. For all intensive purposes, we are a guild of like-minded individuals with specialized goods and services to aid the those in need"

"I'm sure that spiel is what you tell the Guard," Nora said.

"Absolutely," Arvo said, "While it's all technically true, our members are all products of the civil wars across Stromshire. Our prerogative is to reverse the damage done to the community, and to take on jobs the law disregards… or started in the first place."

"I assume you've got a lot on your hands, then," Nora said.

"You have no idea. What's worse is these days our work can lean towards the unordinary."

"How so?" Ber asked.

"You saw it yourself. Warding off poachers and beasts, harboring all sorts of rare creatures… Back in the day, it used to be easy. With the demand for aura being so high, practically no one's safe."

"Why were those hunters after you in the first place?"

"I was helping someone escape— Weird, I guess that's what you ended up doing, too!" Arvo laughed, "But then of course, those fools also see me as a target. My power is about as weak as they come, but the demand for fire in the blood is high."

Arvo continued, "If you don't mind me asking, what brings you to the area? Doubt you're here for the tourism."

"Oh, we're just passing through. We've business in Saint Evedis," Nora said.

Arvo chuckled, "Don't we all… Is it for sanctuary?"

"No— Yes and no. It's complicated," Nora answered.

A quiet beat passed.

"It seems you have business elsewhere but I will ask… Would either of you be interested in joining our guild? This is not a cut-and-dry job position, but rather an agreement– 'I scratch your back, you scratch mine' kind of situation."

Ber tilted his head.

"Why are we scratching backs, now?"

"Ber, not like that..." Nora said.

"I'll be blunt. We need the help, and we can't afford to advertise as it runs the risk of exposing ourselves."

"I don't know, Arvo. Nor and I have some serious business we have to attend to as soon as we reach the Capital."

Arvo smiled.

"I understand. At the very least, I could have you meet my partner, Edvard. If you need a place to stay, I'm sure he would let you, once he hears you saved my ass," Arvo chuckled.

Nora and Ber exchanged looks. Neither could deny a good rest at this point.

—

They made the brief walk back to the tenement. Arvo left to check in on his partner, returning a minute after.

"Ed's ready to see you. He can be... abrasive, but I promise he's a nice guy! Just be sure to call him Edvard," Arvo said.

Arvo opened the door for Nora and Ber to a room surrounded by wooden book shelves. Only one was actually used for bookkeeping, as the remainder were used for material storage and glorified work tables.

"Are these the ones you were talking about, Arvo?" Edvard asked.

His eyes remained glued to an odd gadget he was fiddling with– spindly parts with little blades. Whatever it was, it looked dangerous. He seemed older than Arvo, with dark skin and golden eyes, a shade Nora thought resembled a wolf's. At his feet lay the largest dog Nora and Ber had ever seen. The scruffy, grey animal remained in a peaceful sleep, unbothered by the strangers.

"Yes, this is Nora and Ber. They were quick to take action when I needed help," Arvo said.

Edvard spoke, half attentive to the conversation.

"I appreciate your help. If you need it, you may stay for the night, but no longer."

"We really appreciate it, sir. We have urgent business in Saint Evedis, so we will be out of here first thing tomorrow morning," Nora said.

Edvard said nothing. He continued to tweak the joints of his contraption. Unappreciative of the man's disregard to their conversation, Nora was tempted to kick his contraption off the table. She remained patient.

"... Saint Evedis, huh? Hope you have papers. They won't take most folk in otherwise."

Nora felt a twinge of guilt, as the thought did not cross her that Ber's status would be an issue at the gates.

"Papers?" Ber her asked.

"Saint Evedis will need proof of your citizenship at the gate."

"I don't– I'm not exactly…"

"Not from a place with those? Lucky for you, we have a contact that makes those kinds of documents," Arvo paused, "I have an idea. Maybe you could help us out tomorrow, in return we could put those papers in for you… Assuming you don't have couple hundred gold to spare."

Edvard sighed, placing his contraption aside.

"I don't like this plan. Arvo, are you certain these two can even be trusted?"

Arvo's eyes narrowed, "Saints, Ed, if you paid a bit more attention, you'd know they very likely saved my life today."

For a moment, Nora noticed a flash of guilt came and went from Edvard's face.

"… Fine. I'll assess your skills tomorrow. If it all turns out, we will head out for a mission. Be ready by dawn. We'll have much to discuss."

17

Chapter 17

Arvo prepared cots for Nora and Ber's stay. Nora tried to get rest for whatever Edvard had planned for tomorrow. She eventually gave up and moved to one of the armchairs by the fireplace. The fire's red flames continued to support its size, while still giving little warmth.

Nora let out a quiet sigh from another long day. *At least we're sleeping indoors...* She wrapped herself in the large blanket slung across the chair and picked up a yellowed book from the adjacent side table.

Compared to most things in the room, the blanket was of superior quality. It was thick and densely woven, and made with bright, beautiful colors.

Nora looked around. Their tenement was dingy (as were most others), but had nice touches here and there. It was as if someone was really trying to fix this place up.

When she examined the pages of the book she held and found that it was written in a different language. From the words she could decipher, she read title 'ONE: Study of *Ujai-ek* and ...... Behind the *Korrua*' Nora skimmed through the first few pages and found the word 'Korrua' many more times, along with illustrations of various beasts.

She assumed that it was a research book of some kind, but she couldn't figure out what *Ujai-ek* meant. She skipped a few chapters to find an explanation, but the fading ink became unreadable. The pictures she did find, however, were unnerving. Compared to the background, the beasts pictured were *massive*. Each one she came across had white, featureless eyes.

Distorted from water and age, the rest became indecipherable. Nora set it down and tried to rest. Not long after, she heard the muffled sound of singing coming down the alley. Moments after, someone burst through the door, causing Nora to jump.

"… And now after it all, we still stand—!" Sung a woman at the threshold. Immediately she saw Nora and slid a silver mask over her eyes and nose. For a brief moment, she seemed just as bewildered as Nora.

"… Oh, *you're* new. Tell me, is the old man asleep?"

Nora, who had nearly fallen out of her chair moments before, got to her feet.

"Eh- Edvard? I think so."

A smile spread across the woman's face.

"Joyous day! He tends to stay up just to yell at me about something, so this is refreshing."

The woman brought the second armchair closer to Nora's. She was dressed in a crimson cloak, paired with fancy ankle boots. Curly blonde hair stuck out from her hood, and her mask glimmered dimly in the fire's light.

"I had to deal with him earlier this evening, too," Nora commented.

The woman snickered and patted Nora on the back.

"It's alright. He's hard on all the newbies. You can call me Hel."

"I'm Nora."

"So Nora, what keeps you up so late?"

"Stress, I reckon."

"I see… If you could entertain an old lady like me, would you care for a palm reading? I haven't practiced my work in a while, and I could use the fresh meat."

"Eh, go ahead."

Nora held out her hands. The ashen grey had worn off days before, bringing color back to her hands. A quiet moment passed as Hel scanned her palms. Nora typically did not allow others to touch her hands, but

Hel's touch was light enough to not set her off. She wondered how well Hel could read her palms, or see in general, behind that mask. Nora tried to make conversation with her.

"So… what do you do for Edvard?"

"I don't do anything *for* him, but he likes to think that. But I do work as the guild's seamstress, and I do this kind of stuff on the side. Weird combination, right?" Hel laughed, "You won't believe how often these kids destroy their clothes and armor."

Hel continued, "My ability allows me to vaguely read a person's spiritual history. What people don't realize is that the spirit realm interacts with us more often than we think. With that said…" Hel put down Nora's hand, "… You've gone through some strange shit, haven't you?"

"You have no idea."

Hel stood, arching her back to stretch out the kinks. "Well Miss Nora, you are an interesting one! It was a pleasure, but I should leave you to get some rest for tomorrow."

Nora thanked Hel as she took her leave. The hearth's fire was embers now. In the dying light, Nora looked at her own palms, wondering whether Hel's work was all a fluke.

18

Chapter 18

Nora woke with regret from sleeping crookedly in a chair. To Ber's displeasure, she shook his body awake when she heard movement from outside.

The two stumbled into their boots and headed out the door. They found Edvard and Arvo, still setting up. Arvo greeted them warmly and Edvard, Nora assumed was not a morning person, wore a deep scowl.

He might not be an any-time-of-day person, Nora considered.

"There's a vacant warehouse a few blocks away. We'll be using it for training purposes," Edvard explained.

After a quiet morning walk, the four entered the warehouse through a pair of unlocked windows. The building made for a perfect makeshift arena. It was vast and empty, save for some trash and scrawled obscenities on the walls, likely left by the local youths.

"Are you sure you don't need some kind of pick-me-up or something, old man?" Arvo asked, winking at Edvard.

Edvard's joints audibly cracked as he stretched, almost in response to his jab.

"No, let's just get started."

Ber leaned into Nora's ear, "How old do you think he is for the cracks in his back to echo that much in here?"

Nora snorted, distracted as Edvard chose his first opponent.

"Ber," Edvard said, "since you're awake enough to be cracking jokes, you can humor this old man and spar with me first."

To this Ber smirked, "Of course."

"Hold on, is what we're doing today dangerous enough to be warranting… this?" Nora asked.

"Probably not. But you can never be too careful," Edvard answered.

Ber and Edvard paced to the center of the warehouse, their weapons readied. When Ber took a step, Edvard took four, deflecting his heavy axe and kicking him down.

"Want to try that again, boy?"

"Yessir!"

Slightly off-kilter, Ber lifted himself up with the help of gusts from his palms. Edvard remained unphased, holding a readied stance. Ber marched towards him again, striking Edvard's short sword.

Edvard struck again, and again, trying to take advantage of his opponent's heavier weapon. Each time, Ber met the blade with his axe with surprising speed. Ber gained a formidable stance, an opportunity, and took the chance to lunge. Edvard matched his blade to his own. Ber applied more force to his strikes, and could have sworn for a moment that Edvard was wavering.

A shrill clang rang through the warehouse. Edvard and Ber reached a standstill.

"Interesting style you have," Edvard said, "Were you military?"

"I was going to ask you the same thing," Ber said.

"Yes. Navy."

Ber felt Edvard's force give, but Edvard sidestepped, striking again and again. Finally, Ber tumbled back. His face was met with Edvard's blade pointed at him.

"Your martial style serves you well. But you rely too much on brute force," Edvard said, "I would test your magic as well, but we are in city limits. I don't particularly feel like being persecuted today."

Edvard shifted his attention to Nora.

"It's your turn."

Nora ignored her pounding heart as she prepared herself, wielding a standard sword against Edvard's own. She figured her feather-sword situation would not be best for this fight. Edvard stood at the ready. Something about his perfect posture and fighting prowess came off as smug to Nora. She had the temptation to wipe the prideful demeanor from his face.

Edvard launched himself at Nora, and Nora struggled to keep up. She met each swing of the sword with her own. She knew better than to use all her energy, like Ber.

Nora held her ground, but in the end, she was still not well trained in the blade. Her sword met Edvard's, and with a twist of the blade and a thrust of his arm, Nora was sent tumbling to the ground.

Edvard shook his head, "No good. You'll need far more practice than your companion."

Nora was not one to start fights– she did not think so, anyway. However, she thought now would be a good time as any to sink a dagger into Edvard's thigh. *Perhaps not.*

"At the very least, you can both hold your ground," Edvard said, "I will allow your assistance with our mission this morning. I could use the extra hands."

Ber cheered, but Nora could not bring herself to that enthusiasm. Something about the fight left her unsatisfied. She of course wanted to prove Edvard wrong. Another part of her, which she found quite annoying, felt she needed to prove her worth to him, her strength.

To Nora's displeasure, they again trekked on foot to the outskirts of town. Away from curious ears, Edvard explained their mission.

"We received a tip that imports of semi-precious metals are going missing. The trade checkpoint is under new management by stationed troops… but I've got a hunch they're dipping into the town's supply."

Nora grabbed Ber's attention, "Might not be the only hunch he has."

Ber went pink as he stifled a chuckle. Arvo joined in, Edvard seemingly unaware until he straightened his back.

"You forget that we're the same age, Arvo… And if we're done harassing the 'elderly,' I'd like to get in position. The shipment should be coming in soon."

The team set up an informal stakeout at the town's trading post. They found ample space to hide amongst the barrels and crates in the shipyard.

Minutes bled into hours as they waited for the shipment to arrive. The group let down their guard when they realized no one would be entering the shipyard anytime soon. Even Edvard's perpetually tensed shoulders seemed to relax, though his eyes remained on the post.

"… This shipment is scheduled for *today,* correct?" Ber asked.

"Yes. But with the fog being unpredictable these days, it could come much later– tomorrow even," Arvo answered.

Nora sighed, "I'm starting to regret agreeing to this– at this rate, we'd have lost two days of travel."

"Is what you're relaying to Saint Evedis really this urgent?" Edvard asked.

"*Yes,*" Nora and Ber said in unison.

Before Edvard could express his doubt, he spotted the target– an armored caravan. It made a steady pace towards the checkpoint.

"It's here," Edvard said, "Let's get going– Keep quiet and follow my lead." Edvard descended the ladder down to the main platform first.

"… I'll be right behind you, don't worry," Arvo added, ushering Nora and Ber to follow suit.

They approached the checkpoint station and hid among the numerous crates and barrels. None of them dared to make a noise as they watched as the transaction took place. A lone, bored-looking guard took her time reviewing the driver's papers. She shuffled over to check the goods, and spent a brief moment checking the undercarriage before giving the driver a signal to carry on.

Edvard's brows furrowed.

"There's something we're missing."

The group followed the caravan back into town. The streets were much more lively now, with the afternoon rush of merchants and artisans alike. Nora and Ber trailed behind as they took turn after turn, until the roads began to clear of people.

The caravan took a corner. In an instant, a cacophony of clattering metal rang down the alley. Edvard pushed Nora and Ber towards the noise.

"Go, go!"

Nora's heart pounded as she sidled down to the source of the noise. When she laid eyes on the scene, all that remained was an emptied caravan and a spooked draft horse, the driver gone.

There was no time to dwell on the scene when the trail was hot. She took a chance and ran into the alley. Ber and Edvard followed suit but seemed to lose sight of Arvo.

They made it to a fork in the alley. No sign of commotion could be seen, but a shadow from above. Nora craned her neck to find Arvo above them, jumping from the rooftops.

"Take a left!" He called out.

They did just that. With Arvo's help they had a lead. He guided the group through the alleyways– right, right, left, *stop*.

The dead end of the alley held a single back door. Edvard moved ahead of Nora and Ber.

"Move aside and stay behind me."

In one swift kick, Edvard kicked the door in. For a moment, everyone on the other side of the door was still. Among the clutter and stolen metals in the room stood the thieves. All three were clad in masks obscuring their faces.

"You meddled in the wrong alley, mate," The one closest to Edvard spoke, before swinging a club to his head.

Before Ber or Nora could even process the scene, Edvard clutched the club midswing. He barreled into the thief, shoving the man with enough force to make a crater in the wall.

The other two were already upon him. Ber swung his axe between them and Edvard. The axe was lodged in the wood floor, leaving Ber with just a short dagger to work with. That would not do, so he sprouted a better plan. One of the thieves left their front open, to which Ber kicked square in the chest. He used his magic to add wind force to topple him back towards Nora.

Nora acted quick, grappling the man from behind. Before her and Ber could address the final thief, he had already joined his friend in the wall.

"Nice catch, Nor!" Ber praised.

"Yeah, you *threw* him at me…"

The body in her grasp went limp. Nora realized she gripped her attacker a little too hard as he fainted, nearly bringing Nora with.

"… Whoops."

Edvard waved it off, "These guys are just grunts. They would not have had any valuable information, anyway. Bar the door. We've our own investigation to sort through. I'd rather not have prying eyes."

Arvo finally caught up to them, a moment too late for the fight. He left to make sure no guards came their way. Nora and Ber looked at what was left of the door on the floor once he left. They shuffled to each side to prop the door back into the entryway.

The three turned the place upside down, tearing through ledgers, receipts, anything they could find in the drawers and cabinets. Nora taught Ber a few basics in Common script, but he still could not read anything they could find. When Ed's back was turned, he handed Nora any papers he found to go through.

Nora came across one of the last untouched drawers, when she came across something she was not expecting.

"Edvard, take a look at this."

Together, they went through hundreds of identification sheets of civilians. The papers described appearance, approximate age, and last known location. Some even held occupations, addresses and mugshots. The one descriptor they all shared sent chills down Nora's spine.

'AURA CONFIRMED: Y'

Nora jumped when she heard frantic knocking, coming from inside the tenement. It did not take them long to find the source. Locked away in a storage locker they found the driver, gagged and bound.

Edvard quickly cut the rope and fabric tied around his mouth.

"Oh… Oh thank the Saints. I thought I was going to die in there."

"What happened?" Ed asked.

"I don't know. I was knocked out before I could figure out who attacked me."

Ed tilted his head at the man. He shuffled through the papers he gathered and revealed one of the few with a mugshot.

"Would this be you?"

The man grasped the paper.

"How did they…?" The man mumbled, visibly shaking. He shredded the paper, "… To hell with the shipment. I'm alive. Thank you all so, so much."

Edvard looked around at all the cargo.

"I can help you load this back up, if you can keep a secret, sir."

"Sure, whatever. Anything."

—

"Nora! Eyes ahead!"

Nora turned back around. Her and Ber were stationed on opposite sides of the alley. They watched for incoming traffic and guards, as Edvard and the driver loaded the carriage back up. Nora caught glimpses of Edvard hauling the metal, using his own magic to lift it in quickly.

When they wrapped up, Nora caught bits of Edvard's conversation.

"… Are you sure?"

"Absolutely. It's the least I can do."

When the driver drove off, Ber and Nora met Edvard back in the tenement. The thieves remained knocked out, now tied up for when the guards make their rounds.

Edvard did not move from where the remaining files lie. Before Nora or Ber could inquire, he spoke.

"Hearth is something Arvo and I created. We built it on the backbone of the guild that came before us, with the hope we could carry on what they accomplished— To protect the vulnerable. To provide solace for those with no help, no state, no one to turn to."

He continued, "Our team remains small, and that is my fault. Aside from the law finding us out, it has been my fault why we do not have many members," Edvard turned to Nora and Ber. "But we can't make progress without some risks. If you choose to accept, I would like to officiate you both as members of Hearth."

"I'm honored, truly. But we *do* have business in Saint Evedis," Ber said.

"I know. In earnest, that helps us a great deal. We do not have any intelligence in Saint Evedis yet, and starting something in one of the largest hubs on Ibe would be a great leap forward."

Nora toed the debris on the floor. She looked to the men hung over the concave of drywall.

"We won't have the time to be vigilantes there, Ed."

"I wouldn't ask you to throw up your cause– All I ask is to send information you find to us, anything pertinent to the cause. Of course, this means you have access to any information we can pull for your own mission."

Nora did not have to reflect long to consider the offer. Any information on the fog they could gather would be beneficial. It was work she could do, and she needed any help she could get.

"I'm in."

"Me, too," Ber chimed.

Edvard smiled. Something small, but it appeared genuine. Nora did not know he was capable of that. Still she found herself keeping the mental picture in her mind after the moment passed.

"We should get going, before the Guard comes. Besides, Arvo'd be elated to hear this."

19

Chapter 19

Edvard underexaggerated Arvo's response to the news. The man demanded to throw an impromptu party at their frequent spot, a pub called Rock's Toss. With the promise of a good time, a few passing members joined in. Among them was Arvo, Edvard, Hel, a prematurely greying man covered in scars, an individual with wild hair and circle-rim glasses, and a woman who, Nora swore, looked just like a member of Alice's own crew.

They enjoyed themselves from the corner booth of the pub. Being a not-so-legal operation, Hearth kept a low profile at any gathering. It helped that the barmaid, too, was a member, keeping watch over patrons and any prying eyes and ears.

"So! Kids," Hel said to Nora and Ber, "What's your next step from here?"

"After Ber gets his papers, we'll take our last leg of the trek to Saint Evedis. Fortunately, it looks like it will be a straight shot from here."

"How exciting! I'm jealous, you both are seeing the big city before me!"

"I have to remind you, Ber, there's a possibility those papers might not work. There's a reason Saint Evedis is so elusive and notoriously difficult to enter. I implore you not to go that route if you don't have to," Edvard said.

"I–"

Ber was interrupted by Hel.

"What do you suggest he do, then? Declare refuge as a Stateless?"

"*Yes*," Edvard said.

"*Yes*," Hel echoed, "Because that's worked *so* well for the thousands of others that tried that route. Saints, why didn't I think of that?" She spat.

"You probably could! Your magic is so damn strong, they'd practically *beg* you to come!"

Hel rose from her seat.

"You know *damn* well why I can't go, Edvard."

Tension grew so thick, Nora could see it– Hel held surprising control, but Edvard had bent a fork nearly in half without touching it. The greyed one, Nora learned to be Garrett, leaned to her and Ber.

"Looks like mom and dad are fightin' again," He grinned.

Nora offered a shy smile, but the two went on and on.

"Saints, Hel, every goddamn day you make me wonder why I keep you around."

Hel hummed. She appeared cooler, but Nora was sure she was still fuming. "It is because no one does what I do– Without me, you'd be screwed. No one else with my talents would tolerate your sorry ass."

"Enough!" Ber and Arvo shouted together.

Nora had seen Ber lose his temper once or twice in their travels, but she was not expecting Arvo to flare up. Apparently, no one had, as the table went dead silent.

"... Sorry, you go ahead," Arvo muttered to Ber.

"No, you go ahead," Ber said.

"You sure?"

"Yeah."

"Alright," Arvo inhaled, "You two should know better than to throw a fit at each other, especially during a celebration for new members. You need to make up, walk it off, or fight elsewhere."

In the ever-stoic Edvard, Nora swore he had a hint of remorse on his face from disappointing the man before him.

Arvo did not wait for their apologies. He spoke again, in his cool, rasped tone, "Ber, this is your call. What do *you* want to do?"

Ber thought for a moment.

"I could take the document, just in case. I'll try to find another way, but it's better than nothing."

"That settles it, then. Nora, will you need papers?" Arvo asked.

"Thankfully, no."

Nora was grateful that despite her rush, Nora had remembered how crucial those documents would be.

"You Evedan?" The wild-haired member spoke.

"Where I come from hardly counts, but yes."

They gestured between her and Ber, "Want an easy way in? You could always get married."

Edvard snorted, feeling the burn of ale rise up into his nose. The table fell into laughter. Mood lightened, Hearth enjoyed the remainder of the evening at Rock's Toss.

20

Chapter 20

Ber's request for his forged papers would take several days to return, so him and Nora chose to help around Hearth's headquarters in the meantime. It was a decision Nora began to regret, as now she was being led through a dark cavern. According to Arvo, one of their horses broke loose the night before.

"My surveys showed poachers are still loitering around Houndsmouth. Sorry to take you an odd route, but you can never be too careful. Ed and I are coming with, but we all should keep an eye out," Arvo explained.

Carved in the bedrock laid a traversible path. The rest of the cavern was clustered in jagged rock. Rifts of weak light trickled in from above, but the path remained rather dim.

From atop Arvo's forearm sat a hawk of his collection they were unfamiliar with. The hawk's head bobbed with each of Arvo's steps. On occasion, it swiveled its head upward to stalk the hordes of little bats.

The path hit a dead end. At its end stood a ladder and a steep formation up to the surface of the cavern. One by one, they scaled the ladder to the top. They reached a watchtower, obscured by the mountainside.

They met Edvard inside. He kept watch while half-mindedly tinkering with a crossbow.

"See anything today?" Arvo asked.

"No. S'been pretty quiet." Edvard said. He turned to Ber and Nora. "I assume you explained the situation, then?"

"Of course," Arvo said.

Edvard handed Arvo the bridle that belonged to the astrayed horse. Arvo brought the bridle to the hawk. The hawk took immediate attention to the object, its eyes dilating as it took in the scent.

The bird cried out, batting its wings with excitement. It flew off into the woods with a set direction. Within a moment, the hawk was gone.

"It shouldn't be long, she lands her scent fast," Arvo said, readjusting his gauntlet.

Nora, Ber, and Arvo sat with Edvard. Edvard unraveled a worn map across the table. Stains and faint markings blemished the majority of the parchment.

Edvard signaled to a path on the map.

"I'm thinking that the mare ran off in this direction. There's a prairie a ways out."

Arvo shifted his attention away from the map and groaned. "Edvard, all that equipment isn't just for this mission, is it?" He asked.

Edvard shrugged, "It's better to be prepared than defenseless."

"We're finding a horse, not going to war. If you really care that much, I know Hel would be more than happy to help and—"

"*No*— no, that's not necessary," Edvard interrupted. His face, usually stoic, grew flustered. "... You're right. I guess we can just have Nora and Ber pick what they want and leave the rest here."

Together Nora and Ber searched through Edvard's collection of deadly toys. Nora chose a couple of daggers and a whip, and Ber selected a large, heavy crossbow.

Not long after, Arvo spotted his hawk. It circled and area just beyond the hill. The group set off in their search, scaling down from the watchtower and into the woods. Edvard insisted on silence just in case of a potential ambush. With Ber, this did not last more than a few minutes.

Ber, realizing that he had never even held a crossbow before, asked Arvo for some tips and tricks in archery. Arvo happily obliged, and proceeded to teach Nora some basics on using a whip, as well.

"You all are going to give us away if you keep up the chatter," Edvard warned.

Before Ber could interject, Arvo spoke up.

"You're right. We should keep it down, just in case."

They found Arvo's hawk. Arvo called to his bird, but it refused to descend.

"He needs more training," Arvo complained, "At least our horse should be around here somewhere."

The wind shifted, and Nora picked up something *rotten*. Nora wondered if maybe her senses were off.

Edvard gave them a signal to wait while he checked ahead. He peered into the forest clearing and dodged back down, mouthing *Shit*. His face held more expression than Nora or Ber had ever seen before.

They crouched over to Edvard to take a look. The clearing held a familiar sight to Nora and Ber. A hyena-like beast, of the same kind the poachers they encountered used, sat with it's intimidating talons sprawled upon a large carcass.

Under closer examination, the beast's victim was the guild's lost mare. What was odd, aside from the situation altogether, was that the beast consumed very little of the mare's flesh. The beast used its hooked, translucent fangs to siphon the fluids from the horse's neck.

The beast halted and stood, revealing its true size. It's dark, beady eyes were difficult to read. After a few flares from its nostrils, the beast looked in their direction.

Arvo looked over to Edvard. In a careful, quiet motion, Edvard loaded his crossbow and repositioned himself for combat. The beast crept closer and let out a snarl.

"Ed, we need to leave. *Now*," Arvo urged.

"Ber and I have dealt with these things before, there's no outrunning this beast. We should try to hide and—" Before Nora could finish, Ber chimed in.

"He's getting way too close— I'll take care of him!"

Ber hurdled over the brush towards the beast, its teeth already bared. He bared his teeth back. He brandished his battle axe with both hands. Gaining momentum and aura with a few spins of the weapon, he released the energy at the beast. A force of clouds and gusts blew it back. The animal, however, was not phased. It tore up the earth as it clawed its way towards Ber.

"Damn it, Ber!" Edvard and Nora shouted, almost in unison.

Ber searched for his lent crossbow and shot most of its bolts at the beast. The few that did manage to hit hardly halted its charge. Edvard shoved Ber back and took more precise shots. Arvo and Nora followed close behind.

"Spread out!" Edvard commanded.

Arvo followed suit with a few shots of his bow, but again to no avail. Its thick fur and hide made it difficult to land an effective shot. Nora prepared her whip, hoping to scare it off before going into actual combat.

The beast had its target set on Ber, approaching him with fangs exposed. Ber swung his axe and shouted at the beast to intimidate it, but he only succeeded in holding it back.

Nora whistled for her dragon, praying that she would hear her call from wherever she was. She lashed the animal from afar, landing minor slashes to its limbs.

It turned to Nora and switched its target to her. She unsheathed her blade and prepared for a true fight. The beast launched itself at Nora to try to land a bite. She stumbled backwards but defended herself. One false move could mean becoming victim to it's unforgiving jaws, and her fight would be over.

Nora felt chills from her arms. Ink-black aura leaked from her wrists. She took the opportunity to slash the animal with her magic. If this power could scare her, maybe it could scare the beast, too.

Nora, facing the furious, bloodied beast, dashed toward its heart to land a hard blow. She dodged a swipe from its massive claws and slid below it, digging into its chest.

Despite her direct hit, the thick hide made the damage only skin deep. The mark her aura made, however, spread from where she hit. The affected flesh turned black and cold. The beast struggled to get at Nora from over her and kicked Nora out from under, *hard.*

Nora coiled up and clenched her side. Her shadowy aura continued to spill from her wrists. From her magic grew curved nails and hardened skin.

Saints, not now...!

Nora panicked, struggling to shake the shadows from her hands. She heard Ber's voice from overhead.

"Get away from her!"

He spun his axe and wound back to strike. Arvo intercepted Ber before he could act. His hands were full with red flame.

"Ber, get back and pull out your bow." He ordered.

Ber seldom saw Arvo summon fire, let alone one this large. He nodded and heeded his order. Edvard approached Ber, bow in hand, to give him an oiled set of bolts.

"Fire the whole set as soon as they are lit. We have a plan, but there isn't much time."

Arvo lit both of their bows. They set fire at the same time, igniting the beast. It roared with pure rage. Fire still in hand, Arvo fanned it out in front of them. He created a wall of flames between them and the beast. From the smoke, the shadow of the beast backed away. All they could hear was the roar of the brush fire.

"I think it ran off. Let's douse this fire before we get any more attention," Edvard said.

"You alright, Nor?" Ber asked, helping Nora over to Arvo and Edvard.

"Yes... I think so."

Nora took a moment to gather herself. She did not feel any broken ribs, but she knew her chest was going to be bruised for days. The moment was cut short from a disturbance in the brush.

From the fire, the beast charged once more. Ber ducked below the animal, taking Nora with. Edvard dodged the charge just in time. Arvo, however, could not escape. He found himself pinned beneath the animal, its sickle claws forcing him to the earth. With Arvo immobilized and unable to control the fire, the flames began to spread and intensify.

Hooked fangs hyperextended from the beast's jaws, preparing to make him into its next meal. Two of its talons dug into Arvo's thigh, and one on his forearm. Arvo let out a primal scream.

Nora's gut sank. She sprinted over to Arvo. Her body flowed with aura but she did not care. She forced her entire being into the monster, hoping to end its life with her blade.

Her force—much to her surprise—knocked the beast back. But her blade was never drawn. She realized that her original plan was not going to be an option.

Nora's aura changed her form. Clad with long fangs and scaled talons of her own, she too was a beast.

Arvo ran to safety as the beasts toppled over each other. Nora pinned the animal to the ground. Fire crept precariously close as they fought, and Arvo struggled to keep the flames at bay.

Nora's urges fought to dominate over her rational thoughts, and her jaws longed to wrap tight around the beast's neck. She gripped on with all her strength, but was kicked off. The beast paced over to attack, but she stood her ground with risen fur and bared teeth.

What part of "leave" do you not understand? Nora called to the animal.

The beast did not respond. Nora roared.

Answer me!

The beast lunged once more, taking in bites of hair and flesh. Entangled with tooth and nail, Nora realized that it's wrathful eyes were milk-white. Patches of gnarled, discolored skin and protruding tusks signified one thing; this beast was not normal. It became clear no amount of intimidation would cause the beast to flee. It would not be satisfied until she and her team were dead.

Edvard, Arvo, and Ber hurried to gain a distance from the brawl. Their throats grew raw from the suffocating fire and smoke. Edvard turned to Ber, his golden eyes lit with fear.

"Ber, I demand to know what in the hell is going on— What is that thing?!" he asked.

"It's a long story that I promise I'll tell you later—Trust me, Nora is still in there," Ber said.

"Are you sure we can trust her?"

Edvard's grip tightened around his bow.

Ber swallowed hard; the creeping fire began to take a toll on their breathing. He locked eyes with Edvard.

"Without a doubt."

"Let's help her out, then. The least we can do is not have us all die in my fire," Arvo said. Ber gave him a grin. With a solemn nod, Edvard followed alongside them as backup.

Even in her new form, the beast dwarfed Nora. They thrashed about, tumbling over each other while ripping at flesh. Her endurance dwindled as her opponent tore into her skin. Regardless, she held onto its trachea in hopes to bleed it to exhaustion. Her fight, she prayed, was not to be won with strength, but with resilience.

Nora's opponent dug its talons deep in her chest. She howled and writhed in pain. Despite her efforts, Nora let her grip loosen for just a moment. The beast kicked her off, her body leaving a deep crimson trail. She lay close to the wall of fire, the flames singing her fur.

Nora staggered to her feet. She was at her wit's end. Her team made significant work on lowering the flames, but needed more time. However, there was not much more time to buy.

The beast approached her, driving her more into a corner. Nora's only idea was to attempt to throw the beast in the fire, but there was no possible way she could pull off such a feat of strength against it.

Her opponent tackled her, preparing her for a final strike. Unbearable pressure from its claws pressed on her chest and head, leaving the neck pinned.

Then in an instant, relief came to her body. Like a flash, the weight was swiped off of her. From the air, Lotte struck the beast in full force.

The beast, even under normal circumstances, was no match for a dragon. Lotte spared no mercy on the animal. They clashed with claws and teeth intertwining their bodies.

Nora limped over to help, but Ber held her back. The animal landed some cuts to the dragon, but it did not deter her ferocity. Lotte's long, obsidian-plated body soon dominated over the beast's. With a crunch audible from across the field, the beast went limp, and its suffering finally ended.

Nora made her way to her party. Ber pulled her in and wrapped his arms around her. He let her go, and Nora's eyes met Arvo's, and then Edvard's.

"… Nora?" Edvard asked.

Nora gave a slow nod. He exhaled in relief, and Nora swore that for a moment he smiled.

He looked up to her.

"As… unexpected as this is, I expect that you will give me a full explanation once we return to camp."

Nora let out an aggravated huff.

Lotte came to Nora's side, nudging her head over and offering her body for support.

Arvo and Ber made quick work of the remaining fire. Arvo lowered what he could while Ber humidified the air and blew out the flames.

A horse's whine turned their attention. Edvard's already dour mood sunk lower once he realized that it was a familiar pest. Atop the horse sat Hel, her gaze bewildered from the amount of destruction.

"What happened here? Do I want to know?" She asked.

"Probably not," Arvo admitted.

"Glad you guys are still kickin'. That dragon was going haywire in your coop, so I let her out before she could destroy it and followed her here." Hel said.

She dropped down and proceeded to sling an unwanted arm around Edvard. "This is what happens when you leave me uninvited, Eddie." She chimed. Edvard cursed through gritted teeth, and Hel could not help but laugh.

She turned to Nora, who was still in her beast form. After a moment, Hel recognized who it was.

"Nora I must say, you make a dashing monster!" She said, her tone hiding a genuine compliment.

Nora rolled her eyes.

"You look a little stuck. I'm not exactly an expert, but I can help you switch back—if it is what I think the problem is," Hel said.

Nora agreed and knelt beside her. Hel placed a palm atop her head. The web of faint aura around Nora—the source of her changed form, dispersed. She felt a wave of serenity, and then fatigue. What she could withstand as a human was minuscule compared to her beast form. She fell back, but Ber caught her. She was in poor shape, but nothing some rest and a stitch or two could not fix.

Arvo looked to Nora, and then to Ber.

"You don't turn into anything, do you?" Arvo asked.

Ber gave a chuckle, "You're too funny."

To this, Hel giggled to herself.

21

Chapter 21

"Are you sure you are up to this?" Arvo asked.

That shook Nora from her haze. She was lucky from yesterday's encounter, but the wounds on her chest were still very fresh. Unable to rest comfortably, she was mentally exhausted, as well.

She agreed to help Arvo in the aviary today. She figured it was the least she could do, for taking Lotte in— Though it was entirely Arvo's idea.

Nora rubbed her eyes and eased herself off the bench. She found Lotte looming over her. She gave the beast a good scratch. Admittedly, she had not been much help. After a bout of sweeping, she found herself winded and sat down. She did not remember resting her eyes, however.

"Sorry— Yes, I would have gone stir crazy, otherwise," Nora said.

Arvo understood.

A variety of birds, from canaries to raptors– *actual*, semi-scaled raptors, were housed in their own habitats. In the aviary, Lotte seemed in her own element. She bobbed her head and stretched out her wings at her fellow roommates.

"Is she… communicating?" Nora asked.

"It's probable. Dragons technically avians, after all," Arvo answered.

"You don't say… This place really is beautiful, Arvo."

"Thank you. Most beasts in trades can be released and rehomed, but birds can be so fragile… The ones I can't release just yet live their lives here."

"It's nice that little places like this exist, taking care of those without a voice."

"Speaking of beasts, what is the story behind Lotte, anyway?"

Nora turned to check on her dragon. She allowed the oxpeckers to rid of old skin, and grackle-raptors to take loose scales back to their roosts.

"There's not much to tell. I found her with a broken wing and brought her back to health. When I needed saving, she returned the favor. We've been a pair ever since."

Arvo smiled, "Animals are better company than most folk."

"Perhaps all."

"Perhaps all," Arvo repeated, laughing, "I suppose you can commune with them easier than others given—" Arvo stopped himself.

"I'm sorry, I do not mean to assume…"

"It's okay," Nora said, "You're right, it *is* easier in my other form."

"May I ask… what it is like? You don't have to share. It is just fascinating to me."

"You're not freaked out like the others are?"

Arvo shook his head, "It is still you in there. I can tell."

Nora smiled. She wanted to say something, express her gratitude, but she found herself choked up. She took a few deep breaths, when her throat allowed, and Arvo was patient, patting her back.

"It's… an experience, for sure. You're right, it is still me. It it just a different part of me," Nora said, "Maybe more unfiltered than I would prefer, but I am still getting used to it."

"So this is new?"

Nora nodded, "It started happening after the fog."

"So this is a side effect, a condition?"

Nora sighed. Nora had to bend the truth.

"Kind of? I haven't gotten a solid answer yet, but… Whatever this is, I've an aching suspicion it might be just… part of me."

A little kestrel perched on Nora's shoulder. She cherished the moment, before it hopped onto her head and plucked loose, frizzy hairs and flew off with his nest material.

Arvo lost himself in laughter, trying to apologise between the fits.

"I'd be offended, but this says more about my current state than anything."

Nora tied up her 'bird's nest' before any other birds partook. They sat there for a while, sharing knowledge on the wilds, and the beasts they had encountered. Arvo was still visibly drained from the day before— Losing one of the guild's horses took a serious toll on him, but he tried not to show it. He saw the worry in Nora's eyes.

"… We sent Garrett to take a look at the beast from yesterday. Given its illness. Just to be sure we're not dealing with some kind of outbreak."

"He's a doctor?"

"He was a veterinarian ages ago."

Nora nodded solemnly. She tried to lighten the subject as they left the aviary to return to Hearth.

"You have any other zoos you'd like to show me?"

Arvo shook his head, "Not currently. We have exotics come and go, but it's just the horses and Ed's whalehound. But remind me someday to take you to our base in Oxbrow, you'd love the kelpie!"

Nora stopped.

"… You have a *kelpie*?!"

—

It was rare for Arvo to have a slow day, so he made the most of it by getting ahead on the rest of the chores. What he did not expect was Ber to be in the stable.

"You don't have to do that, you know," Arvo said.

Ber turned to see Arvo leaning on the stable door. He gestured to Ber shoveling out the dirty bedding.

Ber smiled, "It's really no trouble at all! It helps me think, muscle memory, I suppose."

"You did a lot of work like this before?"

"Yep. Military."

His words were brief, common in Nora but certainly not Ber.

"My business here can wait, if you would like to be alone."

"No need," Ber said, "I'm happy you're here, my man. Being alone with your thoughts does things to ya."

The hotblood stood beside Ber in the stable, unbothered and grazing on freshly replenished oats.

"You didn't want to post this one outside the stable? Fabi can get pretty feisty."

Arvo remembered an incident with poor Ed getting bucked, his head nearly split by the same beast. The look in that horse's blue eyes, Arvo swore, was utterly unapologetic.

"It's alright. He knows I'm in here for a job."

Arvo chuckled, "I never thought I would be blessed with *two* folk who are so comfortable around the beasts. It's no wonder too, why you and Nora stick together."

Ber turned from him, scooping more soiled hay from the stable floor. "You should see our friend Alice work with beasts– *that's* impressive!"

"You have my interest piqued– but don't try and change the subject!" Arvo teased, leaning in further.

Ber ignored him, forcibly changing the subject once more. "Actually, what you're doing here makes me happy, caring for these beasts with such care. Not everyone does the same."

Arvo sighed, "Don't I know it."

Though, he knew he only knew part of it. Edvard told him some of the terrible business he was involved in during his service, but Arvo knew he held back the details. Who knows what Ber had seen.

"Let me help you with the other stables."

Together they made quick work of the barn. It did not take long for each stable to be refreshed.

While shoveling waste, Ber spoke, "I had a beast once– technically, I mean."

Arvo turned to him.

"You did?"

"A snow drake. I'm not sure you have them here."

"I don't think I've heard of those."

"Before anyone knew what I was capable of, I was a private in charge of the stables full of war beasts. This drake, he and I just clicked, you know?" Ber smiled to himself, "Some nights, I would sneak in and play with him for hours. I'd get on his back and pretend to fly. It was the best both of us could do to see the sky."

Ber continued, "I was promoted, and became a personal assistant to a higher-up. Everyone in the barracks hated me for it. I can't blame them. But the worst part was being away from him. When I had enough, ready to meet whatever fate had for me, I bust open every door in that stable. It was the least I could do."

"Most aren't bold enough to stand up to powers like that. It's admirable," Arvo said.

"Depending on who you ask, it can be a blessing or a curse," Ber laughed hollowly. "I gave those creatures a shot. At least, I gave my boy the chance to see the sky without fire, and while his mind was his own."

Arvo felt a shiver. Though curious, he did not want to know what he meant.

"Nora does not know of this, if you could keep this between us. She is kind and beyond understanding, but I do not want to put this guilt on her."

"Of course, Ber," Arvo said, "What was his name?"

"Rocco. I called him Rocco."

22

Chapter 22

Clamorous laughter echoed from the main room. Nora entered to find Arvo, Hel, and Ber around the main table. The air reeked of cheap ale.

"Is he alright?" Nora asked, looking at Arvo.

"Ol' lightweight?" Hel scoffed, "He's fiiine! See?"

She prodded Arvo, eliciting a light giggle and muttered words out of him.

"Nora," Ber said, hanging on the last syllable, "Come celebrate with us!"

Ber had finally received his papers. They had gathered to celebrate earlier, but Ber proved fond of an afterparty.

"I think I'll pass, I'm exhausted."

"No!" The three shouted.

"You're not gonna tell Gramps I'm draining his supply, are you?"

Nora rubbed her eye, "I really don't care. Just keep it down, I'm going to bed."

"Nora, *lodse*" Ber sang, "Please?"

Nora stood over Ber. She took the glass from him and took a swig. "...Maybe another time. Don't drink yourself too stupid, yeah?"

Nora left for her quarters. Arvo hiccupped. "I should probably turn in too, while I can still use my legs..."

Arvo sauntered off, hitting the corner of the wall before stumbling into the hallway. Ber and Hel were left alone together. Hel smiled at him warmly, raising her glass.

"You did great today, kid. Ed doesn't show it but I'm sure he's relieved to have a force of nature like you around."

"Thank you, Hel," Ber took another swig. He mourned how much Nora had taken from his glass. "I've got a question for you."

"Let me guess, palm readings? Casting bones? No– I *know* you want to know about your true love!" Hel's brow waggled.

Ber flushed more than he already was, "Can you do that?"

"Ha! No."

"Oh."

"Well, what is it, then?"

"It's just– Well…" Ber struggled to put his thoughts into words, "… With the spirit world, do you know if it is segregated the same way yours and mine is?"

The secret had come out the day before. Hel snagged him for a palm reading, and the truth spilled out from there. Hel promised to keep it a secret. 'For now, at least,' she had said with a wink.

Hel hummed, tilting back in her chair.

"It's hard to say. Legend tells of two spirit guardians that patrol the door between Shadow and Light. Ebi and Ibe. They defend their respective veils from any threats. However, it is not specified whether the line is drawn on the living…"

"I've an idea," Hel said, "I will tell you an old, *old* story: There was once a man so infamous, so cunning that he became world renowned. Kings and beasts alike would do his bidding. He had everything in the palm of his hand, all the while working in the shadows of the multiple kingdoms. One day he was struck down, not by a nemesis but a fallen rock. Some say it was divine intervention, as the legion of Saints deemed his gift too powerful. In death, he was given a form that suits his nature— the Serpent. There is discourse to whether his influence is always 'evil,' but it always instills disorder. There are clerical accounts– old ones, but of this century– of tempted individuals being visited by this Serpent."

"I- I know that one, the whole story is the same, too!" Ber cheered.

"I would guess then, it's probable the spirit world inhabit the same space."

"It's nice to hear," Ber said, "even if it is a possibility. It's nice to know someone that knows me is looking after me here– or at the very least I am not alone!"

Hel smiled. *A surprisingly vulnerable moment from the loud one. He is just a kid, after all...* In all her drunken wisdom, she simply laid a hand on him, patting his back. She had no idea what this man went through, so she prayed this would suffice.

They were closer now. Hel noticed the necklace diving deep into his shirt, and some odd material at the hem of his shirt. Even with the hindrance of her mask, her sight was excellent. When she focused, her eyes widened.

"Ber, were you consumed, too?" Hel asked softly.

"'Consumed?'"

"Possessed, taken over. By a spirit." Hel pulled back Ber's collar by a tad.

Ber seized her hand in an instant. Hel removed her hands, uttering an apology.

"It's– no, it's not that."

"What is it then? I'm not a healer in the classical sense, but maybe I could help."

Ber sighed, "I doubt it would help– I got this when I was in the fog, it's something that developed after long exposure."

"Has it worsened?"

"No, thanks to this," Ber gestured to the stone at the center of the necklace.

"… Any idea what this might be if left untreated? If you were separated from the necklace?"

"Yes."

A silent acknowledgment was reached between the two.

"… Sickness from the fog is new territory, but I will look into it," Hel said.

"Thank you, Hel."

The stone caught Hel's eye. The room was bathed in a dim, coppery light, except for the necklace's odd charm.

"Does Nora know about this?"

Ber finally chuckled. He took a swig. "We've been traveling for months now. You think she hasn't noticed feathers on my–my chest?"

"Suppose you're right. You never did strike me as a chaste man."

Ber laughed, just a tad too loud.

"What I mean is, have you told her what you told me?"

Ber smiled, but his gaze was far away, far from Hel. She could feel his guilt. "I have not. I don't want to worry her any more than she has to."

"That's stupid," Hel said, "She's going to find out one way or another."

"Yep!" Ber heaved himself from the chair. Exaggerated force made him wobble nearly face-first into the table. "But tonight's not the night. Speaking of, I should probably heed her advice and get to bed before my bed is the floor."

"It was nice getting to know you tonight, Ber," Hel said in surprising candor.

"Feeling's mutual! Say, could I see your face without the mask?"

"Maybe. But tonight's not the night," Hel echoed.

Ber chuckled, "Goodnight, Hel. Don't stay up too late."

Hel shrugged, "It's what I do."

23

Chapter 23

That morning, Nora and Ber left for their final leg to Saint Evedis. To Nora's surprise, Hearth left the two with ample money and supplies. Arvo pulled the two in that morning.

"Sorry, he's a hugger. And a crier…" Edvard said.

"You have helped us more than you can imagine. This is the least we can do," Arvo said, "Come back when you're sick of city life, okay?"

—

Just two days in, they made past two more towns, though not under the best reasons. Nora's not-so-human characteristics were found out in the second stop, spurring the two to be run out of town.

All the while, Nora followed the guide Viviane gave for… whatever she needed the herbs for. The task proved to be more difficult than Nora originally thought. Most botanical shops did not carry what she asked for, so she foraged for most of the ingredients in passing.

"How do you know what you're looking at?" Ber asked, "It all looks like grass to me."

"I told you, my old lady used to do this kind of thing. I also had to pull some of this crap from my sheep's mouths."

Ber nodded, then stopped, "Did I know you had sheep? Also what's a sheep?"

Nora did not have the energy to answer that. She cut the red weed she found growing on a fence post just outside of town.

"It's getting late. Why don't we find a place to stay?" Nora said.

They arrived at Warcove, another bigger town that hugged the Evedis River. Nora noticed the closer they reached Saint Evedis, the more illustrious the towns became. *Why couldn't Ghleanne have had a trolley?* Nora thought bitterly. They reached the main hub when Nora heard a familiar voice.

"Good evening, my servants!"

Approaching them were their former captors, Captain Alice and Viviane. This encounter, at least, posed less of a threat than before. The two came without their crew, sticking out like a sore, opulent thumb.

"Oh Saints it's you," Nora said to Alice, "Good evening, Viviane."

"Alice, Viv! What are you two doing here?" Ber asked. His tone came off as though they were childhood friends rather than criminals.

Alice shrugged,"I was convinced to wreak havoc in my homeland a little while longer before we make our expedition." She wrapped her arms around Nora and Ber. A toothy grin spread across her face, "Tell you what; why don't I treat you two to a drink so we can catch up?"

"I suppose a warm tavern does sound nice…" Nora said.

"It's decided, let's live it up tonight! Who knows, this place might have a club with *two* floors!" Alice mused, "Imagine that!"

After a brisk search around town, the reunited travelers settled upon a tavern dubbed 'The Chapel.' Stained glassed adorned the façade in a cheeky nod to the name. The music and bright lights penetrated the stillness of the streets. Alice led them through the doors of the building, greeted with a few cheers.

The band near the bar enthralled most of the patrons and even some of the workers. A trio of men, perhaps too well dressed for the occasion, captivated the room with their alluring, upbeat songs. Along the walls had varying paraphernalia— lager advertisements, criminal bounty posters (including Alice, of course), and some campaign posters. One of the posters showed a second familiar face:

'Vote Suryc Harland for Stromshire Chancellor: Man of the Folk.'

Given the number of posters with his wretched face on it, it looked like he ran unopposed. Nora brought it to Alice's attention, and she waved her off.

"Every town around here's got the same setup. Don't you worry your pretty little head, my white whale ain't taking office while I'm around."

"Sure, but what about *your* posters?" Nora muttered.

Alice flashed a wicked grin, "I want to see someone try!"

The group settled upon a cozy booth in the corner. While Alice left to fetch their first round, the group unraveled as they took in the tavern's unexpected warmth. While she was away, Nora showed her findings to Viviane.

"It's not everything, unfortunately," Nora said.

Viviane shook her head, "No, this is perfect. Thank you two for all of your help while we were away. You have no idea how important this is to me."

"It was really no trouble."

"Even so, you have my utmost gratitude. If you need anything from me until we part ways at Saint Evedis, let me know."

"I remember Alice telling me that she doesn't want to go anywhere near Saint Evedis."

"That may be true, but we'll see how far I can drag her along," Viviane winked.

Alice returned, her arms full with beer and food. As she set the bounty down on the table, Ber and Nora could not help but notice how much she struggled to lower it down. Her grasp faltered. Viviane acted quick, grasping the tray.

"You two look like a couple of starvin' dogs so I'm treatin' ya!" Alice declared.

Nora stared down at the platter before her. With such a gorgeous display of perfect roasted fowl on a bed of buttery vegetables, it took every bit of her will to hold back.

"Alice, you really didn't have to—" Alice cut Ber off.

"We're friends now. As your friend I demand you to enjoy! Now if we can get started, I'd like a nice family dinner, meaning this dinner will end in us getting absolutely plastered!"

"How did you even find us, anyway?" Nora asked.

"It wasn't that we were stalking you, but you made it too easy," Alice said with a cheeky grin, "We figured this would be your next stop."

She slid over an envelope for a familiar invoice, featuring Ber's name and signature— both forged by Edvard, as his handwriting in Common was still atrocious. Nora could not believe her eyes.

"If you needed papers, Ber darling, you should've just asked!"

—

They spent the start of the night indulging in their meal and multiple rounds of drinks. Alice lost herself in ale. She lazily fed her stoat from under the table as she sung to the music. Nora found it strange, taking in this much comfort among thieves. She found herself on a swivel, in case there was any trouble— Alice was a wanted woman, after all. The feeling soon passed, and she unraveled to enjoy the company and beer.

Viviane set her drink on the table, her finished glass nearing the size of her head.

"Why don't we move this party elsewhere? We've a whole ship to cruise to the next tavern, after all."

"You're, like, so right Viv," Alice said, not allowing any personal space between her and Viviane, "I'm not even drunk yet!"

"Alice, dear, you're actually the only one who's made it that far."

Nora and Ber agreed. Leaving a hefty sum on the table, they stepped away from the tavern. Shortly behind them, a few more steps followed.

—

With the moon on the rise, the team of thieves and runaways jaunted their way to the *Coral Fang*. They swayed to the singing of shanties all the way to the beachy riverside.

Viviane caught the slightest movement from the corner of her eye. She took a double take, checking behind her. Not one, but two pairs of wideset, glowing eyes peered from the dunes.

"Change of plans," Viviane spoke, "We're being followed, get to the ship."

Nora swallowed, "Ship's blocked."

From either side, they were approached by creatures creeping from the shadows. Man and beast alike came closer, brandishing fangs and blades. Alice, though inebriated, was first to draw her blades, followed by Ber and Nora. They all inched back until the black waves licked at their heels.

Their company emerged from the shadows. Upon their faces coming to light, it was certain that they had encountered the same group before. A familiar, unsettling voice came from the shadows.

"Where do you ladies think you are off to at this hour?"

A tall man appeared, clad in a prim suit and tied up hair. Steel blue eyes pierced straight through them. He walked straight to Alice, and Alice refused to move an inch.

"It seems that we need to discuss some payment for a debt… with you destroying my ship and caravan and all."

The urge to flee was strong the moment Viviane saw glowing eyes. But now, it sang in her bones, and for a good reason. She and Alice always escaped from their treacherous escapades. Not one enemy of the *Coral Fang* had yet to challenge her to a rematch. And of all enemies, it had to be the Bachelor.

With one swift motion, Viviane slashed sand into the man's face. She took Alice's hand and fled, only to be caught by the man by the wrist. He clenched harder, causing Viviane to hold back a scream.

"Captain, *this* is the crew you've chosen to protect you? I would have expected more, considering your reputation."

"Let her go, *now*," Alice spoke through grit teeth.

The man ignored her, twisting Viviane's arm so she would fall and succumb to him. Before Alice could lunge for his neck, her arms were bound by the poachers around them, along with Nora and Ber.

"It's a shame you keep this one around. Scrawny, obviously feeble with aura… and an outsider, above all else. Absolutely worthless."

It was not the man's words, nor his force that shocked Viviane. Nora and Ber could not believe what they were seeing. Brilliant green light surrounded them as it spilled from Alice's eyes. Though her body was anchored still, the ocean waves behind her danced and rose. Capped in sea ice, their points directed to Viviane's captor.

"I will not ask again. Let. Her. Go." Alice roared.

Nora almost missed it, as Alice was struck at the base of her shoulder with an object she could not identify. In an instant, Alice was down.

The man smirked, "No, I don't think I will. However, I do believe I'm done toying with you, for now. Let's go."

As quick as the waves rose, they fell, along with Alice. Black blood spilled onto the sand. Ber lunged and Nora felt her strength raise, but they too fell.

24

Chapter 24

Nora and Ber awoke in a large, vaulted room. Outside a storm brewed. Shelves of books lined the walls, all of which seemed to be abandoned for a long while. They found themselves bound alongside Viviane and Alice. Viviane laid limp, despite Ber's coaxing.

"Nora. Ber," Alice spoke, hardly above a whimper, "I don't know what that bastard stabbed me with, but I don't think I can put up a fight like this…"

Alice sat beside Nora, her upper body collapsed over the table. The only viewable movement from her lethargic form was the labored rise and fall of her chest.

Their captor stepped in, dressed down from their encounter on the beach.

"That was all you, Alice. I just sped up the process," He said, adjusting the cuffs of his buttoned shirt.

Alice's eyes widened. She wished her glare could stab as deep as her daggers.

Below the table, Ber felt Viviane's hand slip into his. He stole a glance. She still seemed unconscious. He pretended to pay no mind, but tightened the hold.

"You're making a mistake. My crew will find and kill you," Alice said.

"Perhaps we should keep things civil. You can call me Suryc," He glanced at Nora and Ber, "You two look familiar, actually…" Suryc said.

"Does it matter? Why were you hunting us in the first place?" Nora asked.

"If I tell you, you won't believe me."

"I've heard that before. Try me."

"I suppose I have time to spare. I've been honorably appointed as Chief Director of some underground operations including a reassignment of… let's say a few bureaucratic offices and resources."

Ber spoke, "Those are some big words, pal. You could just say you're overthrowing the government. And, correct me if I'm wrong— you are taking and exploiting people to accomplish this goal."

"This should not come as a shock, your government does this, too," Suryc said, "I understand the claim is outlandish, but my colleague's forces are unlike any others I've seen. And Alice would know I've been on the scene for a while."

"You—you're working for Serkan, aren't you?" Ber paused before laughing, "The man must really be scraping the bottom of the barrel, if he's got you in charge! No offense, sir, but you have no idea who you're dealing with."

Suryc approached him.

"Quiet, fool! I won't hesitate to end you where you stand."

"If you touch him I'll rip your face off…!" Alice growled. An empty threat, Alice's condition made her far from intimidating. She could barely hold herself up, and her weak voice was close to nothing

Suryc turned his attention to Alice. A sickening smirk crept along his face.

"Now, something tells me you are more than just a pretty little thief," Suryc cupped her face in his palm, "Is this true?"

"So I've made some mistakes," Alice tried, "It was a mistake to not drop that chandelier on you in Saint Evedis. And it was a mistake to shag you that one time in Silpor."

"I— you—" Suryc's eyes were blown wide. The second part was news to him.

"You don't remember? Or are you *that* bad with faces? It was mediocre at best— I hope you're okay with us staying enemi—"

Alice's entire face cringed. She coughed up blood, an involuntary action that she was glad to spew onto Suryc's tunic. To add insult to injury, Satya peaked out of her coat collar to bite the man's hand.

"… You asked who I am. I'm the thief that decimated your ship. Now fuck off."

Suryc coiled back. He grabbed the back of her shirt collar and pulled, revealing intricate lines starting from her shoulder and down her spine.

"You know, I had suspicion upon our last encounter, but even now I cannot believe I landed such a big catch! I'm glad I prepared for such company. My apologies for such rude behavior, Princess Alice." He said, bowing in a mocking manner.

Nora and Ber's heads swiveled, *"Princess?"*

It all clicked at once, and Nora felt foolish. Thousands of women and girls were named after the missing Princess, and it was not unusual to come across a lookalike in Stromshire. But looking back at the missing posters, the resemblance was obvious.

"You didn't tell your friends, your Highness? What a pity."

A guard entered the room, "'Caravan's ready for the Collector, sir."

"Change of plans," Suryc said, "Set the course for Orson's Ridge. I expect the Heir would be most pleased with our cargo."

This made the guard stiffen. "A-Aye, sir."

Suryc met his eyes. "With grace, this all will turn the tides in His favor."

The guard nodded, gingerly excusing himself from the room.

Alice forced herself to meet her captor's steely eyes. "You 'prepared…'" Alice repeated, "You ambush during a new moon when my magic is weakest. You targeted my right arm when we fought… Just how planned was all this?"

"Yes, I know who you are, and the research on you wasn't hard, either. The whole damned kingdom has heard your story," He paced back to his own desk, pouring himself an opaque liquid from a crystalline decanter. "You had *such* a hard life up in that lofty palace that you and that scullery maid of yours decided to run away. But what *I* know is that lo and behold, turns out the castle has defenses."

Suryc stood in front of her. He yanked Alice's injured arm. She shrieked, the pain shooting through the rest of her body as she pushed back tears.

"So I can imagine that one of those lovely spellbound plants around the castle nicked you here, and that's the reason you are bleeding on my freshly polished floors," Suryc said.

"Now, here is what is going to follow this pointless conversation: We're going to see if any of you have anything worth extracting, and Princess here... well, I believe she would make a great key to infiltrate Saint Evedis, wouldn't you think? Of course, there's the problem with your arm..."

"You're looking for magic blood, right? Want a sample?"

Ber grunted, heaving his entire body upward. He lashed out towards Suryc, spitting gusts and ice to force him back. From the force, Suryc blasted back into the wall. As satisfying as it felt to make a Suryc-shaped dent in the wall, Ber felt more fatigued than usual for performing such magic. Still on his feet, Suryc paced back, adjusting his cuffs. Viviane's grip on Ber's hand tightened.

"You filthy punk—" he stopped once he realized that the lights in the room grew dim. His gaze shifted to Nora, her eyes illuminated and her teeth extended from her mouth.

"It'd be best if you didn't lay a finger on either of them again," Nora threatened. An empty threat was better than nothing, she considered.

Suryc took a step back. He sneered and spoke, "... I've changed my mind." He called for his guards, "I'm not having my months in this hell be for nothing—I'm dispatching you immediately."

Suryc brandished a curved knife and aimed it towards Nora's neck. The searing heat radiating from the blade flushed her skin. As he charged more heat into the blade, it grew unbearable.

Suryc muttered into her ear. The calmness of his voice was beyond unsettling to Nora. "My superiors instructed me to cauterize anyone I can't take in alive. I will make this quick, but that doesn't mean you won't feel it."

A panicked series of knocks interrupted his advances. Suryc let out an exasperated sigh.

"Just come in, damnit!" He said.

They tried the knob. The knocks continued until they grew to bangs. The urgency drew his attention to the door. Fibrous, woven vines melded the door shut. He traced the vines to a seemingly inanimate Viviane, then to his own feet.

Viviane tilted her head up and met his eyes. Aura tapped from Ber seeped from her hands behind her back. With a turn of her wrists, her trap set into place. Her chain reaction caused him to fly across the room once again, knocking him unconscious this time.

Viviane echoed his word to him under her breath. "Worthless…"

The bangs at the door grew louder. Suryc's guards began to make progress in nudging the door open. Viviane looked to Nora.

"We don't have much time, and me and Ber are drained. Nora, is there anything you can do?"

"Yes but… I need you to be *very* open-minded, okay?"

Nora focused. She had never willed herself to transform before, but in her fearful state, it came quite easy. With newfound talons, Nora tore the ropes around her wrists. She proceeded to unbind her friends. When she unbound Alice, her entire body lay limp and she took strained, heavy breaths.

"She looks bad…" Ber said. He lifted Alice onto his back.

They could not barrel through Suryc's poachers in this condition. Nora peered to the only other opening in the room. With the heel of her boot, Nora shattered a window.

"We can call Lotte from the roof," She said, offering Ber a hand. Laden with Alice, Ber took his time securing safe steps.

The hinges on the door loosened, and the vines holding them in place gave way. The shouts of Suryc's poachers were no longer distant muffles. In one swift movement, Nora helped lift Viviane. Viviane left to ensure that Alice was delivered to the roof.

To Nora's fortune, Suryc was foolish enough to simply throw their belongings aside. She grabbed them on the way out. Nora hoisted herself out of the room. She heard the door collapse followed by the stomps and shouts of poachers. She climbed faster.

Nora, Viviane, and Ber carrying Alice managed to clamber to the roof. The heavy rain made the tiles slick and tedious to traverse. Nora called for Lotte, praying that she could hear it through the rainfall.

Ber set Alice down. Her face grew much paler and sunken. Ber formed a thin shield from the rain. Viviane kneeled beside Alice, unscrewing a bottle containing a thick liquid from her belt. She gave her the liquid and comforted her between sobs.

"This—this should stabilize you for a while longer. Alice, I need… I need you to stay awake. Please…"

Alice gazed at her and forced a weak smile. She wanted to hold her closer.

"I'll be fine, dear. Now bugger off…" She said.

Viviane returned the smile, brushing Alice's red hair behind her ears.

Stomps grew louder and louder as the hunters approached. Viviane held Alice closer, knowing she could do nothing more. One by one the poachers surrounded them, armed with magic and spears. Ber grew weary from forcing them off the roof, and Nora did all she could to defend with her blade. Her human form began to falter.

Despite their efforts, Nora and Ber lost their ground. They receded closer to Alice and Viviane. After some short, clumsy combat, Nora slipped. Her face met with the head of a spear.

Ber fended them off until a poacher snuck up behind him. He went still when an arm hooked around his neck. A dagger pricked against his back.

Before the poachers could apprehend them all, a small quake shook the building. The quakes became bolder with each passing second. The poachers by the edge of the roof awaited the darkness below with spears and blades.

The guards flew back effortlessly from the whip of a long tail. Lotte approached the remaining attackers. She bore her fangs, taking swipes at the bolder enemies until they retreated for reinforcement.

Without a moment to spare, Nora and Ber hurried Alice and Viviane onto the dragon's back. But the problem remained that Lotte could not take them all.

"What about you and Ber?" Viviane asked.

"We'll be right behind you," Nora held Lotte's face in her arms, "Find shelter. Please."

Lotte hesitated, but obeyed and flew low over the trees. Nora turned to Ber.

"It's your turn to be open-minded, Ber."

Nora transformed before Ber's eyes. Her form changed from the first time they met. Even on all fours she was taller than him. She vaguely resembled a bear or a wolf, but she was something else entirely.

Are those feathers...?

Ber did not have time to dwell on it, as Nora grabbed him and jumped off the roof.

—

Once they landed, they rushed Alice a vacant cabin and onto their makeshift bed. Viviane rushed to prepare everything she had to save Alice. Nora and Ber were not far behind. It took Ber a moment to calm Nora down into her human form. He needed the moment, too, before what they were stepping into.

"I need rags and water, *now*." Viviane said as soon as they entered.

Nora and Ber did so, fetching the items as quick as they could. Alice left a trail of blood all the way to the bed. She was barely awake. The dark mark spread across her shoulder and arm, leaving the limb colorless.

Viviane worked to get her fever down, but her skin was hot to the touch.

"Ber, take over. Nora, I need those plants."

Nora obeyed. Viviane kept vials and alchemical tools on her person. She was grateful that Suryc thought that too was "useless." She administered what she had into Alice, forcing her to swallow the contents. Nora stepped in to tend to Alice. Ber pulled Viviane away so she could catch her breath.

"It—it's just not enough..." Viviane said, her voice broken, "... Even if we were to make it to town, no amount of medicine can reverse the damage done."

Viviane held onto him as she sobbed, curling into herself. Ber looked to Nora, her face just as red and tear-stained as his. A thought spurred him.

"Maybe we can find help beyond medicine."

"No spirit will help us. Not in this cursed place—not anywhere," Viviane spat.

"This is your call, Viviane. But if there's nothing else we can do, we should try."

Viviane had seen enough to believe the spirits and Saints do not care about the suffering of the living. If Ber was honest with himself, he felt the same. Two months in a hellish fog is a long time to wait. But he forced himself to believe someone was looking out for them.

Viviane considered Alice's condition. She would not last for another ride, nor would she last in the cabin. Viviane swallowed hard.

"… You're right. Let's get going."

They carried Alice to the nearest body of water, a wide, black lake. Its surface was violent and layered with a white mist from the downpour. Given her water aura, they figured their best bet would be a water spirit. Ber carefully set Alice in. They all stood around Alice, soaked and waist deep in the black water. None of them knew what to do from there. So they prayed to whomever would listen.

Viviane bent over and broke down. She sobbed into Alice's chest. Her breaths were few and far between. The inhales became far too shallow, then she was still.

Viviane's trembling hand brushed back Alice's hair. She recoiled her reach and covered her face. She shrieked into her palms until her voice went hoarse. The noise rung through Nora and Ber. It was a noise that would haunt them for a long, long time.

The rain lightened to a drizzle. The sound of rain was replaced by swaying reeds and the eerie howl of the wind. The clouds parted in the black, moonless sky.

From the distant bulrushes came a disturbance. Nora through red, watery eyes averted her gaze to the bank. What was first the faintest glimmer grew into a radiant light that filled the bank.

A sliver of light emerged from the brush. The light shaped itself into a small, spindly creature. It skimmed across the water, giving stillness to everything in its wake.

This spirit hovered before them, silent and peering into each of them. Its pale eyes stared down, unblinking. The spirit's mouth opened but no sound could be heard. Instead, the wind picked up once more and rushed between the thickets and reeds. It revealed a reverberated message in the form of a supernatural melody.

These waters of old transcribed to me.
The joys and the woes of your history.
And from my power I give this child
The one of the churning tides and wild
A chance to reverse the damage once more.
Thus from these waters my healing will pour.

The spirit directed it's attention to Viviane. She gazed up, her eyes wide and body shaky. She, Nora, and Ber lowered themselves into a bow as much as they were able to in the water.

You, my child of the Flora. You must do what you can once I revive her. My blessing cannot be regenerated. Drain the poison, and she will start her life anew. Do not let this blessing be in vain.

The spirit's eyes closed as it descended into the water. It dissolved into a luminous, indistinct form and entered Alice's body. The lake began to dim.

Soon after, Alice's eyes creased, and released tears of pure black. Viviane welled with tears of her own. She took Alice back to land, with Nora and Ber alongside Alice.

To Viviane, the spirit's instructions were clear. She did not rejoice just yet, for she knew what she had to do. With trembling hands, she prepared herself to remove the poison sown deep within Alice's body.

Nora laid a gentle hand on Viviane. Viviane took a deep breath. She drove the poison out from Alice. The poison's composition and resistance made the removal more difficult than it already was. She made slow, tedious progress to revive Alice, but at this rate, her efforts were not enough.

Ber lent a gentle grasp around Viviane's wrist, giving her aura support. Together they extracted the poison. Alice's body contracted and coiled in an unnatural form. The involuntary wriggling of her pale flesh nauseated Viviane, yet she continued. With every pump of poison out of her body,

Alice's face regained color, and the dark marks faded.

Once the final drop was extracted, Alice jolted. She gave into a fit of rapid, exasperated breaths in a desperate attempt to fill her lungs with air once more. Viviane, too, felt like she could finally breathe. Viviane helped her sit upright. She could feel weakness in Alice's struggle to get up by herself.

Viviane's forehead met with hers as she sobbed. She brushed Alice's soaked hair behind her ears as she tried to speak.

"I thought—I thought I was going to lose you, and…" Viviane's words trailed off.

With her stronger arm, Alice wept Viviane's tears away. It took all of her strength to have her lips meet with Viviane's. Viviane smiled into their kiss. A long silence between the two ensued as the gentle breeze sung.

"Please, please don't cry. I'm alive, aren't I?"

Viviane chuckled to her response and held her in a long embrace.

25

Chapter 25

Back at the cabin, Viviane, Nora, and Ber did not sleep. Viviane tended to Alice's aftereffects of her illness and stayed by her bedside throughout the night, while Nora and Ber took turns being on patrol in case Suryc's men returned.

On occasions Nora or Ber came to visit Alice and help Viviane with whatever she needed. What she needed, however, proved equally demanding as patrolling the area throughout the night.

Light returned back into the sky after what seemed like forever. Alice fell in and out of consciousness for most of the night, but regained enough strength for the party to travel somewhere safer. Nearing the end of the final patrol, Ber caught a familiar face soaring above, the *Coral Fang*'s raptor. He grabbed Viviane to call him down.

"The crew's looking for us..." Viviane said, setting Ian down on the table. She looked to Alice, unconscious and still deeply ill, "... We have no choice but to decommission. Alice is in no condition to sail."

"What about the crew?" Nora asked.

"Robbie is second- eh, third in command. He will square everything away. The crew will be pissy, but there's nothing we can do..." Viviane said while writing a letter to send back, "Actually, I'm more worried how this one will respond when she comes to."

—

They set off again in search of medical help. They traveled in stealth, walking through the woods with Alice asleep on Lotte's back.

They entered first town they spotted outside of Warcove. Along a stream nestled the large mill town, simply called Mill Town. Nora took charge of holding Alice when Lotte retreated back into the woods.

They did not step far into the town when a kindly merchant offered his assistance to the town's infirmary. Upon the doorstep of the infirmary, Viviane turned to Nora and Ber.

"Don't worry about payment, we should have enough on us for a few days here," Viviane assured.

Upon entering, many of the bustling nurses took a second look at Alice as they passed. Though her condition improved since the night before, Alice's face remained pale and sunken. She could do little other than grip onto Nora. Nora realized how her slender fingers, usually akin to the daggers along her belt, bore little strength. At the front desk, a couple of nurses greeted them.

"Good morning! How can we help y—oh goodness..."

"She is... sick, please, can you help her?" Viviane asked.

"Of course, I will get her situated right away," The nurse said.

Alice was situated in a small, bright room. Despite its rather cramped conditions, the natural light let in made the room much more comforting. The nurse asked Alice a series of medical questions, to which she could not answer well. Even speaking grew tiresome to her, a feeling she never felt before.

The nurse turned his attention to Viviane, Nora, and Ber. "There is an inn just down the street from here. I'm certain they have a vacancy," He advised.

The nurse picked up the blatant concern amongst them, especially written on Viviane's face. He placed a hand on her shoulder.

"Many of us here are the best healers on this side of the province. I assure you she is in good hands," He said, giving a soft smile.

"... Thank you," Viviane said.

Viviane knelt beside Alice. Viviane found it strange how she did not put up a fight with being put in an infirmary, let alone being left in this room. Viviane brushed Alice's hair back and kissed her forehead.

"Please, get some rest."

To this, Alice smiled and nodded.

"We'll be back really soon." Nora said.

"Don't think this gets you out of our rematch!" Ber added, trying to lighten the mood. As they left, the nurse shot Ber a questioning gaze.

The moment after they left the steps of the infirmary, Viviane gave into tears. Nora and Ber sat by her side to comfort her. After a few minutes, she gathered herself.

"I- I want to thank you… Thank you, for everything. I don't know where I would be without both of you. And Alice…" Viviane choked on her words.

Ber pulled her into a warm embrace, and Nora joined in.

"Viv, I think we've been through enough for us to have each other's backs. You've done the same for us." Ber said.

Nora added, "I may not know much about being part of a family, but I think our team is pretty damn close."

"I… I think so too," Viviane said.

They dispersed from their embrace. Viviane, still wiping the tears from her face, fell into a warm smile.

"You know, after all of this is over, I'm having you all meet my family. Trust me when I say you're going to have the best damn meal of your life when that day comes!" She laughed.

"I'd really like that," Nora said.

Viviane continued to clean herself up. She wiped away more tears, as well as the remaining makeup streaked on her face from yesterday.

Together they sauntered along down the street. The closer they traveled to Saint Evedis, the more extravagant the towns became. As far as the eye could see, the streets lay covered in perfect, polished stones and lined with ornate street lamps. On each side, earthy red bricks constructed grand buildings, each ending with at least one or two spires grazing the sky. Each structure seemed to be placed in aesthetic perfection.

Between the food markets and bakeries were specialty shops, some of which Nora had never seen before. Along the streets, advertised with fancy lettering and giant display windows, were cafes, hobby shops, and pet stores. Nora had to physically hold Ber back from running into the dessert shops, though the scents tempted them both. Not even a few blocks later, all three gave into their empty stomachs and stocked up on various non-pairing foods.

Sitting on the street curb, they enjoyed their feast, stuffing in unhealthy amounts of sugar and meat. No one seemed surprised from their hoard of food. It seemed that a group of youths eating food on the side of a street like a pack of rats was a common site here.

They continued on to their other errand to secure a place to stay. Ber, now full of energy, sparked conversation.

"So, I gotta ask. What's the story behind you and Alice? Were you two always an item?" he asked.

"Ber, you're asking the wrong questions," Nora hushed her voice, "Is Alice really *the* Princess Alice?!"

Viviane looked away, her face flushed with color. "… Yes. I think I owe you an explanation. I much as I hate the man, Suryc was right about a few things."

Her eyes remained misty from earlier as she spoke, "When I was young, I was taken away to work under the Crown. That's when I met Alice. We were alone in different ways, so we just clicked. We always dreamed about going on adventures. When we escaped, we did just that."

Nora asked, "You were taken away?"

"When this nation's youth was subject to the draft, the commonwealths were not exempt. How I ended up in Saint Evedis of all places is kind of a long story…" Viviane said, "…You know, it's funny. I always thought she wanted me as a friend, and I was fine with that. But she proved me wrong, and—" Viviane caught herself, "I- I've said too much! Don't you *dare* tell her any of this."

"You have my word. Though I can't speak for Ber, I'd watch him if I were you.." Nora said.

"That's not true! Don't listen to her slander, Viv." Ber said, "I never spilled your secret on you being a shapeshifter, have I?"

Nora's head fell into her hands.

Viviane could not help but laugh, "What am I going to do with you two...?"

By the time they checked into the inn and traveled back to see Alice, the sun dipped low in the horizon. As they walked, the shadows cast from the buildings stretched and filled the streets.

When they entered Alice's room, her attention was turned to the window. With a sleepy gaze, she greeted her visitors.

"Oh, it's you freaks again."

Already by her side, Viviane grazed the side of her face. Though Viviane's eyes remained misty, she grinned from ear to ear.

"How are you feeling?"

"Like utter shit," Alice answered.

"Well, I know what will make you feel better."

Viviane revealed her stash of sweets from her bag. Alice lit up, her entire body reaching for her bag. Just as she seemed to be returning to normal, a sharp pain struck her chest. She coiled and fell back on her bed.

"Ah. Seems I am still dying."

"Don't say that, we *just* brought you back to life," Viviane piled the food onto her lap, "Have you been obeying the nurses?"

"Hardly. She's fought every medication we've given her," A nurse said in passing, overhearing the conversation.

"I took 'em eventually, didn't I?" Alice said.

To this, the nurse rolled her eyes and moved on. Viviane shot Alice a look.

"I'm sorry, I am really trying. It's just... It's been a while since I have felt this feeble," Alice admitted.

Viviane sighed. She placed Alice's hand in hers.

"I know."

Viviane sparked an idea, and began to forage in her bag once more.

"Saints, what else do you have in that thing?" Nora asked.

Viviane revealed a small, travel-sized mess kit, complete with a quaint tea set. She rolled up her sleeves and began to set everything in place.

"I feel like we have all had our fair share of dour evenings. So damnit, we will be having a pleasant one today!" Viviane announced.

"Even if were in an infirmary, and one of us almost died?" Nora asked.

"*Especially* if one of us almost died," Viviane gestured to Nora and Ber, "Now, I need your able bodies to raid the nurse's lounge while I set the table for tea."

Nora and Ber exchanged each other a glance, but did as they were told. Together they all set up tea time in Alice's room. They passed the rest of the afternoon in pleasant, lighthearted conversation.

Night crept forward. Nora let out an eased, quiet sigh.

"I think it's about time I head back to the inn. You coming with, Ber?" she asked. She gave a slight head tilt, suggesting they give Viviane and Alice some time alone.

"Sure. You comin', Viv?" Ber asked.

Viviane showed a warm smile, "I'll meet you there, I'm going to stay a little while longer."

They bid their farewells for the night, wishing Alice a peaceful rest. Nora shut the door behind them.

Alice locked eyes with Viviane's, honey gold in they dying light.

"I suppose we need to talk."

26

Chapter 26

Soldiers turned to the echo of irregular footsteps in the vast chamber. A man sat on its opposite end, attentive to a set of worn dice in his palm.

No need to be this on edge, Suryc continued to tell himself.

He felt the crease on his forehead form, as he struggled to maintain a perfect posture with his limp. He had a history of talking himself out of trouble with ease. But this, he knew, could turn out much different. The Light was not known to be forgiving, after all.

"You are late, Mr. Harland," The man, The Light spoke.

"My condolences, Master," Suryc replied. He tried for a lighter approach, "You would get a kick out of what I just—"

"Would you care to explain what we needed to discuss on such short notice?"

"Ah, yes…" Suryc mulled his words over carefully, "I made great strides towards infiltrating the Evedis nobility circle. What I discovered is that, get this— I found the Princess. Better yet, she's gallivanting with practically no defenses around Stromshire. I'm hot on her trail. Once her capture is done with, 'negotiation' with the Queen should be quick and effortless."

"I have one question for you," The Light said, "If you know all of this, why is she not already in your possession?"

"That, Master, is the one, *temporary* setback I regret to inform you. Upon capturing, she was accompanied by some ragtag trio of magicians. Her little posse allowed the Princess to escape her imprisonment."

The Light's jaw tightened before speaking, "Harland, stop me if I am incorrect. I have expended more than an ample supply of my resources to you. And yet, after *months* you have nothing to show for it?"

"Master, pardon my boldness, but I have done everything in my power to overturn this damned nation. The supplies and connections I've gathered say it all, many of these big cities *love* me!"

"While your words may have some inkling of truth behind them, my quarrel is this: you have made no progress into Saint Evedis, and yet you have the audacity to speak to me in this way after you clearly were beaten by these 'ragtag' magicians." Suryc held in his breath. He began to regret his loose tongue.

The Light continued, "What I am hearing is that this 'temporary setback' is insincere. Tell me what you know of these magicians."

Suryc obeyed. He relayed descriptions of the three. He explained how regrettably, he did not gather their names. He felt foolish now, even forgetting Viviane's name.

"I will admit that I underestimated these people. Master, you have my sincerest apologies. I *assure* you that I will not fail you again."

The Light showed a reserved smile.

"... I understand now. It's quite alright, my son. You know, I believe I found something that we can agree on." He said, placing his dice aside, "*You certainly will not fail me again.*"

From outside, the soldiers at the door heard the blood curdling shrieks of Mr. Harland, and then an audible, bodily *crack*. Silence filled the chamber.

Suryc's body laid limp on the marbled floor. The Light stood above him, rearranging the cuffs of his suit. He addressed the soldier that began to rid of the body.

"Don't allow Mr. Harland here to go to waste, send him to Bastel. Once you are finished, call for Arel. We've some new matters to discuss."

27

Chapter 27

"How is she doing?" Nora asked.

"Better. Though she is further from recovery than I thought, I'm afraid," Viviane said, "Perhaps while we are here, we can make some plans for when we are able to travel again."

Viviane unraveled her map on a coffee table. Marks of her and Alice's travels dotted the page, along with circles of areas of interest. One area in particular was curiously marked, a city in Rinesant, a nation southwest of Stromshire. Before Ber could ask, Nora pointed to another circle close to their current location.

"This right here, Orson's Ridge. This is the place Suryc mentioned, right?"

"Yes. I took note as soon as I could so I wouldn't forget. He mentioned something about an "Heir," so I would hope that if we pursued Orson's Ridge and found this heir, maybe we could put an end to this people-hunting business. However…" Viviane moved to trace the ridge, "The Heir being here isn't possible. We have information that Orson's Ridge is covered in fog. I doubt that's changed."

Nora's eyes met Ber's. With the glance, they knew they shared the same insane idea. "Actually, me and Nora have been inside the fog before, so…"

Viviane leaned forward, locking eyes with Ber. It took her a moment to respond. "How—how is that possible? People aren't supposed to come out…"

"They're not," Ber stated, "not without the proper medium. There's a lot we need to catch you and Alice up on."

Viviane watched Alice's sleeping body. Her body still heaved with each breath, but she slumbered in peace.

"What happened to Alice—what's happened to many others, I never want to happen to anyone again. Is this something we can prevent?"

"I don't know, but we can try."

Alice shuffled in her sheets. She rubbed her eyes and asked, "I heard my name, did I miss something?"

"Saints, Alice, are you some kind of demon? I mentioned your name and you just pop in."

Alice grinned sleepily, "Aww Viv, that's the sweetest thing you've ever said to me!"

"Actually Alice, I'm glad you're up for this. Me and Nora have some things to tell you," Ber said.

Viviane and Alice sat and listened as Nora and Ber told of their involvements prior to their meeting. Ber told of the origin of the fog, a different world where he himself is from. He told of the transformed creatures, the tortured souls that lay trapped within the fog. He also explained as to how 'keys' from this other world do exist, allowing someone to traverse the fog in relative ease.

Nora told them of her entrance into the fog, in which she and Ber met and managed to escape. She took a deep breath, reluctant to continue. She explained the link between her aura and her inhuman form, and how the form kept her composure through the fog.

Throughout their explanations, Viviane nodded intently. Alice even seemed to abandon her snide comments.

Ber continued on, "... With that being said, we could pursue the 'Heir' before the trail gets cold. I'm willing to do this if we can end this all sooner."

"I'm willing, too. But, we are a team now," Nora looked to Alice and Viviane, "What do you think?"

Viviane froze in thought.

Alice placed a hand in hers and asked, "As much as I don't want us to separate for this, I fear it may be our best choice. But this fog, it's something I've never heard of *anyone* surviving… But you two aren't just 'anyone', are you?" Alice smiled, "We've beat one of these bastards before, so if you have confidence to do so again, you have my full support."

"I have faith in both of you." In the same breath, Viviane pulled out her bag and said, "But as we all have seen, faith can only take you so far. I want you to take my medicines. We won't be needing it while we are here, anyway."

"… Are you leaving now? Should you not go at dusk?" Viviane asked.

"The sooner we leave, the better. It's always dusk in the fog, anyway," Ber said.

Viviane's lips quivered, but she forced herself not to cry. She pulled them into an embrace.

"Be safe, won't you?"

Alice nodded to them. Her shaking was visible, "I just died and I do not recommend it. If either of you die, I'll kick your ass."

Nora chuckled, "I'll take note of that."

Ber scooped them all into a hug.

"We survived the fog before. It sucks, but we can do it again," He assured, "See you on the other side!"

He left the embrace, nodding to Nora. With an exchange of goodbyes, Ber and Nora hit the road once more.

28

Chapter 28

Even on the back of Lotte, the trip to the Orson's Ridge fog took several hours. Nora landed Lotte a little ways away from the fog so as to not spook her. She bid her farewell to her dragon, though Lotte was hesitant for her and Ber to leave.

"We'll be back, Lotte. Promise," Nora said, brushing Lotte's cheek.

Lotte hesitated, backing away before dashing off. Nora looked up at the familiar wall of grey before her.

Nora turned to Ber, "Any official plan?"

"Get in, take down the 'Heir', get out. In regards to details, that's something we will have to find out when we get there," Ber answered. "Are you sure you're okay with this? You will be a beast again until we leave…"

"I will be okay. I was going to ask you the same thing."

"I'll be fine, I survived last time. As long as we got each other's backs, we'll be fine." Ber smiled, and Nora found it to be contagious.

"One last thing– You'll be needing this." Ber untied the stone from around his neck and handed it to Nora. His body began to change once her stone was out of his possession. The patches of scales and feathers like the ones on his chest emerged from his face and arms. Nora watched with intrigue, though she felt rude for staring.

Betram stepped into the fog, concealing himself aside from an open, clawed hand. Nora took his hand, and the two returned to the fog.

—

Nora got to her feet, realizing she had blacked out. Before her newly formed body stood Ber. His own transformation ceased once he entered the fog.

"Glad you're okay!" Ber said, "You look different from last time— a better different!"

Nora tried to examine her own body. Her body seemed to stabilize,as this time it was one, uniform piece. As before, four scaled limbs adorned with talons replaced her arms and legs. Her sense of smell heightened, overstimulating Nora, as she was still new to the sensitivity.

"We could try to get a vantage point from the ridge. I can't see anything down here," Ber said.

Nora nodded, following suit.

Nora and Ber continued onward, approaching the ridge. Inclined terrain turned to land steep enough for Ber to have to scale on all fours. Nora scaled the ridge with relative ease on already acclimated limbs, jumping from ledge to ledge.

They stayed on the alert for monsters in the fog. Nora could smell the distant rot of the creatures downwind. Nora figured the one perk of treading through rough terrain was steering clear of those terrible things.

"Feels just old times! Right, Nor?" Ber paused, "I forgot you can't speak. I'll assume you agree."

To this, Nora huffed.

Upon reaching the top of the ridge, the haze thinned just enough to grant a general scope of the land. On the other side laid a valley, narrowing into a canyon.

"When we left, I was under the impression that this base wouldn't be impossible to find." Ber said, "If you have any ideas other than looking at every tree with suspicion, let me know."

Nora closed her eyes and tried to pick up something, anything. Her ears swiveled to hear any kind of activity. Instead, her senses were filled with the whipping wind and the rustle of trees down below. No birds or insects sung from the land below. The eerie air left Nora greatly unsettled. At the very least, she did not smell any predators, either.

She struggled to pick up and decipher the spectrum of scents around her. The most prevalent seemed to be Ber sitting aside her, who smelled of hay grass, and now sweat from scaling the ridge. The strong odors from Viviane's medicine bag overwhelmed Nora's senses, so much so that she paced away to get a chance of picking up anything else. She smelled the grasses and woods below, and the dust from the open earth under her feet. And yet, something seemed off. While the wind blew, the world within the fog smelled stagnant, and almost *rotten*.

With a shift of the wind, a hint of metal traced the air. Nora followed the scent, with Ber in tow.

The trail led her to some mounds of stones atop the ridge. Within these stones Nora weaved between the rocks, trying to find the source. Ber called her over, and what she saw took her a moment to process. Before them was what they hoped would lead them to the Heir, a man-made passageway into the ridge. It seemed fresh, as clean cut dirt and rock formed a perfect rectangular shaft descending underground.

"This is not something your people made," Ber said, "many of our military bases and hangars are made within the protection of mountains and valleys, and this was made recently with powerful magic."

With hesitation, they entered the passage.

With each new set of stairs, the air grew thicker. Strange fixtures emitted a dim teal light, just enough to see a few stairs ahead. The two picked up speed to escape the passage's cramped, almost suffocating environment. Nora forced back her instinct to dash back to the surface.

The two began to feel a slight draft. After a couple more flights, they made it to a large chamber. It was stocked with crates of supplies and rations. Below them stood a handful of knights in deep conversation. To Ber, there stood a friend from a world away.

Nora bared her teeth, awaiting the go-ahead to attack. Instead, she found a halting hand in front of her.

"There's more to to this situation than I thought… We aim to incapacitate, understand?" Ber asked.

Ber prayed he was making the right decision. The Knight in the center, a brick wall of a man with long black hair was undeniably his old friend. A wave of relief hit Ber under otherwise bleak circumstances.

Nora and Ber crept closer. They searched for any vantage point to counter the knights but to no avail, finding more knights in the chamber.

Why would he be here *of all places?* Ber struggled to understand. He strained his thoughts, repeating to himself to focus on the task at hand. *Protect Nora. End the operation... Talk with Arel.*

Hearing approaching footsteps, Nora dashed to another set of stairs. Ber followed suit. They slunk low, fearing they were too exposed. The two snuck closer, dashing from pillar to pillar. From the ground floor they gauged just how large the structure within the canyon was, looking up to see a dozen more floors, and each wall lined with long halls.

Nora and Ber halted behind a pillar, just out of earshot from the knight's low murmurs. Nora's heart pounded, still a strange feeling to be so low in her chest while in this form. They followed the black-haired one from the overhang to a vacant room. Ber told Nora to wait while he took dropped down to meet him.

"Hey, Arel."

"B-Ber!" The man ran up to embrace him, "Where did you go? What happened to you?"

"Got sent to one of these," Ber gestured to the fog around them, "Indefinitely."

"What... what are you doing *here?*"

"I'm finishing what I started, Arel. It's what we always talked about."

Arel faltered for a moment, backing away. Ber had not seen Arel in months. Why now was he looking away?

"I... I'm afraid I can't let you do that."

Nora crept closer to the two. She could not understand them in their native tongue, but she anticipated she would need to act quick. What she did not anticipate, however, was Arel's hand reaching to cup Ber's face.

"Ber, come back to the Knighthood. I can work something out for you.

Please."

"He… He never told what I did, did he?"

"I've heard some outlandish rumors. Whatever you did could not have been that bad!" Arel heard the other Knights approach and he took a step back, "You know he gets into his spats. Please, just come home."

In a stagnant hangar, the air picked up. Ber's eyes reflected briefly a silver-blue before returning to brown. "No, Arel. I cannot return. I will not return. I— I still care for you, Arel. So I am giving you one more chance to think this over, before I remind you why I was Serkan's favored."

The Knights rounded the corner. They clocked Ber and surrounded him in an instant. He was kicked directly in the stomach and he fell.

"Watch your tongue before His Majesty," said the Knight.

Ber forced out a dry cough before catching his breath. "… Nice to see you too, Leo," He groaned weakly. He rolled to his side to relieve the deep, unrelenting pain in his gut.

Nora was instantly on his attacker, pinning him to the floor. Her toothsome maw opened over the man's neck, but she halted at Ber's command.

"Nora, wait, please!"

It was a bad call. The Knights got their chance to gain full advantage, forcing a distracted Nora off the man and retaining her in a prison that jutted from the ground. Sharp fractals of crystals, all the same pale hue, surrounded her. In the same breath, Ber was apprehended as well.

"I really don't have time for this game, 'friend.' You came all this way for what? A hope for my change of heart?" Arel asked, "… And what's with the weird dog?"

"The weird dog is a friend. What… What *happened*?"

"That, Ber, is a loaded question. In short, I'm your 'Heir,' now." Arel said, letting out a soft chuckle, "You *left*, Ber. The Light moved on, and I happened to be next in line."

Ber leaned towards Arel, ignoring the spearhead at his neck, "Please, Arel, this isn't you and you know it."

Arel looked away briefly before he spoke.

"Think of this as a new start. Ebi will be powerful and united again. In history, what we are doing will be marked as a transition towards a glorious revolution. Perhaps in a few years, our realm will finally understand true peace and prosperity."

Arel stepped beside Ber, "You know, it can be a new start for you as well," He smiled, "Please, Ber. Let me help you out of this. Perhaps you can even be the success story of your tribe."

The muscles in Ber's face tightened.

"How- how *dare* you?! Arel, for fuck's sake, think about our families! Think about the destruction Serkan has done already! Do you honestly think that this—all of this, is worth whatever is gained in the end?" Arel frowned, but he listened. "I'm not sure what all you've been told, but even if I wanted to go back, I can't. I'll be at *least* killed for what I've done. Give Serkan or his men one reason to not like you, and you'll be done, too. Even if you do your job well, do you really think Serkan will place you in any political power when this is all over? You'll be a figure head, at *best*. If and when something does go wrong in this 'revolution,' all of Ebi will want your head."

"Ber, what... what happened to you? You were the Light's right hand man. What happened?"

"Try 'servant' or 'accessory.' Pride is a trait your 'Light' treasures, so I understand why he hasn't told you..." Ber paused, "... What happened is I tried to kill him."

Ber and Arel were at a standstill. The Knights were waiting for the Heir's command. Nora was forced to watch, and listen in vain to their unknown language.

"... You saved my life once, Ber. I will not forget that. Consider this me returning the favor. I want you to walk away, and never show your face to me again. If you know what is good for you, you will not stick your nose where it doesn't belong. Understand?"

To this, Ber mocked a stiff salute, then a deep bow. He looked up through his mussed hair, locking eyes with the man.

"Yes, my Heir."

Hesitantly, the Knights shuffled aside, leaving a path to the exit. The crystals around Nora descended. She too hesitated when Ber ushered her back up the stairs.

Nora felt beyond confused at the whole ordeal, and now, the Knights below them argued violently.

But Ber understood.

"I adhere to the Code, Leo! Make no mistake!"

"You let a fucking criminal walk! *Our* code does not tolerate treason."

A thunderous crash rang out, so strong the earth beneath Nora and Ber's feet rumbled.

"… Let this be a lesson to you all. I am the *HEIR*. I am *SECOND IN COMMAND*. You will listen to me, or you will be *REPURPOSED*."

29

Chapter 29

Nora and Ber breached the fog. Like before, Nora returned to her human form.

"... I assume you have questions," Ber said.

"What *was* that back there? I thought we were putting an end to this."

"We are. This just got... complicated."

"I could tell. It sounded like you had history with the dark-haired one," Ber flushed. Before he could respond, Nora continued, "I don't care what kind of history you two had. I just need to know that I can trust you."

"You can trust me, Nor."

"But... But you worked for those people, didn't you? You served the people that cursed this land. That cursed *me*."

"Nora—"

Nora stepped out of the tree's shade. She was changing form, partly, as her limbs became dark and clawed. She spoke, while she was still able.

"You... you were the first person I was able to trust in a long time. You have no idea what I have been through, before even all of this. You think I wanted any of this?! I didn't know who I was when I left, and now I share a soul with a fucking monster! Tell me what merciful god would believe that to be fair! I never wanted this! I never wanted any of this! I ran away from a cage closing in, only to be put in another prison. It just doesn't. Make. Sense."

Nora had covered her face as she sobbed. Her already rasped voice grew hoarse. When her claws moved from her face, it had become fully canid.

"You were my closest friend, Ber. I thought you were different."

The words seared Ber's heart. Regardless, he brought her in close and held her for a long moment as she cried.

"… For what it's worth, you are *my* closest friend, too. I'm sorry, Nora. I should have told you sooner."

Nora clung to him for a long while, tears running down her beast face. After a while, the transformation receded and her human form returned.

"I… I was drafted, Nora. It was part of a deal, to keep my city, my tribe safe from Serkan's further interference. I was a stable hand, but when Serkan discovered my power, he made me his 'right hand man.' But I was just his personal servant."

Ber continued, "When I found out what they said was a lie, and my city was invaded, I did not think. All I could do was act. I went to kill Serkan and put an end to it all. Of course, that did not work and I was arrested. Not even an hour later, he sent me to where you found me. He said he would have use from me sooner or later."

"He put you in the fog to transform…" Nora realized.

He nodded, "You saved me that day, Nora. I will forever be grateful for that. Please, please don't ever connect your judgment of me to my past. Yes, it's something that happened, but I wish it never did."

"I'm sorry," Nora said, holding onto Ber, "I'm sorry."

"It's alright, Nor… You give great hugs."

Nora laughed through her sobs, "Thank you. If it is alright with you, I… I think I'm ready to tell you how I entered the fog."

30

Chapter 30

-Nora-

"Season's ending, Reed. Do you have everything ready?"

"Yes, Selene."

The old woman had called Nora 'Reed' since as long as Nora could remember. She was thin, and always a tad taller than the other children.

"Remember the fog's spreading. You might have to change routes this year. I would leave a day or so early, if I were you."

Nora smiled, "I always leave early, anyway. It should be no trouble."

The two wrapped up their chat over tea. Nora considered it kind the old lady still checked up on her for the annual movement. Each year, she was tasked with herding Selene's sheep to the depot way out east. There they were sheared, showed, and sold. Nora took on the duty years ago, when her caretaker's health began to decline.

"You know, there is one more thing we have to do before you leave," Selene said.

Nora frowned as she faced the sink, "I know."

—

Nora left to the field to ensure everything was ready for her journey. Really, it was an excuse to escape the house. With her chores done she took to the woods to see Lotte.

The beast waited for her every day in the same place. She bounded to Nora, despite her injury.

"Easy, girl! I missed you, too."

Lotte bellowed over Nora, blowing her hair over her face.

"You know the routine. 'Gotta check you over before your snack."

Nora examined the makeshift cast she set on Lotte's wing. Lotte moved the limb with little issue. A good sign, given Nora's approaching leave.

She found the beast worse for wear, and against her better judgement nursed it back to health. Nora spent her childhood caring for sheep, so making a splint on something other than a lamb came with its challenges.

Nora still felt stupid for the decision. She was already magic folk. Harboring a beast, let alone a dragon, was a serious crime. But when she looked into the dragon's eyes for the first time, Nora had a revelation: She too was afraid, broken, and alone. Not where they were supposed to be. She felt foolish for thinking it, but Nora still wondered if Lotte shared that understanding.

Nora removed the splint in place of some looser bandages, just to encourage Lotte to keep it in place a little while longer. Lotte examined Nora's own bandages in her wrists. The herbal scent made the beast sneeze.

"Don't you worry about me. Worrying's *my* job..." Nora said, "Selene refreshes these. It keeps my magic at bay, so she does not have to worry about me when I'm away," Nora said, "Though I could go without the side effects..."

Lotte turned at a noise Nora did not hear. Nora felt the muscles beneath her scales tense.

"It's probably nothing, Lotte, but you should run off, just in case. I'll come say bye before I leave town, alright?"

Nora hopped back to the path back to the village when she noticed a pair of footprints that were not there before. *No one's ever over here...* She tried to push her worries away as she made her way back in time for dinner.

—

It only took that evening for word to spread. The local Guard was informed and they took action. Nora could hear the rumbling of footsteps as they made their way upstairs. Vibrations shook her room, causing hanging oil lamps and small trinkets to tremble. There was nothing she could do but wait and pray that she could talk her way out of the trouble she was in. Of course, talking was not her strong suit.

"Nora Ní Dyr," A familiar voice called, "We come to issue your arrest. You will be charged with the practice of witchcraft and of harboring a beast."

Nora's head spun, but her body froze. Des. She always mentioned wanting to join the Guard, but for some reason recruitment never came. She left for Bend for training, and returned different. Now, Nora's closest friend was arresting her.

And Selene... why did she not stop them?!

"Stay away from me!" Nora shrieked, causing her throat to close and ache. A symptom of her caretaker's treatment.

It was easier to keep magic under wraps if one does not talk, lest something slips, the woman had said. But Selene was wrong.

The bandages around her wrists dissolved. Nora's magic poured out, and filled the room in a swirling web of shadows. Lanterns throughout her room dimmed in submission to her power.

Before they could put Nora in chains, a dark mass bursted through the window. The mass slashed the guards back and surrounded Nora. Before the guards could regain themselves, the creature encased Nora and leapt back out the window.

Within the clutches of her beast, Nora was swept away from the ranch, away from Ghleanne. She looked back when she knew she should not have. Time seemed to slow. The lights from the ranch grew smaller. She watched as guards flooded out from her house, a few of which childhood friends. She thought it may have been a trick of the light, but she saw a figure in a white gown emerge from the house. Selene.

Nora wrenched in pain as she shrieked. Tears were swept away from the wind just as soon as they formed. Everything in her life seemed so *decided,* yet now, she had never felt more helpless.

—

Nora told Ber the basics of it all. Nursing Lotte back to health, being 'treated' for her magic, escaping her arrest. Ber seemed pensive. He had many questions, and many folk he now wanted to maim. He did not want to overwhelm Nora, but one slipped out.

"You never told me why you entered the fog in the first place. You thought it was a shortcut, I reckon?"

Nora did not answer. The silence said it all.

"Well, whatever the reason," Ber said, "I'm happy I got to meet you."

"Me too."

31

Chapter 31

Viviane found herself alone with her thoughts, a place she always dreaded. She was in Alice's hospital room, watching over her as she slept.

The bed sheets rose and fell with each breath Alice took. It took Viviane off guard at first, to see her partner so peaceful. The rising sun peeked through the window, casting light on Alice's tanned skin and coppery hair.

Viviane drew the curtains closed to not interrupt Alice's much needed rest, though she left a gap to peek through. The sun made its steady ascent from the hills. Though less than a day passed since Ber and Nora left, she began to worry– more than she already does for the two.

She shook the feeling to watch as nurses and chambermaids alike rushed across the courtyard below to their daily chores. She knew the hustle well, and part of her yearned to help out. Viviane caught Alice's reflection in the glass as she shifted to her side, still sound asleep. She was stable now, but Viviane could not help but think that if she left, something would turn for the worse. The rational part of her reckoned it was unlikely, but unlikely things tended to happen to Viviane. Unlikely things, Viviane considered, had also saved her and Alice just two nights before.

The memory was branded in her mind. Wood floors wet with rain and blood-soaked rags. Shallowing breaths and necrotic skin. Black water, white light, then a miracle.

Viviane looked at her hands. Rope burns around her wrists were still red and fresh from that night.

Viviane had accepted her predetermined life of normalcy. Her hands could craft baked goods to her heart's content, but nothing more. Even if she was not as talented as the others, that night had proved just what she was capable of. She had the vial of extracted poison to prove it.

With Nora and Ber gone to bring down an unknown threat, and the fog becoming an inescapable danger, a sobering thought dawned to Viviane– Her parents may have fallen victim to this 'Heir.' Even more, she knew the search for them would have to wait.

She tried to tell herself her fear for her family was irrational. Why would anyone pursue a nonmagical couple of bakers from a tiny island nation? But since the draft, she learned a sobering lesson that anything was possible. Even more, the fog was spreading, and does not discriminate on its captives.

She turned to find Alice shifting, still sound asleep. Alice's breathing had steadied, but Viviane still found herself counting respirations. She heard a soft rap at the door, and a nurse entered with arms full of sheets. The nurse stopped a moment when she met eyes with hers.

"Miss Viviane," the nurse said, "Alice is stable. You may retire at the inn, if you'd prefer."

"Thank you, Madame. I think I fell asleep on the bench, again..." Viviane lied.

"Well, I'll be adjusting her fluids"

"Wait."

The nurse turned.

"I want to be taught– I want to learn how to heal. I... I want to be of use. Is this something you can help me with?"

The nurse hummed to herself, "You folk must live a dangerous life, out in the country..." She started to say something, but paused, fighting the urge to pry further. "Well, I'd be stupid to turn you away– we certainly need the extra hands. It will be a lot of manual labor, but when care is needed you may shadow me for treatment."

Viviane beamed, "I'll do it!"

"If you're ready, I can take you now."

Viviane nodded and followed. She looked over her shoulder to find Alice, still sound asleep, before quietly closing the door.

—

Alice awoke to being stabbed– it was her initial thought before she came to. She jolted in bed, cursing her lethargic state. In her former state she would have leapt from the bed, snatched the sharpest nearby object and returned the favor to her attacker tenfold.

Her panic melted away when the masked figure grazed a familiar hand along her cheek.

"Sorry to scare you, dear. Here's hoping this is your last set of fluids."

Alice blinked, "… Why does the Doc' got my girl's voice? Am I still dreaming?"

Viviane's blushed from behind her mask at being called her 'girl.' Either Alice was trying her hand at being forward since their talk, or it was the drugs talking.

"No my dear, this is real. I'm taking on some medical training for next time we're in a pinch."

Alice took a good look at Viviane. She looked like an entirely different person, in the hospital's blue garb and white apron, but the chatelaine she always wore was still at her side.

"The fit suits you," Alice said, "Could do without the mask, though. How am I supposed to kiss your pretty face?"

"… How drugged are you, right now?"

"Bone dry," Alice said, hanging on the last syllable, "'Only hurts a little, though.'"

She checked to be sure the other nurses were out of earshot, "I thought you liked a bit of mystery, dearest?"

"This is taking me back to our summer at Dragon Shores. But if I recall right, *I* was the Doctor…" Alice mused, "Hey, have Nora and Ber returned yet?"

"No. I'm starting to get worried."

"You worry too much, Viv. The two are tough as sheep-steers. I'm not convinced Nora *isn't* one, with that mess of hair," Alice said, "How long has it been? The mind's a fog, being near comatose and all."

"Close to a day, now."

Alice paused for a moment. "Maybe you *are* worrying about the right amount. I'll look for the–" Alice doubled over. When she sat up from the bed her body aches shot up to searing pain that branded her to the core.

"Not in your condition, you're not. I want nothing else than to go out there myself but– but…"

Viviane sat at the edge of her bed. Alice hated feeling useless, but she loathed when Viviane felt that way. She placed a hand on Viviane's thigh.

"I know."

"Wait a minute…" In an instant Viviane shot up, "We're literally sitting on the solution!"

Alice did not follow. Viviane dug through Alice's belongings beneath the bed to pull out a holster containing Alice's pistol. Viviane gingerly unsheathed the weapon and presented it to her.

"I'm not a fighter, but…"

Alice considered her proposal. The last thing she wanted was to send her out alone, but she could admit that Viviane proved a good shot. *Hell, with more practice she'd be better than me…*

Hailing from the reserved nation of Gheni Sahel, gunpowder was notoriously expensive *and* hard to come by. Landlocked until further notice, Alice could no longer restock ammunition from seedy, less-than-legal vendors on international waters: Whatever was in that belt was all they had left.

"We're really in dire straits, huh?" Alice said. Her face steeled. "But someone's gotta get those two. If you find trouble, you *must* make them count. Follow the road to Orson's Ridge but I *beg of you,* do not step anywhere near that fog. You are to come back to me no matter what. Understood?"

Alice welled with tears, more so than Viviane had seen in years. She put the pistols aside, kissing her tears away.

"Of course my dear–"

Viviane froze to the sound of heavy footsteps approaching from down the hall. Just when she thought they passed, a knock and a half rapped on the door before someone inharmoniously barreled in.

To their delight and horror, Ber and Nora appeared. Like Viviane, the two had not slept. Their endorphins dwindled to zero. Nora collapsed on the floor, and Ber staggered forward.

"… There's *no* way it's okay in this country to have guns in a hospital."

Directly after, he passed out, face first onto the foot of Alice's bed.

32

Chapter 32

Alice was released from the hospital later that day. She found herself bored, as the rest of the party slept off their exhaustion— At least Satya kept her company. A foolish part of her yearned to cause trouble, but her soreness kept her at bay.

The following day, the party set forth on their final stretch to Saint Evedis. Lotte could not carry them all, so they opted to walk. Beyond the valley lay their final destination. Fortified in grand stone walls was a city overflowing in impossible, marvelous structures and magic.

"We didn't die," Ber said, "We made it to Saint Evedis, and we *didn't die!*"

He fell into a fit of his signature maniacal laughter. He reached for Nora's hand and gave her a lopsided spin. Relieved and exhausted herself, Nora caught his contagious laughter.

"Well, congratulations. You've made it to the gilded hole of despair," Alice sneered.

"Alice..."

"Oh Viv, you're right! Our work here is done! We best be on our way, then."

"Alice, we promised safe *entry* into the city," Viviane reminded her.

"Viv, have you considered that we are also *wanted?*"

Viviane shot a discontented face. Alice relented.

"... I'll keep my word, I suppose."

Before even entering the gates the city's beauty spilled into the leading roads, streetlights, and watchtowers. The guards on patrol spurred Nora to think about her dragon. The local merchants seemed comfortable using uncommon beasts around the magical hub, sporting draft beetles, king elk, and raptor mounts. Still, Lotte stuck out.

"What do we do about Lotte?" Nora asked.

"Beasts are allowed under certain circumstances, but dragons… It might be best we leave her at the gate," Viviane said.

Hesitantly, Nora unleashed Lotte. It should not have been harder than shooing her off at any other town. But this felt more significant.

Alice laid a hand on Nora's shoulder. Her gentleness caught Nora by surprise.

"It's a hike, but we can always skip town to check in. S'not like we're locked in or anything," Nora said.

Locked in echoed in Nora's mind.

"That reminds me," Nora said, turning from Lotte. The dragon rested her head on her shoulder– clearly neither wanted to split just yet. "Do we all have papers? Non-incriminating ones?"

"Cute. You think this is our first rodeo?" Viviane said, "I should have told you earlier, but until we're past customs, call us by our 'legal' names."

Viviane showed her their papers. Watermark and all, they appeared legitimate. But the names…

"'Florence Fae'goeh,' huh? Wait a minute, Alice– *Why* is your name still Alice?!"

"What matters is I changed the last name," Alice said, "Besides, it keeps folk off-guard when I tell them some fake anecdote about how obsessed my imaginary family is about the Crown. It worked for my crew… when Viv and I accidentally gave out our actual names. *That* was our first rodeo."

"She's onto something, here. You already *look* like the Princess. Having a totally different name might actually draw more attention," Ber said.

"I hope you're right," Nora said, "Ber, you have yours?"

Ber smiled but said nothing. He did nothing to hide the panic in his eyes. "You're joking."

"I'm so sorry! It must have gotten loose when we were rushing into Mill Town!"

"Do you have any idea how important those papers were!?" Nora took a step back, swearing under her breath. She turned to Alice and Viviane, "You lot have any bright ideas? Any spares, maybe?"

"Let's see," Viviane searched through her seemingly endless bag. "Looks like I'm out of certificates but–"

Viviane stopped. Nora tried to read her face, still, but the corner of her mouth twitched, like she was fighting back a smile. "… Eh, I have an idea. But you're not going to like it."

Viviane wore *that* smile. The one, Nora learned, should make her nervous.

"I have a marriage license."

Nora dwelled on Viviane's words for a beat. Then it hit her.

"*No.*"

"Stromshire law states–"

"I *know* what the law states, Viv. That can't be our *only* way in."

Ber waved, "Heya! In case you all forgot, *I* don't know what the law states. Care to fill me in?"

Nora sighed, "If a foreigner marries a Stromshire citizen, they can be granted citizenship."

"Oh!" Then it clicked, "Ohhh."

Alice elbowed Nora's side, "C'mon, Nore-Bore–"

"Not my name."

"Be a good sport! S'not like it's real."

"Though if it were real, this would be less risky…" Viviane mused.

"Not helping. Why do *I* have to marry Ber?"

Alice and Viviane looked at her with a lesbian gaze.

"… Fine."

Begrudgingly, Nora signed the false certificate. It was a small price to pay, after all. Ber followed in signing. His wild hair drooped over his face, but Nora could tell his face was flushed, as pink ears peaked out.

"You all right?"

Ber hummed, "I, eh… I haven't had much practice with writing. And–

and do I make a new signature?"

"Good point. Let me help." Nora leaned in, assisting in tougher letters while making sure it all appeared legitimate. "You were actually doing quite well writing yesterday… Alright, it's done."

"Congratulations!" Alice cheered, "Nothing better than a honeymoon in the Gilded Hole. Should we have brought a gift?"

"For consolation on being an insufferable pain in my ass, maybe."

"One more thing, and I'm not sure how to put this…" Viviane said.

"You only say that when you're trying to be polite," Alice pointed.

"Well… Nora, you are not exactly the most affectionate person. I'm not worried about you, Ber, but Nora might need to play the part a bit more."

"As long as I'm not sucking face, I guess I can do that."

"Is sucking face totally out of the question?" Ber asked.

"Let's get going before I change my mind and divorce you."

33

Chapter 33

The party made the short hike to the Office of Customs. The office was held in a massive hall flanking the city wall. Guards stood at every hub, every exit and entrance. Immigrants to the city filled the hall to the brim– single folk, couples, and many, *many* families. Nora knew when she began her travels she was not the only one seeking asylum, but never guessed this many people shared the same need. Her eyes jumped across the room. An unaccompanied boy with scars running up his arm. An exhausted mother alongside two teenaged children. A young woman, speaking a language even Nora was unfamiliar with, tucked beneath her arms numerous embossed folders. She wondered what their stories were.

The office held a variety of beasts as well. A handful of folk came with what looked like smaller household pets, but most appeared to serve a purpose. Mounts, cargo holders, and personal messengers of all types were held close by their owners. The Guard, too, held a variety of scent 'hounds.'

Nora mourned having to leave Lotte at the gate, but she could fend for herself now, and bringing a dragon into Saint Evedis would cause more problems than it was worth.

Minutes bled into hours. The party stood in a line with no end in sight. When they thought they could see the end, they were ushered into yet another line. *Maybe Alice had a point to hate this city so much,* Nora considered.

They neared the true end of the line to multiple kiosks. In typical administrative fashion, only two were open. Slowly the line shuffled on. Alice was called first, then Viviane. Out of earshot, Nora and Ber watched as the two spoke to different clerks. They watched as Alice's clerk *laughed*.

"Guess it's going well," Ber whispered to Nora, his breath tickling her ear.

Nora and Ber were next. An unspoken agreement fell between them, as they prepared to act the part. Ber approached her– close, but not too close– and placed a gentle hand at the small of her waist. Nora expected the touch, but it still made her jump.

"It's alright. Take a breath, sweetheart," Ber said, moving a thumb in a small, side-to-side motion.

'Sweetheart.' He's really playing the part, Nora laughed to herself. Still, Nora admitted the simple, comforting gesture at her side felt nice.

Together they approached the kiosk. A stony man stood behind the desk, leering down at them. "Papers, please," The man said, monotone.

They obeyed. Nora handed in her papers and the certificate. The man frowned, his eyes furrowed.

"And where are *yours,* sir?"

"I'm stateless, sir," Ber said cooly, "I am claiming citizenship via marriage."

The man stood from his desk to get a better look at the two. He waved a fountain pen in Nora's general direction.

"Why does she look so cross? You in the doghouse?"

"Me and the Mrs. are just worn from travel, sir," Ber said, "But yes, I'm always in the doghouse. You might as well call me 'Spot!'"

At this moment, Nora wondered why she did not ditch this man at the gate.

The man barked a laugh, "Been there, kid! Go ahead into the next room. The clerk there will interview you separately."

Ber went first, exchanging a worrying glance to Nora. After a few agonizing minutes, Nora was ushered into an empty office. More waiting. Nora wondered if remaining sane was part of the test. She then realized her papers were never returned to her.

After a while, a woman came in. "Good afternoon, Mrs. Ní Dyr. My name is Ms. Kadlec and I will be reviewing your case and asking a few questions."

"Yes, madam."

If not prepared for anything else, Nora was ready for this. Alone with her thoughts for a long, long time, she imagined every possible inquiry the clerks could have.

"What is your purpose for coming to Saint Evedis?"

"I am here to claim sanctuary."

"And for what purpose do you claim sanctuary?"

"I am magic folk under threat of persecution."

"And is there a reason you never applied to the Guard?"

Nora blinked. "They never came to my town to recruit, madam."

The clerk's pen scritched at her notepad. Nora could hear more laughter coming from Ber and his clerk. *At least his interview is going well. Lucky bastard.*

"We reviewed you and your husband's certificate. I am happy to say we can affirm the validity and affirm Mr.Blødek's citizenship," The clerk said, deadpan, "Will you taking the last name? I can make that change for you."

"*No.*"

Nora did not care if that would harm her case. She would rather die than give Ber the satisfaction, or Saints forbid Alice.

The clerk continued, "For documentation purposes, I will need to note your aura type."

Nora instinctually retracted. "Why?" She asked, before she could stop herself.

"This is standard procedure. We put every city immigrant's aura on file in case of criminal activity."

"*Just* the immigrants?"

The clerk said nothing.

Now was not the time to fight. Nora hesitated a moment more. At least in this moment, the clerk was patient. Her hand was outstretched, waiting. Only one way forward, Nora forced her wrist into the clerk's hand. For a moment the clerk glanced at the marks along her hands and wrists, but said nothing. She began to do her work, infiltrating her power into Nora's body.

Breathe in, out.

Nora put her focus into breathing, ensuring she did not overreact and turn the office pitch black.

"… Just smoke?" The clerk said, "They ran you out of town for *this?*"

"… Ms. Kadlek," Nora said carefully, "How do you know of my exile?"

"Mrs. Ní Dyr, Saint Evedis serves as a central hub for many things, including information. We collect information on all magic Stromshire citizens."

"… I understand."

"Fortunately for you, Crown Law does not lie in my hands. The City demands magic folk like a body demands blood. Despite your records and… quality of blood, the Law still protects you," The clerk continued, "But I will usher this warning to you: Should you cause *any* trouble during your residence, another exile for you would be your best case scenario."

The clerk stamped Nora's papers with a loud *thud.* "May the Saint Evedis watch over you. Enjoy your stay."

Left with an ominous message, Nora was unsure whether the clerk's remark was a blessing or a threat, she finally left the Office of Customs and into the City.

34

Chapter 34

Nora was the last of her party to make it out. As Nora passed through the gates into the city, above her stood great buildings and towers with garnet roofs.

As impressive as it was, Nora could not see much of the city from where she ended up after admission. Aged brick and stone of less charm lined the dusty streets. The flock of surrounding people impaired her vision. The sun was already beginning to set, making her wonder just how much time she spent rotting in Customs.

Ber spotted her from within the crowd and went to retrieve her.

"Hey, check who they let in!" Ber chuckled, "Told ya it'd be alright!"

"Hardly. I think I was threatened...?"

"That's classic 'Nora Luck' for you. What matters is you got in," Ber winked, "Right, *sweetheart?*"

Nora's nerves were trod on enough that day. She punched his stomach– not hard in her eyes, just enough for the man to double over.

Ber groaned, "Too far?"

"Too far."

Parting through the bustle, Alice came in with Viviane in tow. "About time you got through! Thought *I'd* have the most trouble."

"Never mind her, she's hungry and had her toys taken away," Viviane said.

Alice grimaced, brandishing an especially fine dagger. "Not all of 'em!"

"How were you hiding that…? Nevermind that, put that away!" Viviane sighed, "… It seems we all need a moment to rest and refuel. We will need to leave the slums if we want to find something edible."

It was difficult for Nora and Ber not to crane their necks at the city. Bold, flawless architecture surrounded them. The designs were so intricate and alien (even to Nora), they wondered just how old this strip was. Something Nora did not anticipate was the sheer number of bridges everywhere in the city. They stretched not just over the winding canals, but from tower to tower, street to street, overlapping each other in layers.

"Tourists…" Alice muttered to Viviane.

The group stopped by an outdoor café for a light dinner. They were still not in a great part of town, but this little corner shop was an exception. Alice explained that the nobles of the city often go out of their way to dine in what they call the "rustic parts" of Saint Evedis.

Though they all changed into more professional clothing for their entry into the city, they still appeared out of place. Lavishly dressed women greeted and ushered them to a table.

"Well, I hope you lot are enjoying the Evedis experience so far, because it only gets shittier from here," Alice warned.

"I think it's nice!" Ber said.

"While we're all in one place, we should start a plan of action for jobs and housing and what not. To be honest, my money will spread thin here pretty soon."

"Then why are we eating here, of all places?" Viviane asked.

"Listen, I gotta treat myself sometimes. You can't deny we've had a rough few weeks, especially me!"

Viviane, with a mouthful of sandwich she snagged from a cart, nodded in admittance.

"Hold on, why can't we head to the palace now?" Ber asked.

"If it were that easy… That palace is on high guard, practically air tight. Even if you wanted to fly over, there's strict protocol to shoot any violator down. That's why we need a solid game plan for this."

"Alright," Nora said, "What do we suggest we do?"

"Viv and I should be expecting the *Fang* to send over my savings. With my funds we can keep a shitty tenement for *maybe* a few weeks. But we need to start thinking about how to rake in some cash."

"You're acting as if you won't be stealing left and right while we're here," Ber winked.

"It pains me to agree with Viv on this, but given my… track record here, I need to keep a low profile."

Their waitress stepped outside to check on their table.

"More tea, madam?"

"Oh, yes please!" Alice said.

"This might be odd to say, but have we met before? You seem terribly familiar."

Alice tilted her head slightly, "Hmm. I'm sorry, but I can't say that we have."

"You sure…? My apologies for prying. Your food should be out soon!" The waitress excused herself to head back inside.

"… Case in point."

"I think I saw a sign for an open tenement down the street. It's not the best place in town, but it will have to do for now," Viviane said.

One hefty check later, they left for the tenement complex. To their relief, booking a week in the dingy complex was quick– In a place like this, it seemed the landlord did not care much about background checks.

Nora could not bring herself to unpack just yet. Her plan was to shamelessly drape herself over the dusty chaise lounge until morning. She figured, however, she could treat herself to a long, hot shower after today's endeavor. Ber already beat her to it. He was clad in only a towel when they crossed paths in the hall, heading towards the bathroom.

"… You had a long day, why don't you take the first shower?"

"Pretty sure we all had a long day. You sure?"

Ber nodded.

"… Thank you, Ber."

They swapped places. Nora winded down as she soothed her muscles in the surprisingly hot water. Cleansing her hair in the cheap products supplied, she swore she plucked out leaves and twigs from a different biome.

Nora thought back to her and Ber's quick exchange. *This must be his way of apologizing,* she thought, smiling to herself.

Later, she met Viviane and Alice on the 'porch.' The only tenements available were basement level, so their view was limited to roofs and occasional passerby above them.

"Heads up, between Ber and I there might not be a lot of hot water," She warned.

"I wouldn't worry too much, dear. Even in the outer ring, the City's got more power than they know what to do with," Viviane assured.

"That's nice... I think." Nora leaned on the wall beside them. "You got any pointers for where I should try for work tomorrow?"

"The day market might be a good idea. Maybe a general store or a restaurant might need some help."

Nora nodded, "It's funny. I've spent years dreaming of this day, getting into Saint Evedis. Now that I'm here, the relief hasn't really washed over me yet."

"Give it time. A lot has changed in your life in a short time. Staying in one place for a little while will do you some good."

"It'll do us all some good," Alice commented.

"We touched on this earlier, but do we have a plan for how we're getting to the Queen?" Nora asked.

Alice and Viviane looked at each other, "We're working on it," Alice said, "First thing we should take care of is submitting a formal request. Worst case scenario, we can fall back on bureaucratic bullshit.

It was not the answer she had hoped for, but they had done more than enough for her. She smiled, "We'll think of something. I'm turning in early, so if I don't hear ya come in, have a good night."

Alice and Viviane bid her goodnight. They stuck around outside for a little longer.

"... You *do* know this plan is flawed, right?" Viviane asked.

"I know. I'm still thinking on how to get them in."

"You think you're going to tell them? The 'easy' way?"

Alice shook her head, "If they wanted to turn me in they would've done it by now."

"I know they would not do that. I'm saying the *other* way."

"I'm hoping I won't have to."

35

Chapter 35

Submitting a formal request fared easy for the party. However it did not come without frustration.

"Four months!?"

The clerk behind the desk nodded, "Unfortunately seeing the Queen is quite the lofty request. Typically this kind of audience can be pushed back up to a year."

"We *really* don't have that kind of time," Ber reminded anyone who would listen.

"I understand whatever it is troubling you is urgent. Could I maybe pencil you in with a local representative? It looks like that turnaround is only about two months–"

That was Alice's cue to lift herself off the wall she had been leaning into and listening.

"All right, that's enough. Shall we?"

Alice gestured for the door. Crestfallen, the group followed.

The party conspired over breakfast. Their next steps remained hazy, nevertheless they brainstormed every and any idea. There was something about the pause in Alice's speech that puzzled Nora. She could not put a finger on it, so she pinned it to nerves.

Sneaking in was impossible. Bursting through was out of the question. And apparently, The Queen did not receive any letters directly, for security purposes.

"... I got it," Alice said, "Two birds, one stone– why don't we search for jobs that have clearance to service the palace?"

"That's actually not a bad idea. I could strum up a list of old vendors and see if any of them are hiring!" Viviane said.

"What does that have to do with birds and– it's another weird saying, isn't it?" Ber asked.

"Yes, you're catching on!" Nora could not help but laugh.

Viviane did just that, bouncing off Alice to jot her memory of anything from bakers to farriers that served the Crown. Nora took the list to make a copy of her own, and another for Ber. They finished their meal, and Viviane directed Nora and Ber where to go.

"If you get lost, remember Saint Evedis is just one big circle."

"One big, stupid circle," Alice echoed.

The party split once again. Nora and Ber strode together through the wide streets, and in and out of marketplaces. Boisterous merchants called from their stores, city folk discussed new products and the latest gossip.

The two picked up bits and pieces as they passed.

"You stocked up for the next week?"

"Think so. I can never really tell the year's turn up."

"Well, ya better set up at the courtyard soon, it'll be getting packed."

Once they got a lay of the strip, the two agreed to separate to cover more ground. They exhausted their list much quicker than they had anticipated, so they resorted to just landing a job for now. They visited every store in the strip, only to be turned down at each one. Deciding to call it quits for the day, Nora returned to the market's center to find Ber.

"Any luck?"

"Nah, but I might ask the factories nearby tomorrow. I heard they're looking for aura wielders. Want to come with?"

"I don't think I can. Mine's not the most desirable. I'd rather not cause a scene while I'm here." Nora said, "Besides, it's not like mine can be used for any jobs."

Ber nodded solemnly, "Hang in there Nor, You'll find something!"

Nora appreciated his enthusiasm. However, nothing could qualify her for any skilled jobs in Saint Evedis. Farm hand jobs were not exactly plentiful in the city. To Saint Evedis, she was an unskilled, untrusted newcomer to the city, without a useful aura to claim.

The two watched as banners were draped across overpasses and lights. Just down the street, not a single corner was left bare. Ber and Nora decided to follow the waves of excited crowds to investigate.

Even from blocks away they could hear the announcer and low roars from the stadium. As they got closer, the announcer became clear.

"I welcome you all to the tryouts for Slatir Det Ostrucin! It brings me great pleasure to host this ancient game once more. As in year's past, the rewards remain the same. Winners of each game will receive a cash prize. This prize will only increase as the games progress. The Champion gains an audience with Her Majesty herself, our gracious Queen Maeve, as well as a luxurious dwelling within the Inner Wall!"

Nora and Ber shared a glance.

The arena was made from a vast, repurposed area of a park. Despite its temporary construction, it was made from flawless stone, banners and flags of every color hung from the posts and rafters. Surrounding the stadium stood gorgeous statues of warriors and beasts.

Ber marveled at the arena. On one side was an ice witch, an old woman with no particular flashiness but had incredible skill and power. On the opposite side was a boy of earth and stone, clad in shining armor. Aided by his comparative youth and speed, he sped around the arena with light, rapid attacks while the woman took precise aim with large chunks of ice.

Ber called Nora over, "Wow! Nor, look!"

Together they watched the match from start to finish. The witch won by a landslide. She sent a straight shot to the boy's chest, his body tumbling hard onto the ground, but had time to soften the blow.

"Amazing..!" Ber turned to her, "Do ya think that maybe-"

"Before you finish that thought, absolutely not," Nora retorted.

"Hm. Agree to disagree."

"Please don't be Alice. There's a better, less deadly way to make money."

"But, meeting the Queen…"

"Ber…"

Nora thought he made a valid point. Ber was talented, but surely not talented enough to take a city full of prime magicians.

"Fine, I'll *consider* it until the end of the tournament."

"This isn't a negotiation!"

The announcer came onto the scene once more.

"That about wraps up our today's tryouts! I'm giving a last call for anyone who would like to try their luck with our competitor here!"

"Now's my chance!" Ber leapt over the gate, not realizing the gates were open.

The announcer braced Ber's arm in a firm handshake. He was a thin man with finely coiffed hair, and the most stunning mustache Ber had ever seen.

"Congrats kid for your courage! That could not be me, this woman terrifies me," The man smiled with rosy cheeks, mustache curving with it. He backed out of the ring and commenced the fight. "Good luck!"

Ber realized something in this moment. Ber had no desire to fight an elderly woman (unless it was Nora's old caretaker). He was not given much time to think, as the woman sent a spear of ice straight towards his head.

He caught the spear and tossed it aside, but not without his maniacal scream, as the woman pursued him.

"You filthy rat! This was my win!"

Nora was at a loss for words, as she watched this man run for his life around the ring.

"I really don't want to hurt you, lady!"

"Then sit still so I can hurt you!"

"I don't want that, either!"

Ber kept dissipating her attacks. When it appeared the two ice magicians were at a stalemate, Ber failed successfully. He broke apart a fractal, a chunk redirected straight to the woman's forehead. It was enough force to knock her out. Ber rushed over to break her fall.

Onlookers cheered and hollered at Ber. The announcer approached him once more.

"That was… unprecedented, but it made me laugh! Don't worry about your contestant, here. Her and her sister compete every year. I can't wait to see how you fare in the next round!" The man caught movement in the smal crowd. "Wait, what's this?!"

Through all the excitement, a woman was glaring at Ber as she approached the edge of the ring. She appeared to be a carbon copy of the woman Ber just beat. She locked eyes with Ber. He could hardly hear her shout towards him, but her lips read an unmistakable message: "You're next."

36

Chapter 36

Over dinner, Nora addressed Ber.

"You want to explain what just went down this afternoon?"

"Thanks for reminding me, Nor! We went down to that tournament arena and I entered, so hopefully we can make bank!"

Viviane's fork dropped.

"Oh, sweet!" Alice praised

"Oh, sweet Saints…" Viviane muttered.

"I was actually thinkin' of going in myself, if it wasn't for the whole 'missing nobility' garbage. But hey, it's just what we need! I can teach you a few things to prepare for and—" Alice said before Viviane interjected.

"Alice, do you not remember what the tournament is like? This is *bad.*"

"What, is it hard?" Ber asked.

Viviane tried to be gentle, "Well, people don't die, but they can get seriously injured."

"How about the guy that exploded?" Alice asked.

Ber's stomach sank.

"Then there was the Buttercup Incident…"

Viviane stopped Alice, "They should've known better than to eat their way out of a cage of plants. Ber, is this really something you want to do?"

Ber shrugged, "I mean, it's worth a shot! I was a soldier, after all."

Viviane mulled his words over.

"Well, at the very least, we have some chance to get money and see the Queen."

"As the master of this house, I decree we support our brave boy for this chance. Viv, would you be open to helping Ber with his injuries?" Alice asked.

"I suppose as open as his wounds will be." Viviane responded.

"Wait—"

"Nora, could you help me train him? He's goin' to be against multiple people at once, after all," Alice asked.

"Now hold on, what happened to getting a job? Just in case this doesn't work out, we need money."

Alice hummed, "Then help me while you're jobless!"

Alice and Viviane took the liberty of explaining the rules of Slatir Det Ostrucin, or lack thereof. Ber stumbled into the beginning rounds of the tournament, where anyone is free to compete. The tournament tents take place across the City simultaneously. As the tents lessen around the city, so do the number of contestants in the ring. Occasionally a rule is added, or subtracted at random, to 'keep things interesting.'

Ber's head spun as he tried to retain this information. Nora positioned a hand on his shoulder, gentler than normal.

"There's no shame if you want to pull out of this early. We can find another way."

Alice remained silent.

"Let's see how far we can take this, Nor. You know me, I'm sturdier than I look!" Ber said, "Besides, it wouldn't hurt to rake in some good money. If it starts looking like I might explode, I'll forfeit."

-

The following morning, Nora and Ber made their way to the bare patch behind the tenement to train. Alice spared no time for Ber to prepare himself. In mid-stretch, Alice lunged at him with full force.

Nora watched them as they began to spar. She could not deny it was good entertainment.

Nora noticed how different Alice and Ber moved, despite their similar powers. Alice performed quick, light attacks while Ber protected himself and made slow, precise blows. She was impressed, wondering how long they would keep up this pace.

The following days ran into each other, as Nora alternated between her job hunt and training Ber when Alice got tired. Viviane found positions at a local bakery the two could apply for. It was not a job affiliated with the Palace, but it would make do.

"Wait," Nora had asked, "Shouldn't you be keeping a low profile, too?"

"I'm not sure if you noticed, but the wanted posters have kind of forgotten about me," Viviane chuckled, "No one would expect the Princess' accomplice to be back in the City. Call me Florence, and it should be fine."

Nora reflected on it all. She started her first day at the bakery alongside Viviane. Despite knowing little on baking, it seemed like a good fit for now. Kneading through swaths of dough proved to be almost relaxing to Nora, though it did leave her with sore arms. The first week in the city was not even over yet, yet everything moved so fast

Nora was pulled out of her thoughts with a sudden blast of sleet. Blades of ice stuck into the tenement wall behind Ber.

"What the hell, Alice? That could've *killed* me!"

"Well it didn't, so quit complaining!" Alice chided as she prepared another attack with her arms coated in water.

With a yelp, the fight ended. Ber washed up close to Nora and Viviane in a pool of muddy water. Alice swept her hair back.

"That was fun!" Alice strode up to Ber and pinched his nose. "S'not a total failure, Ber. This serves as a great example of what *not* to do."

$$37$$

Chapter 37

Ber's first tournament came. Hours before the event's initiation, Nora walked with Ber to the arena, both unsure what to expect. Ber was given loose instruction where to find his designated arena. Just like before, they followed the trails of banners and flyers that lined the streets.

Their path led across the park where the first tournament took place. What struck Nora and Ber was that the entire arena left without a trace. Even the arena's wide patch of dirt was refurbished with lush, green grass, as if nothing ever happened.

"That's so strange," Nora said, "why would they move an entire arena? This was at the center of the district..."

"They probably like to move it all over the district so everyone can see it. That or they are doing so in a way of flaunting," Ber answered.

"I'm going to bet on the latter."

After a few dozen more blocks they arrived at the tournament. This one, however, was held in a vast courtyard. Unlike the first arena, this one sat upon a mosaic of flawless, coloured bricks.

Across the courtyard stood large, flamboyant tents where most staff appeared to be checking in. Looking around, the two felt more out of place than ever before within the walls of the city. Men and women alike were dressed to the nines, sporting colorful attire. Their plumed hats reminded Nora of Arvo's aviary.

Ber scratched the back of his neck, "Viv and Alice are running late… It's making me a bit nervous."

Nora felt the same, but she did not want to tell him that.

"I'm sure they'll show soon," She assured.

Before they entered the tent, a man in a perfectly tailored suit ran up to them. They identified the man as the same announcer from the last tournament, judging by his unmistakable mustache.

"You there!" The man called out.

He began to run over to them. His fine shoes clacked louder as he approached. The distance between them and the relative silence of the courtyard made for a much more awkward moment in waiting for the man.

"… We can meet you over there, if you'd like," Ber said.

"No… my good sir… I insist!" The man panted.

By the time he reached Nora and Ber, he was out of breath. Nora offered him a hand, but the man recomposed himself and bowed.

"Honored competitor, and guest," He began, "Welcome, to Slatir Det Ostrucin. I am your esteemed host, Sir Huan Jun. Please, allow me to take your equipment for you!"

"Thank you, sir. What does Slatir Det Ostrucin even mean, if I may ask?" Nora asked.

"It's ancient speech for the Trials of the Sacred Saints. These trials have been passed down for generations, but it is only here in Saint Evedis that you can witness such an extravagant show!" Huan Jun said, "Now before we get in that tent, are you folk outsiders? You two seem *super* fresh."

"Is it that obvious?" Nora asked.

"I knew it! I just got a sense for people. Now don't you worry, most everybody here isn't city-born. I only ask because everyone *loves* an underdog story."

"I appreciate the gesture, but I'll let my skill do the talking," Ber said.

"That!" Huan Jun pointed, "*That* is the moxie I'm looking for. Tell me, what are your names?"

"I'm Ber, and this is Nora." Ber said.

To this, Huan Jun grinned. "Nora, Ber, allow me the honor to show you the competitor's tent."

The tent seemed much larger and classier than its outer appearance. The interior was paved with glossy tile, and furnished with sofas, tables, chairs, and counters with an array of refreshments. Scattered across the room stood groups of people, competitors and their supporters alike.

To this the two were delighted. Ber and Nora restrained themselves from digging into the food to listen to Huan Jun.

"Here you will prepare for the fight. After I show you around please take part in anything you desire," He said.

He led them to the first subsection of the tent. Many of the people they passed greeted them in jovial tones. Only a few exchanged dirty looks. Ber considered himself lucky, for he had not seen the nasty old lady from the first tournament yet.

Huan Jun uncovered the intersection in the tent. Inside were metal tables and carts full of medical supplies. Some nurses stood by, preparing for the game's aftermath. The sight made Nora cringe.

"When you need some patching up after the game, we selected the most qualified personnel in the region to help," Huan Jun said.

"That's relieving… Don't you mean *if* I need patching up?" Ber asked. Huan Jun let out a hearty laugh, patting his back.

"You're one funny lad, Mister Ber! Everyone gets at least a flesh wound or two! Don't worry yourself none, folks find scars sexy!"

Next on his tour was an even bigger room than the first. Though it was dim, luxurious décor bordered every edge. The center was left bare, with tilework of the nation's emblem.

"If you so choose, you may come here for the after party of each game. Here you may mingle with whomever you please, for all folk are allowed here."

They moved to the final room, a cluttered space lined with mahogany stalls and filled with leather and plate mail. The workers here seemed much more occupied, rushing about with arms full of material.

"Since you're here early, why don't you check out the changing room and get fitted into some armor? We don't want you getting impaled on the first day," Huan Juan asked.

"Sure thing!" Ber said, striding forward into the room. He paused for a brief moment and turned, revealing pinkish ears and cheeks, "This is where I leave ya, Nor..."

It was not exactly a mystery with Ber, but Nora understood he was growing anxious. Having to be measured for armor she imagined did not help either.

She patted Ber on the shoulder and said, "Make sure the tailor makes something real flashy, alright?"

To this Ber smiled and nodded.

—

The tournament was well over an hour away, and most of the arena was already filled with spectators. Snacking on the roasted leg of an animal Nora did not know the origins of, she kept an eye out for Alice and Viviane. Eventually they turned up, both dressed in higher fashion for the event but somehow worn ragged. Alice appeared to have specks of blood scattered across her sundress.

"Saints, what happened?" Nora asked.

"What matters is that I won." Alice brushed off the question, "Listen love, we're really sorry for being late. I promise I didn't start the problem, not this time."

"How is Ber?" Viviane asked.

"I think he's getting a bit nervous. I just hope it doesn't get to his head..."

Horns and roars from around the stadium drowned out Nora's voice. From above the sky grew littered with bright, colorful comets of lights and an unnecessary amount of golden glitter. The glitter danced in a single spotlight at the center of the arena. From under that spotlight Huan Jun emerged from the very earth. He was dressed in a suit even more flamboyant than the last. He stayed in the air under some floating stones for only a moment before landing with grace, placing the stones back perfectly. He removed the hat obscuring his face and inhaled.

"Good evening, Saint Evedis!" Huan Jun shouted.

The audience cheered in unison. In solidarity some magicians in the audience shot small bursts of magic into the air.

"Once again, I am your esteemed host, Sir Huan Jun. I know we kept you waiting, so why don't we dive right into our second tournament?"

The crowd responded in more cheers.

"But, I have an announcement! As always, we invite a handful of newcomers into the first games to shake things up. Please allow me to introduce these lovely folk onto the floor," He cleared his throat, "Give it up for our well-renowned, well-seasoned ice witch, Miss Gerda Jannes!"

A black iron-cast gate rose, and from the chamber approached the old woman from the end of the last tournament. Shoulders rolled back, she strode across the arena with a trail of swirling, flawless ice. Her expression remained stoic as she walked to the center and bowed.

"*Another* ice witch? I don't blame Ber for being scared of her, that woman gives me the chills," Nora said.

"Is it because she's an ice witch?" Alice asked, "Ah? Get it?"

Both Viviane and Nora were unamused.

"Next, please welcome our iron-fisted fighter, Solon of Bren!" Huan Jun announced.

A large, bearded man appeared. Clad in only pants and body paint, he vogued his way to the center. With a raised fist, a thick sheet of metal wrapped up his arm, forming a spiked gauntlet.

"Now, give it up for this pharmacist of harm, the lovely Eskarne Thames!" Huan Jun said.

A thin, bronze skinned woman paced over. Her piercing gaze gave a hint of intrigue and mystery. From beneath her sleeves sprouted dense, intertwined vines. She bowed with an open palm towards the sky. The vines swirled far above her and branched into a fibrous, web-like design.

Nora leaned over to Alice and Viviane, "Exactly how many contestants are in the first round?"

"Oh, there's only one round. This is the second game, so there are nine fighters total," Alice explained.

Nora felt her heart pound in her throat. "Did either of you happen to tell Ber just how many people he's up against?"

"I may have forgotten the specifics," Alice gave a nervous chuckle. Nora rested her head in her hands cursing the situation under her breath. "Listen, the first two games are child's play. He'll be *fine!*" Alice insisted.

The fighters following to center stage were another two herbal witches from the night market, a water witch from Viviane and Nora's work, an earthen man from the city's outskirts, and a mage's apprentice sporting fire.

"Our final opponent," Huan Jun spoke, "is a brave soul that joined us during our last game. He's a hurricane of a man, and it takes more than a torrential downpour to bring him down. Saint Evedis, please welcome our new competitor, Ber Blødeks!"

Alice, Viviane, and Nora sat at the edge of their seats. The three had no way of telling how well Ber would perform, let alone if he would return in one piece. Nora balled her fists on her lap.

From the chamber, Ber strode to join the rest of the competitors. He was dressed in a flowing, crimson cloak that obscured his face. Beneath the cloak he was covered in fine leather armor. The segments on his shoulders and forearms were constructed into upward facing points. Though expertly crafted, the armor seemed to care more for aesthetics than functionality.

With a swift motion, Ber flung the hood off his painted face, puffed out his chest, and raised his arms. He created a cyclone of clouds around his body. Once dispersed, trails of small clouds shot in every direction.

Ber shot a wide grin and inhaled.

"SAINT EVEDIS, LET'S MAKE SOME NOISE!"

To this the entire audience hooted and howled. Alice, Viviane, and Nora stood and cheered, relieved for Ber's courage. Most of his fellow competitors watched in awe and applauded his performance, while a few sneered, especially Gerda.

"Yeah, that's my boy!" Alice screamed, "Show 'em up, Ber!"

Huan Jun stepped in once again. His full, youthful cheeks grew even rosier with Ber's performance.

"I think on that note, we should get started!"

The competitors set themselves in a circle, to which Ber lagged behind on forming. Their weapons of choice lay in front of each of them. For a long moment, all was still in the arena.

Ber's eyes wandered to the spectators, straining his eyes to find his friends. He shifted to his fellow competitors. Gerda in particular set her continuous death glare on him. Ber felt his pulse rise.

If his life truly depended on it, Ber could let loose. Folk here have seen traditional magic, sure, but he could really give a show by going berserk. He prayed it would not have to come to that, for the other competitor's sakes.

Huan Jun raised a slender arm to the sky. With a graceful, rehearsed motion, he spoke, "And… BEGIN!" With that, he disappeared underground before the chaos ensued.

Ber grabbed his axe and took a pace forward before freezing. The burlier folk joined at the center to clash while those who were lighter evaded and chased each other on the sidelines.

He did not know where he stood. Though he did not want to admit it, he was unsure if he was strong enough to face the group at the center head on. At the same time, he did not want take the chance of running into Gerda on the sidelines.

Before he could make a decision, Ber was disjointed from the ground by mangled, writhing vines.

Once he stumbled to his feet, he spun and dodged his way around the fighters. He watched as one of the herbal witches soared over him, landing hard near the edge of the ring. Medics from the tent were already congregating to the witch.

He made his way to another fighter who lay limp. From afar he heard crowd chanting, followed by Huan Jun's voice, "Lance, unable to rise in the time allotted, is out!"

"Lance, are you alright?" Ber asked crouching beside him. Lance gave a pained attempt of a nod. His eyes shifted away from Ber's.

"W-watch—" Lance said.

Ber's ears pricked from a grunt coming from behind him. He took a clumsy roll just before Eskarne could land a blow on him with her vines.

One of the nurses called out to him.

"Kid, get your head in the game before you lose it!"

He took their advice to heart. He was terrified, but he lacked options. He raised his axe above his head and screamed at Eskarne.

Her stern eyes widened and she stumbled back. She rose what was left of her vines in defense as Ber ran to take some swings of his axe. She landed some slashes to his body to slow him down, but he pushed forward. He took a swing, creating a burst of wind to blow her far off.

As she went flying, Ber's stomach sunk.

"I'm really sorry!" He called out.

Eskarne landed just barely on all fours. Before she could recover, the fire mage burned what was left of her vines and kicked her back down. She too was out.

Ber kept himself light on his feet. He noticed that there were three other competitors left. Though the arena thinned out, he knew better than to grow brash.

The dust cleared by a significant degree. Ber examined that the ring lay ruined in foliage, scrap metal, scorched patches, and large branches of ice. The fire mage, the metal worker, and the ice witch were all who were left.

Gerda threw off the metal worker when she made eye contact with Ber. Her cold glare made it seem like she was staring through him, like he was an inconvenience to destroy. Distanced a just few paces away, she made her way to him.

The fire mage interfered, landing wild swings at her. She fell back for a moment, and then returned in full force. She crouched before he could take another swing and began to pin his feet in ice. The boy's eyes widened, and he grew fiercer with his attacks. She dodged the attacks and within seconds pinned the boy. In the process some of the ice grew through the flesh in his limbs. The boy howled in agony. Ber was certain that it was not an accident.

For her final blow on the mage, she spun aura above her and hurled a small-scale glacier at him. The block of ice shattered his bounds, but knocked him out in the process.

Ber screamed, pushing gusts towards Gerda. She persisted, shooting spears of ice at him. She landed the spears with devastating accuracy. Ber fell back, and the spears tethered him to the earth in an icy cocoon.

His body lay trapped under a dense block with his hands bound tight to either side of him. There was some room by his legs, but otherwise he was sealed tight. His head, however, remained free, but he could not help but think there was a reason for this.

Ber, however, believed he was far from finished. Combined with his aura, he struggled to kick his way out of the solid chamber of ice. He was able to shave off a few thin sheets at a time, but much to no avail.

"I warned you, boy," Gerda said as she approached, "You had your chance to leave. But now, I will make an example of you."

She formed a dagger in her hand and drug it along his cheek, letting blood instantly. He screamed from the top of his lungs and squirmed to prevent Gerda from carving him anymore.

"Not the face, you bitch!"

Nora could not watch any further. She stood to take action but Alice and Viviane held her down. The last thing they needed was Nora's beast emerging, so they tried to calm her down.

During his pathetic attempt to escape, light from the sun blinded him from passing over a mass he did not notice before. Above him stood a rock formation made by another contestant.

Ber's eyes shifted to the mass above her. The formation began to buckle and give way. The debris from the cliff gave way to larger rocks. Ber took a deep breath. He was not going to die at the hands of an old lady and a pile of rocks. He belted out a scream and kicked as hard as he could.

A thunderous *boom* rolled over the arena. Gerda went flying, but to Ber's surprise so did the rock to the opposite side of the ring.

"Incredible, Blodeks wins by landslide!"

Ber was met with a roaring applause from the audience. Unsure what to do, he took a bow. The crowd's response nearly ruptured his eardrums.

Like the match, the aftermath was a whirlwind for Ber. He was ushered back into the tent to assess his injuries. Ber was so exhausted he could not put up any fight for them to look him over. Fortunately his wounds appeared all superficial. The one thing he fought the crew on was keeping the armor. Begrudgingly they obliged, returning the pieces after a quick cleaning.

Nora, Alice, and Viviane came to his side the moment he exited the tent.

"You did *amazing*, Ber! Where did you learn to fight like that?" Viviane asked.

Looked away to Nora, giving her a knowing glance, "I've been around!"

"Think you can keep this up for another four weeks?" Alice asked.

"… Four weeks?"

"Sure! I think you could pull it off. Not to mention too, you have solid support," Alice leaned back to peek past Ber's shoulder, "Nora, are you going to add to the pep talk or are you gonna keep ogling our champion?"

Nora knew better than to take the bait. Still, she could feel her cheeks redden. She admitted to herself the getup complimented Ber's form well, but she was more involved in the material itself.

"This is really impressive craftsmanship. It's a shame the leather's on the thin side. But, I could patch it if you plan to keep going."

"That's great! Because I don't think I'll get another set," Ber chuckled, "But I do get this!"

Ber brandished a little, embossed envelope. Alice took it to find its contents– a generous wad of cash.

Alice whistled low, "Great job, Ber! My little cash cow!"

"Maybe this plan could work," Nora said, "But Ber, are you *sure* you are comfortable with this? We can always find another way." *I don't want to see you hurt,* she wanted to say, but she held her tongue.

"Are you kidding? That was the most fun I've had in ages! Plus I get to blow off a lil' steam."

Ber did a double take at Nora. To Nora, she had done nothing to change her expression. Stony, as always. But still, she wondered if he had seen something.

Shaking Nora out of her own thoughts, Viviane clapped her hands together.

"I'm sure our champion is ready for a break! Why don't we find a nice place to celebrate?"

The party let Ber pick the spot. The man had expensive taste, as they all felt wildly underdressed upon making it to a little bistro in the inner ring.

"Ber, you know I love ya. But why here?" Alice asked.

"I saw an advertisement for the drinks– They do fancy sculptures in each glass! And I'm nothing if not a sucker for a good drink and craftsmanship in ice magic."

"I stand corrected, I want to see this!"

The two rushed in.

"I fear this is going to give them bad ideas later..." Viviane said to Nora.

Nora shrugged, "We'll add it to the list, I suppose."

They sat at the corner of the bar. A man greeted Ber's party from behind the bar. He looked sharp in every way, from his dress, eyes, and perfect-cut jawline.

"Good evening, sir! For drinks, what do ya recommend?" Ber asked.

"Our establishment works a little different here, kind sir," the man answered. Alice's eyes rolled, *oh boy here we go.* "You see, I am specially selected to 'read' every patron and craft an experience perfectly suited for the individual. Who would like to go first?"

Ber volunteered himself, inching closer to see the man's magic at work. His face dropped comically, in disbelief as the man revealed a katana. The bartender went to work, shaving an obelisk of ice into fractals. His final result was what appeared to be an uncut gem, jutting from the earth in little spikes. He placed the sculpture in the glass, spinning the glass for dramatic effect. Nora wondered if she was ever getting dinner at this rate.

The bartender crafted a peculiar cocktail for Ber, a silvery liquor among muddled wolf apples and a suspended, glittery substance. Of course. The man flourished the concoction over the Ber's end of the bar and got to work on the others. Ber took a sip, and his eyes widened.

"Nor, you have to try this!"

She obliged and took a sip. It was *heavy* on the fruity notes. Definitely crafted for Ber. Soon after the others were prepared– a honeyed mix for

Viviane, a blood-red mystery for Alice, and a molten bronze drink for Nora. Reluctantly, she took a sip. Second to a Saint Evedis coffee, it was the best thing she had ever drunk. Looking at Alice and Viviane, it seems they had a similar experience.

"Please, excuse me as I take a brief leave. Please take a moment to look through our dinner menu," The man said.

To their relief, ordering food proved much less of a fanfare event. The party chatted amongst themselves over dinner as the world outside dimmed, and lamplighters made their rounds to light the streets. Other patrons trickled out as they too winded down for the evening.

Alice leaned back at the high top stool and stretched, "Well, I'm turning in for the evening. Are we ready to go?"

"Nor and I will be right behind ya," Ber said.

"You know the way back, yes?"

"I got Nora, so I'll be fine!"

Viviane and Alice gathered their things and headed home, leaving Nora and Ber alone.

"Everything alright?" Nora asked after their leave.

"Wha– Oh, yeah! It's just… I wanted to check in on ya."

"'Check in?' How do you mean?"

Ber took a swig of his second drink, "… I know you're concerned about this whole tournament thing. I wanted to let you know I don't plan to do anything rash for the sake of this game. If it gets too much, I'll pull out."

"That's big of you, coming from the man who throws his axe before thinking," Nora quipped, "But… Do you promise?"

"You have my word."

"Thank you, Ber. I didn't want you thinking you had to do this or anything."

"And you're alright with training me for the time being? I know Alice kind of threw it on you."

"I don't mind, really."

Nora took a drink. What she said was true, but he did not need to know how much she enjoyed sparring. Unintentionally, Ber took a drink from his glass at the same time.

"I don't think I ever tried your drink. Could I give it a try?"

"Be my guest."

Ber took a sip, "Huh, tastes like Nora."

Nora chuckled, "Odd words from an odd man. How do you know what I taste like?"

"I don't," Ber smirked, "'Guess I could find out."

Nora choked on her drink. She pushed herself off from her stool and head for the door.

"… Alright. Bye."

"Nor, wait–" He stood too quickly, tripping on the leg of his chair, "I was just kidding! Don't leave, I don't know where our house is!"

38

Chapter 38

The group fell into routine. Ber trained for the weekly tournament through-out the week. Alice made regiments for him, occasionally recruiting Nora for extra help when she was off the clock at the bakery. This left Viviane with patching up Ber after matches.

Alice, having the night off from training, ran some errands along with Nora after the fight. Despite Alice's protests, Nora insisted she accompany her. 'A wanted criminal *and* a runaway Princess shouldn't be alone, in the Capital of all places,' Nora had said. Alice displayed some rude gestures to her, but she knew she had a point. Begrudgingly they headed out, leaving Viviane and Ber alone.

"Are you sure you know what you're doing?" Ber asked, his worn smile began to falter. He had faith in his healer, until Viviane pulled out a curved needle and began threading.

The tournament tent came with medical staff for on-site injuries, but his options were limited with an after-hour rip in his sutures and low coin.

"Do you have such little faith in me, Ber? I'll have you know no one's died on me yet." Viviane winked.

"I'm sorry, it's just my second run-in with needles today. I've been feeling… nervous since the first round."

"Would it help if I talked you through it?"

"Yes, please. I'm sure Nora has filled you in on how much I like to talk."

Viviane smiled, "Just take a few deep breaths for me while the numbing kicks in."

Ber obeyed. Viviane watched as his bound chest rose and fell. He began shaving and plucking the patch of feathers that grew there in preparation for the tournament. She matched her own breathing to his and got to work.

For once, Ber struggled to make conversation. He was too focused on the pinch points.

"So… you're a baker? Before all this, I mean."

"I was, yes… hold that thought, please." Viviane felt his heartbeat pound beneath the skin, his face pale. She fetched some pillows to prop his legs up. "Better?" Ber nodded. "Yes, my whole family were bakers. Not much to tell, really. What about you, before military life?"

Ber thought for a long moment, just long enough to worry Viviane that he was passing out again, "… Would you take the answer of 'brat?'"

Viviane laughed, "I'm sure you weren't *that* bad!"

"No. I mean, not on purpose. Pops was gone a lot, and Mom tried her best, raising me to be a 'man of the people,' she called it."

Ber continued, "But I'd get bored. I'd make storms in the banquet halls. I'd play with the chancellor's prized steeds, even the toothy ones. It's not that I didn't care, I just…"

"You were a child. Children make their own fun, even if it is destructive," Viviane said, "No wonder you and Alice mesh so well. This all sounds awfully familiar."

"You can't tell me you never were a bit of a hellraiser when you were a kid."

"Nope! I was a perfect angel. I'll tell you this, though– Hopping a ship and raiding the coasts wasn't *all* Alice's idea."

"Really?"

"Mhm. And can I tell you something else? We're done."

Ber craned his neck to look at her work. "You really are a miracle worker, Viv." He said, "Between matches, you and I should cook together sometime. I'd love to learn some new recipes."

"Why? Are you trying to impress someone?"

"I– That's not *exclusively* the reason…"

"I'm only teasing, dear. I won't pry… tonight. I'd love to cook with you! I could always use some help. Who knows, maybe you could show me some recipes from your world!"

"Heh, maybe…"

Ber smiled, but his gaze laid elsewhere. Viviane realized then, acquiring whatever ingredients would be impossible.

"I have an idea," Viviane said, "Why don't you make a list of ingredients that taste like foods from your world? Maybe between the both of us, we could make a mock recipe?"

"That's very kind of you, Viv."

"Well, it's the least I can do. You've already done so much to help us get an audience with the Queen."

"'Us,' huh?"

"Alice might not admit it, but this is our mission just as much as it is yours, now. I might not be welcome on palace grounds, but until then you have my support."

—

Nora pounded on the bathroom door. "Are. You. Done."

"One more minute!" Ber sung.

"You said that twenty minutes ago. Ber, we're going to be late if you don't get out of the damn bathroom, *now.*"

The next game was the second to last before the final. Nora could not believe Ber got this far. The man was skilled, sure, but sheer dumb luck carried their party to the top. Nora admitted it was nice to not have to worry about finances for once. Viviane and Nora did their part, and with Ber pulling in the extra cash, they were able to afford better furniture and better food for their tenement.

Ber opened the door, releasing a large cloud of steam from the room. Dressed in the tournament's uniform, he stood tall and proud.

"How do I look? Sexy, right?" He asked, still primping his hair.

"Whatever. Sure. Can we go now?"

"Let me put on some dust first."

"I'm sorry, what?"

Ber displayed a tiny jar of glittery powder. "Huan Jun gave this to me, he said lots of competitors use it to look pretty."

It was part of Huan Jun's job to prime his competitors. But with their matching flamboyant personalities, he and Ber meshed seamlessly.

"Viv and Alice already left to find seats, so we're leaving too," Nora reminded.

Ber tried to wave her off, but stood at the entrance of their kitchenette. "Nora."

"Yeah, Ber?"

"Which clock were you referring to?"

"The hall clock," Nora stopped, "… Is that one slow?"

"Yep."

"Shit."

There was no way the two could make it to the tent before the game started. Nora scanned the street for a trolley, a carriage, *anything* to get them there on time. Through a dark shop window, she spotted the glint of a wheeled contraption.

Nora pulled Ber across the street to the shop. She opened the door to a store full of the same machines. From behind the counter an old man peeked over.

"Eh, we're not open just yet, folks," He said.

"Please—how much for the cheapest one of—of these things?" Nora asked.

"This bicycle here is a popular, less pricey pick."

The man observed Ber's outfit.

"I'll give it to ya half price, too, if ya give ol' Lee's place a shout out at the tournament today."

"Sold, and consider it done."

Nora dumped her money onto the counter. Frustrated with counting the exact amount, She pushed the remaining bills and coins to the clerk.

"Keep whatever's left!"

The two stepped outside with the thing.

"Nor, what is this?"

"A 'bicycle,' apparently. We didn't have them back home, but it doesn't look *too* hard…" Nora mounted the seat, leaning her weight to one foot. "What're you waiting for? Get on."

Ber carefully balanced himself behind her. In a half-crouch, he pondered how the machine worked, and if Nora executed it right.

Stomping on the pedals, the bicycle teetered left to right. Their progress towards the tournament was worse than if they walked.

"Lemme try something," Ber said.

Holding onto Nora, he stretched his other hand back. He created gusts of wind, balancing the bicycle. In addition to Nora's pedaling, the two gained momentum.

Nora grinned, "Great idea Ber! Keep it up!"

Ber did just that and created gusts to propel them forward and upright. But it only worked if they kept the momentum *fast*. Nora and Ber flew up and down hills, cutting tight corners, flying through alleys. Their speed grew out of control. The sparse crowd grew denser as they followed the banners to the tournament. Townsfolk craned their necks in confusion as they flew by.

"Out of the way! Out of the way!" Ber shouted, "Nora, the brakes!"

"I'm trying!" She spotted the spires from the tournament just past a few buildings. What mattered now was not dying. She wrapped her fingers around what she hoped were the brakes and pushed hard.

The bicycle grinded to a halt, but not without Ber flying off the back. Throwing the bicycle aside, Nora ran to him.

"Saints, Ber, are you alright?"

Ber coughed up the dirt from his lungs, "Next time… we should find a ramp."

Nora helped him onto his feet and dusted off his uniform.

"Well, I'm just glad I didn't kill you. Is there anything else you need?"

"Other than you and the other criminals to cheer me on, I don't think so."

Before Ber could enter the tent, Nora stopped him. She fished a small, glittery container from her pocket. "Are you sure?"

Ber gasped "My dust! Nor, you're the best!" He pulled her into a tight hug. *Ow.* "Alright, I really have to go. Thank you for being insane!"

"No problem. Good luck out there, and don't die!" Nora shouted before they parted ways.

—

The spectators began to go wild as the competitors entered. Huan Jun ran through introductions quickly, as everyone knew the remaining three competitors by now. Before they could throw flowers or shoot magic into the air, Ber signaled them for their attention. He called for Huan Jun, who reluctantly gave him the microphone.

For a moment, the microphone rang a high pitch tone throughout the stadium. Once it faded out, Ber spoke.

"An old man named Lee told me to tell all of you about his bicycle shop. I think it's near this district's plaza…?" The microphone gave a low whine over a murmuring audience, "Please check it out, and thank you for listening!"

With that, the match began. Ber only had a moment to assess his foes.

Both competitors held fire aura. Unable to control water the way Alice finesses her magic, Ber would be at a disadvantage. Fire magicians worked fast, so Ber would have to be faster. He spilled the water vessels alotted to the arena. He crafted an ice rink around the arena, where he skated amongst the other fighters to land quick shots.

Alice and Viviane sat beside Nora, their mouths agape.

"Did you know he could do that?" Viviane asked Nora.

Nora laughed, shaking her head. *What a fool.*

But his work was not enough. He was among the final three in the ring. A magician caught up to him, hurling a ball of fire his way. Ber narrowly dodged the attack, but wiped out immediately after. The other fighter tripped him. Ber was sent flying to the edge of the ring.

What happened at the exact same time as Ber's wipeout was the fire magicians firing at each other. Distracted by Ber, they too went down. The crowd was in hysterics, unsure what to make of the results.

"What a turn of events!" Huan Jun said over the speaker, "Sit tight folks, as we review the footage."

Nora and Viviane were already hopping over the ring to check on Ber, despite the scolding medics. Alice knew better than to make a scene for this, so she suffered in silence on the bleachers, praying Ber was alright. Nora kneeled over him. He hit the wall hard and she could tell. She was unsure whether he was concussed. She erred on the side of caution and slapped him.

"C'mon you fool, stay on the side of living, please," Nora tried to joke, but her tone betrayed her.

Ber held her hand against his face with a ghost of a smile. If he was in pain, he was trying to hide it.

"Did we win, *lodse*?"

"Why do you keep calling me that—? It doesn't matter, Ber. Let's get you patched up."

Then, Huan Jun's already-loud voice came back on the speaker.

"Good gravy, folks, that was a close call! So close, in fact, our producers can't make heads nor tails of it! It looks like we will have the audience decide who moves forward."

First Huan Jun raised the fire mage Arwen's hand, then the fire mage Keno's to rally cheers. When Huan Jun raised Ber's limp arm, the crowd cheered the loudest.

Nora did not have time to process the victory until Ber was in the clear. As she waited for his discharge, she noticed his photos from the event had already been printed and passed around. She never realized photos could be made en masse so quickly. She snatched one, she could not help but laugh. They managed to capture Ber's essence in a single, monochrome glimpse. It caught the moment Ber dodged the last fire ball, his form dipping impossibly low while skating one-footed. He was screaming, and Nora just knew it was in that maniacal pitch he jumps to when he panics. It was now no wonder the crowd chose him. Since she met the man, Ber set a change of pace in every way. The City appreciated it, too. Nora smiled, tucking the photo into her shirt pocket for safekeeping.

39

Chapter 39

The following week the final fight came. The party tried to keep tensions low, but the game changed. Now, it was clear they had the chance to meet with the Queen. If they win, Nora and Ber's could finally put their fog business behind them— or at least put it in the hands of a capable power.

Nora began to wonder what life would look like after their ordeal came to an end. Surely Alice and Viviane would leave, and Nora would not blame them. Alice's missing posters were plastered in every depot, after all. That left Ber, a bigger question. Would he try to return home? Would he seek his revenge on Serkan? Would he try to have a fresh a fresh start in a new world? They had not had the conversation yet.

She was pulled from her thoughts when Ber, somehow, got louder.

"Noraaaaa—"

"Saints, what?! You drone like a damn mosquito."

"Ya looked zoned out."

"It's because I was. What do you need?"

"Oh, I don't know. Wait, yes I do— Can I tell you a secret?"

Becoming a bit of a celebrity, Ber left for the tournament far earlier than the earlier games, so the streets were empty. Still, Ber looked around before leaning into Nora's ear.

"I'm fucking *terrified*," Ber admitted.

He straightened back up, standing taller than Nora thanks to his platformed boots. He looked like a typical warrior in Nora's old storybooks, armored, strong, capable, but his watery eyes and weak smile broke that narrative.

"… Fine, come here, needle-noggin."

"'Needle-noggin…?'"

Nora hugged him. He melted into her hold and let out a sigh. They had time, so Nora let him hang on as long as he needed.

"Better?"

"Much better, *lodse*."

"Good, 'cause we gotta get going."

Nora escorted Ber a final time to the competitor's tent. With only two competitors now, the tent seemed far less empty but still buzzing with excitement. She stayed with him for a while he got ready and dressed in the final pieces of armor.

She pulled him into one more hug before leaving, "See you when you win, alright?"

—

Nora joined Alice and Viviane in the stands. It was a while before the match started, but the seats filled out surprisingly quick.

"How's our Champion doing?" Viviane asked Nora.

"He's nervous, but he'll be alright."

Nora noticed Alice's attention on the theater box across the stadium. It remained vacant throughout the tournament. Now it held the head guest of the show: Her Majesty, Queen Maeve of Stromshire.

Nora had only ever seen Her Majesty from newsprint, and of course some newer coins. From their position, though, all she could make out was her tall figure in a green dress with long, red hair.

Alice's eyes were still trained on the woman, hardly hiding her resentment.

"My sister…" Alice said simply, "I should have prepared for this, but I'll just try to ignore the wench."

"Are you safe here?" Nora asked.

"Don't worry yourself. She's not looking for me in all these spectators."

It became clear how bothered Alice was for the unexpected family reunion. Viviane slipped a slender hand in hers, and Alice's shoulders untensed a bit.

Huan Jun entered the center of the ring.

"Welcome, all, to our final tournament of Slatir Det Ostrucin. What a season we have had, folks! As always, I'm forever grateful we got to partake in this tradition together. It is something I cherish more than you all will ever know."

The crowd cresendoed into a loud cheer.

"Now who's ready to see some blood, huh?!"

This got an even louder applause.

"I can't imagine we really need introductions at this point, but let's do it one last time! To my left is our new gem, our Typhoon Berserker. Let's hear it for Ber Blødeks, everyone!"

The audience screamed as he entered in a swirl of mist. He dispersed the mist, voguing before falling into his now signature pose from the tournament before. He bent back with surprising flexibility. He dipped low to the ground one foot, while kicking the other high in the air, and the crowd ate it up.

Nora, Alice, and Viviane laughed at his stupid display. *At least his nerves aren't eating him up entirely*, Nora considered.

"And to my right is last year's electrical storm makin' a comeback! Please welcome our esteemed Bruno Adela!"

A young man about Ber's age entered the ring. Unlike most competitors Bruno spared the theatrics. He did however saunter towards Ber, staring right through Huan Jun and at him with bright green eyes. If Huan Jun sensed the tension, he clearly ignored it.

"Two storms in the final ring! This MUST be a first— I hope you all are ready to take shelter!" Huan Jun clapped a hand on Ber and Bruno's shoulder, "Now, I *would* say I want a nice, clean fight. But that wouldn't be true. Just don't kill each other, because I don't want to do the paperwork. Alright?"

The two gave a quick nod. Huan Jun raised a slender arm to the sky.

With a graceful, rehearsed motion, he spoke.

"And… BEGIN!"

Bruno and Ber moved at amazing speed. Ber tried to land a heavy blow to slow the other man down, but it proved to be a mistake. The moment Ber was no longer on the defensive, Bruno struck his side. Electricity coursed Ber's system, he stifled a scream as his body of contracting muscles doubled over. Bruno began to summon another shot, but Ber managed to roll out of the way.

Another shot, and Ber was not just out. He sparred with this kind of magic before, but this caliber of power could stop his heart. Judging by the cold look on Bruno's face, he did not care about Huan Jun's paperwork.

Ber lost his footing, and he was pushed closer and closer to the edge of the ring. He had one more trick up his sleeve, but it was not something he could get away with the whole city watching. So he allowed Bruno to take his win, but Bruno was playing it safe, too.

Ber tried to communicate with the man through his spasms but to no avail. Bruno kicked him down and held him in place.

"I'm not letting another *filthy* transplant take this win. I deserve this money— I *need* this money. So be a good girl— boy, whatever you are, and know your place is in the ground."

Bruno leaned close to Ber as he prepared a final blow.

Nora, Alice, and Viviane's hearts sunk as they watched the scene unfold. Viviane's words slipped from her mouth.

"Oh Saints, he's actually planning to—"

Nora stood, "Viv, Alice, I'm about to do something stupid. Please don't follow me."

Despite her request, Viviane grabbed her bag and prepared to follow.

In tandem they tripped out of their seats. They looked down to find that their feet stuck to the stadium floor from ice.

"What the hell…?" Nora muttered.

"I think Alice has different plans," Viviane squeaked. The two scanned the stadium, but Alice was already gone.

—

Alice made her way through the crowds to the arena gates, hood drawn over her face. She ducked and dodged through the waves of civilians. Her heart pounded and her breath grew heavy. She tapped into her old persona, keeping each step to be methodical and almost elegant. Much to her favor, her small stature kept her suspicious path to the gates hidden. Her fingers wrapped tight around her daggers, ready to start a fight.

The guards securing the gates confronted her. No turning back now, Alice repeated to herself. She wept one to the side with water from an adjacent fountain. She stabbed the other in the thigh, hindering her movement. The guard shouted for backup, but there was no need in Alice's plan to stop it. Alice scaled the gate into the arena. A horde of guards followed her in, but she was faster.

Alice saw Bruno muttering to Ber while charging his final attack. She began to sprint, and yet everything around her seemed to slow. She drew a dagger, then another three and took a deep breath.

With devastating accuracy, her first dagger struck Bruno's wrist. Aura flowed in entropic surges from the cut, and his grip on the blades failed. Bruno looked at the intruder with so much rage he did not recognize her at first. Before he could raise his other hand, Alice pinned his other arm with another dagger. She inched towards his face armed with even more daggers.

Ber looked up to Alice, his face pale. His fear for her escaped through his teeth.

"A-Alice, don't do this…"

Alice ignored his plea.

Alice's lips almost touched Bruno's ear, "Make another move and I won't hesitate to make a new kind of show for all these people. You wouldn't want to ruin their appetites, would you?"

Bruno froze, too afraid to make another move now that most of his aura flow was cut. Alice kicked her victim down with a heel on his neck. Stadium guards flowed into the arena from every direction.

She rolled her eyes and removed her hood, "That's not a very proper way to greet your Princess." She conjured all of her courage to make it look like she knew what she was doing. Her plan worked out, and one by one, the guards dropped to bow before her. "Hand me a microphone," She ordered. A guard did just that.

Alice could feel her sister's eyes boring through her. But she pressed on. Alice tapped the device.

"Hello Saint Evedis... nice to be in our gracious City once again," She lied. She forced her eyes on the Queen. "Queen Maeve, I will make this brief: I return so that my affiliates may have an audience with you... And I assume that the price on my head is an equal trade off," Alice announced, "I want to assure you—all of you, that my affiliates had nothing to do with my actions today. And I apologize for disrupting your regularly scheduled bloodshed."

With that, Alice raised her hands in surrender, dropping the microphone and her daggers and stepping off of Bruno. The guards encased Alice, forcing her out of the arena.

Nora followed Ber to the infirmary and Viviane followed. Nora turned to her.

"You need to go— While you still can," Nora said.

"I can't leave her. I can't leave you."

Nora breathed in. "... Let's get going, then."

While Ber was saved from heavy damage, he needed immediate attention for the electrical burns. His series of burns and spasms paled in comparison to the storm in his mind. *If only I had been stronger...* He thought.

Viviane and Nora were not in a much better place. Nora forced her focus on comforting her friends while refusing to think about the one she just lost, or what was to come next. Viviane, however, sat shaking. She struggled to hold herself together, but would fall into waves of tears.

Everything seemed to go by so fast. Soon after a team of royal guards escorted them to a carriage waiting outside. From the brief walk to the carriage, citizens and the press alike swarmed around them. From all sides Nora, Ber, and Viviane were pushed forward.

Once escorted to the carriage, two guards sat on each side. No one dared to speak. The walls of the carriage, at the very least, offered some comfort and privacy from the situation at hand.

Not long after, they passed the gates to the castle. Even from the small portholes of barred windows they could see the massive amounts of reinforcements; beside the intricate gates stood groups of guards and large spires. The carriage slowed to a stop. The guards once again escorted them into the castle. Nora had never seen an impressive piece of architecture like the castle, at least this up close. It stretched far across the courtyard, and far into the sky.

Poor Viviane seemed helpless to her entire situation. Forced on all sides, each step towards the castle led to more uncontrolled shaking. Nora and Ber noticed this. The castle was the last place she ever wanted to return to.

They entered a vast, elegant chamber, working as a main vein to a series of stairs and corridors. Holding their breath, Nora and Ber expected to meet a wrathful monarch at any moment. Through twists and turns, the guards led them to a more discrete part of the chamber. They paced to the door at the end of the hall. She turned to question the guard behind her, but noticed Ber was gone.

"Where's Ber?" Nora asked. She loathed how small her voice was.

"Your compatriot will be down the hall in a guest room until morning. The same will go for you," The guard beside her answered. The guard held a relaxed but firm grip on her arm. With her other hand she unlocked the door, "Tomorrow morning, we will retrieve you for questioning."

Nora nodded. She was put into her 'cell,' a lush, palace guest room. To her surprise, the guards did not lock the door, but she could tell from the shadows beneath the door that they remained just outside.

She took in her surroundings. The room held a canopy bed, an empty wardrobe, and a washroom with a clawfoot tub and shower. She stepped to the window– barred, of course, in elegant cast iron architecture. A willow blocked much of her view, but from below, another pair of guards were posted outside. *What a beautiful cage...*

Nora took a long, hot shower. It felt wrong to indulge in a creature comfort, but what else could she do? Her mind went to Ber, hoping what the guards said was the truth. *He's probably shaken, he almost got really hurt today...* Nora wondered if anyone would have stepped in had Alice not entered the ring. She wished she was faster. That she thought to keep Alice in place and go to Ber's aid.

The day's light already reached its end once Nora was finished. She flipped a switch by the bed. A pair of flameless lamps lit the room. Nora marveled at the little contraptions. Curious if it would respond the same way fire would, she extended her shadows into one of the lamps. It flickered before snuffing out entirely. Nora recalled her aura, relieved she did not break the mechanism.

Stripped of her belongings, she wandered her posh cell to find something, anything to keep her occupied. To her dismay, it was practically barren.

Nora gave up and chose to retire for the night. She slid into the sheets of what rivaled the most comfortable bed she had ever laid in. Still the air felt desolate, and she knew why– she was truly alone for the first time in months.

She wondered where Alice and Viviane were put. *Given their crimes, surely nothing like this.* Then the thought hit her hard– She did not know where her friends were or the state they were in. The rational part of her brain told her they were probably fine, but it was not knowing for certain that haunted her.

She felt pressure behind her eyes as tears threatened to come through. Nora finally was in the City she desired, and finally in the right place to warn the Crown to put this business to rest, but it was only now she came to realize just how unprepared she truly was.

Curling into herself, she quietly wept into a pillow. Her eyes grew sore and red, but she could not help but cry more, until sleep finally took her.

40

Chapter 40

Arvo cursed below his breath. His words were directed to himself rather than anyone else. On days with so much to do, he tended to revert to stasis, collapsing in his quarters.

He found himself absently stroking the cheek of his beloved bird. His beast, one of several, stood tall and proud on Arvo's chest as it readily accepted the attention. The bird's talons dug into his skin, but he did not mind.

The bird's head swiveled to a click from the door. Arvo placed the bird aside to be greeted by Edvard. Edvard gave a once over to Arvo before averting his eyes.

"You're not busy, are you?" Edvard asked, his voice strained.

"No. What's going on?"

Arvo remained curious of Edvard's odd behavior, until it clicked to him that he was in a partial state of undress. He slipped over a shirt. His fingers fumbled on the buttons.

"… Listen. Hel picked up some strange readings nearby. We need to make a quick survey to make sure it's nothing. You in?"

Arvo raised his brow. "You're working with Hel now?"

"Like I said, it's probably nothing. Can't be too careful these days," Edvard said, "Can you be ready in fifteen?"

—

Edvard, Arvo, and Hel left under the cover of night. They traveled on horseback, silently out of the city. They quickened the pace as they entered the steep, weaving paths into the valley. Both Edvard and Arvo struggled to catch up to Hel until she pulled the reins.

"You hear that?" Hel said.

"No," Edvard and Arvo said in unison, but their steeds sure did.

Then from across the valley they saw packs of beasts, one group black the other white. The dark ones nearly blended in with their surroundings had it not been for their heads reflecting the moonlight.

"Are those... Mirror dogs? I never knew they chase prey this far from their territory," Arvo commented.

"They don't," Hel said, "These things must have got them riled up for a good reason. See if you can get a better look with the scope on your bow."

Arvo did just that. He closed in on the pale beasts. Arvo thought himself at least a capable naturalist, but with these he could not make heads nor tails of them. They moved too fast, in a stampede of scales, tails, feathers, gossamer wings.

He shared the scope with Edvard, then Hel.

"I've never seen anything like this... Could these be the fog beasts Nora and Ber were talking about?" Arvo asked.

"I'd say so," Edvard said, "Why don't we help these mutts out?"

Hel quietly agreed, handing Arvo back his bow. He lined up his shot, moving with the rampaging beasts. "I'm not one to meddle with the natural world like this," Arvo began, "But these things aren't natural, are they?"

His finger hovered over the trigger, hesitating for just a moment. He exhaled as he squeezed the trigger, sending a set of three bolts flying. None of the bolts struck the pale beasts directly, but instead scattered them. In the disarray, the dogs made quick work of the stragglers. Those quick enough to escape fled into the brush.

Edvard whistled low, "Good shot."

"Maybe we can come back during the day to study one of the dead ones— if we can find the pacck's cache."

"I have a crazier idea. While those dogs are busy, why don't we check out their ruins?" Before the men could reject Hel continued, "We're not far from it, I can feel it. I'm certain it's where I'm feeling these dreadful vibrations."

"*That* wasn't what you were feeling?" Arvo asked.

"No."

Arvo relented, and Edvard struggled to argue after that. They followed Hel over the valley's crest. They kept their heads on a swivel in case the dogs decided to return early.

Like Hel promised the gravesite proved to be a short trip. She dismounted her horse. She weaved through the site, gingerly avoiding the graves. Judging by the old arches and pillars, she figured it could have been a small, private temple, or an old village grave.

Hel closed her eyes. Her ears twitched incessantly. With her condition, she had a skill (she would call a curse) to pick up frequencies in the spirit veil. The curse, however, was a struggle to pinpoint *where* they were coming from.

She opened her eyes, brows furrowed, as she searched around for clues. She did a double take of a grave, rather the remnants of one. She stepped over to investigate. The grave sunk into the ground more than the others.

"Graverobbers?" Ed asked, "Or, maybe the beasts were getting into the site. That'd set the dogs off for sure."

Hel shook her head, "The grass is pretty undisturbed. It looks almost concaved."

"Sinkhole?" Arvo suggested.

"Reasonable thought, but no dice."

"Then what is it?" Edvard asked, the edge of his voice tinged in frustration.

"Don't know," Hel fetched a shovel from the side saddle of her horse, handing it to Edvard, "One way to find out!"

"No. Absolutely not, Hel! What is wrong with you?! Aren't you the one that finds all this sacred?"

"Yes. But these are desperate times, Ed! Now put your big, stupid muscles to work!"

"Hel, are you sure this is right?" Arvo asked.

Hel sighed, exacerbated, "Just trust me on this, alright?! This feels– it just feels *bad.*"

Hel and Edvard's eyes met. Edvard stood over her, but she stood her ground. Finally Edvard sighed.

"I swear if this gets me cursed or some shit…" Ed muttered, shovel in hand, "Someone get the light."

Edvard got to work, swearing under his breath. He paused his digging to wipe his brow. The light from behind him danced and jittered.

"How hard is it to hold the light straight?" He turned around, "Sweet Saints, seriously?!"

Hel stood above him, hand hardly containing a ball of raw, chaotic electricity. Arvo stood sheepishly beside her.

"The lamps were low and my fire's no good…" He said.

Edvard softened, "… I'm almost done anyway, I think. Just keep your death ray far away from me."

With the grave compromised, Edvard made quick work of it. It was not long before he hit… nothing. Edvard scraped around the area to find some loose jewelry and a robe. Indentations marked the excavated earth, though Edvard was unsure whether that was his doing. Someone *was* buried here, but the remains were nowhere to be found.

Edvard looked to Arvo, his brows knit together. "Is there a bone-eating creature I don't know about, Arvo?"

Arvo frowned, "Nothing that leaves a grave unscathed. If they weren't dug up, then where did the bones go?"

"I think there's really only one other option," Hel said.

She took Edvard's shovel to point at the innocuous marks. Small as they were, it was evidence– the bones were drug *down.*

They stood in silence for a long moment, part in prayer, part in shock. In the distance, a lone howl sounded out, then a harmony of more. It was enough to shake the team from their spell.

"We should be going…" Edvard said, "… Are the kids in Saint Evedis yet?"

"Yes, Nora sent us a message yesterday with their new residence," Arvo answered.

"Guess it's as good a time as any to write them back."

41

Chapter 41

Nora woke well before the morning light seeped into her room. Unable to fall back asleep, she stared at the crystal chandelier above her bed that she could not figure out how to light last night. For a moment, she considered prying off a few crystals for some pocket money when she could leave. *If I can leave...* She mourned.

Hours passed until the Guard came to collect her.

"Nor!"

Making it to the end of the hall, she was paired again with Ber, but no sight of Viviane or Alice. Still she breathed a sigh of relief, happy to at least see a familiar face. Judging by the dour expressions worn by the guards that flanked Ber, she could tell he must have talked their ears off. She prayed it was not any damning information.

The two met with a single servant. Based on her dress and posture, she seemed to be a rank or two above the other servants.

With a graceful curtsy, the woman greeted them, "Good morning, my name is Cherie. In honor of our Gracious Queen, I would like to welcome you to Saint Evedis Palace. I hope you found your accommodations acceptable," Ber opened his mouth to speak, but Cherie spoke up, "I understand that you have business with the Queen. Allow me to escort you to Her Majesty and go over a few guidelines."

"Pardon me, Miss Cherie, but where are Alice and Viv?" Ber asked.

"Her Highness and Miss LeClair are being questioned separately," Ber opened his mouth but she continued, "When you meet with the Queen, you are to call her 'Your Majesty.' Please only speak to her once spoken to," She said, glancing back at Ber.

They left the hall and out of the wing, further and further into the palace. Nora could not fathom how a building could be so huge. She struggled to lull her nerves, when with each step brought her closer to the head of the entire nation.

Nora and Ber were brought to the end of a wide hall to a large, intricately carved door. Cherie stepped to the side and bowed her head.

"Her Majesty is expecting you. You may enter."

Nora breathed in, trying to soothe herself, before entering. Her hands still shook as she pushed the door open, entering the throne room.

The room was nearly radiant. Windows lined two walls entirely, reaching high to the vaulted ceiling. Before her, in a large, ancient throne sat the Queen of Stromshire, Queen Maeve.

The first thing Nora noticed was just how alike the Queen and Alice appeared. She was paler, and with longer hair, and something about her gaze seemed much more unyielding than the Princess.

Behind her hung an utterly *massive* oil painting, depicting Saint Evedis himself alongside his beast, a wolverine with fur like sunlight. The painting looked so real, Nora could almost feel their eyes on her. She took a brief second in the confines of her mind to pray. *May the Saint Evedis watch over you,* the voice of that Customs officer echoed in Nora's mind.

A similar beast was at the Queen's side, but a reddish hue and rosettes in its fur. It rested its huge head on her armrest, unbothered.

The Queen spoke.

"Good morning, and welcome! I take you found your accommodations acceptable?"

"Y-yes, Your Majesty," Nora managed.

"I want to apologize for not greeting you last night. Needless to say, I was quite busy with the tournament's activities." Her words, though the largest understatement of the century, felt relaxed and genuine. Nora found her impossible to read.

From behind Nora and Ber the door squeaked back open. They were elated to find Viviane peeking in. *Thank the Saints she's okay.* She smiled at the two, but her dread was quite obvious as she entered the room.

In an instant, guards surrounded her, halberd spears trained on her neck. Almost unphased, Viviane bowed.

"Your Majesty, please excuse my intrusion."

"Ah, Miss LeClair. Please, come in!" the Queen smiled.

"For you, your Majesty." Viviane handed the Queen a striking bouquet of amaryllis and daffodils, accented with sprigs of basil blooms.

"Thank you, dear. Did you grow these yourself? You've become quite skilled since I have seen you last." Her ivy green eyes glinted over the bouquet, "Please, make yourselves comfortable. I believe we have some matters to discuss."

Queen Maeve ushered her guests to a table. Her crossed legs and straightened posture gave her the appearance similar to a preying animal— graceful and confident, dangerous.

"I will not deny that I was caught off guard from last night's events. However, as scheduled, I will still be hosting the Slatir Det Ostrucin Champion's Ball. You may not have won, but I would love it if all of you were able to come join the festivities." The Queen leaned in, "It's a *total* rager. Even in mild years, we have to replace the ballroom's chandeliers!"

Viviane was taken aback. It was clear she was not expecting a party invitation, of all things.

Ber spoke up, "Your offer is very tempting, Your Majesty. But before we go any further, we have some very important matters to discuss."

"Yes. Your Majesty if you would please excuse my boldness…" Viviane interjected, "… but what did you do with Alice?" Queen Maeve frowned and rolled her shoulders to the back of her chair.

"Your questions will be answered soon enough, I assure you. But if you do not mind, we need to discuss the plans for you three." She responded, her tone went cold, "Before we continue, I would like some confirmation: Were any of you involved in the planning of yesterday's events?"

Ber, Nora, and Viviane answered no. Quietly, Queen Maeve assessed each of them. Nora felt like she was being seen straight through. The air of the room seemed so heavy it was hard to breathe. They told the truth, but the Queen did not know this. Only her judgment could decide. A long moment passed before she relaxed herself once more.

"Alright. I believe you. I have a knack for reading people. But if, for whatever reason, I guessed wrong, well…" She said, "I have my ways of finding out."

The Queen turned to Ber with a warm smile. The sudden change of mood was unsettling. Her voice softened, "Now… Ber, is it? I must say you fought rather admirably until the very end of the tournament. It truly does pain me to see your competitor win. But please, do tell me. How did you learn to wield your aura with such power? It's like nothing I have ever seen."

Queen Maeve's words struck a nerve in Ber. The last time his aura was mentioned in such a way, he lay at the mercy of another ruler's cruel hands. Ber struggled to string together the right words. "W-well… I've traveled lots, and between learning how to protect myself and learning techniques from other magic users I've met, it's a style I developed over time," He answered.

"Is that so…?" The Queen mused. She turned to Nora, "As for you, Miss…"

"It's—It's Ní Dyr, Nora Ní Dyr," Nora answered.

The Queen nodded, "It's a pleasure to meet you, Nora." Something about the way she spoke made Nora shiver. "I will get to the point. Your potentials should not go to waste. Should you and Ber accept recruitment into the Saint Evedis Militia Academy… Well, you may earn a favor."

Nora felt like her heart stopped. She could understand recruiting Ber, but why her? She wondered just how much research the Queen did on her party, on her.

"I understand that you may need some time to mull this over. But please, let me know as soon as you can. Regardless of your answer, I will be happy to host you until after the Ball," She said.

A castle guard gingerly entered the room. "Your Majesty, we need your guidance."

"A minute, please!" the Queen said.

"If I may have another word, Your Majesty," Nora tried, "we still have yet to discuss our reason for being here. It's incredibly urgent, and the whole reason why we entered your city."

"Those topics, unfortunately, will have to wait. Ber, Nora, you are dismissed. It was wonderful to finally meet you, and I loved our little chat. If your matters are truly urgent— which I assure you they are already being handled, you may find me at the ball," The Queen said, "And please, consider my offer and let one of my servants know. Miss LeClair, would you stay a moment, please?"

Nora and Ber bowed, thanking the Queen for her time. They excused themselves from the chamber, exchanging a worrying glance to Viviane before leaving her alone.

The Queen sighed. Taking her neglected cup of tea in hand, she unwound herself to the company of a familiar face. Viviane remained statue still. She slid her tongue between her teeth to ease her clenching jaw.

"Viviane, you look well. How have you been?" Maeve asked.

"I have been… better. What about yourself? You seem as illustrious as usual, your Majesty."

"Thank you, dear. I've been well…" The Queen took a sip of her tea, "… You know, I do miss your spinach puffs. Any chance I may have the recipe?"

"Per-Perhaps we can discuss that some other time. May we talk about what is both on our minds?" Viviane asked.

"Yes, yes you are right. Please, go ahead."

"Your Majesty, I apologize for my brevity, but you must understand my concern—What did you do with Alice?"

Maeve took a moment to respond. She set aside Viviane's flowers blocking her view, "*You* must understand that she was a threat to state by pulling her little stunt yesterday. Currently, she is under interrogation for her disruptive behavior and treasonous actions," She answered.

"Maeve, I know where this is going. You and I both know that you don't have to do this. I mean for all that's holy, she is your *sister.*"

The Queen frowned, "Bold of you to talk to your Queen that way, Miss LeClair. Have you no respect for the laws of this land? Only the Saints know what atrocities you and my sister committed upon your desertion." Her unrelenting gaze pierced straight through Viviane. Viviane stood statuesque in fear, but held her ground. She kept her eyes locked with the Queen.

The Queen sighed. She continued, "It is clear to see that you have learned nothing since our last encounter. Like any other criminal to the state, Alice will be interrogated, judged, and be given punishment befitting for her deeds. Her blood has no play in the matter."

"If… If I were to take her place, would you let her go?" Viviane asked.

Queen Maeve let out a small chuckle, making Viviane much more uncomfortable. "Curious, adorable even. I heard she requested the same for your situation. Don't think you're off the hook just yet. The only reason why you're here and not behind steel bars is that you were in the right place at the right time."

She continued, "Miss LeClair, the Court will not turn a blind eye to you being an accomplice. But luckily for you, the press seems to feel differently." She slid a copy of that morning's newsprint across the table, "You and I both know how decisions can be swayed by this. The public could have an uproar if I were to punish Alice properly."

Viviane took a moment to view the front cover. In bold black letters the print read, 'THE PRINCESS RETURNS! Her Highness Makes Appearance At Ostrucin Final, City Rejoices.'

Viviane swallowed, "… I understand."

The same guard from before entered once again. Softly he cleared his throat, "Your Majesty—"

The Queen stood. "A minute, *please!* What could possibly be so important that you feel the need to interrupt me *twice?!*"

The guard in response backed out of the room and out of her sight.

"Thank you once again, Your Majesty, for meeting with me and my friends. I believe my questions have been answered." Viviane said, attempting to take her leave.

"One more thing before I excuse you, Miss LeClair," Queen Maeve placed a hand on her shoulder. "I had a lot of faith in you. Don't forget who got you your position in the first place. Allow me to give you one more piece of advice: Stay away from my sister."

With that, Viviane bowed before escorting herself from the room. "Good day, Your Majesty."

42

Chapter 42

The palace guards would not allow Nora and Ber wait in the parlor for Viviane. Fortunately for the two they were not wanted criminals like Alice and Viviane, but they were still being closely watched. They managed to find a secluded spot in the next hall. They perched at a bay window, overlooking one of the Palace's multiple gardens.

"Ber."

"Yes, Nor?"

"There's a lot we need to talk about."

"I agree."

"Before we jump into anything, I think we need to lay out exactly what's on our minds. Then, we'll come up with a plan of action."

"You go first."

"Alright…" Nora breathed, "… I never thought I'd be saying this, but I'm willing to take the offer. But I don't want you to feel pressured to join."

"Nora…"

"If I were to obey the Queen's request while you gain her respect here, we could—"

Ber took hold of her shoulder.

"Nora," Ber said sternly, "I'm coming with you. I *want* to come with you. Nothing could make me change my mind— if this is how we get results, I'll go along with it."

"Are you sure? I know how you feel about coming back to something like this..."

"I'm certain," Ber pulled a thin smile, "Besides, the Queen described it with a bunch of fancy words, right? Something along the lines of... a super-special military academy? If anything, it sounds like a police academy."

"Yeah, it probably is," Nora said, unconvinced, "Just... tell me if you change your mind, yeah? You've already done enough." *You have been through enough,* she wanted to say.

"Funny, I was going to say the same thing," Ber winked, "Gods, we're both so stubborn!"

Nora gave Ber the grace to move on from the topic. For now, she could afford him some peace.

"Did you think the Queen seemed a little... off?" Nora asked.

Ber nodded in an instant.

"Do you think she's, like... into me?"

Nora grimaced, "I think it might be a bit different than that, Ber. The way she talked about you and your 'power...'"

"It was uncomfortable."

"This whole situation is uncomfortable," Nora smiled, "But at least for once, we are in the right place, and relatively at the right time."

From the corner of his eye Ber caught sight of Viviane's honeyed curls. He caught Nora's attention and they rushed over.

"Viv, Viv!" Ber called out.

Viviane turned, clearly on edge. She took a glance around before pulling Ber and Nora into a hug. Her lashes dusted over Nora's sleeve, tears wetting the fabric. She escorted the two into another room. They descended old stone stairs into what Ber assumed was an archival room.

"No one ever comes in here. We should be safe to talk here," Viviane breathes, "It's such a relief to see you both."

"Viv, what's going on? Are you alright? Is Alice okay?" Nora asked.

Viviane smiled, "We will be alright, dear. Alice is being held for questioning. As to where, I do not know."

"I don't understand, why aren't *you* being held for questioning?" Ber asked.

"I was, or I am. But I'm not the Princess. According to the Press, it seems I was overlooked. I was put in a cell last night, sure," Viviane grinned, "But the Queen underestimated me, again. So I got out."

Nora blinked. She figured she underestimated her, too. She had forgotten just how bold the ex-pirate could be. Judging by Ber's incredulous look, he must have been impressed, too.

"How?"

"Miss Maeve doesn't know just how many friends I've made when I served here. I cashed in a couple favors to expedite my meeting with her Majesty," Viviane winked, "Too bad the witch hates my guts. Per usual, she would not take me seriously."

"Viviane, there is something the Queen offered to us," Nora started, "She said we could earn counsel with her if we were to join the Militia Academy… Should we take the offer?"

"I… I don't know. I only have fleeting experience in infantry. I simply don't know enough to urge you one way or another. I'm sorry," Viviane sighed, "What I *can* recommend is to learn from my mistake, and make friends with the Queen."

"I don't understand. Why doesn't she like you?" Ber asked. Nora and Viviane turned to him slowly.

"… I seduced her sister and ran away with her."

"Ah! I see."

"Listen," Viviane said, "The ball is tomorrow evening. In my opinion, this is the best opportunity you have for Maeve to listen to your plea… Putting in a good word about me and Alice during the ball would help an awful lot, too."

"Of course, Viv. It's the least we can do," Ber said.

Viviane smiled. She pulled them into another hug.

"Thank you, dear," Viviane pulled away, "I should go. I told the Queen I would return from my breakout."

Viviane parted ways, leaving Nora and Ber with much more to think about.

—

Queen Maeve descended the stairs to one of the many winding chambers of the palace. It was by design, but she had memorized the palace inside and out.

Repetitive clangs of metal echoed down the chamber. The Queen met with her sister, disheveled and chained against the chamber wall. Alice laid slumped back, kicking a thin portion of sleet against the metal bars.

"So, you finally want to talk to me face to face?" Alice asked. She paid half attention to her sister while she continued to hit the bars.

"I aimed to talk with you personally as soon as possible. In the last twenty-four hours, I had to jump through hoops just to pacify the public from your little stunt." Maeve said, already struggling to keep her even tone.

"What did you do to Viv? I swear if you did *anything*–"

"Relax. She already managed to get out of her cell to bother me this morning. You two need to start taking this seriously, because this disobedience will not help your case."

"Leave her out of this. I left on my own accord."

"That's for the Court to decide, Alice."

Alice said nothing. She instead concentrated on slicing the bars. The *tink, tink, tink,* of the bars made Maeve's pointed ears twitch.

"You didn't come here just to make a scene, no matter how much you make it look that way." Queen Maeve felt her temper burning away as she endured the silent treatment. *Tink. Tink. Tink.* She rested her head in her hand, "Just—what do you *want?*"

Alice exhaled. She noticed just how much she wished she were not sober. Or here. "I want you to listen to me, for once."

"I'm listening."

"Well… You're right. You know better than anyone else here that I wouldn't come back here unless I had a damned good reason. I'll cut right to it. There is something threatening the countryside, and it's coming here—"

"Foolish…" The Queen cut her off, speaking half to herself, "I *knew* this was a fool's errand."

"I'm not kidding, Maeve!" Alice growled.

"Alice, what threat could *possibly* get past these walls? We've the strongest defenses in Ibe. Has the scoundrel's life tainted your mind so much that you've forgotten where you come from?"

"I think it's *you* that's forgotten that *I* snuck past these walls. Consider what might happen if someone with more power and ill intent were to come through."

Maeve shook her head, "I'm done with you. I'll return once you learn to properly converse with your Queen."

"You came down here for another reason," Alice said, "You wouldn't have come just to have an argument. You only ever speak to me when you need something."

Maeve ignored the dig, but she could not ignore that she was right. Just this once.

"... I'll be blunt. Somehow, the Press is absolutely enamored by your return. The whole city's in hysterics over it."

"It's because I am a delight," Alice said, "Wasn't expecting an ego boost from you of all people, though. What does this have to do with me?"

"It's the ball. Press will of course be involved, and some people of interest have already asked about you..." Maeve sighed, "It's forcing my hand to have you attend."

Alice groaned, "Seriously?! I'm already locked up! Isn't that punishment enough?"

"I don't want you there, either! But all this attention on you has my hands tied."

"Did you forget you're the *Queen?* Just tell them I'm not coming– Make an excuse!"

"It's not that easy, Alice. Also, you forget this is *my* night, and I'm not about to get badgered all night about my sister."

"And if I refuse?"

Maeve gripped her staff, "There is no refusing. You are going. You will answer diplomatically to the nobility, and you will be watched the entire time to see that you do."

White oak roots grappled the ground and spread. Not far, but enough for Alice to panic. She scrambled as far back against the wall as she could.

"Th-that's not fair! What if I panic and mess up?" Alice cried.

Maeve watched as Alice trembled. The younger sister's eyes, the hue matching Maeve's, were trained on Maeve's magic. She did not put it past her to pull dramatics to get out of her duties, but this…

Maeve retracted the roots.

"Just… make an appearance so everyone can get off my back," Maeve sighed, "After, I can have the guards escort you to your old quarters."

Alice mumbled, something of semblance to a 'thank you.' Queen Maeve turned, stomping up the stairs away from her sister.

Alice called after her, "Maeve, we're not done! If you don't listen, Saint Evedis could be–"

Maeve did not turn back to hear the rest. She shut the door to the chambers and moved to more pressing matters.

43

Chapter 43

Nora expected the preparations for the Champion's Ball to be suffocating, in its nicest term. Nobles and clergy alike rushed up and down the hall outside her door, laughing and shouting over the night's festivities. Yet otherwise, everyone left her alone to prepare, even Ber. In lieu of how long he took to get ready for anything in the past, she decided to leave without him if he was not ready in time.

Servants dropped off essentials the day before, along with effects for the ball. Within her wardrobe hung a variety of outfits for this night. Among them was a standard suit in crisp black, accented with white. Behind the suit hung an array of party gowns, some slim and elegant, others full and dramatic. One that caught her eye was a deep blue ball gown, relatively simple compared to the others. Its low sleeves left Nora's shoulders bare.

Nora sighed. She could not deny how pretty the dress was, but it just did not *feel right*. One more article flagged her attention. She donned a uniform-type garb. It reminded her of a royal guard's coat, with its sharp collar and lined with golden buttons and braids. What differed was its embellishments and how the coat tail billowed behind her. The uniform was paired with black pants and boots and a half-cape, no less. She forwent the cape, but all else fit just so perfect. Nora did some final touches. She pinned up her hair and attempted the makeup tricks Viviane had taught her. When finished she carried herself tall; for the first time in a while, her appearance sparked confidence in herself.

Nora knew Ber would be fretting *far* longer than she in front of the mirror, so she chose to fetch him instead. She stepped out of her room and knocked on Ber's door, smiling to herself. To her surprise, there was no answer. After a few more attempts she turned away and left towards the ball in hopes to find him there.

The ballroom proved an easy place to find. Music and cheers rattled through the palace, and all she had to do was follow the noise. At the end of a vast chamber stood tall mahogany doors cast wide open. This chamber seemed crowded enough. Nora wondered how much more dense it was inside.

Though foreign, the ball seemed almost welcoming to Nora. Upon entering, she was bathed in soft, golden light. As told by Queen Maeve, massive and intricate chandeliers hung from the vaulted ceiling. Guests from the inner ring mingled with each other. They lined the stairs and balconies, overlooking pairs of dancers on the main floor.

The night had just begun, yet some guests already indulged in their fair share of wine. The drunks happily jaunting about made Nora feel a bit better for her lack of skill for dancing. She aimed to stay on the sidelines this evening, saving her energy to converse with the Queen. A band kept the ballroom mood upbeat with a kind of swing music also foreign to Nora. At center stage it seemed like the main band left for the time being, leaving the other musicians to their own devices.

She picked up an intoxicating scent just past a series of large pillars. Each table was covered in roasted meats, pastries, and some items Nora could not identify. *No use negotiating with the Queen on an empty stomach,* she considered.

Halfway into shoveling her third mouthful of food, Nora noticed Alice and Viviane standing before her. Alice sported a slim, black and gold party dress, adorned with tassels and jewels. Viviane wore an elegant, dusted pink dress, its folds grazing the ballroom floor. Nora was utterly taken aback by their beauty. Apparently the feeling was mutual.

"Nora, holy shit..." Viviane said.

Alice whistled low, "You clean up good— I didn't know you could do that. Where's Ber?"

"I haven't seen him, I was hoping one of you would," Nora said.

Viviane tilted her head. "He did not take you to the ball?"

"No… Should he have? We both know where the ballroom is."

"Right… It left my mind that this is your first ball," Viviane said, "You look stunning, by the way."

Nora could not help but blush. "You think so? I appreciate it…"

"Yeah, you're hot as hell!" Alice shot a wide grin, "Come with us. I just lost my guards, and these walls have ears."

The two led Nora through the crowds to an emptier spot in the lounge. Some traffic passed by, but to Nora's surprise they did not seem to care too much about the Princess.

Alice plucked the food from Nora's platter as she spoke, "You're probably wondering why we're here and not still locked up. I needed to make a 'public appearance' for good publicity, or whatever."

"And I'm just so good at my old job. Maeve had to let me back in to oversee the food!" Viviane winked, popping a tart in her mouth.

"With that said, both of us are being watched like hawks tonight. Technically I'm not supposed to even be on the main floor, but making a plan takes priority," Alice said.

"Given our… relationship to the Queen currently, I'm sorry to say you and Ber will be on your own negotiating with her. God help you," Viviane added.

The three left the lounge to find Ber. A familiar voice rang through the hall. The three of them turned, watching the main band return to the stage.

"Hello once again, Saint Evedis! It's your esteemed host, Huan Jun, back at it again!"

"Saints, the man does music, too?" Nora asked.

"Me and these sweet boys have made it our sworn duty to deliver you sweet jams alllll night. Are you ready to WALTZ?!"

The crowd shared a few conflicted woots and cheers. Most stared in silence.

"ALRIGHT!"

The band began to play a series of string instruments in a low hum. Its sweet harmony began to soothe Nora's mind, until guests in pairs began to bump into her. She drifted away until she could no longer see Alice and Viviane.

Nora hung a right around a corner. She caught her breath and took a moment to observe the ball. Under crystalline light and gentle, entrancing music, people danced together in pairs. They danced slowly, smiling to themselves as their flowing gowns caught the air.

Nora found herself smiling. Though a gathering of this size was too busy for her taste, she understood why the city looked forward to strange festivities such as these. Even under the surveillance of guards, she could feel herself unwind.

Descending from marble stairs came a figure Nora almost did not recognize. Clad in a flowing, royal blue cape came Ber. Alongside his white, militaristic suit and knee-high boots, Nora admitted he looked almost princely.

Ber caught Nora's eyes and approached her. Her feet paced towards him and onto the ballroom floor. Ber smiled wide. He bowed low before her.

"May I have this dance?"

"Shut up and take my hand."

She pulled Ber to his feet, and they began a clumsy dance. She followed Ber's lead into a spinning dance somewhat like the others in the ballroom.

Ber looked down at Nora and winked. "I see both of us have the same taste in outfit. One of us will have to change."

"So I noticed…" Nora said, "Where have you been? I've been looking all over for you."

"I'm really sorry! I wanted to take you to the ball, but some… devotees chased me off."

"What is it with people *taking people* to this ball? We *all* know where it is!" Nora said. Ber was unsure how to respond. "Anyway, I'm just glad you're alright. You say the word, and I will be more than happy to be your personal body guard for tonight." She smiled, imitating the cracking of her knuckles.

Ber chuckled, his face dusted pink, "I appreciate it, Nor."

Nora took care to follow Ber's steps and spins. She grew accustomed to the steps in unison to the soft rhythm.

"When did you learn how to dance like this?" Nora asked.

"I was forced into a lot of these kinds of events back home. They were fundamentally the same, but also so different… Hopefully this isn't too much for you."

"Not at all," Nora assured. However, she was unsure if he was referring to his unorthodox dancing, or dancing with him in general.

Nora stole glances out at the ballroom. "We really should start looking for Alice and Viv…"

"I think we can afford to dance to one song. What do you think?"

Nora thought it over for a moment. It had been a long time since Nora felt this carefree. She nodded.

She held onto Ber with one hand in his, and the other on his opposite arm. Following his steps, Nora swung and spun as the music swooned. Nora tripped from their shuffling feet, but Ber caught her each time.

As they music picked up in speed, so did they. Ber circled Nora, and Nora followed suit. The two made a game out of their dance, attempting to outdo the other with twirls and spins around the other without toppling over. To no one's surprise, Nora failed. Ber tripped, himself. He lunged foreward, managing to catch Nora at the waist. Upon Ber catching her, she could not help but fall into a fit of laughter. Ber found himself laughing as well.

When Nora was pulled back up, they stood still for just a moment. They rested their arms on each other's shoulders, realizing they were out of breath. Their shoulders, usually tense from travel, seemed to soften. In this moment, the worries from months of travel, from years of pain, melted away. They held each other close.

The band's tempo picked up, and horns began to blare. Huan Jun with his large brass instrument, as well as the rest of the band shifted to a tune with more speed and swing.

Ber's eyes lit up. "Now *this* is something we can dance to!"

"As… as much fun as this was, we've some business to do. We need to find Alice and Viv."

Ber's eyes glinted up. "Looks like they found us first."

Alice literally twirled in alongside Viviane. The two seemed like absolute naturals to the event. Their steps followed one another in sync. If they were not criminals to the state, they would have fit in perfectly.

"Ber, Nor!" Alice sung, "Enjoying the festivities so far?"

"It's grand. I believe we have matters to discuss elsewhere now that we have Ber?" Nora asked.

Viviane shook her head, "Our best bet is right here. We're kind of surrounded."

"Oh no, guards?"

"No, drunks."

Nora looked around. Crowds of people sealed every exit. Watching their haphazard dancing was almost dizzying. It made Nora feel better about her own grace, at least.

"This works out, actually! The guards are around the perimeter, and the crowd's too dense for them to follow us," Alice said.

"With that said, we had an idea, in case of curious ears." Viviane said with the slightest smirk. Alice too grinned.

At the same time, Alice bowed to Nora, and Viviane to Ber. "May I have this dance?" The two said. Nora and Ber placed uncertain hands upon theirs, and they began to dance. Alice and Nora spun off, almost losing sight of Viviane and Ber.

"Don't worry, I'll give her back!" Alice called out.

Alice took the lead of Nora, picking up in speed and skill. Nora just hardly caught up and resorted to most of her moves becoming idle steps and turns. Alice's tassels and jewelry flew with her, catching the light like little stars. It was strange for Nora to see Alice in accessories that were not stolen. *Maybe they are.*

"You're taking this social event with people you hate awfully well," Nora noted.

"Glad it looks that way. I thought I would 'behave' until your business with my sister is done. Don't worry though, I have some tricks up my sleeve before the night is over."

Nora gave into a grin. "I thought so."

Alice held her hands and led her into a shuffling movement.

"So, here's the plan," Alice started, "I'm gonna help you try to find my sister. Chances are she's chatting it up with some snot-nosed nobles by the outer lounge. See this?" She flashes a wide, flirty smile.

"Y-yes?"

"*This* is fake. That's how fake you need to be when you talk to her. Can you do that?"

"Yes."

"Alright. Butter her up with some jokes and stories; casually ask for her to walk with you. I want to stress how important it is to try to get her as alone as possible. She can be quite... impressionable on her decisions around her advisors."

Alice twirled Nora, and brought her in close. "Do this right, and Maeve just might listen to you... Or maybe just have Ber do the talking. He's better at that."

Her eyes batted up to meet Nora's; something she realized Alice did not do much.

"You can do this. SWITCH!"

With a dizzying spin, Nora was handed to Viviane. Viviane's hand's wrapped around hers. She craned her neck back to Alice, now arm-in-arm with Ber.

"Enjoying the party, dear?" Viviane asked.

"I am, actually."

"That's great to hear, I know these things can be a little awkward." She looked up to Nora. Her smile seemed to warm the entire chamber. "Would you like to lead?"

"Viviane, this is my first time doing any of this. I'm not sure if that's a great idea..."

"It might be fun to try!" Viviane suggested. To this Nora gave into a nod.

Viviane led her hands into position. She allowed Nora to lead, taking careful steps. Viviane may not have stood out as a royal or with extravagant accessories, but she seemed to shine in her own way to the rest of the ball.

"So… what does the Queen plan to do with you after the party is over?" Nora asked.

"This palace may not be very just, but we will be fine. I'm sure they will keep us on the grounds until matters are settled… In the meantime, we will do everything we can to help your case, as well as ours." She smiled sadly, but picked up her tone. "As for speaking to the Queen, I suppose you need a few more pointers…"

Viviane continued, "She seems to be rather intrigued with Ber. While he should be the one to really win her over, you need to get to know her as well so she can trust you, too."

"What do I do?" Nora asked.

"How good are you at pretending that someone's past actions did not hurt you?"

"Very much so."

"Good— for this, anyway. Pretend you have nothing but respect for her, and get her to talk about herself."

"Got it."

Viviane brought Nora in closer. Her hold as always was warm and gentle. "Me and Alice may not always be able to help, but remember that you are not alone in this fight."

"That means a lot. Th-thank you."

Nora could feel her eyes get misty, and shook the feeling away. The last thing she needed was her makeup to run.

Viviane gave a little devious smile, "This goes without saying, but even if you want to be alone in this, you're too late. I like you way too much and you'll never be rid of me!"

Nora laughed, "The feeling's mutual."

"See you soon, dear. SWITCH!"

"Wait—!"

Once again, Nora spun to Alice. The Princess' hair went loose and wild, and she seemed sweatier than before.

"I am going to hurt Ber," Alice huffed.

"Why?"

"We made a competition and… long story short, he dipped me too far and threw out my back."

"Alice," Nora groaned, "we just got you out of a hospital. I'd rather not go back."

"You don't understand. When someone bets me on anything, I *have* to win."

Nora smirked, "But you didn't win, did you?"

"Fuck off."

The two passed by Viviane and Ber, the folds of their dress encircling each other as they danced. Alice and Ber exchanged a glance, and then a couple of rude gestures.

"My, how unladylike of me!" Alice mocked, and Nora laughed.

Alice and Nora continued their dance. Nora grew accustomed to Alice's quick pace. However, her finesse stayed much less elaborate than Alice's.

"I realized I forgot to mention Maeve's 'tagalongs.'" Alice said, "She is more often than not walking around with her advisors, the same pricks that make her so impressionable—and somehow more insufferable."

"It's odd to me. She seems so… self-accomplished," Nora said.

"She makes a great façade, doesn't she? Sure, she is well read, but under all that fake confidence is a child trying to be a ruler. Those advisors realize this, so they walk her through basically everything. It's been like that since we were kids."

Alice sighed, "They work directly under Parliament, and I assume none of them are particularly thrilled for us being here."

"Great." Nora said.

Alice gave an assuring pat. She pulled Nora in, and their spin felt faster. "If there's anything I've learned about my sister, it's that she can be swayed, if the conditions are right," She said.

With a stretch out across the dance floor, Alice twirled Nora back, dipping her low. She looked down to her and said, "Don't you worry your pretty little head, Nora. From what I've seen, it seems like you're already in good graces with the Queen."

She pulled Nora back up. A grin spread across Alice's face when she noticed that Nora's pointed ears dropped low, something Nora wished she had more control over. "You're a cute dance partner, but I think I'll be giving you back to Ber now."

With one last "SWITCH!," Alice and Viviane pushed Nora and Ber back together. Alice and Viviane once again took each other's hands. They spiraled around each other, and back into the crowd.

"What... *was* that just now?" Ber asked.

"Beats me, but I'm guessing they discussed how to see the Queen?" Ber nodded. "Then let's get going, it's going to take forever getting through this crowd."

Ber peered the room for an opening. Instead, he spotted Huan Jun, enthralled in the music as he performed a solo for the song's finale. "Wait right here, I got an idea."

He weaved by a few dancers towards the main stage. After the song, Huan Jun leaned in to pull Ber into a choke of a hug. Ber whispered in his ear, and a smile covered his face.

As Ber returned to Nora, Huan Jun got the attention of the ballroom floor. "Attention, my beautiful guests," Huan Jun began, "I just got a special request from a good friend. This smooth piece goes out to all you lovers out there!" The band began to play, their melody lulling soft and sweet.

"Ber, this is sweet, but—"

"Nor, watch!" Ber said. As the music slowed, so did the dancers. They spread out, creating paths away from the dance floor. "Now's our chance. Let's go find the Queen!"

Ber took Nora's hand as he led her through and out of the crowd.

—

Everything about Viviane never ceased to amaze Alice. From her calm disposition hiding her fiery interior, to her quick intuition, she could not shake the feeling. Hell, even her scheming tendencies outshined Alice's most times. It almost pissed her off.

To Viviane, Alice was absolutely exceptional. For someone who craved peace and stability, Alice was the exception. Alice was her key to chaos and adventure, and she enjoyed every minute.

They were lucky enough to avoid most pestering nobility for the evening. Alice, however, did not want to push her luck, so she took Viviane to the mezzanine to overlook the festivities. Viviane sprung an idea, escorting Alice to the "washroom." Guards were placed everywhere; they could not escape from responsibility, but she proved an expert in finding secluded places to rest.

Viviane took Alice to a hall, closed off for renovations. Swooning music could still be heard, muffled through the walls. Viviane took Alice's hand in hers.

They stayed hooked to each other in a dance they had done many times before. The two followed in time with the music, their movements complimenting each other's. Viviane led the dance this time, with one hand in Alice's, and the other rested at the small of her waist. She guided Alice across the hall in graceful turns and spins.

Viviane tilted her head. "You look like you are plotting. What's on your mind?"

"Just thinking…" Alice drifted, "… what our plan is for after this."

"After this dance?"

Alice shook her head, "After this party. They have us under such close surveillance. At least when I was behind bars, there were less eyes on me."

She continued, "So, I was thinking that we should try to clear our names—as much as we can, anyway."

"What an odd thing for you to say," Viviane paused, "… I see now, you want to help Nora and Ber."

"It's more than that. It's true that I don't give a rat's ass about conserving my reputation, let alone the family name. But I happen to live on this planet, so I'm not keen on having it destroyed."

Viviane smiled. She pulled Alice in just a bit closer. "You want them to listen to you."

Alice spoke quietly. "… Yes."

"Well, *I* am listening to you, Al. How would you like to do this?"

"We tell them everything."

"And when Parliament tries to twist our story…?"

"We twist 'em right back. I'm not turning a new leaf here."

Viviane sighed, "… I also have an idea, but you're going to hate it. I think you should have a talk with Maeve."

"No. Our last chat was… less than satisfactory. The one thing we agreed upon is how much we despise each other. In fact, I'm hoping to meet with Parliament while she is busy."

"Alice, I dislike her, too. But that does not mean she is not all bad news. She believes in fair trials, does she not?" Alice listened. "I'm not saying to make up with your sister. That, frankly, is impossible because she is terrible. But, I think it would not hurt to find some common ground."

Alice met Viviane's eyes, "I'll think about it."

Despite their best efforts, the two were found by straggler guests at the end of the hall. A small crowd began to gather, not bothering to be subtle in ogling the royal and her old servant. No doubt this gossip would spread city-wide.

"I believe we've caught some attention…" Viviane said, her voice almost shaky.

Alice cupped the side of her face. Barely above a whisper, she spoke, "I wouldn't be surprised if they were all looking at you."

Viviane's immediate blush turned to a fit of laughter, turned to downright cackling. Between her gasps for air, she said, "*That*—was so terrible! Even for you!"

Alice's smile cracked into laughter as well. "Don't call me out like that, I was trying to be *romantic!*"

Viviane continued to laugh. "'I wouldn't be surprised if they were all looking at yoooou!'" she mocked.

"You are such a dick!"

Alice took Viviane into a fast, spinning dance. The music brought the finale up into a dramatic crescendo, and the two spun faster. They took turns lifting each other in the air.

At that moment, Alice and Viviane did not care about the guests staring. They did not think about the Ball, or the Queen, or anything, aside from each other.

Alice and Viviane took turns stretching away from the other, only to pull back to the beat of the swooning strings. When Alice tried to pull Viviane back, Viviane pulled instead. Alice found herself in her soft arms, weak in her grasp. Viviane dipped Alice just slightly, falling into a tender kiss. Alice deepened the kiss, and everything else melted away. When Viviane pulled away, Alice ran out of breath. She restrained herself, despite how much she craved more.

Viviane straightened herself. Though her entire face flushed red, she spoke with certainty. "You took the first move. I just thought I should make it even."

Alice was uncontrollably giggling—actually *giggling*, while she held onto Viviane. Viviane did not fare much better, muffling her careless laughter as she tightened their embrace.

Viviane caught the stares from the guests. "Seems like we are making a scene..."

"Oh, I'll show 'em a scene," Alice mused, "I've realized that these pesky chandeliers are still mounted to the ceiling. We should fix that."

Alice shot her a devious grin, and with Viviane's nod, their fingers intertwined. Together they ran past the crowd, ready to start utter discord.

44

Chapter 44

Nora and Ber found Queen Maeve with much more company than they anticipated. She sat in a chaise lounge alongside her guests, and some older suited men Nora assumed were her advisors.

The Queen's gown made the her appearance alike to a perfect bust. Its sleeves rested off her shoulders, leaving them bare aside from delicate strings of diamonds across her neck. The delicate folds of her myrtle gown lay gently strewn from the lounge to the marble floor.

Before the two could discuss their plans for speaking to the Queen, she caught their gaze. She lifted and held the sides of her gown as she rushed over.

Her energy caught Ber and Nora off guard. "Sir Ber, Miss Nora! I was wondering when I would see you. Come, there are some guests that would love to meet you!"

Queen Maeve dragged them over to a group of guests, many unable to contain their excitement. The Queen spoke, "Ladies and gentlemen, it is my honor to introduce our most recent celebrity and guest, Sir Ber!"

Her guests cheered, raising their voices to ask Ber a series of questions. "How does it feel being the Queen's honored guest?" Asked one. "Are you disappointed about losing the Tournament?" Asked another. "What are your endeavors moving forward?"

Nora noticed Ber freezing up. She breathed in, brandishing a fake smile.

"You will have to excuse us. This is—is our first time at such an exciting event!"

The crown built up again into a small roar. "Who is this? Ber, is this your lover? Is this your agent?"

"This… *agent's* name is Nora," Nora said, swallowing her embarrassment, "and actually, we are here for you, your Majesty."

"Is that so? I'm flattered!" Queen Maeve gestured to them to sit beside her. "Allow me to introduce my advisors."

Nora's head spun as her and Ber were subject to the welcoming committee of men. Nora made a mental note to try to remember their names. *Ali, Barclay… Devon? No, Delvin.*

"Lastly, I'd like for you to meet my right hand man, Sir Jamesson."

A colorful man turned to the sound of his name, pouty, like he was already annoyed. Jamesson stood out like a gaudy jewel, clad in a violet, three-piece pinstripe suit and a dramatic pompadour hairstyle. Nora thought the most obnoxious hair she ever witnessed was when she first met Ber, but this took the stupid cake.

Jamesson did not hesitate to speak up, "'It's a pleasure,' and all that. Maeve, can we be done with this? I'm bored."

Shocked silence ran through the crowd, but Maeve seemed less than phased at this man's back talk. Instead, she shot a tired look that screamed "Shut up."

"He's right," Ber spoke up. The guest's heads turned, and Jamesson's brow rose. "We're all acquainted. Why don't we live it up while the night's still young?"

"*Exactly*, Ber! Come, sit!" The Queen beckoned. She grabbed the attention of a server for a round of drinks.

Nora and Ber complied, sitting across from the Queen. Nora's hand slid over Ber's arm under the cover of the table, and he felt like he could breathe again.

"So," Nora's voice broke. Now was not the time for her broken voice to cause issues. She cleared her throat, "I've heard about you, your Majesty. But to be blunt, I feel like I don't *know* you."

Maeve smiled, "Actually if you don't mind, I'd love to hear about you two. Coming to Saint Evedis only last month, traveling from who knows where, by fate or chance meeting my *sister...*" She met Ber's eyes, "I'd love to hear *your* story."

Nora watched Ber open his mouth. His expression was the same kind she had come to know well, that he would not stop talking for a long, long time. She assumed (or hoped) that she and Ber were briefed the same instructions by Alice, and that he would obey. *This could turn out good or very, very bad.* Nora took a drink.

—

That night, Nora learned Ber could spin a marvelous story of technical truths. It was true that he traveled from far away, seeing the 'wonders of the world.' It was true that she and Ber teamed up to fend themselves from the wilderness. It was true that they met up with Alice and Viviane after a botched kidnapping, and were able to hitch a ride towards Saint Evedis. But of course, Ber left a *lot* of such details out that would have had them imprisoned in an instant.

The Queen seemed enraptured in Ber, in more ways than one. She shifted from the back of the chaise to the edge of the seat.

"What did you do?"

"How does that even happen?"

"She did *what?!*"

Ber took his time to answer all her questions, and expertly obscured sensitive details. A monarch and her advisors did not need to know Ber was a step beyond a foreigner, or about Nora's *affliction,* after all.

The night drifted on and the drinks kept coming. Tales of grandeur turned to increasingly silly anecdotes, to which Ber had endless.

Something in Queen Maeve shifted over time, something Nora found difficult to pin as to what. *Was she getting bored? She can't be, with how she's been ogling Ber all night.*

The Queen clasped her hands together, "I could go for some fresh air. Ber, Nora, won't you join me?"

"Your Majesty," An older advisor said, the one Nora remembered to be

Mr. Reynolds, "Why don't you take an advisor and a guard with you? You can't be too careful."

"I suppose you're right… Jamesson, come along."

Reynolds smiled politely, but his eyes portrayed that was not how he wanted the conversation to go. Jamesson swung his long legs off the chaise and followed into the garden.

They strolled a well lit path along the outskirts of the garden. The path was narrow, so Nora and Jamesson walked behind Maeve and Ber. Upon getting up to walk, Nora realized how drunk she had become. Every step was like walking on a mix of air and moving ground. She looked to Ber, glad that he appeared to be holding his liquor better.

Attempting to sound sober, Nora spoke up, "Your Majesty, this is a pretty garden, especially when it's dark out!"

Whoops.

To her surprise, the Queen laughed, "I'll take that as a compliment, Miss Nora. All of the plants here are cultivated by yours truly."

Ber whistled low, "You've got talent!"

"You'll see I'm a woman of *many* talents, Ber."

What. The quip nearly took Nora out, and she tripped but caught herself. Jamesson caught her attention, and he quietly mimed vomiting at Maeve's words. Ber chuckled nervously. Nora could not break her promise to be his personal guard for the evening. She thought of something to break the tension.

"Your Majesty, I've been meaning to ask. Where is your Champion this evening?"

Before the Queen could answer Jamesson spoke up, "He took the cash prize and ducked out… But I saw he took an extra prize on his way out, and left to be dicked down by one of the Guard."

"Jamesson! Don't spread such inflammatory rumors."

"Not a rumor if it's true," Jamesson said, flashing a sharp smile.

At the very least, Nora was relieved by the news. Ber was severely electrocuted just days ago. She was not exactly keen on seeing the man, let alone warding him from Ber.

They stepped deeper into the garden. In the clearing sat a small tea table and some iron chairs. It felt secluded, but dimly illuminated by street lamps shining through the trees. The Queen gestured for her guests to sit.

"You and Nora have entertained me long enough, Master Ber. I believe I owe you some of my time. It's only fair I entertain you." The Queen said, "I am giving you five minutes."

Nora felt like her heart stopped. *Is she serious?* "B-but, you said earlier—"

The Queen hummed, "I'm feeling generous, maybe it's the wine. But I reserve no promises to act on the 'important news' you have to tell me. I'd hurry though, time's ticking."

Together, Nora and Ber told her everything— everything they could in that time, that is.

Queen Maeve listened, tapping her nails on her champagne flute that had been long since empty. Once they had finished, she tilted her head to look at them. It was a trait, Nora noticed, that she and Alice shared.

The Queen finally spoke, "… To your knowledge, is what you told me— everything you told me, the truth?"

"Yes," Ber answered.

"Listen. Both of you," The Queen began, "I expect you two are smart enough to know what you are getting yourselves into by giving this information to me."

"Yes," Both said.

"I cannot understate the repercussions for you if you were to be fabricating any detail in this alleged threat. Is there anything else you may want to add before I make up my mind on the matter?"

"Yes," Nora said, "Your Majesty, I have traveled very far and faced many dangers just for a council with you. Do with me what you will. If you take the time to investigate this, it will have all been worth it."

Queen Maeve paused, in shock of the quiet girl's boldness. In this brief moment, Nora realized how much she resembled Alice. They seemed so different, because of two, maybe three years separating her and her sister.

Despite his past demeanor, Nora could now understand why the Queen chose Jamesson to be the advisor by her side. He stood beside her, statuesque and unmoved from this information. She could not tell what he was thinking. Perhaps it was a good thing, for when Maeve wished to make up her own mind.

The Queen spoke, "… Alright. If I happen to have some spare time between now and my sister's court date, I will indulge in some research on the matter. Only if you agree to my past condition, of course."

Nora could feel her face lift. She wanted to say so much, but cut herself off. "Of course— Thank you, Your Majesty. You won't regret this."

Maeve mustered a faint smile, "I should hope so. Now if you will excuse me, I will be taking my leave. Have a good evening, you two."

Jamesson helped the Queen from her chair. Nora gave a deep bow, and Ber followed suit, offering once again their thanks. When Nora looked up again, the Queen and her advisor were gone.

After a moment, Ber looked over to Nora.

"… That—that worked? Did that just *work?!*"

Nora flashed a grin so wide, it hurt her cheeks, "Yes, I think it did!"

"Something went right! That doesn't happen much– we have to celebrate! I mean we *are* at a party," Ber rambled, "Wait, maybe we should go and tell Alice and Viv first—I don't know, I don't know! I didn't think we would get this far!"

The two gave into a fit of laughter that turned into cackles. Out of breath, Nora spoke, "No, no, you're right. We should find Alice and Viviane before anything."

Nora and Ber began to make the walk. At about the same time, they lost their balance. The alcohol was really hitting, now.

"Ber, just how much did you drink?"

"I don't know. I got nervous and kept taking them, so I lost count."

"… Yeah, me too."

"Alright, alright, change of plans. We find Alice and Viv, we cebelate while we do that—"

"Don't you mean 'celibate'?" Ber interrupted.

Nora snickered, "No, 'celibate' is what you're going to be if you keep acting a fool."

Ber flushed, his brows furrowed, "Once I get a dictionary in front of me, I just *know* I'm gonna be so mad…"

"Yes but shut up— and we *don't* take any more drinks. If we can't find them, we go back to our rooms and call it a night. Make a plan in the morning. Sound good?"

"… Yes, I think."

Despite being inebriated, weaving through the crowds became much easier as other guests left for the night. Huan Jun and his band left some time earlier, leaving the stage to a band playing low on string instruments.

Nora was thankful she did not stay by the table of nobles any longer. Her own body seemed controllable enough, but her words fell out of her mouth alarmingly often, sometimes against her own will.

"I just realized something." Ber began, "I don't think I've ever seen you drunk before. You're kinda floppy, an' it's—it's pretty funny!"

"First time for everything, yeah?"

A loud, static thumping filled the ballroom, followed by Alice's voice. "Is this thing on…? I'd to alert all guests and *maybe* a few nobles to evacuate the dance floor."

Nora and Ber craned their necks. This felt familiar. Atop a gaudy and unnecessarily large chandelier sat Alice, dagger in hand.

"Who's ready for this fucker to fall?!"

While some guests stared in fear, veterans of these events hooted and howled. As instructed, everyone fled to the adjacent chambers, watching in anticipation.

Alice cut a few cables, and then leapt to one of the theater-sized curtains. She rode the fabric down to a waiting Viviane, who hoisted the Princess away from the crime scene.

The rest of the cables suspending the chandelier snapped. Its mass dropped at the room's center, every crystal shattered, scattering across the room in all directions.

"Seems like we'll have to check in with them later," Nora said.

"Agreed," Ber said.

From afar, Ber caught the eyes of a few women and men. Aghast, one of them pointed to him, "Is that Master Ber?!"

Many heads turned in his direction. Ber had been lucky thus far not to have been terribly bothered by fanatics— he was not the true Champion, after all, and there were many more important figures there. But with the party thinning out, more attention trickled to him.

"Nor, remember how you said you'd be my bodyguard for tonight?" Ber asked, "I'll be cashing in that favor. Like, right now."

Guests came rushing over, and the two ran into the hall. *Where are the guards at a time like this?* Nora thought. Nora and Ber, dizzy from their drinks, had to pace themselves slower in fear of falling. After several lefts and rights, they lost track of where they were. Many of Ber's fanatics still followed close.

"Keep going. I got an idea to hold 'em off," Nora said.

She did not have to tell Ber twice. He kept running, knowing she could handle it.

She stopped, almost falling over with offset momentum. She pulled a couple of side tables towards her to blockade the guest's path.

She needed to intimidate the crowd, without doing anything too weird. Before Ber's fans could topple her, Nora pressed her palms against the walls. Her eyes emitted a faint glow as she puppeteered 'smoke' to creep along the wall. The lights flickered before dying out completely. *Whoops, too much.*

"You should probably turn back," Nora said simply.

They did not need to be told twice. Ber's pursuers scattered, screaming down the hall.

45

Chapter 45

Nora wandered forward until she found Ber. He sat upon the stones of a pond, fixing the wrinkles in his suit.

"Thought I'd find you around here somewhere," Nora offered Ber a bottle of wine she found abandoned in the hall, "I know I said to stop drinking for tonight, but you look rough after all that."

Ber gave his thanks with a mischievous grin. They sat together, finishing the remnants of the bottle under the dim lantern lights. Muffled music and chattering from the halls sung through the garden.

"Thank you for scaring those fanatics off. That was… unexpected," Ber said.

"I made a promise to protect you, didn't I?" Nora smiled. She glanced down at his uniform, now in tatters. "Did they still get to you?"

Ber leaned back into the grass. "Some got pretty close, but I'm alright." He looked over and smirked, "You're, eh, pretty intimidating in that uniform. It's no wonder they ran off."

Nora tucked a few stray locks behind her ear, "You think so? I hope I didn't scare those people too much…"

Ber shrugged. "They should be fine, I'd be surprised if any of them remember tonight. They all *reeked* of booze."

"We do, too. I'm not looking forward to the headache tomorrow…"

Together they sat in the moment, enjoying the quiet. Though perfectly manicured, there was a familiar comfort in sitting amongst the willows and elms, much like they did in their travels only the month before.

Nora found that along with her words, her body movements also seemed loose. Feeling the drowsiness set in, she rested her head on Ber's shoulder, snaking her arm beside his. If she was sober, she would have noticed his breath hitch at her touch.

The two took in the peace of the garden before deciding to sneak back into the dormitory wing. To prevent further encounters, Nora sent herself ahead to check the halls. The party was mostly over. At this point, most halls were left barren.

"I think I know why the Queen wants you," Nora said. Ber's face flushed even more so than with his prior drinks. "You are the governor's son to your city, are you not? I've also got— got a hunch you've been the center of events like this before. On top of all the fancy dancing and your— your getup, you're almost *princely!*"

Ber groaned.

"No, I'm serious! You mingled with nobility all night, everyone adores you—"

"I'm *not* a prince."

"Then tell me, were you next in line to be in charge?" Nora asked.

Ber blushed. "I- I wasn't necessarily *next* in line…"

"My point still stands!"

"Shut up!"

Nora gave into a deep bow, almost toppling herself over. "Forgive me, Your Highness, I forgot my place."

"Whose side are you on, anyway?"

Nora laughed, "I'm sorry, you're just so fun and easy to tease."

Ber smiled, "Now you see why I do it."

-

Nora walked Ber to his chamber door. They were lucky enough to not run into any more guests. Ber turned to Nora, but failed to speak.

He cleared his throat and started again, "… You know, it was pretty fun being someone different, even if it was only for tonight."

"It was," Nora said, "Talk to you tomorrow? That is, if we're not miserable."

"Of course." Ber closed the door behind him. Nora followed suit, shutting her own door down the hall and breathing a sigh of relief. She was finally able to rid herself of her costume.

Nora had a few buttons down her front when she heard knocking again at her door. She opened it again to find Ber. His eye contact faltered for a moment when he spoke.

"…It's been lonely having a room to myself. I was wondering if I could sleep in here with you…?"

"You may."

It was an easy decision. Since her separation from her friends, she struggled to sleep. It was odd to her now, that for so long she traveled alone.

Ber's face brightened and he thanked her. He sat beside Nora on the bed and clumsily pulled off his boots.

"I'm going to miss that look on you," Nora commented.

"Funny, I was going to say the same thing."

"Even if I'm 'stealing' your look?"

"Nah, not when you look so pretty—" Ber's pointed ears drooped low when he caught himself, "M-may I call you that? Pretty?"

Nora stopped from taking off her coat. She turned to Ber.

"You may," She said, "As long as you know what that means, alien boy."

"I do. It means gorgeous. Lovely. Beautiful."

Nore felt heat rise to her cheeks and her head spin. She tried to blame this and his honeyed words on the alcohol.

"It's late, and we're drunk. Maybe we should just go to bed, Ber."

"Whatever you want to do, *lodse*. I'll follow."

"And what is it that *you* want, exactly?" The words fell too quickly from Nora's mouth.

Ber was quiet for a moment. His pupils were blown wide, to the point they were more black than brown.

"… I'll take whatever I can get."

Nora did not know who closed the gap first. It did not matter. She felt the press of his soft lips on hers. The wine they shared lingered on his lips. She did not usually care much for wine, but now she chased the taste. Ber was gentle and sweet, and surprisingly graceful in his movements despite the lack of sobriety. It made Nora wonder just how much of his life she did not know.

Nora gave an inch, and Ber took a mile. His tongue teased the entrance of her mouth before slipping in. Nora slipped in her own tongue, much to Ber's delight. He groaned into it.

He playfully pushed Nora down on the bed. He straddled her at the hips, hovering over her as he dusted her face and neck in kisses. He made his way down the remaining buttons of her silk shirt. Nora's heart pounded, and she reciprocated the action.

Nora became lost in Ber's sweet words and wandering hands. Their limbs tangled together. His breasts pressed against hers. What she loved most, beyond his warm embrace and the nibbles at her long ears, was when his fingers intertwined with hers. A simple but sweet gesture. In this moment, it meant the world to her.

As sweet as their moment was, and as much as Nora wished to stay close to Ber, something in her screamed *stop*. She did not remember speaking it aloud, but she must have. Ber pulled away from kissing a trail down her chest, breaths hot and heavy, awaiting instruction. Such a sweet sight. But Nora could not take it.

"I… I don't want this," Nora panted, "Why don't I want this…?"

"That's alright. Did— did I do something wrong?"

"No— I like this. I like *you*, Ber. So why don't I want this?"

"I moved maybe too fast, I'm sorry, Nor."

"It's not that. You did nothing wrong. Hell, I loved *all* that, so why not— not… What's wrong with me…?"

"Nothing is wrong with you, Nora."

Nora tried to protest. She thought there was a lot wrong with her— her magic, her affliction, the fact this was not the first time this had happened, the fact she could not even be feminine enough for a damn dress.

"I like you for *you*, Nora. This does not mean that much to me, at the end of the day."

Nora sniffed, she did not remember when she started crying, "You don't mean that."

"I wouldn't lie about this kind of thing, Nor."

"Promise?" Nora said, her voice growing small.

"Of course. We can take a pause on this, if you want. I can head back to my room."

"Would you stay for the night? I— I don't think it's smart to continue… whatever this is, while we are in the palace, sweetheart," Nora said, "But for tonight, would you like to pretend for a little while longer?"

Ber shivered at being called 'sweetheart'— Should he have liked it that much? He cupped the side of her face gently with his hand as if holding something precious.

"Of course, *lodse*," Ber smirked, "Now, c'mere."

The two held each other close for the rest of the night. Nora meant to ask Ber what 'lodse' meant, but sleep took her and Ber before she remembered to ask.

46

Chapter 46

The following day passed in utter headache for Princess Alice. *No regrets...* She tried to tell herself through the pangs in her brain, through the thoughts she would be found out about the chandelier incident. At the very least, she got away with being fucked within an inch of her life in her sister's most beloved flower bed. She smiled. *No regrets.*

Still, Alice's childhood bedroom brought no comfort. In her youth, her chambers felt so vast, almost desolate. It was unnerving that now grown, the room felt the same. Unwilling to stay idle any longer, she got out of bed. She had already flipped through every old book and drawing in the room. She had smiled, seeing how every item in her old collection involved seafaring– even from a young age, she knew what she wanted.

At the very least, she was not totally alone. After being released from her cell she was reunited with Satya. Now the stoat sat on her chest, its little red whiskers tickling her chin. Like her, the beast could not sit still.

Alice heard a quiet sneeze from the other side of the door. The Queen stationed guards at the door and below her balcony. She had lowered security around Alice after gaining a shrivel of trust in her sister (if only she knew who was behind the chandelier incident). Still, it did not help that Alice still felt like a prisoner in her former home.

Alice considered the pair of guards below her. They were young– surely not wise enough to know the palace shortcuts, nor wise enough to know of Alice's tricks.

She slipped on an old favorite pair of boots and toed up and out of the balcony. Years of sidling roofs and ledges made her descent seamless and quiet. She slipped for just a second down the spout, its bronzed metal creaking under her weight. She looked over her shoulder– to her luck, neither guard noticed.

Slinking down to the bottom, Alice stood and stepped into the garden.

Like Alice's bedroom, nothing seemed changed since her last visit in childhood. Since the start of her involuntary visit home, she felt frozen, in a chapter of her life she preferred to forget.

She passed by ancient oaks and elms that were once her and Viviane's playground. She stopped at a bridge, masterfully woven from live vines and roots. Alice peered into the black stream below her, the same source where she first heard her aura sing in her veins. Its gentle waters reflected a portrait of herself. Her frame and face left a bitter taste on her tongue. No matter what, Alice could not shake the damning similarity of her and her parents, of her sister.

Finding the eerie silence insufferable, Alice paced off. *Anywhere but here.* On her way out the garden, familiar roses loomed over her. Its bundled twists and thorns left a phantom pain in her arm and chest. She paced faster.

Alice took the lift up to the top of a spire. *Maybe looking at scenery this is not that damned garden will help.* Multiple lifts were scattered across the palace, most of which Alice thought resembled dainty bird cages. She found the resemblance suiting.

The lift took an unexpected stop. The doors slid open to Queen Maeve. *Of course.*

Even to Alice, she was not used to her sister dressed down at all. The Queen was clad in a simple, silk night gown. She hitched her gown to step into the lift. Alice noticed she wore the same, old boots.

"Going down?" Maeve asked.

"No."

Maeve shrugged, and hitched a ride anyways. Alice broke the moment's silence in the lift.

"What are you doing up? Got an early morning meeting?"

"No, actually," Maeve said, "I haven't slept much lately…"

"Makes two of us."

"I looked into your case. I found your wanted posters."

"Hm. Which ones?"

"The pirate ones, you fool. I oversaw making the other one," Maeve said, "How did no one connect the dots? *Why* would you still go by Alice?!"

"… No one expected it?" Alice suggested. "Yeah, I fudged that when I got on the scene, but I just kinda winged it."

Maeve scoffed, "Stupid luck…"

A gentle creak resonated within the cabin. It rose to a screech, and the lift halted to a stop between two floors.

"No… No, no, no! Are you kidding me?!" Alice cried.

She leapt to the cabin doors to try to pry them open, but to no avail. Maeve sighed.

"Don't be so dramatic. It's happened before." The Queen pressed a button, ringing a bell. "Someone should be here soon… of course I have to be stuck with you, of all people."

"Hey, I was thinking the same thing!" Alice sneered.

Despite Maeve's words, Alice refused to stand still. Instead, she scoured the cabin for something to pry the doors open. Unsuccessful, she stretched her arms outside of the lift, trying to grasp any water within range. In her attempt, she only attained some dew from the walls.

"Will you stop that? You are making this incessant headache worse with all of your struggling."

Alice huffed, her arms hanging limp outside the lift. "I'm stopping. But not because you told me to."

They stood in silence for the better part of three minutes, until Maeve's own impatience took over. She too reached out of the cabin through the metal bars, trying to grasp nearby foliage. Even with her stronger aura, Maeve failed to grab anything of use. She cursed herself for not having her staff on hand.

Maeve turned to find her sister already sitting out their wait. She joined her on the mosaic floor of the cabin. Neither spoke for a while.

"So... you couldn't sleep either?" Maeve finally asked.

"I wouldn't give this place the credit of 'haunting' me, but it does have a bad air to it," Alice said.

There was a pause.

"You didn't have to leave, you know," Maeve said. Alice turned to face her. "You didn't have to leave. We could have worked this all out. But instead, you decided to go off and play pirate, while I took care of the kingdom."

"Do you not think I considered that? You always thought you were better than me, and so did everyone else." Alice's voice went shaky, but she found her tears had run dry. "It was *suffocating,* Maeve, and a thousand-fold more for Viv."

Another pause. Alice huffed, turning away to look out the cabin. Maeve knew if she went down that route about Viviane, she would lose he sister completely.

Maeve took her attention to the revealed scar along Alice's shoulder. Though shrunken and no longer coursing with toxins, the star-shaped mark still laid deep in her flesh, permanently branded to her shoulder and arm.

"I've been meaning to ask what happened to your arm," Maeve said, changing the subject.

Alice turned back to face Maeve again. "You don't know? Not a long story, really. Me and Viviane were hopping a garden wall, and a nasty thorn got me– struck me on the way out. It felt like a little sting at first, then I got deathly ill. If it weren't for Viv, and the other two 'guards' you're trying to recruit, I wouldn't be here." The Queen stayed quiet. "Always loved what you did with the garden, Maeve. Those protective roses I think were a sound choice."

Maeve was taken aback by her words. "Alice, I—"

"Hey, I'm just glad no one else got hurt in your fit of paranoia." Alice said, turning away.

A painful silence ensued between the two. The early morning's lament of whippoorwills began from deep within the garden.

Finally Maeve spoke, "Alice, I've come to realize over the years that you and I grew to become very different people. I realize now that no matter what power I possess, I would never be able to bring you back to your life before—" she felt herself stop, but pressed on, "And as your sister, no matter how distant we've become, I do not want to keep you here against your will…"

Alice looked to the Queen, her sister. Alice could tell that she wanted to say so much more, but fell short. Alice continued to listen.

"… But as your Queen I would advise you, I am unsure as to what the Court will say in your case. Just know I will do everything in my power to keep your trial fair."

It was not quite an apology. Alice figured, however, it was the closest she was ever going to get to one.

"Thank you, Maeve."

Having enough of the conversation, Alice took out a small flask. Where she pulled it from, Maeve had no clue. Regardless, they shared its contents.

"We've yet to find her family, you know," Alice said solemnly.

Maeve frowned. "I assumed so."

"You wouldn't know anything that might point us in the right direction, would you?"

"I promise, I don't," Maeve said, "It's so strange… How does a whole island go missing?"

"I mean it's not *missing,* but–" Alice stopped.

Maeve did not know. Maeve did not know anything that was occurring outside the city walls. She cursed herself for getting lost in her own feelings–how could she forget the whole reason she was here?

"Maeve, were you able to talk with Nora and Ber last night?"

"Yes, they had some outlandish claim about a 'fog' shrouding the countryside."

"… Maeve, there's a lot you need to know. I need to tell you what's all happened since—"

Before she could say anything more, Alice was interrupted by a team of guards and maintenance workers forcing open the cabin doors.

"Our sincerest apologies for the delay, your Majesty, your Highness. Are you two alright?" A guard asked.

"Yes, yes. We're fine." Maeve stood, straightening her gown. "Now if you will excuse me, I'd like to head back to my quarters."

Alice hesitated, but spoke up, "Maeve, about what's happened…"

The Queen turned and smiled at Alice. "I would prefer 'Your Majesty'… and it may be best if your information is held until court."

As she walked away, Maeve muttered something Alice could not hear. Alice read her lips, "Later, Alice."

"'Night, Maeve."

Equal parts numb and disappointed, Alice retired to her room, not that she had much choice in the matter with guards escorting her back. She fell onto her bed, praying, at least, the night's escapades were exhaustive enough to lull her into sleep. And it was.

47

Chapter 47

Following the ball, Nora and Ber signed the agreement to accept their role into the Saint Evedis Militia Academy. The morning for initiation came, and Nora rushed across the palace grounds to Central. She almost left Ber behind— leave it to the man to sleep in on an important day.

When they arrived, their jaws dropped. The colossal, gothic building towered far above them. Black spires stood so tall they threatened to pierce the heavens. Nora wondered if at some point this had been a place of worship long ago.

Ber whistled low, "This place is… big. You think it's bigger than the palace?"

"Vertically, maybe," Nora thought aloud.

Guards stood beside the entrance, a pair of massive, iron-braced doors. The interior was even more elegant than the outside; intricate arches lined the main hall and corridors. Nora wondered just how long it took to build the place.

A long-eared man sat behind the desk. He did a once over at Nora and Ber.

"You're Maeve's picks, I take it?"

"Yes, sir," Ber said.

"Very well, follow me."

The man then escorted them to Central's innermost courtyard.

"Her Majesty had your paperwork already sent through," The man explained. The courtyard was already full of initiates. "You will be assigned to Troop 409. An Officer will be addressing you all shortly."

Nora and Ber offered their thanks, and the man smiled and left. They filed in between rows and rows of soon-to-be-soldiers. Among the first things they noticed in the sea of recruits, was that these soldiers were older than other troops they had seen.

Like a wave, the rows stiffened into a straight posture. They caught on and proceeded to do the same. In came what they assumed was their Officer, along with a couple of high ranking officials. All was silent, save for the pounding boot heels. The pounding stopped in the dead center of their group.

Nora peeked from between a few heads to spot this woman. Though her eyes scanned the entirety of the group, Nora felt as though the woman's eyes pierced right through her. She was clad in a long, grey coat, decorated in numerous medals and cords. Though she stood upright and confident before her soldiers, her expression sported weariness and obvious disinterest, highlighted through her aged and scarred face.

The woman cleared her throat, "Attention. I want to welcome you to your first steps into duty. I am Lieutenant Amund. I will keep this brief— My Officers will conduct the bulk of your training, as well as process you through initiation. As for your more specialized training, I will teach you personally. May the Saint Evedis watch over you. I have faith that all of you can keep this city safe."

As Lieutenant Amund strode away, Nora observed her. Inside Nora something twinged. She figured she had seen the woman's portrait before, somewhere within the palace.

From a distance Nora heard indistinct shouts and commands. With a nudge from Ber, she realized she lost focus. Sticking close to Ber, she followed her fellow recruits towards initiation.

Ber kept walking. His entire body stiffened. Nora noticed his eyes turn glossy. She figured returning to a military force, even if it was 'voluntary,' was consuming him. Hidden in the chaos of moving bodies, Nora held onto his hand. He could not spare her a look, but he gave her an affirming squeeze.

They lined into compact files, leading to a few large buildings outside of the academy. There Nora and Ber separated. Both were given paper work, measured, and given training uniforms, a grey drab.

From there, their work was far from over. The entire troop endured a series of physical tests until well into the evening. Nora felt each of her muscles extend and contract further than they could handle.

As she scanned the other recruits, she realized, at least, she was not the most ill prepared. Nora thanked her ill circumstances of running from things trying to kill her for that. However, she was also far from the best in her group. This branch sported folk desperately wanting to prove themselves, and for good reason– training in the Inner Ring came to those who had connections, were excellent in their field, or were very, very lucky. In this crowd, her and Ber (more so Ber) were no longer considered "famous." Nora was grateful for that. She considered it would be best to stay where she was, average enough to not draw any attention, but efficient enough to not get kicked out.

One by one the recruits were dismissed for the day. Nora's legs quivered, threatening to give way. She counted herself lucky for lodging so close to the institute. Of course, staying at the palace will be a topic she kept to herself. Just outside waited Ber, already apart from his uniform. She approached him gingerly.

"Everything alright?" Nora asked.

"Of course. Nothing I haven't dealt with before."

Nora's eyes went to what remained of his hair, "What happened to this mess?"

She mussed out his hair, happy there was still some length at the top.

"Yeah, I asked for it. No more of the 'forest cretin' look for me!" Ber laughed, "… Do you like it?"

"Sure. I might miss the mess, though."

The walk back to the palace was quiet. Even Ber seemed too tired to speak up.

"How are you feeling?"

Nora knew it was a weighted question. She was patient with Ber to respond.

"I mean… I feel much better about this than last time I was drafted!" He managed a chuckle.

Nora gave a small smile, "I'm glad. I know what you went through can't be compared easily, but I'll take it as a good sign."

—

Nora and Ber parted for the evening. Nora closed the door to her room behind her, taking in a ragged breath. She tugged the buttons of her shirt to loosen the chafing grip around her neck.

She caught herself in the reflection of a vanity mirror, and she could hardly recognize herself. Her hair was kept in a once-tidy bun, and her face seemed thinner. A proper grey uniform and brand new, blister-wielding jackboots gave her a different form altogether.

Nora could not seem to remember the last time she looked in the mirror for this long. First, her hands, then her body. Again, and again. She searched the mirror, knowing she did not look like herself, but not fully knowing what she was supposed to look like, either.

She relented. She changed into night clothes and flopped onto the bed after a long shower. She did not even bother to move into the sheets before drifting into sleep.

—

Dawn rolled in much sooner than expected. Nora met Ber just outside of his door.

Before Nora could head off, Ber stopped her. "You forgot something." He latched a loose cord on her jacket to the underside of the lapel. Their eyes met for just a moment, a calm moment in the chaos.

"Well… Shall we?"

The morning crept along slowly. Nora and Ber were separated once more for various types of training. They now considered themselves lucky for yesterday's relative ease. This day served more than their fair share of physical labor.

After lunch, Nora and Ber were finally put together in their training. Nora sat on the courtyard steps, catching her breath from her exercises. She watched as it was Ber's turn for the same set.

Since she had grown accustomed to combat, Nora considered her skill at least comparable to Ber's. But now, looking at the way Ber eases his way through sets, she began to have doubts. He was focused, almost mechanical in his movements, as he sent his spar mates to the ground. She wondered if he had been holding back, or if this skill was subconsciously coming out in this environment.

It was no surprise when his drills drew in a crowd. Ber was as safe as he could be, Nora told herself, but it did not stop her thoughts from racing.

Nora scanned the crowd, before her eyes followed a rogue stone Ber kicked from his opponent's grip. Had she not followed the stone, she would have missed an onlooker. From the balcony of an old building stood a blonde woman, too far too recognize, staring not at Ber, but her.

<h1 style="text-align:center">48</h1>

Chapter 48

The weeks passed. Nora and Ber did not see much of Alice or Viviane, putting the two on edge. They did not know what was to come of Queen Maeve's 'investigation,' as she too became sparse.

Just as they grew accustomed to general training, Nora was pulled off the training grounds. When she arrived to a little meeting room, she was met with the same blonde woman from weeks prior. Dread sat in Nora's gut like a lead weight.

"Did I do something wrong?" Nora asked.

The woman chuckled at that, "Not that I'm aware of, Miss Dyr," She gestured to her to sit, "No, I will be conducting your magic check today."

"I actually wanted to ask about that, Officer…"

"Barras. Go ahead."

"Officer Barras, with all due respect, I offered administration my papers. Why would the academy need to check again?"

"Customs does as much to identify what each immigrant has. We test the type, efficacy and nature of your aura to ensure your best placement in the academy," Barras continued, "Her Majesty insisted on your placement in the Inner Ring Guard, but we run this test to determine your particular position."

"All right…"

Again, Nora handed her arm to the officer. Like before in Customs, her proctor produced her aura in smoke-like wisps. With Barras' free hand, she wrote the results. Then, her hand repositioned to sink her fingers further into her skin. Nora's aura began to change shape.

"What are you doing?"

"Miss Dyr, this is a standard part of the test."

Nora tried to remain calm. *In. Out. In–* Her tempo faltered as she watched in horror when her shadows twisted to a heavier state. Like a viscous liquid, the shadows crept along the table, staining its path in black. She wondered, uselessly, if she could still convince the officer it was smoke.

Then, Barras' grip dug *in*. Nora felt the intense flow of the officer's aura flow into her. Almost immediately the shadows poured everywhere. The room grew cold and black. Barras turned her attention to the lights that began to flicker and dampen.

This much attention, this much expulsion of Nora's magic made her crack. The circumstances were different, she tried to tell herself. But no reasoning could talk her down. Barras' tight grasp, Nora's loss of control, the spilling blackness, was all too familiar. All she could feel now were Selene's thin, wrinkled hands holding her magic in, readying 'bandages' to stop the flow.

She tore her arm away. Her arm turned pitch black as her budding claws dug into the table.

"ENOUGH."

Surely, Nora thought, she would receive disciplinary action for this. She did not care. Through teary eyes, she watched Barras pause her writing. Nora struggled to read what she was thinking. This was a beyond rare power, and this all was enough to elicit a stronger reaction than just a pair of raised brows and an annoyed expression.

"… We'll have to change your records from 'Smoke' to 'Shadow,'" Barras said plainly.

"What now?" Nora spat out, "Will you call the Guard? Put me away?"

"Watch yourself, Private. I understand you are emotional, but there is no need for all that."

Nora steeled herself. She reeled back to show no emotion. Under the table, she gripped her lap until her claws dug bruises into her legs.

"Here in the Guard, your aura and power can be a valuable asset, Miss Dyr." Barras gathered her papers and walked Nora to the door.

"Forgive me, Officer Barras. Most folk do not take well to a magic they have not seen before."

Barras waved her off, "I've dealt with worse, Dyr. It's not like I've never seen something like this before. Take a break. Take a breath, then finish up your drills for today."

Nora saluted as she was dismissed. She obeyed her orders, though still spiteful over the whole ordeal. She escaped to a washroom– not to 'control her emotions.' Leaning over the sink, she splashed cold water in her face, and let the water run over her taloned hands for a while. Eventually the talons and black receded, leaving slightly ashen skin that was at least within the realm of normalcy.

At the end of each day, Ber or Nora would wait for the other and walk back to the palace. This time she asked Ber not to wait up so she could make the walk alone.

"Is everything all right…?" Ber asked as Nora walked away. She knew Ber deserved an answer, but she could not bring herself to speak further.

She shut herself in her room. Nora thought for a long while. *Maybe Barras was right. Maybe I was too emotional about it all.* Despite this, she found herself sobbing into a clutched pillow. She was trapped again, and there was no flying away from this.

Nora eventually pulled herself off the bed. She washed off and changed into some clean clothes. She watched the dirt, sweat, and shadows spiral down the drain. As she changed, she replayed the conversation between her and Barras in her head, again and again.

She tried to rest but something Barras said drifted to the forefront of her mind. *I've dealt with worse, Dyr. It's not like I've never seen something like this before.*

Wait.

Nora shot up from bed. *What did she mean by* that? *Had she seen my aura before?* Nora sighed, *That's not possible– Maybe she meant other, rare powers?*

It was a logical answer. But the comment still ate at her mind.

Nora got to her feet– if anyone had a good answer about her aura, it would be Ber. She opened the door to find Ber already there, caught by surprise.

"Nora! I was just about to check on ya."

"Ber, my aura is not found here naturally, correct?"

Ber paused for a moment, "… Sorry, wasn't expecting that. That's correct– but Nor, what's going on?"

She looked down the hall before pulling Ber into her room, shutting the door.

"It's Barras," Nora said.

"The Officer?" Ber's eyes hardened, "Did she do something to you?"

"No– Well, yes, but it's not that. She tested me today, tried to reason with me, poorly," Nora said, "She said 'It's not like I've never seen something like this before.'"

"'Something like this,'" Ber repeated, "Could she be referring to just… weird powers in general?"

"That's what I thought, but… Is it possible there are others here like me?"

Ber searched his mind for the right answer where there was none. He spoke truthfully.

"It's possible. But the chances of that are very slim, Nor. It's almost unheard of, even where I'm from. I'm sorry I don't have a better answer for you," Ber said.

He paused, "Can we talk about what happened today?"

"I'm fine, Ber. Barras just went a little rough on me. I panicked, needed some alone time after that, that's all."

"Nora. Many folks get nervous on those tests. But you take them very poorly. Do you wonder why that is?"

Nora knew why. Hell, she told Ber about it just weeks ago. So why was it so hard to bring it up now?

"I know *why*," Nora said, "But it's not the most violent thing a wean can go through. I just have to… work on it."

"I don't think this is something where you can force yourself to get better."

"What do you suggest I do, then?!"

Nora turned her head away. She quickly wiped her eyes with the edge of her sleeve.

"… I don't want to be like this, Ber," She said, hardly above a whisper.

Ber delivered the truth, and he hated it. Nora deserved better than a half-baked answer.

"I don't know." Ber sat beside her on the bed. He offered his hand. Nora took it. "But we can figure it out."

Wordlessly, they shifted on the bed. Nora rested her head on Ber's shoulder, and Ber wrapped that arm around her. They stayed like that for a while. Nora sniffled quietly while she collected herself.

"… Have you eaten?" She asked.

Ber could not help but laugh, "Yes, Nor." He hoped his stomach would not betray his lie, "I assume you have."

"Of course. At the very least, I'm not the type that skips meals."

Laying there with Ber, the position felt familiar. The memory was not totally lost, though the specifics were foggy. Stumbling through the garden, a long talk, lips on her neck, her mouth. The man's surprisingly sharp teeth… She felt heat rise to her face. She was grateful her face was already red from crying.

Now was not the time to dwell on such frivolous things, Nora thought. But she could not help but wonder what Ber thought of that night.

Nora felt Ber beside her, his breaths slow and evened out from drifting to sleep. It did not take long for Nora to follow suit.

49

Chapter 49

It did not come as much of a surprise when both Nora and Ber received assignment letters so soon. Their letters read the same:

POST: Inner Ring

POSITION: Third Guard, Magic Class

Despite this change, Nora and Ber's days began to blend into one another. Their day started like many before. They crawled from their beds at the first hint of daylight, meeting each other in the hall and rushing across the courtyards to begin service.

Nora found their 'service' redundant, as their drills grew more and more monotonous. Their laps around the palace, strength training, and classes made their occasional 'shift' outside the palace feel like a field trip. The only drill that still proved to be entertaining was their sparring sessions. Something about jabbing a fist into one of the many pompous men in their class brought Nora some much needed relief. Even Ber seemed to ease up as the weeks went by.

As they performed their daily morning run around the palace, her mind began to drift. She made it a habit to try to search for Alice or Viviane, but to no avail. She wondered if somewhere in the towers, they could see her.

She leaned against the cool stone wall at the end of their lap. She chatted casually with her cohort, waiting for Ber to finish. She would laugh at how no matter what he tried, she was always a hair faster.

Ber hung around the final corner. Out of breath he asked, "How long were you waiting…?"

"Not long."

"Good."

"When you were taking your time around that corner, did you catch if the shifts were posted yet?"

"Yer hilarious, Nor," Ber said dryly, "I don't think so."

"If I get bank security one more time, I'm begging one of you to trade shifts with me," said one of their cohorts, Arc.

"Sure. Better than the private school– I didn't sign up to be a baby sitter…" Nora said.

"That's nothing, try the train station," Ber said, "Why does the Inner Ring act like they've never boarded a train before? And how do they get lost? The track's a *circle*!"

"Talking your team's ears off again, are we, Blødeks?" Officer Hare said. He laughed when Ber jumped out of his skin and into a stiff salute, and the others followed suit. "At *ease,* Saints, you lot are jumpy."

"Any news, sir?" Arc asked.

"You're not going out this week, if that's what you're wondering. Your troop's getting started on combat training with aura today."

They were gathered in the courtyard with the others in their troop. All other training had been pulled off the courtyard for the time, but it did not stop onlookers from staying for a free show.

It's the tournament all over again, and I'm in it, Nora dreaded.

They went down the list, picking randomly from the line to spar with nothing but their magic. First up was Arc and Declan, a classic fight between ice and fire.

Hare stood between them in their arena. "We're testing your team's strengths and weaknesses today. Give it your all, but I want a good, clean fight. Is that clear?"

"Yes, sir!" Arc and Declan said in unison.

Hare stepped away, and gave the signal to begin. Chaos broke out in an instant. Arc and Declan danced around each other, trying to outspeed the other and gain the upper hand. Even on the sidelines, Nora could feel the waves of cold, then intense heat.

The two were Evedan-grown. Eager to prove themselves skilled mages, eager to prove their worth in the Guard. Soon, the fire burned too hot. Arc could not keep up, and he too exerted his magic. He lost his ground, then lost his footing on his own ice.

Declan stumbled into victory. He had no more energy to burn. He knelt over his opponent, pinning Arc to the ground.

Hare called the match. Declan grinned, expecting praise, but instead was delivered criticism. Nora heard pieces from where she stood.

"Sloppy. Both of you… can't just rely on your hands. You have to use your whole body like a tool…"

Once he was done berating the two, Hare addressed the rest of the troop, "I expect you all to be watching and learning. I want to see improvement while we move down the list."

Next was Sera and Will, electricity and flora. Then Erin and Nikita, another fire and earth.

Finally it was Nora and Ber's turn. They stood, facing each other in the arena. He flashed a wicked grin Nora's way.

"I'm not going easy on ya just because we're friends, Nor."

"I'd hope not."

Hare gave the signal, and Ber came barreling towards her. He was easy enough to avoid. Nora knew him long enough that she predicted most moves.

Nora also knew his methods. Ber used catastrophic gusts of wind to knock her off her feet, and excessive clouds to blind her. But she knew she could not dance around him forever. She needed to find an out. She considered getting wiped out instantly. *I'm not a great actor...* She figured too, she'd rather not get reprimanded, or worse face some kind of inquisition. Hare snapped her out of her thoughts.

"Dyr! Quit messing around and get on the offensive!"

So many eyes on her. But she had to follow orders. Nora exhaled, and did what she had to do.

Nora spun her magic, expelling from her hands billows of 'smoke.' She did not truly know what getting on the offensive meant with her magic. She would rather not find out in this setting. Ber was trying to blind her. Nora figured she could do the same, but much more effectively. She struck her magic into the earth, let it grow, and ran straight into the storm.

Nora watched how in a split second Ber's face went from focused to dumbfounded. She adored it, catching him so off guard.

They began to truly spar, throwing wind and shade at each other in such close proximity.

"Coming out of the shell, are we?" Ber asked within breaths.

"A bit...!" Nora managed.

He smiled, he was having *fun* with this. She wondered if she was smiling, too.

Ber, having more practical training, still had the upper hand. At the least Nora learned that in a pinch, her magic could be used as a shield against his own. Nora would have time to wonder about that later. She used her shield to get even closer, make the shadows even darker.

He's experienced, but he's never dealt with this before. I could catch him off guard if I tried–

The dark cloud around the two dissipated. The mist still lingered, until Ber dropped it entirely. He watched someone approach from behind Nora, frozen. Before Nora could turn, she felt a hand land on her shoulder.

"Enough."

Nora craned her neck to find a tall, blonde woman. Lieutenant Amund. She was the same figure who made a brief appearance in her initiation, decorated in many, many cords.

Her dark eyes met Nora's, "Would you come with me for a minute?"

A command painted like a request. Nora did not know whether to be less or more afraid. She voted for the latter, and followed the Lieutenant.

—

Nora sat alone in the Lieutenant's office. It was decorated similar to the palace's many reading rooms, but notably devoid of any personal touches. She spent the time looking down from the partly drawn windows. She watched Lieutenant Amund berate Officer Hare, but more so the other Lieutenants. Nora took a chance, opening the window ajar to hear the dispute. Amund was yelling. "I expressly told you if… and you deliberately disobeyed my orders. Give a goddamn reason why you thought that was a good idea to… I don't care. You should have… Enough. I'm not done with you all. I will be finding you all again later today to discuss further. Clear your schedules because this is getting fixed TODAY."

The Lieutenant began marching back up to her office. Nora wondered where her fate would lie after this interaction. She was merely a guard-in-training, she was just following orders. *It doesn't matter. I'll be reprimanded for being involved.*

Nora wondered if she was put to death in Saint Evedis whether she would at least get a pretty gravestone. The door was unlocked. For a moment she considered making a break for it.

Lieutenant Amund rapped on the door before entering. She made a brief nod to Nora before setting her gaze out the window.

"Seems you gave everyone quite a show, Miss…"

She appeared calm. Too calm. Nora tried to relax, but only Saints knew how long until Lieutenant Amund blew up at her.

"Ní Dyr, Lieutenant Amund," She managed to answer, "Troop 409, Inner Ring Third Guard. Magic class."

Amund hummed, her tone remained neutral, "I don't usually hear that prefix to a name like that."

"I come from North Stromshire, Madam. Ghleanne."

"You've come a long way, Miss Ní Dyr. What brings you here?"

"I wanted to better serve my nation, Madam."

Lieutenant Amund hummed an acknowledgment. Nora knew she did not buy it. Nora figured (or hoped) it did not matter, it was the acceptable answer.

"Lieutenant Amund, if I may…?"

"Go ahead."

"Am I in trouble?"

"Looking at your options, you would either be reprimanded for not following orders, or be reprimanded for showing the magic given to you," Amund thought aloud, "No, you're not in trouble. Actually, I owe you an apology."

"An apology?"

"With onboarding so many recruits, I neglected my duty to review their papers. It is something I do personally for numerous reasons. Main one being so I may oversee magic training. Especially if we have a special case like yours."

Grand. I'm a "special case."

"Moving forward, I will be training you in magic personally," Amund said, "We will meet here every day, at dusk. Don't consider this change a promotion or special treatment, however."

"Yes, Madam."

"Furthermore, I'm pulling you from your shifts until we get your magic under control. Frankly, it's a mess. Chaotic."

"Yes, Madam…"

Lieutenant Amund finally paced away from the window and sat at her desk.

"Miss Ní Dyr," She said, facing Nora.

"Y-yes?"

"… That will be all."

Nora tried to search the Lieutenant's face. Was she going to say something more?

Regardless, Nora obeyed. She gave her superior a salute before closing the door behind her.

50

Chapter 50

Maeve started her day like most before. Outside her chamber, several maids exchanged pleasantries with her as they poured her morning tea. They exchanged small talk with their Queen while they brushed out her long, auburn hair.

An unexpected chill filled the air. She braved the cold to sit at her favorite balcony, overlooking her garden.

"A cold front this early in the year..?" Her maid said as a gust bellowed in, "Care for your coat, Your Majesty?"

"Please," The Queen observed the skyline of the city. Dense clouds cast the city in a violet shade. "It'll pass. Saint Evedis isn't known for agreeable weather, after all."

She shrugged into a hooded coat, cloaking her thin frame. Her wolverine came up from behind her. He put its blocky head in her hand before dashing ahead for their morning walk in the garden. Before leaving, Maeve was met with a disgruntled Jamesson. Strands of his usually primped hair hung low over his eyes.

Maeve's head tilted, "In a bad mood already, Jamesson? This might set a new record."

"It's f-fucking cold," Jamesson shivered, "Here's today's agenda."

He shakily handed the Queen a letter. Upon reading the letter, Maeve's brow creased.

"… Which advisor is this from?"

"Reynolds."

"I don't recall appointing Reynolds to make my agendas. This letter suggests I stay in and do busy work."

"You never appointed him in general," Jamesson said bluntly, "Anyway, why not do so? It's a *perfect* day to stay indoors."

You never appointed him in general. She knew this, but those words dwelled in Maeve's mind longer than she intended. She frowned, folding the letter and stowing it away in her coat pocket.

"Come along, Jamesson. We're going for a walk, and we've plans to discuss."

Jamesson turned, clenching his sides for warmth. *"We?!"*

"Is there another Jamesson, Jamesson?"

Jamesson huffed. He hailed for a spare coat and followed along.

He caught up with Maeve at a knoll of flower beds. Maeve set her staff aside, finding its power redundant for plants so small and fragile. She hovered a hand over the bed. She felt each flower as if they were connected to her. They stretched and breathed, though impossible to catch with an untrained eye.

Maeve could feel the bed as it began to cower from the cold. She pulled back her sleeve and breathed. In unison, the flowers sprung from their rest, growing taller and brighter.

"At least this bed is better than the last. It almost looks like…"

"Like a couple took an especially rowdy tumble?" Jamesson grinned.

"Saints help me if I catch whoever did this…"

"At least they got fertilized."

"Utterly vile, Jamesson."

Jamesson allowed Maeve to finish her work before riling her further. She spun her magic with graceful expertise. The bed sprung back to life, and shed a few broken leaves before new buds grew.

"So, I suspect you're not following that agenda today?" He asked.

"Correct," Maeve returned the letter to him, "Look for yourself– Answer nobility inconveniences, assess Inner Ring plights, *another* banquet…!"

"What are you doing instead?"

"As I see it, it seems like I have a light day of work. I will be doing some routine checkups on our broader offices. The Department of Trade, the Department of Defense, the city's representatives…"

Jamesson gave a loud sigh, "*Why* are you such a sucker for punishment?! You know that's well above my pay grade, right?"

"And you're aware that talking to me like that is a pay grade that doesn't even exist, right?" Maeve reminded.

Jamesson grinned. "But the thing is that you let me."

Maeve knew he was right, but she was not going to entertain him with a response. She finished patching up a weak sapling and turned to Jamesson.

"Anyway, I am well aware that your expertise lies within palace walls. You're finishing this walk with me, but you may stay in the palace today if you wish."

"Oh, thank the Saints."

"You sure you won't miss me today?"

"I'd miss you like I would this cold, your Majesty." Jamesson said, curling into his coat.

—

The Department of Trade made for a brief walk from the palace. As The Queen recalled, it had been almost a year since she took lessons in this building.

When she entered, every member's head turned. A woman rushed to her and bowed.

"Your Majesty! What an honor to see you!" She said, "My sincerest apologies for our surprise. We'd no word of your expected arrival. Would you care to speak to the Head of Trade?"

"I suppose I should have given notice. That is my fault," The Queen spoke, partially to herself, "I can return at a better time if preferred."

"Do not worry, Your Majesty. Mr. Hendricks would love to speak with you at any time!"

The woman led her down the hall to Mr. Hendrick's office. Even with Maeve's long gait, she found it difficult to keep up with her guide.

The woman opened an office door before Maeve could knock. Behind a cherry wood desk sat Mr. Hendricks, halting his progress in paperwork to wonder why the Queen was at his threshold.

"Miss Irving! What an unexpected surprise! Please, come in." He called.

"Good morning, Mr. Hendricks. I thought it was about time I did some routine checkups on some of the departments," Maeve said.

"Certainly a good idea, Miss Irving. Always a sound plan to brush up on your studies."

Mr. Hendricks began searching his manicured shelves for relevant reports. Maeve watched as her former mentor searched his office. In the year since their last meeting, Mr. Hendrick's hair had gone almost completely white. She considered his tone to be too informal for her taste. But in a way, it was almost refreshing that he treated her as a student rather than his superior.

"This goes beyond my studies, sir. My judgment needs to stretch beyond the walls of the city. In order to do so, I need to know Stromshire's current conditions."

Mr. Hendrick's eyes met hers, "Of course. My apologies, Miss Irving, I did not mean to offend." He did some further digging. He slid a stack of files across the table to Maeve. "These are my most recent reports on trade patterns between provinces."

They sat in mutual silence as Maeve reviewed the papers before her. With each page her confusion grew. Finally, she faced the paperwork toward her mentor and spread them across his table.

"Please correct me if I am wrong. I want a clear understanding," Maeve began, "Between all provinces—not just our own, trade has fallen. I'm sorry, but between our new routes and train systems this makes no sense. I established open door policies, and this is the result."

"We've found much of our struggles are from rising civil disputes, thus the blocking of trade routes. Those political topics, unfortunately, are out of my expertise. I cannot not tell you what the step should be, as much as I want to help you…" He carefully explained, "There are things in this line of work that are out of our control. I remember your mother and father inheriting similar concerns. They persevered, and so will you."

Maeve stood from her chair. Mr. Hendricks followed suit, shaking her hand. "Thank you, Mr. Hendricks. I have what I need to know. I will get to the bottom of this."

"I know you will, Maeve," Mr. Hendricks said, "Stay warm out there."

Maeve left Mr. Hendrick's office, now with more questions than answers. She paced to the Department of Defense at Central, papers clutched in hand. Maeve knew this reeked of suspicious business somewhere within her council, and she refused to rest until she found the source.

—

Unlike with Trade, Maeve could not even remember the last time she stepped foot in the Department of Defense. Defense was both a topic she did not consider fascinating nor was it pushed on her in her studies. 'A redundant study for an era of peace,' an advisor once told her. She could not remember which one.

The Queen strode across the Department's courtyard, its flawless elegance reminding her of her own garden. She marveled at the building's spires and architecture for just a brief moment. She felt peering eyes on her, and moved onward.

Upon her entrance, she caught the immediate attention of a clerk. "Y-your Majesty!" The man stammered, bowing so fast Maeve thought he was falling forward, "How may I help you?"

"At ease, sir," The words fell from Maeve's mouth with less cadence than normal, "I must speak with the Senior Lieutenant."

"Of course, Your Majesty. Come with me."

The clerk ushered Maeve up a series of stairs and halls. They caught Lieutenant Amund leaving her office, seemingly in a huff until she met eyes with the Queen.

"Lieutenant Amund," Maeve's guide saluted, "Her Majesty is here to speak with you."

The poor man looked like he was about to burst. Maeve could not blame him, unexpectedly being in the business of his superior's superior, and the actual Queen. Amund must have seen it, too, and dismissed him.

"… That will be all, Tore, I will take it from here."

The man saluted and excused himself from the room.

Amund raised an eyebrow to the unlikely presence of the Queen. Even at her position, she was not often visited by nobility.

"Queen Maeve, s'been a while. How can I be of service?" Amund asked.

Maeve analyzed the woman before her. Maeve was a lot smaller the last time she spent time around the Lieutenant. She considered that if she were not Queen, her nature would be much more intimidating.

But there was something on Amund's mind. It did not need Maeve's expertise to see it.

"Is everything all right, Lieutenant?"

"Yes, something came across my desk today I was not expecting… Personal matters. I won't bore you with the details."

"If you're sure…"

"Yes, Your Majesty. What can I help you with?"

She seemed happy to change the subject, and Maeve allowed it.

"It has come to my attention that we have been dealing with increasing civil disputes and blocked trade routes. I've come to troubleshoot and put an end to the matter."

The Lieutenant observed Queen Maeve. She had questions, but she left it be. "… Very well. Come with me."

She led Maeve into a windowless room. At its center sat a large, ancient war table, nowadays used for less violent means. Amund took a pointer and directed to several markers on the map.

"These are the routes that are currently inaccessible. Here, here, and here are where we've seen the most civil unrest."

Maeve studied the scattered marks scattered across the map, "These events, and the routes. Are they not directly correlated?"

"Correct. Though the unrest isn't helping economically, I'm sure."

Amund's affirmation raised more concerns to Maeve. "Pardon my bluntness, but what is stopping troops from stopping this little rebellion?" The Queen asked.

The Lieutenant shook her head. *Now* this *sounds awfully familiar.* "If only it were that easy," Amund mused, "The common folk do not take well to organized oppression. Despite my say against it, we have tried to silence them with military presence. And we have failed."

There was a pause.

"… Lieutenant Amund, if citizens are not the cause for the blocked routes, then what is?"

Amund's stone-like expression fell. She tilted her head, "Is… is this some kind of test?"

"I'm afraid I don't understand. Why would this be a test?" Maeve straightened herself. She grew tired of these games. "Amund, I am your Queen. When I ask you a question, I expect it to be answered with absolute honesty."

The Lieutenant took a moment to respond, not out of fear, but rather uncertainty. The time when she felt threatened by her superiors had *long* since passed.

Amund answered, "The truth is, we don't know. The troops my men have sent come back with all sorts of strange stories. Some say it's beasts, or criminals. Hell, I've heard spirits. One thing these stories all shared was talk about a wall of mist or fog."

Maeve's eyes widened. She retained her calm tone, "… A fog, you say?"

"Yes, Madam. I apologize for the miscommunication. As you know, the State established the 'All Sound' policy a few years before your reign, banning all officers from talk of potential threats not officially addressed by legislature. I figured this was some kind of test."

The Queen frowned. "No, Amund. I did *not* know of such a policy. Why was I not trusted with this information?"

"I don't know. And I'm afraid that is not my place to speak," Amund said.

"There's disloyalty in our system, and I *will* snuff it out," Maeve said, trying to even her tone, "Thank you for your honesty, Amund… I *can* trust you, can't I?"

Amund found her vulnerability in her voice a surprise, and almost off putting. "Think what you will, Maeve. Just know I've nothing to gain from lying to you," She stated plainly.

Before excusing herself, Maeve stopped herself. "One more thing. Exactly how long have you known of this 'fog?'"

"The first report was about a year ago. Legislature disregarded my pleas to address the concern…"

Queen Maeve forced a pensive smile, "I'll make it right."

With a solemn nod, Amund saw her Queen off.

—

Confusion and pent up rage stormed inside Maeve. She struggled to make sense of the information she was given, but fell short of any understanding.

Maeve took note of her interactions with Mr. Hendricks and Lieutenant Amund. She always took pride in proving one's dishonesty, but now she had doubts in her ability. She replayed the scenes with the two in her mind over and over again, desperate to find an abnormality in their body language, or perhaps how they spoke.

If what Amund and Mr. Hendricks was saying were true, how could her advisors hide such crucial information from her?

She considered that her rule was not as feared and respected as she had hoped. She also considered that her youth likely played a role in their disrespect. The youngest heiress to the throne in over a century must have raised some question to her rule, Maeve figured.

Maeve dreaded the thought of inferiority. After decades of peace that her parents ruled over, their early absence left a near impossible seat to fill. For just a moment, Maeve began to tremble. The Queen shook her head. *Now is not the time for weakness.* She carried on, hastening her steps back to the palace.

Unlike Central and the Department of Trade, Queen Maeve knew exactly where to find her advisors. She felt as her presence formed a wake of followers and whispers behind her. She ignored the pleasantries and questions from her servants and headed upstairs.

She found the two youngest first , catching the two between fits of laughter. "Cairn. Lenor. Come with me, we're having a mandatory meeting." They two exchanged looks and followed suit.

She found three more in the next room, Ali, Barclay, and Delvin, lounging beside their afternoon tea.

"Meeting, *now.*" They too followed.

Mr. Reynolds, her head advisor, had a history of being the hardest to flag down. *He is the only one that ever seems to do work,* she considered. Coming up empty, she accepted Reynold's absence and found an empty room for her discussion.

She was not even going to try to find Jamesson— despite being an advisor, he shaped his own role more into a domestic one, tending to palace needs. Still, Maeve knew he would not be exempt from her reckoning.

"I will make this brief," Queen Maeve began, "After checking up on a few of our departments, it seems that some information I have been given does not cohere to what I've been previously told."

Maeve spread the information she gathered across a table. Advisor Cairn was the first to speak up. "Your Majesty, you must be joking if you think we could read all this in a 'brief' meeting!"

"I don't expect you to read it all, I expect you to listen," Maeve answered, "Now, what I discovered is that—"

"Oh, Your Majesty, you must be mistaken!" Advisor Ali started, "Whatever you were told, I'm certain it was a lighthearted mistake. We've only told you the truth since your coronation."

The Queen approached Ali. She stood over him. "I expect you could be a more than capable judge as to whether or not this is some 'lighthearted mistake,' if you were to shut up and *listen.*"

With reluctance, Ali's agape mouth closed shut.

Maeve began once again, "I received concerning reports of blocked routes throughout the nation. Upon further investigation, it seems the common factor between every case is an unexplained fog." She looked across the table at her advisors, "Now, not only am I considering punishment options for not a single one of you alerting me of this phenomena, but also for hiding this 'All Sound' policy from me."

She felt heat in her chest as her temper began to rise. She forced down her rage, but certainly not all. "How *dare* you defy me like this? I've half a mind to terminate each and every one of you, and ensure I never see your faces in the Inner Ring again!"

The Queen evened herself. She resented such a display of distress, but she was at her wit's end. A lifetime of seeking fairness through sheer emotional neutrality and reliance on her advisors seemed to be for nothing, she thought.

Before anyone could answer Queen Maeve, she heard a small click from behind her. A smiling Mr. Reynolds, the absent member to her council, stood at the doorway. Maeve had a cluster of thoughts, mostly of anger, distress and almost relief, upon his arrival. However, all she could muster to say was "… I thought I locked that door."

"I spend an awful lot of time in these halls, Your Majesty. It's only sensible that I own a few keys to these rooms," Reynolds mused, "Speaking of which, it's a pleasant surprise to see you here, and you herded these hooligans into one room—I'm impressed!"

"Mr. Reynolds, thank the Saints you are here. Out of all of my so-called peers, I'm certain you can help me."

Mr. Reynolds walked towards a seat, unbothered by his compatriots' uncharacteristic silence. Maeve continued, explaining her discovery of the nation's blocked areas, of the civil unrest, and of the fog and threats associated with it. She remained careful to not name Amund or Mr. Hendricks for confidentiality's sake. She paced beside the table to steady her mind.

As she went through the details, her glances to the audience would catch their attention, catching them off guard in their obvious discomfort. Maeve's report was brought to an end, but she found herself speaking again.

She slammed her hands on the table. It shocked her advisors, and even herself, but it felt *good.* She spoke, "I want to know what I have done to lose your trust. I've done everything in my power since I could *walk* to please most of you here. You treated my parents with the utmost respect, while I stand here, struggling to get a fraction of your time. I deserve the same! What could possibly be the advantage of keeping me in the dark all these years?!"

Unless…? The thought hung in her mind. Every instinct in Maeve turned to something more sinister occurring within her council. *No,* she shook off the thought, *everything happens for a reason, there must be a logical reason behind all of this.* As always, she remained patient, awaiting the facts, awaiting her council's response.

Reynolds was the first to respond.

"Your Majesty, I understand your qualms, but there is so much more we must look at for the big picture. The civil disputes in Saint Evedis alone have taken so much of my time personally to sort, I've no time for troubles outside our walls."

"He's right, you know," Advisor Delvin added, "With the troubles in the city, it's important we investigate inward before we work on the rest of the nation."

Queen Maeve breathed in. There was no time for pleasantness. "You're wrong. That is not how you run a country. If someone is ill, a doctor does not merely focus on the head– they focus on the source. It is the same concept here."

Advisor Lenor piped in, "Your Majesty, I apologize, but I can't fathom the meaning behind all of this. Your council is making their best efforts to keep this city safe and under control. That is part of the reason for the 'All Sound' policy. It's the fact that—"

"I'll take it from here, Mr. Lenor." Mr. Reynolds interrupted.

To Maeve's relief, Mr. Reynolds stood to her side. "Maeve, you have my deepest apologies. For all of this. You did not deserve all of this pressure from our late King and Queen to fall upon your shoulders. In this political climate, we are *all* struggling. I can only imagine what you are going through."

Being called just 'Maeve' by Reynolds, or anyone aside from Alice and Jamesson for that matter, caught the Queen off guard. Regardless, she appreciated the sentiment.

Mr. Reynolds continued, "It's for this very reason that I highly advise you to cease investigation, and take care of yourself."

Queen Maeve blinked. She feigned ignorance to Reynold's words, tilting her head. "I'm—afraid I don't understand. What would you wish for me to do, if not to address these national threats?"

"I think your place would be to tend to the nobility," Mr. Reynolds said, still smiling. He placed a hand on Maeve's shoulder, and it took everything in her to not snap at him. "Living and taking care of the people, *your* people, in the Inner Ring, I think would best suit you."

"Alright, that's enough!" the Queen declared, partially to herself, "My *people* are the people of my nation, not just the nobility—and how *dare* you 'advise' me to learn my place within the walls?!" Queen Maeve breathed in. She dug her palms into the table with a heavy slam, her wild aura warping the wood at her fingertips. "I will not stand by as your little revolt continues any longer. I am having all of you incarcerated. Once the legal system has their way with you, I will personally make sure that you are all BANISHED FROM MY CITY."

"My Queen," Mr. Delvin spoke, his voice several pegs too calm and monotone for an enraged monarch, "I'm afraid you have it all wrong. You forget where our jurisdiction lies. I suggest you adhere to Reynold's advice."

As Maeve stood above her mutinous council, she considered for just a moment that, perhaps, violence was a viable solution.

"Guards!" She shouted. In no time at all, a small troop rushed in. "Arrest these men for treasonous intent. The next and last time I want to see their faces is in court."

The guards froze in place. Still and silent, they glanced at each other.

"What are you waiting for? Arrest them!"

"What they are waiting for, Your Majesty, is *my* command." Mr. Reynolds answered, "As Mr. Delvin explained, you forget where jurisdiction lies."

The head of the guards looked to Mr. Reynolds, "What will you wish us to do with Her Majesty, sire?"

"Certainly nothing too brash, though this… display, is a little too barbaric for my taste." Mr. Reynolds gestured to Maeve's aura, branching across the room in roots and vines. "Please escort Queen Maeve out of east wing, and ensure that she stays in the palace for the rest of the day."

Arms wrapped around her own. Her guards had never even touched her before. Such an unsolicited feeling caused her to jolt.

Within the hour, every lesson, every struggle for perfection and respect, every minute shared discussing and studying, every laugh shared with her advisors left Maeve with regret. She grew absent, looking within herself to find something that was truthful, that was *real*. Her title meant nothing, and it was all obscured by those she held close, perhaps closest. Losing her parents, then her sister, she understood now why she turned to books and politics and her advisors for comfort.

As she was taken away, she made eye contact with Mr. Reynolds. With one last look at the sly, greying man, Maeve changed her mind. Perhaps it wasn't *all* for nothing. *No time for weakness,* Maeve repeated.

"Hey, Reynolds!" Maeve shouted. She began to understand Alice's tendency to make a commotion. It felt *great*. "You and your little organization are going to regret this."

"I highly doubt it," Mr. Reynolds said passively, "What makes you so sure?"

"I think I'll adhere to Saint Evedis tradition and keep it a secret for a while. Let's just say I won't take your teachings for granted."

As the guards pulled her from the room, Maeve felt as her face curled into a grimace. "It seems I'll be taking my leave now. Thank you, gentlemen, and have a *great* day." With that, the Queen was discreetly escorted out of the east wing.

—

Queen Maeve paced the length of the palace halls. Passerby servants dared not get in her way as her heels echoed down the chambers.

Maeve knew her quickened pace was for nothing. Maeve feared if she did not occupy herself, she might do something she would regret. Pairs of guards stationed every exit she came across. Maeve laughed to herself. *Reynolds wasn't bluffing when he said he'd keep me inside.*

Her eyes came into focus upon seeing Jamesson, avidly rearranging flowers on a table. She wondered how long she had been on a rampage to have already made it to the end of the west wing.

Maeve grabbed Jamesson, shoving him against the wall. Jamesson's brow raised, "Maeve what the *fuck*? I was busy with something."

"Jamesson, I need a straight, honest answer out of you."

"What's this about?"

"Trust me when I say I really, *really* need an honest answer from you. *Please,* Robin."

Jamesson looked to his side. Maeve's hands shook—Strong, wise Queen Maeve was *shaking.* Jamesson swallowed. Something was terribly wrong.

"What is it you need to know?"

Maeve asked her loaded question. "What is the All Sound policy?"

Jamesson answered carefully, though he was unsure what she needed to hear. "The All Sound policy assures, eh, a noise ordinance is in place—"

Maeve's expression soured, "You're an awful liar. You will tell me what you know. Now."

"I- I don't know!" Jamesson panicked, "I don't know about that policy, I've never even heard of it! What's this all about?" Maeve eased off Jamesson; he was nervous, but it was clear to her he honestly did not know what she was talking about. "This is about Reynolds and his cronies, isn't it?"

Maeve said nothing. She slunk back, finding herself sinking into a chair. Copper strands of hair fell into her face from behind her ears.

She cursed under her breath, "Is *this* what I've blindly led our nation into? Is this what I've led my family name to, to be just some useless public figure?"

Jamesson walked away, but did not leave the room. "That doesn't matter now." Maeve turned, waiting to hear his justification. He returned with drinks in hand. "You know what does matter? Getting back at them. Make sure they regret what they've done, what they've done to *you.*"

Maeve took the drink. Such a kind and gentle offer from perhaps the Crown's boldest advisor. "While that's a sound plan and all, I am still subject to the law."

"You're a clever woman, Maeve. You and I are far too smart for this court of fools. We'll figure something out." He helped Maeve up to her feet. "But not tonight. I suspect Reynold's men are watching these halls like hawks.

"... What should I do now, then?" To this, Jamesson laughed.

"You're asking *me* what to do?! I feel like I should be flattered for you to finally be listening to me, but what you do next is your call."

He was right. Maeve remembered this was why she hired him years ago. Jamesson was not afraid to speak his mind, even if it made him unpopular with the others. Maeve straightened herself.

"… If you will excuse me, Jamesson, I've much work to do."

"You never give yourself much of a break, do you?"

She muttered a 'thank you' just loud enough for Jamesson to hear and left for her quarters. He was left alone, yet he could not help but wonder if Maeve would ever call him 'Robin' again.

51

Chapter 51

Nora walked through Central to Lieutenant Amund, alone. Amund had asked her to come by her office, rather than the training grounds. She rewound that afternoon's conversation with Ber in her head.

'This is great news!' He had said, 'Maybe with a little help from a specialist like the Lieutenant, it will help you understand your magic.' Nora smiled to herself. This could be the change she needed.

When Nora arrived, Lieutenant Amund's door was open. The Lieutenant was focusing on a dusty book. Her face looked more tired than usual. Nora stood at attention, but Amund waved it off.

"All that won't be necessary, Dyr."

Nora relaxed. "Is now still a good time, Lieutenant?"

"Good time as any…" She answered, putting the book aside.

She offered Nora water, but Nora declined. Even from across the table, Nora could smell the contents of the Lieutenant's mug. It was not coffee.

"… Close the door. There's something I need to tell you."

Nora obeyed.

"There is not exactly a good way to tell you this, so I will just… Try to say it. Were you wondering how I might train your shadow magic, if it is practically unheard of?"

"Yes, Madam…"

"Well wouldn't you know it, you found the second only person in the world who has it."

Amund merely stretched her neck, and the world around them darkened. Light peering through the blinds petered out, before Amund allowed it back in again.

Amund could see the shock in Nora's eyes. Their specialized vision cut through the shadows, a pair of dark eyes meeting the other.

"How… How is this possible?" Nora asked.

"Promise to keep a secret? You're not the only Ní Dyr, either. Though you can drop the 'Ní.'"

Nora squinted at "Lieutenant Amund." *Could we really be related?* She figured they shared some resemblance, namely in the eyes, sharing the same, colorless hue.

Nora's voice carried faster than her thoughts. "What are you to me?"

The Lieutenant took a sip from her mug, "… This might answer your question."

She presented to Nora an old letter, dated well over a decade ago. The old Ghleanne Post crest marked the front, alongside 'Return to sender.' Nora gingerly pulled the letter from the old envelope and read the contents:

My dearest Nora,

I can't believe my daughter already another year older! How have you been? I hope this letter finds you well. I'm sorry you had not received my last letter for your birthday, as it was returned to me multiple times. I figure I would try again.

I hope the ranch is doing well. I'm sure you are growing so tall by now— When I was your age, I was already at the shoulder of your grandmother!

There were pages more but Nora stopped reading. She felt sick. She had enough.

"Why… why now?"

"I know it's hard, but please understand—"

"Understand what? That you left your child for you to hide away in some castle?"

"Nora, it wasn't like that."

"Then tell me. Tell me exactly what happened. Tell me what led to you thinking it was best to leave your child with a-an incapable guardian in a town where she had to hide her entire life, like some little monster?!"

"It wasn't that easy! I cried for months and months. that my daughter would not have her mother, and that I could not bring you up how I wanted, but… but there is so much you don't know. So much you would not even believe."

This sounded familiar. Nora was not about to beat around the bush for answers.

"We're… You're not from Ibe, are you?"

Lieutenant 'Amund' looked at her daughter with wild eyes. She too had questions, but she owed her daughter more.

She spoke of a powerful man she dared to stand up against, one whom she once trusted. She fled to Ibe alongside folk she helped escape. But the man still found her, inflicting the first, brief occurrence of the fog and its monsters, the Night of Stormfire. Seeing an entire town turn to ash, she knew her daughter would not be safe as long as she was a target. She sent word to an old friend to take care of Nora.

"… After losing you, I came to realize I could never truly escape from Serkan, so I went to where I could be most helpful against his forces. For some time I was successful, despite this city's efforts to remain oblivious. Once I became a Lieutenant, I set as many orders as I could to protect against any upcoming forces while ensuring that our army could stay efficient," Amund said.

She continued, "As you know, with constant incoming threats we overexpended our reserves. Those above me forced my hand to recruit younger and younger soldiers… This is where I stand now, giving these children as much of a chance against danger as I can, while still being the monster who turns them into killing machines."

Lieutenant Amund exhaled. Her eyes were glassy.

"Nora. I do not ask you to forgive me, or to even ever see me as your mother. I understand that opportunity is long gone. What I do ask of you now is to tell me everything you know about the fog, and about Serkan's forces."

"… I have to go. But I will, later."

"I understand. I will be here, should you still take my offer on training."

Nora did not honor Lieutenant Amund with an answer. She descended the tower and took a walk.

Nora kept walking. She left the confines of Central, exiting the Inner Ring. She paced past the Middle and Outer Rings. She focused only on her steady pace, until she reached the gates of the city.

She did not carry her papers. A guard acknowledged her drab, granting her a paper for reentry. She had half a mind to tear it in two.

When she was out of sight and out of earshot of anyone around, she felt herself unravel. The shadows began to seep from her hands. She let them. The shadows drenched her upper arms, but its magic seeped further, until they saturated the vessels up her neck and to her face.

The shadows formed into a very familiar set of claws, and she gladly used them. She tore through the woods, through the brush, the grass, the earth. She ruined everything in her path and left a wake of deep, icy black.

In the midst of her rampage, she realized. These shadows, this magic, curse, whatever it was– it was given to her by her mother. It was her tie to that woman, and she could never escape it. She wanted to scream, so she did.

The ache turned into a deep, sharp pain. It did not stop her. Her screams meshed into a roar as her beast form took over. For once, she did not care. Maybe if she was a dumb, wild beast, this would hurt less.

She ran until her limbs threatened to give out from under her. Her rage granted her a second wind. She stood on her hind legs. She began to claw, tear, and slash at a tree. She kept going, chipping away at the bark and into the wood, until it finally gave way. It fell into the brush, and so did she.

Nora had calmed down enough to will her form back. She chose not to. She only rose from her resting spot when she heard something approach.

She breathed a sigh of relief when it was none other than her dragon. Lotte stepped forward, into the black clearing Nora made. She extended her head to Nora, and Nora met her halfway, resting her head on her snout. Even in this form, Lotte was still much bigger.

... I'm sorry, Nora managed to say. Sorry for being away for so long, sorry

for being a mess, sorry for making a mess– She hoped it would all translate.

Lotte moved away. She reared up, flapping her wings. Her magic was on the wings. It swept away the lesser shadows, and muted the rest until the damage was almost unnoticeable.

There is no need for that, little one. Except for maybe the tree.

The dragon curled around Nora. She shielded her from the world with a sprawled wing as she licked her face in an attempt to preen.

You're a mess.

Yes, I'm abundantly aware, Lotte.

Stay with me as long as you need.

Thank you. As much as I'd like to, I can't stay long.

I miss you. I miss our flights.

I do, too. This won't be forever. Though it's starting to feel that way.

Nora and Lotte stayed that way for a while. Nora shed her beast form. She traded her claws for hands. She took time brushing away her beast's old scales for new growth.

The sun dipped dangerously low in the horizon. It would be well after dark when she returned to the palace. Nora resigned herself to leaving the wilds, to leaving Lotte once more, but not before embracing her by the neck. The beast rested her head against her back, pushing her in closer.

—

When Nora returned, Ber was leaning by his door in their hall. She wondered how long he had been waiting.

"Everything all right? You were gone for a while..."

"... I don't want to lie to you, Ber. But I also don't want you to worry about me."

"I'm worried now."

"Sorry. Give me the night. I'll tell you everything in the morning."

"But... You'll be alright for tonight?"

"Of course. 'Saw Lotte today, so I feel better."

"Good, good... Goodnight, Nor."

Nora bid him a good night. She tried to sleep but sleep did not come.

52

Chapter 52

Moving forward, Nora made it her sworn duty to postpone the problem as long as she could. For once luck was on her side, as she was not on duty today.

She took advantage of her free day and went on the hunt to find Alice and Viviane. Spare for the rare passing in the hall, they had not talked much since their arrival. She went to retrieve Ber when she realized she forgot the promise she made last night.

Shit...

Nora was not ready for this conversation, but he needed to know. When she entered his room, Ber was leaning over the coffee table. His ear twitched to the click of the door.

"Nor! I was just about to get you."

"You brought me coffee?" Nora eyed the silver carafe on the table.

Ber shrugged. "Was grabbing myself something, but I figured I'd grab a lil extra for you. Don't think I was supposed to take the whole thing, though."

Nora thanked him and pulled up a seat. Ber watched as she dished out her cream and sugar– hardly enough, for his taste. She took a long sip. All misfortune aside, Nora stayed grateful the coffee here was damn good.

Another rap sounded on the door, and Alice and Viviane entered.

"'Hope we're not too late," Viviane said.

"No you're just in time!" Ber said.

Nora brought the two into a hug. "It's been too long. I've missed you, but I have to ask– is this safe, all of us gathered here? Aren't you both under watch?"

"Funny thing about that," Alice said, "Maeve loosened our leashes, quite a bit! Didn't get a reason, however."

"You should've asked her. She could be looking into the fog," Ber said, "Finally."

"I would, trust me, but she's made herself even more scarce. I didn't think it was possible, but here we are."

"If it's any consolation, Her Majesty would not have told us either way," Viviane said, "Now, I understand there's some... important news you wish to tell us?"

"Is this... Something you're ready to say, Nora?" Ber said gently.

"No. But I'd rather get it out of the way."

Without any further distraction, Nora told them everything. She explained the Amund's confrontation, the letter, and her mother's proposal. Ber remained quiet and listened, only halting the conversation to hand her a tissue.

"... It's funny," Nora said, "I'm not used to you being the quiet one. What are your thoughts?"

"That's a heavy burden, Nora, and I wish it wasn't yours to bear..." Ber tried to stay positive, "Still, I can't believe there's another person here from my world– and on our side, too!"

"I mean, she's not out to kill us, but I wouldn't jump to that conclusion."

"Will you be taking her up on her offer? I think you should."

"I don't want to, but I fear I have to."

Viviane spoke up, "I suppose it makes sense now, why the Lieutenant showed me compassion upon my onboarding."

"She did?"

Viviane nodded, "I was young. But by law, I still applied to the draft. I'm unsure how much say she had in my infantry release, but she helped me prepare for my interview in the palace."

"Are we talking about the same old hag that yelled at me for *accidentally* misplacing her weapons in the war room?" Alice asked, "No offense, Nor."

"Absolutely none taken."

"So… What will you do, Nora?" Viviane asked.

A loaded question, Nora knew this. The Lieutenant had the power to pull her from her duties, even pull her out of the Guard entirely. That would give her undivided attention to train.

It would be the logical course, Nora thought. But she was not going to do that. There was already word of Ber, and by extension Nora's 'special treatment.' She preferred not to feed into that. But if Nora put her feelings into the mix…

"The plan is business as usual. In the meantime of waiting for the Queen, I'll be doing what she wanted, and that is serving the Guard. If I happen to have some spare time, I *may* indulge the Lieutenant and attend a lesson or two."

Alice was the first to respond, "… You know, it might help to get with your mum to–"

"She's not my 'mum,' Alice!" Nora snapped, "… I'm sorry. This topic is not up for debate. This is my plan, and I will see it through."

After a beat, Viviane spoke up.

"I think we could all use a break. I know a spot, if you all are up for it."

"We gonna sneak out and go gambling?" Alice asked.

"No… But that *does* sound like a riot," Viviane mused, "Come with me, I have an idea."

—

They followed Viviane up numerous floors of the palace until they had to climb the service ladders to the roof. She instructed them to wait for her there. Reluctantly they agreed.

Before long, Nora, Ber, and Alice hear her slowly clamber back up. Slung over her shoulder was a large sack, so full she struggled to keep her balance on the ladder.

"You twit! I could have helped!" Alice fussed.

"Too late!"

She unfurled the sack into a large blanket. She began to set out its contents of fruits, pastries, and other stolen goods from the kitchen.

"A picnic on the roof?" Nora asked.

Viviane nodded, "Alice and I used to do this all the time. Besides, the guards never check the inner rooftops. It's hiding in plain sight!"

Ber flourishes a bottle with bright amber contents.

"Leave it to Ber to find the drinks," Nora laughed.

"What is it?" Ber asked.

"Mimosa. I think you'd really like it, actually."

Ber grinned, popping open the latch. He lined up the four champagne flutes Viviane miraculously smuggled without breaking, and poured to the brim.

The four stayed on the roof until the golden hour began to wane. They caught up after weeks of absence. Nora and Ber received an earful of crimes and general ill behavior Alice and Viviane had been up to around the palace. Nora and Ber's time was not nearly as joyful, though they shared their stories of drills gone wrong and suplexing newer recruits.

Nora joked and laughed for the first time in a while. Ber always carried himself like a carefree man, but Nora noticed that he too was finally unwinding. A genuine smile fit him much better than the one he plastered on.

Nora did not know what tomorrow would bring. So, she took note of this moment– Alice tucking in Viviane's stray, blonde curl, the ruby red rooftops of the city in the golden glow, Ber lazily tracing the clouds as he finishes the mimosa– and saved it in her mind.

53

Chapter 53

Against Nora's will, time marched forward. She spent her days ever acclimating to her new life that had become her work. She made a point to not meet with Lieutenant Amund as requested.

She can stay as mad as she wants, Nora speculated bitterly, *It was a request, not an order. All I need to focus on is staying in good graces with the Queen... Wherever the hell she is.*

Her thoughts clouded as she stepped along her route around the Inner Ring. It would help to stay more alert, she considered, but nothing of note ever happened here, anyway. But she knew it was a blessing. It was dull days like these her psyche needed most. Declan was assigned her partner for patrol. Unlike a certain traveling partner, Declan could find comfortability in the silence of their patrol. For that she was grateful.

Then, a firm hand grasped her shoulder from behind.

"Newbie! Look alive!" A deep voice bellowed.

Nora jumped out of her skin and whipped around so fast, she dizzied herself. Her head stopped spinning and she found Ber in front of her with that stupid, trademark grin. Her partner howled in laughter– he must have seen it coming. Bastard.

"... Asshole," Nora spat, "What are you doing here?"

"Bold. I'm at my post. I should be asking you," Ber said. He plucked the askew cap from Nora's head before setting it back squarely with a pat.

She had not realized her pace already led her back to the palace main gates. He stood in the same uniform as her, a heather grey outfit and simple cap. The brimless, wool cap became Nora's personal bane, as her curls, even when pinned up into a tight bun, made the garment off kilter within minutes of wearing. A golden trim signified their status of Inner Ring Guard. They were decorated with a single badge for rank as Privates.

"Same here, just doing our rounds…"

"Over and over… and over," Declan said, "Like a couple of mill ponies."

Ber laughed along, before asking, "… What's a pony?"

"Ha! Ber buddy, I love the commitment, but this ain't helping with the talk!"

"What 'talk?'"

Arc, Ber's counterpart on duty chimed in, "The Guard's dumb as bricks. In their defense, no one in their right mind would pick a career like this at the rate we're paid."

Nora nodded solemnly– the rumors have a point.

"Oh Saints, what is that…"

Around the turn came a *massive* caravan. Twenty-odd drafts were employed for the sheer size of the cargo. What the caravan was carrying, Nora could not comprehend. As it came closer to the gates, she saw flowers and decorations breaching the cargo. Practically every parcel was varying shades of purple.

"Easy! Easy…" Ber said to the drafts as they jostled to a halt. He pet the whiskered snout of one as he strode up to the driver. "Good afternoon, sir! May I see your identification?"

The driver obeyed. Ber pulled a ledger from his breast pocket, cross examining the information. Nora admitted herself impressed– his reading improved greatly since their last lesson.

"We're contracted to decorate as well, so we will be here for the night. Where do you want our horses once we're done unloading?" The driver asked.

"You'll just pull into that depot. We will board them from there."

"Thank ya kindly!" The driver tipped his hat to Ber and the rest of the guards as he passed through.

The guards rotated, giving Nora and Ber the temporary duty of escorting the cargo and horses. The stable hands finished the day's work, leaving the two alone with the beasts.

"Any idea why they're shipping loads of junk to the palace?"

"It didn't say in the shipment. Hell, it looked like decor for the whole city... Something wrong?"

Nora did not realize she had gone quiet for so long. She went to work situating the horses, all the while brooding. She could not help but think Maeve was prioritizing frivolous things over their plea.

"'Suppose I need some confirmation on this.'"

The stable hands were selected for their skill with Maeve's prized horses, but apparently not much more. They neglected to see the schedule for such large drafts being boarded. Nora spent some time securing extra feed. She gave each a pet on the nose for good measure. Ber eyed the extra amount of food and split the work.

From the open window of a stall Nora glimpsed some movement. Sidling around the horse to get a better view, she saw a woman straddling one of the side gates. She flagged Ber of the situation and they left the stable running.

"Madam, you are trespassing on the Crown's property– Get off that gate and state your purpose," Nora demanded.

The woman turned, her green eyes meeting Nora's. She repositioned herself, crossing her legs while facing the two.

"Well, glad I'm not trespassing, then."

"Alice?! What are you doing here?"

"I'm setting up recreational activities to boost equine morale," She said dryly, "I'm causing problems, what do you think I'm doing?"

Ber ran a hand through his hair, "I don't even know what paperwork to fill out if we apprehend *you,* so would you stop doing that?"

Alice chortled, "Wow, really? They should teach you that on day one. I got a bit of a track record here, if you haven't noticed."

Nora had an idea. She cleared her throat.

"Miss Irving. To avoid further persecution, I'll cut you a deal."

"Oh?"

"You tell us what we need to know, and maybe we never saw you," Nora winked.

Alice sighed, "Can't argue with that. I must uphold my status of law-abiding citizen, after all."

Alice followed Nora and Ber back to the stable. They closed the doors. A soft, metallic jingle came from Alice with every step. Her hands stayed in her dress pockets.

"Alright. What's this about?" Nora gestured to her pockets.

"Wait, am I actually in trouble?" Alice chuckled.

"Depends on the answer."

"Ah, you're no fun. I was unscrewing." Alice revealed the contents of her pockets, a handful of screws and a screwdriver.

"Why...?"

"Maeve's ponies run that side of the paddock. Maybe it'd be fun to watch a few get loose."

"Right," Nora took the screws awkwardly in hand. With nowhere to put them, she stowed them in a spare feed bucket. "Now, what's going on with the caravans of purple shit coming to the palace?"

Alice looked confused for a moment for finding clarity, "Ohh, you mean Plum Day. Forgot it's that time of year, again."

Nora breathed in, "...Alice. What. Praytell. Is Plum Day."

"Like, years ago. My great Nan, said in passing her favorite fruit when traveling Rinesant were the plums. Things escalated to the point where we have a holiday, if you can call it that."

"Would Her Majesty be in charge of something like that, by chance?"

"Certainly. Though, its really just to consult aesthetics, then decorating the palace. Why do you ask?"

Nora hummed, "Just curious. You're free to go, 'citizen.'"

"What, you don't want to grab a bite or somethin'?"

"We're sort of on the clock, remember?" Ber chuckled, "But tell Viv we miss her!"

Like that, Alice snuck back out again. The two finished their respective duties for the evening. Nora kept the conversation brewing in her mind. Was the Queen ignoring her? Was this her life indefinitely?

Later, Ber noticed Nora was nowhere to be seen. He hunted for her and found her in the training room. Her knuckles were bound in protective bandages. In complete focus, she pummeled away on a miserable looking decoy.

"Nora, are you alright?" He asked.

"Yeah— why?" Nora grunted in between punches.

Ber did not want to be in between Nora and her subtle but obvious rage. He chose his words carefully.

"I was just checking… Let me know if ya need something."

Nora's hands, soaked in black aura, clenched and took two more swings at the decoy before turning to Ber.

"You want to know what my problem is?" Ber swallowed, struggling to maintain eye contact. "This whole damn city is my problem! You nearly die in the final tournament and the only action even vaguely in our favor was that we were made into Maeve's dogs. We had one request, and we are put on the back burner until Saints know when!" Nora huffed. Her throat turned hoarse from her raised voice. She continued on.

"Alice was right. I thought we would be speaking to responsible and rational individuals, but no. We are dealing with folks who are more concerned with their personal tastes for aesthetics than the lives of anyone around them!"

She turned to take a final swing to the decoy before storming off. "Do me a favor, Ber, and blow that bitch's doors down."

—

Ber wanted to blow that bitch's door down. He should have known, however, that guards would be anywhere the Queen was. He did not have an appointment. He did not need one. Nora made a point– they had been waiting too long, and they had grown complicit.

In the deepest part of himself, Ber knew what stoked the flame especially hot– he loathed to see Nora upset. He strode to the door, of course to be stopped by the guards.

"Whoa there, Blødeks. Got an appointment?"

"Piss off, Noel. I wouldn't be here if it wasn't important," Ber sighed. He came on too hard, but he needed in.

Noel and the other guard, Holly, looked at each other before addressing Ber, "Her Majesty's personal Guard aren't as friendly. You know that."

"I'm aware."

Noel finally shrugged, "Your funeral."

He and Holly stepped aside. Ber entered the throne room to be immediately met with halberds, much sharper than his own.

"Saints, what now...? Jamesson, see who that is for me?"

"Sure."

The smaller man pushed his way between the guards. He gave Ber a once over.

"It's just your almost-Champion."

"Master Ber!"

As quick as they intercepted Ber, the guards stepped aside. Maeve grabbed his hand, practically pulling him in. She gestured to take a seat, but he stood his ground.

"Your Majesty, forgive my intrusion, I–"

"How are you liking your accommodations? I hope you are enjoying what the Academy has to offer. I see they have been treating you well..."

Maeve stepped around Ber. Even from behind, he felt her eyes on his body.

"I apologize for my intrusion, Your Majesty. But I must speak with you."

The Queen sighed, a tad too dramatically even for her usual, "I suppose this is for business rather than pleasure, then?"

"I'm afraid so."

"Pity. Maybe we can compromise?" She rested a hand on his arm, "Have a bit of both?"

She dismissed her clergy. Ber did not need to focus on Robin to see his face retort as he left the room. They were in 'private,' but Ber knew better than to test that. In her heeled boots, Maeve stood a tad taller than Ber.

She slid her hand up to his shoulder, brushing an adventurous thumb over his collarbone.

"… Is this a test?" Ber blurted.

The Queen *giggled.* A sweet disposition in theory, but Ber found it terrifying. She leaned in for a whisper. Her lips grazed his ear.

"I'm sorry to use you like this, Master Ber. It's the most surefire way to ensure I don't have an audience."

She dropped her hand, easing back. She was still too close, for Ber's liking.

"Your Majesty," He started, "I apologize for coming to you unannounced. However, I must insist on the urgency of the matter we discussed at the Ball."

"You sound just so funny! It's cute," Maeve said, "Where did you say you were from, again?"

"Far, far away."

The room was cold. Why was he sweating?

"You know, I have watched a training or two since your onboarding. Your moves are astounding… Hypnotic…" Maeve said, "Perhaps you can show me those moves sometime. Maybe a private lesson?"

"Your Majesty, I–"

"I must warn you, though. I'm a powerful magician, myself."

He thought she was holding him again, but when he looked down, he found a vine creeping up his arm. With the vine, she pulled him in again.

"I've run into a few hurdles. I'm working on it," Maeve whispered, "I'm… sorry, for not looking into it earlier."

Ber knew the game, now. He cupped her cheek, "Thank you, Your Majesty. I admit, this is a smart decoy."

"You could call it that…"

Before Ber could ask what she meant, The Queen dismissed him. He knew better than to push his luck. With the information he needed, and made sufficiently red in the cheeks, he left the throne room.

Chapter 54

Ber informed Nora of the news… omitting a few details of the meeting. Nora did not know how to respond. Relief, impatience, happiness, and a few things she could not pinpoint the feeling, felt like they clashed in the doorway of her heart. In the end, she just chose to pull Ber into an embrace to thank him.

The two did not have time to inform Alice and Viviane or celebrate-tomorrow was a work day, after all, and it was getting late.

The following day, Ber and Nora were stationed to patrol the Inner Ring. The two tended to not be scheduled together often. But with the bitter cold morning in a strange city, an ounce of familiarity was appreciated.

The morning proved to be slow. A handful of lost merchants, a lost kid, a breakfast break with a generous 'Guard discount' all broke up the monotony.

Ber laughed at Nora. She struggled to wipe the snot off her sleeve from the kid from earlier. The brat insisted on inflicting a vice grip on Nora's sleeve, that wrinkled the ruined fabric.

Nora tossed another ruined napkin in the trash, "Not funny, Ber. What if we have a dress code check today?"

"Officer Hare's got kids. Pretty sure he will understand."

"Knowing my luck, that wean's probably got diseases… You hear that?"

The quiet morning broke with the sound of sirens. It sounded by the border of the Middle Ring. The two dropped everything and ran to the source.

They found themselves at a good vantage point on one of the city's many bridges. Crocodile dogs were chasing a man, and other guards were in tow. Nora figured she could flank the fugitive if she was fast enough. Ber must have had the same idea, so the two ran.

The beasts did not sound like they were getting closer, but a few guards were drawing closer from above. The man must have escaped by the roof.

"Ber, give me a boost!"

Ber did not need to be told twice. Nora stepped onto his threaded palms and blasted Nora up to the rooftop with his magic. Nora hardly landed on her feet but she hit the ground running.

To her surprise her plan actually worked. The man was caught off guard when she tackled him from the side.

"Please let me go, there has been a mistake!" The man cried.

His accent was thick, so Nora had to strain her ears to understand. At the least, the man did not try to struggle once he was in her grasp.

"If that's the case you really shouldn't be running from the Guard, mate," Nora said.

"Th-there were beasts after me!"

"Fair point. What happened?"

"I-I had an interview— a servant job at one of the estates. I must have gotten the wrong one."

At this point the other guards were already upon them. The bulk of the the guards were Middle Ring guards, so Nora was unfamiliar. One of them relieved Nora of the man, pinning him with ice to search his belongings. They found nothing.

"It burns, please, I'm not magic!"

Nora swallowed. She remembered something sliding away when she tackled him. Sure enough, she found his wallet in the gutter. Turning back to the scene one of the Middle Ring officers arrived, and so did Ber. The man tried to explain his story, but the officer was not having any part of it.

"Here's how I see it," The officer said, "You infringed on Inner Ring grounds without proof of purpose, you trespassed on private property, and you lack any proper documentation. You will be taken back to Customs, and enforcement will take you from there."

There was pure terror in the man's eyes. Nora knew enforcement on 'non citizens' was intense, but this...

"Sir," Nora presented the man's wallet, "I found his identification."

Nora read 'Doubek' on the officer's badge before meeting eyes with him. He looked down at her. He smiled, then pushed the wallet back towards her.

"Thank you, palace girl, but Middle Ring will take it from here."

Nora ignored the dig, "S-Sir—"

"We found this man with no identification. As you should know, that is a punishable offense in these times. We don't want word of your subordinance getting back to Officer Hare, would we?"

The sick man had a sick point. But why would he not just take the wallet? Nora could not risk all her work for her cause to be for nothing, but this not nothing. Nora chose to do something that felt morbidly wrong, something that would curse her thoughts for a long, long time. She complied.

Nora looked away from Officer Doubek as she spoke, "No, sir."

The scene cleared up as soon as it was made. The Middle Ring Guard followed alongside Officer Doubek, leaving Ber and Nora on the rooftops with a 'lost' wallet. Nora dug her nails into the leather. They did not have the clearance to follow the suspect to Customs. This left Nora with the hope Customs did what they do best, and take a long time processing the man.

As soon as they could, Nora and Ber rushed to Customs with the wallet. Being members of the Guard, they were able to give the wallet over with no hassle, though the clerks did not give them any information on the matter. At the very least, it was in the right hands (she hoped).

"Nora," Ber said some distance from Customs, "*This* is why I left— part of the reason, anyways. You become a tool for things you swore to prevent. This is why I did not want it to get to this, to get you involved."

"I understand."

"I'm so sorry, Nor."

"I chose this. Don't apologize."

—

The following day, they heard a knock at the door. Despite Officer Doubek's words, word still got around that Nora and Ber were involved in yesterday's events. Nora expected more officer inquiries, but found Lieutenant Amund stepping in instead.

"I understand you had an eventful day."

"Yes…" Nora said carefully.

Amund tilted her head at Ber, who's expression mimicked that of a stunned deer. He was already at his feet in salute.

"Who are you?" Amund asked, monotone.

"Private Blødeks, Madam."

"At *ease,* Blødeks. Good grief," Amund looked to Nora, "I've come to insist again on training with me. People will start asking questions if you're the only Magic Class guard not adept in magic."

"People will talk either way. Is this an order?"

"No."

Nora did not want to take her offer. But it was not about what *she* wanted. It never was. Still, the smallest voice inside Nora appreciated her mother for still making it a choice.

"… Fine. When do we start?"

"Tomorrow at dusk will be fine. Meet me in the courtyard. Your Ebian friend will come after our exercise is complete."

Ber's ears dropped *low.* "L-Lieutenant Amund–"

"*Susta,* Blødeks… " Amund spoke briefly to him, in words Nora could not understand, "… Seriously, neither of you thought of fudging different last names?" Amund did not wait for an answer. "I'll see you both tomorrow."

55

Chapter 55

Ber and Nora were kept in palace walls for their shift the next day. With the investigation ongoing, Nora figured it reasonable, and a relief.

That evening, Nora showed up where Lieutenant Amund requested. She stomped out her cigarette upon her arrival.

Nora tried to read the Lieutenant. Similar to herself, she proved hard to read. All she could gleam was a sense of weariness.

"… Let's get started," Amund said.

She stepped into the center of the rotunda. She began to weave her magic.

"Is this safe to do out here?" Nora asked.

"There's no other place to do it," Amund said, "If you're worried about 'being seen,' nothing's going to happen with me around."

Nora nodded. Her words were almost comforting, but the feeling left her bitter. She shook off her thoughts and watched Amund's demonstration.

Nora understood now why the Lieutenant chose to meet at dusk. In the day's waning light, the shadows stretched. Amund stretched them further, gathering the power into her own.

The performance was familiar to when Officer Barras tested her briefly after initiation. Her magic shifted like states of matter– from a gaseous smoke Nora was familiar with, to liquid, then solid. A couple of training dummies were left out from earlier drills. Amund mowed one down with her magic, almost like a blade. She heaved the large, crafted weapon over her head with ease. In a single, swift movement, she staked her power into the ground. It produced a shockwave of shadows, Nora blinked the darkness and chill away, and for a moment, swore she had seen colors in the black. When she was able to see again, she saw Amund's weapon lodged in what was left of the dummy, a large, beautifully sharp shield, stapling the chest into the earth like a massive spade.

"… This is what you will learn from me, and more," Lieutenant Amund said, "You think this magic is a curse– and it can be. But it doesn't have to be. It is what you make of it."

Nora examined the shield before her. Its form was a flawless black, emanating its gaseous aura. She touched the shield, and its form began to dissipate, until there was no trace of her shadows save for a demolished dummy. Amund appeared from behind the disappearing shadows.

Nora could handle the unwanted company for a while longer. She wanted to learn these skills, maybe then her abilities would not be so unreliable.

Amund stepped aside, gesturing Nora to the center. It was her turn. She held a hand out, waiting for the magic to seep through. But nothing came. She turned from her mother and focused, and that did the trick.

Amund brought over the second dummy. She and Nora locked eyes for a moment, and Nora saw the hint of a smile on her face. She could not bring herself to do the same.

"Now Nora, show me what you've got."

—

Ber made his way to the courtyard as instructed after his shift. He did not know what to think, other than to overthink. Lieutenant Amund spoke to him in Ebian– the first to do so in *months*. That, coupled with her intimidating demeanor and being a *Lieutenant*, made Ber terrified.

Regardless, he pressed on. This was far bigger than his feelings. He stopped at the edge of the treeline when he noticed the two were still training. He watched for a few minutes. Nora swept her magic in big arcs. Unpolished, but still so beautiful. He cursed that she was afraid for so long to use her gift.

They seemed to be wrapping up. Ber figured it was a safe time to walk in. He was wrong.

"…to need a lot of work. Your form isn't just sloppy, it's peculiar. Like you were trained by I don't know what–"

Lieutenant Amund turned her attention to Ber coming their way. In an instant she understood. She did not care to watch the Tournament, but she had seen the man work his magic.

"You."

"E-excuse me?"

The exchange was given in Ebian, but Nora could assume the context. Only when they began to argue did Nora interrupt.

"Can you both cool it and speak in a language I can understand?!"

Ber muttered an apology. Before he could speak up, Amund interrupted.

"I need answers– But not here."

Amund led them back up to her office. Nora was surprised when Ber proceeded to tell her *everything*. He did not hold back on being a deserter of Serkan's, nor on most everything else. For being equal parts brave and stupid, Nora was grateful he omitted her affliction during the wild tale.

"… Gods help me, Ber, if this is some kind of trick or attempt at a coup, you understand I will neutralize you on the spot, yes?"

"Please, Lieutenant Amund, he is telling the truth. I would not have become a military dog if I did not have to," Nora sighed, "Trust me on that…"

Lieutenant Amund took a sip from her 'coffee.' "… I will need some time to figure out what to do with this information. I will have to consult intelligence. Once I get more information, we will reconvene."

"Thank you, Lieutenant Amund, for looking into this," Ber said.

"I wouldn't thank me. You'll have a lot of work to do, moving forward. I will write up an inquiry on every piece of information on Serkan you have. Furthermore, you will be attending Nora's training. *That,* is an order."

"Of course, Lieutenant… May I ask why?"

"You'll work better than a sparring dummy. Also, I'd like to keep a close watch of you."

"Oh."

—

The weeks passed. Nora and Ber spent most days on Palace Guard. They did not return to the Inner Ring due to the ongoing investigation, though the two figured Lieutenant Amund played a role in this decision.

As instructed, Ber showed up to assist in Nora's training. Ber was impressed at how much Nora grew in her prowess. She transitioned from his form and stature to a form similar to Lieutenant Amund's. It was more fluid, a tad quicker, and almost *daunting*. As a child, Ber had only heard stories of those who could bend shadows, from long ago. Now, two trained with him, taking turns exhausting his strength.

Nora still did not like her mother. But over the weeks she learned pieces of her, many of which she saw in herself. She had even gotten her to joke a time or two– an insane feat for such a demanding woman. The feeling was complicated, but Nora could boil it down to respect. At the end of the day, at least she could say she respected her mother. Maybe that was enough.

—

The three had just finished training for the day. With proper training and freedom to finally use her magic, Nora learned quickly. She may not be a master, but she could summon all states of her shadow at will, and do quite a bit of damage.

Even to aloof Ber, something had set off the Lieutenant. She appeared irritable from the beginning of the lesson– even more so than normal.

"Show me," She had said, "Show me that you are strong enough, that you are even a fraction prepared for reversing Serkan's forces."

"You're kidding," Nora said, paying half of her attention to putting down her hair. Just then, a crack shook through the air. Amund, doused in aura, constructed her shield from its very essence.

"Am I kidding now?" Amund asked, her tone far too calm for a blatant threat. With one swift swing of her arm she raised a large, silver sword.

Nora's eyes widened. Of course she was not kidding. Before she could open her mouth to negotiate, Amund lunged forward. Nora dodged her heavy swing, but was too close.

"What's your problem?!" Nora barked. She took a few steps away only for Amund to steal them back.

"You lack proper training for the dangers ahead." Amund said, "It is easy to see that you've learned little from your travels."

"Are you serious?! We fought his forces on the way here—and *won.*"

"Most of the time!" Ber chimed in from the sidelines.

"Stay out of this!" Nora and Amund shouted in unison.

Amund launched herself at Nora. She held nothing back, trying to land heavy blows on her. In the quick chase, Ber followed but lost sight. All Nora had time to do was dodge her attacks and pray her mother would gain some sense.

Even with sword and shield in hand, Amund still managed to create masses of shadow aura aimed at Nora. The magic she formed was vast and powerful; it struck the earth and approached Nora in surges.

Amund's precise lunge forced Nora to stumble to the ground. She landed on all fours. She spent her spare moment to sheath her blade and compose herself to a crouch.

"Stop it now before I kick you down the stairs!"

"I'd like to see you try," Amund smirked, "You lack discipline, strength, technique— It's a miracle how you ended up here in one piece!"

Strike after strike, Nora's strength wore down. So did her patience. Weeks since a true break had Nora's body screaming for solace, but her mind insisted otherwise. This was not a battle Nora could simply outlast and endure. This clicked in her the same second that Amund's blade finally "struck."

Nora gripped the blade, talons drawn. The swing of the blade slowed upon the strike, maybe she did not want her daughter dead, after all. But the blade still struck. Blood trickled down Nora's hand, only fanning the flames within.

Nora stood to her full height. Amund may have ceased for a split second, but Nora would not mistake it for mercy. Blade clutched in hand, she stepped toward Amund.

"IF YOU DON'T GIVE ME MERCY, YOU WILL NOT SEE ANY FROM ME, YOU OLD WENCH."

Nora kicked Amund square in the chest. She grabbed Nora, and the two barreled down. Nora bled out fast, but so did her magic. She had lost her weapon earlier in the fight. If she had not been riding on fumes and fists to finish it, she would have been shocked to find another weapon beginning to form flush to her forearm and knuckles.

Amund managed to slip her sword out of Nora's grip and have a final swing. Nora met her with the same force with a weapon more powerful.

"Nora… look."

Nora had not realized she closed her eyes. The fight was over. She gazed up at what she had done. A large shield constructed out of shadow was poised above her. Instead of the usual ink black aura she produced, the shield was made of deep blues and violets and greens. It glimmered under the dying sun's rays like a black opal. Whereas Amund's weapon resembled a bundle of scales, Nora's resembled a neat line of feathers.

To both her relief and dismay, her mother was still standing. Her weapons and magic were cast aside. *Did I… win?*

Amund approached her, and she was smiling. The woman touched the edge of Nora's shield with one hand, wiping the blood from her nose with the other.

"Are you alright…?" Nora asked. She hated herself for asking.

To that her mother barked a laugh, "I haven't had that much fun in *ages!* So, you can use your 'curse' after all. You still can't dismiss it, though. We'll work on that."

She stepped around Nora, admiring her work. Amund must have noticed the black scales crawling up Nora's arms, but at the least she had the decency not to point it out. Finally the Lieutenant noticed Nora's hand clutching her other arm.

"… Are *you* alright?"

"A bit shaken by my mother trying to kill me, but sure."

"Your arm…" Amund said, "I have a kit on me. I'll get you cleaned up."

Without a word, she began to work on Nora's arm. She set out her supplies. When Nora saw the gauze, her stomach sank. She felt ill, but she pushed through. *At least she's not working on my hands…*

Amund began to wrap the wound. She took extra care in cleaning between the scales. Nora did not know she was capable such gentleness. She should have found comfort in it all, in a mother taking care of her child. But all she felt was *sick.*

Nora stood up before the work was done.

"I have to go."

She did not wait around for her answer. She saw Ber finally catching up, but she pushed past him, too. Keeping a steady pace, she searched for a place to quietly work on the wounds herself. She snagged a kit of her own and sat in the washroom of a remote end of the palace. The wound did not hurt, and her body was not sore yet. So, it surprised Nora when she began to cry.

After a few minutes of fumbling the awkward angle of the bandage, she heard the door creak open.

"… Nora?"

Viviane went from standing at the door to kneeling beside her in half a second.

"I'm fine, Viv. Just a rough day, is all."

Viviane sighed. As Nora spoke, she already cleaned the wound and was finishing up the bandage.

"I had those days, too. I won't ask, unless you want me to," Viviane said, "You've become much better at this, you know."

Viviane referred to the wrapping. Just months ago, it would have been a different story. Nora found some relief in that. They sat in silence for a few minutes. Nora relished in her friend's gentleness, one she was actually used to, and missed dearly.

After a while Nora broke the silence, "What are you doing out here?"

"Ah… Late night reading. I was just coming back from the library next door," Viviane answered, looking away to pack up the kit.

Nora nodded, "Ber has made progress with Her Majes- er, Maeve, and I have with Lieutenant Amund. Hang on a bit longer, I think things might be looking up."

Viviane smiled, "I'm forever grateful, dear. Don't you worry about me, though. I will be okay."

"I owe Ber an apology. Seems I keep storming away from him but I— I needed some space."

"He will understand, dear."

Viviane picked Nora up off the floor. She led her out of the bathroom when Nora tapped her.

"… Looks like you got really into 'reading.' I'd wear your hair low tomorrow, if you can." Nora said, struggling to keep a straight face. She gestured to the bite marks along Viviane's neck.

Viviane reddened. She thanked her before rushing off to her quarters, leaving Nora to walk to her own.

56

Chapter 56

Nora never told Ber what fully transpired the day before. She wanted to, she wanted to vent to him. But Ber could be ruthless. She could not afford amy more animosity than what she already held against Lieutenant Amund.

Now, the two were being summoned by Her Majesty herself. They received individual letters that morning, requesting their presence in the Queen's garden.

Nora felt understandably nervous, but Ber seemed to be on another level.

"You are so red," Nora put bluntly, "'You alright?"

Ber chuckled nervously, "I'm fine! I'll... tell you later."

They entered the same clearing as before, when they first spoke to Maeve privately. She stood before them, tall and illustrious as always. She appeared somewhat dressed down, clad in a long, silk dress and a dark coat.

Before Nora or Ber could muster any words, the Queen spoke, "Good morning to you both. I wanted to personally invite you to take a stroll with me in my garden. No need to worry about your training– I've already pardoned you both for the remainder of Amund's drills today."

Ber opened his mouth, but the Queen continued, "I expect you have questions, I will answer them all once we get going."

Nora and Ber, confused as to what just happened, bowed on instinct. "Yes, your Majesty!"

Queen Maeve smiled. She led the two deeper into the garden, its foliage growing denser. Nora and Ber spent some of their spare time exploring the garden's paths, but certainly not enough to know all of its twists and turns. Deeper in the garden trees grew denser, curling in on the manicured path.

They reached a large grove, surrounded by a barrier of myrtles and old pillars. Maeve's garden held an air of ambiguity in its design. Plants grew wild, yet their growth was controlled and shaped. Some areas allowed overgrowth of moss and vines, while others remained strictly cultivated.

"Just a little further…" The Queen said. The three reached a large creek, its waters sluggish enough for flora to grow. Maeve lay a palm to the creek, and a colony of lily pads grew until they were big enough for her to cross the water. Nora and Ber followed suit.

"This is one of my favorite places in the palace. Did you know I cultivated much of this myself?" Maeve asked, "Though, I suppose I did not invite you here to charm you… It's for privacy. The palace has eyes and ears everywhere these days, it seems."

Maeve turned to face Nora and Ber.

"I'll get right to the point. During the Champion's Ball, you two mentioned a fog engulfing the countryside. Naturally, I disregarded your claim. I thought it to be utterly ludicrous. Well, I found out that an extensive amount of information was hidden from me, including this phenomenon."

Queen Maeve did not change face upon announcing such news. Ber and Nora since grew accustomed to her cold and even temper since becoming her guests, but they expected *some* kind of change in her.

"Listen. I need you to tell me everything you know about the fog."

"Of course, Your Majesty… May I ask why us?" Ber asked carefully.

Maeve sighed. "… It's because you are the only ones I can trust about this information."

The three sat in the garden for a long while– no tea tables, no elaborate parties or formalities. They told her everything.

"… What's the plan now?" Nora asked.

"I don't know. I am bound to the palace. With Alice's court date coming up, I don't have the time nor the resources to any more research," Maeve looked up at Nora and Ber, "But… You could gather the information *for* me."

"We would, but with that mishap in the Inner Ring, we are bound, too. We're being watched as well, mind you," Nora said.

"Lieutenant Amund," Ber said simply, "She could do the research. She has higher clearance, too. Couldn't imagine they'd give *her* any trouble."

"Brilliant idea, if she can be trusted," Maeve said.

Nora sighed, "It pains me to say, but Amund can be trusted with this task."

The Queen sighed in relief, "… Then I will discuss this with her tonight. Thank you both, so much."

As they made their walk back to the palace, Nora's mind dwelled on a final question. Carefully, she spoke, "Your Majesty… You *will* aim to get Alice out of this mess… right?"

"My sister and I had a long chat. She needs to be held accountable for some of her actions, but I will say this: Her acts of good outweigh her petty crimes. I will see what I can do."

The Queen saw her guards off, and went to work.

$$57$$

Chapter 57

An unusual air filled the palace before everyone was expected in court. Queen Maeve arrived at the courthouse early to clear her mind. In reality, her choice only made her mind race with the possibilities for today's outcome. Maeve took a breath. *It doesn't matter.* A lie, of course, but she repeated it to herself. *It doesn't matter. What matters is getting through this to expose Reynolds.*

An opening door echoed through the vacant courtroom. Alice entered the room beside a pair of bailiffs, clad in tall black boots and a long leather coat. *Always the one to make an extravagant statement...*

"It's odd for you to show up early, that's a first." Maeve said to her.

Alice shrugged, "I've nothing better to do," she looked to the court's mahogany stands, "Besides, I need some time to think." Her voice was haunting to Maeve, sometimes sounding so much like herself.

Maeve spoke, "You know, dressing like that won't win you any favors."

"I don't see how that matters," Alice adjusted the cuffs of her seafaring coat, "What's that phrase you always used to say...? 'The truth always finds a way of shining through,' I believe."

"Yes..." Maeve turned her attention to her case files, anxiously awaiting her sister's trial.

People came into the room like a trickle, and then all at once. Members of the Court situated themselves, filling the room with hushed anticipation.

Ber, Nora, and Viviane shuffled into their designated seats. When Ber asked Nora how the judicial system worked, Nora was at a loss. Most cases do not reach the Crown Court unless it is of high importance. Or, of course, a hot scandal such as this. They exchanged looks with Alice across the room. Soon enough, Honorable Judge Hornik settled into his seat, closely followed by Maeve's advisors. Maeve feared what they may have discussed before the trial. *It's not above Reynolds to try and get favors from the Judge,* she considered.

"I'd like to officially call the Court into session. Today, we review our defendant, Her Royal Highness Princess Alice Marja Irving's actions following her disappearance from the city of Saint Evedis," The Judge continued, "Miss Irving, your pending charges include, but are not limited to, treasonous intent, piracy, arson, grand theft, fraud, disturbing the peace, kidnapping, and… impersonation of a doctor…?"

Alice sighed to herself. *I forgot about that one.*

"Miss Irving, how do you plea?"

Alice's brow furrowed. "… Is this a trick question?"

With an exasperated sigh, Maeve's anger rose up her throat. "Alice for all that is holy, just say 'not guilty!'"

Mr. Delvin stood from his stand. "Pardon me your Majesty, but I must interject. I ask for you to cease conversation with the defendant, as she's chosen to defend herself… lest you wish to defend her yourself." He chuckled, "But I'm afraid any more outbursts will lead to contempt of court."

Maeve looked up to Mr. Reynold's podium. He smiled to himself as she was being chastised. She grit her teeth. She did not want to follow any more rules. She did not want to be professional and polite. She wanted, more than anything else, to force that smug grin off Reynold's face.

"Actually, I would!" Maeve announced. "Your Honor, upon reviewing the records, I believe there is enough decisive evidence to prove Miss Irving's innocence."

Soft murmurs rose to an uproar in the court. "Order! I demand order in this court immediately!" The Judge shouted, "Miss Alice Irving, will you allow this change?" Alice reluctantly nodded. The Judge rested his head in his hand. "Alright. I will allow a brief recess for reassessment of the trial at hand. Afterwards, I want no more obstacles for finalizing this case. Understood?"

"Yes, Your Honor," Maeve answered.

"Court dismissed."

—

"Your Majesty, what is the meaning of this!?" Reynolds asked when pulling Maeve aside.

"How come no one told me Alice was without an attorney?"

"She *agreed* to defend herself."

"If I know my sister at all, she likely didn't even know that was an option. Was one even offered to her?"

The air held the briefest inkling of hesitation. "Of course."

"You're *lying!* I don't have time for this, I need to speak with Alice." With the swift turn of her heel, Maeve paced off.

Maeve met Alice alongside her bailiffs in a stuffy side room. Alice looked to her, gaze piercing as if she were trying to read her mind. Otherwise, she remained silent.

"Listen. I couldn't just stand by while you threw away your case like that. Full disclosure, you are very much guilty for a lot of these verdicts," Maeve paused, "but certainly not the ones that could get you killed."

"Back in the lift that night, you said you would keep this trial fair, but *now* you want to prove my innocence. What are you trying to get at? I am well aware everything you do is a scheme to get what you want, so what do you want?" Alice snapped. Almost immediately she lowered her tone, "I'm sorry."

"Don't apologize. This case has become bigger than you, bigger than me. I was given several chances to learn of our nation's threats, and I neglected every one. What I'm doing now... I just wish to set things right."

Alice considered her explanation. Still not an apology, but it was the closest she would ever get from her prideful sister.

"Alright. Tell me what I need to do"

—

Court started once more. Rising excitement charged the air. The Judge briefed through the previously spoken introduction. He focused his attention to Maeve.

"After our recess, I expect both the defense and the prosecution are prepared."

"Defense is ready, your Honor," Maeve said.

"The prosecution has *been* prepared, sir." Reynolds said.

"Queen Maeve Irving, please make your opening statement."

"Yes, your Honor," Maeve began, "At the Slatir det Ostrucin, I warranted the arrest of the defendant, Alice Irving. On the grounds of her possible links to criminal activity, I reserved the right to do so. Upon further investigation, I have found proof of Miss Irving's innocence for her severe charges."

The Judge nodded. "Would the prosecution care to make their opening statement?"

"Certainly, your Honor," Reynolds answered, "With evidence from numerous city criminal records, the prosecution believes there is more than ample proof for Miss Irving's full conviction. Furthermore, we have great reason to suspect treasonous intent in her action against Saint Evedis."

"First and foremost, I would like to assess common law on the grounds of Alice's alleged desertion. Miss Irving was a minor, thus did not hold proper office. So, she cannot be held to the same accountability as an adult at the time of her leave," Maeve said.

"No, there is surely *no* excuse," Reynolds said, "Princess Alice may have been a child, but those laws apply all the same: Anyone who leaves the Crown on their own volition is committing desertion."

"However, this particular set of circumstances would have protected her outside the city. In other words, if she knew any better, she would have never returned," Delvin noted.

Maeve leaned over the table.

"But here's the thing, she *did* know better. Alice would have only returned if she had a motive, if something incredibly urgent occurred." Maeve paused.

She studied her opponents. Not a single one objected. She grew wary as to what they may be planning, but she continued. "Would the defendant care to give reasoning behind her return to Saint Evedis?"

"Yes," Alice said, "I returned with Viviane as well as Nora and Ber upon receiving information crucial to the well-being of Saint Evedis. I was maimed and held against my will by Sir Suryc Harland."

"Sir Harland, of the noble line?" the Judge asked.

Alice nodded. "The very same. He demanded the power taken from him. He planned to infiltrate Saint Evedis while using me as bait."

Believers and nonbelievers alike were taken aback, muttering amongst themselves. The Judge urged for silence.

The Judge spoke, "I'm aware of the Harland family's circumstances, so I am able to entertain such a motive from Sir Suryc," he continued, "However that alone could not possibly infiltrate our defenses."

"But he's *not* alone," Alice explained, "he has backup. From what I've gathered, he's part of an entire underground operation. The others involved had aliases. There was the Heir, the Light, and perhaps another…?" Alice drifted. She urged herself to remember, but her thoughts were interrupted by snickering from across the courtroom.

"I say, Miss Irving, you can spin quite a tale!" Advisor Cairn laughed, "Your Honor, you can't possibly believe all this."

"Actually, her testimony is quite accurate when compared to the other witnesses of this event. Viviane, Nora, and Ber were each asked to give a private testimony. Each one came back the same." Maeve revealed a set of papers, distributing them amongst Judge Hornik and the prosecution.

"This is a well-rehearsed ploy. While there are *many* issues with this story, my main concern is this: In what reality do we trust Miss Alice Irving?" Cairn asked.

"You raise a valid concern. There is simply no way of knowing, not without the right sources." Maeve reached under the table once again.

Reynolds could have sworn he witnessed Maeve's face briefly curve into a smirk. She returned to her full posture, hoisting yet another set of records.

"Being denied many of my duties as of late, I was given time to explore this case. To keep the trial as fair as possible, I took it upon myself to retrieve every record on Miss Alice Irving I could find throughout the province," The Queen explained, "I hope you don't find it rude, but I only printed a spare copy for Mr. Hornik. I thought it a waste of ink to print more of such records."

The Judge tabbed through the pages, "… Quite the collection here. I'm uncertain if I should be skeptical or impressed by Miss Irving…"

"Indeed," Maeve replied, "that's why I'd like to go through these records as efficiently as possible and begin reviewing the witnesses." With a nod of the Judge, Maeve continued, "I'd like to bring our first witness to the stand, Miss Abigail Keene."

Slight shuffling came from the back of the room. Alongside a pair of bailiffs, a tall woman with gold-adorned braids approached the stand.

"Name and occupation if you would, Miss Keene." said Maeve.

The woman cleared her throat, "I am Abigail Keene, a current ship hand in Oxbrow… Though I'm sure you lot are more interested that I was a member of the *Coral Fang*."

"To our understanding, you are free to speak of the experiences during your employment. Is this correct?"

"Aye."

"Would you please explain to the court your entire work history with Miss Alice Irving?"

"Didn't expect to be beltin' monologues today, but I'll see what I can do—anything to get this over with sooner."

Abigail continued, "Two years ago I was down on my luck, so I came into employment with Captain Alice aboard the *Coral Fang*. With a new vessel such as she, I was wary to join, unskilled sailors, 'n all that. Regardless, I joined and was given a number of odd jobs, to say the least."

"Odd how? Could you elaborate?" Reynolds asked.

"Yeah, yeah, I was gettin' to that," Abigail waved him off, "At first, Captain Alice seemed like a lil' lass with money to spend and a hunger to raise hell. Lookin' around, I guess I was right. Me an' the crew was commanded to commit petty theft on a bunch of posh towns."

"Why do you think that is?" Reynolds asked.

"Beats me. Captain kept the *Coral Fang* alive through this 'do what you want' kind of business tactic. It was brilliant, really, albeit accidental success. 'Had to respect Captain's guts, because she found something to pursue beyond our tour of the Stromshire coast. However, that's where we had to split ways. I had business elsewhere."

"You mention Miss Irving went to pursue something beyond our nation's coast. Could you please specify?" The Judge asked.

"It seemed the Captain had more direction toward her attacks over time. We sometimes harbored beasts onboard, despite my arguin' about it. We'd kidnap those of interest to poachers. Captain would talk to 'em in privy, only for them to be let go later. When Captain fell ill, work got scarce, so I left." Abigail looked around, "So, that's about as far as my knowledge goes for ya lot. Am I free to go?"

"Not quite, Miss Keene," Maeve said.

"Yes, I am curious on what you mean by 'poacher,'" Judge Hornik added.

"… Ya lot don't know? Alright… Comin' from a—eh, *past* crook, these folk play dirty. Anybody with anything worth taking, they'll take. They used to only be a problem outside of civilization, now you can find 'em anywhere," Abigail said, "save for here, apparently."

"If I may interject, I would like to briefly inform the Court on the subject, as this was news to me as well." Maeve browsed her papers to find the correct notes. "In recent record from Houndsmouth, 'Sightings of poachers have steadily risen in the last two decades, strictly on the account for the rise in organized crime across all Stronshire regions. These groups travel in caravans, preying on man and beast alike for valuable asssets.'"

"As… frustrated as I am that I just now hear about this threat, we need to postpone this discussion until after our current case," Reynolds said.

"Yes. Now, when you say hostages were let go, could you please go into detail on this?" The Judge asked.

"What else is there to say?" Abigail said, "Our crew'd get the drop on crooks and take their loot. Sometimes the loot would be an actual person, and Captain would just let 'em go. Maybe some deal happened behind closed doors. But if there were, I never got a coin of it."

Reynolds spoke up, "I find this a good time as any to move along to our next testimony. Thank you for your time, Miss Keene."

With a nod, Abigail shuffled out of the courtroom. Maeve eyed Reynolds, wondering just what was up his sleeve.

"The prosecution would like to call Hayden Zeman to the stand."

Unlike Keene, this witness seemed to march, urgently on foot to face the court.

"Name, and occupation, if you would."

"Yes, sir. I am Hayden Zeman, and I own a trade company."

"It reads here you were a witness to the Oxbrow Incident. Please explain to the court what exactly happened here," The Judge said.

"Certainly," Zeman began, "Me and my merchants attended the Oxbrow day market, about three months ago. Some folk were browsing our wares, and of course I paid that no mind, until twenty-odd crooks reared their ugly heads and took everything that wasn't tacked down. It was utter chaos and folks were scrambling for safety. That was when I saw the person before me, directing her crew from the top of a streetlamp before joining the fight."

Ali pitched in, "I would like to add that this incident filed numerous reports from witnesses, all of them the same. A red-haired girl dropped from above to join and direct the attack. Upon further investigation, guards deduced this criminal was none other than the estranged Alice Irving."

"Your grievances are fair, truly, they are," Maeve began, "This is why we need to find out everything that has happened, so that we may set things right, Mr. Zeman."

"Of course."

"To get started I must state that the area under investigation, based on our testimonies, is quite large," Maeve said, "Can you confirm that this is your place of business?"

"That it is. We've expanded in the last few months, so we've taken residency of the entire corner of that market."

"So to specify, your corner, according to the accounts, was Miss Irving's main target.

"I'm not sure. I suppose it's possible."

"Regardless, it seems that your assets appeared to be a primary target. May I ask what wares you were selling at the scene of the crime?"

"We pride ourselves with a variety of artisanal and rare items. Exotic spices, elixirs, things of the sort."

"A reasonable target for a high-roller criminal," Reynolds commented.

"Indeed," Maeve said, "Mr. Zeman, are there any other specifics about your trade that we the Court should know about to further understand the case? I would like to remind you that you are currently under oath."

"No, I don't believe so."

"Very well. Your Honor, I would like to bring one final witness to the stand. The defense would like to call in Mr. Beck Mallory."

A man approached the stand, his blazer ill suited for his thin frame. He stood tall, setting tired eyes on the jury.

"Would you state your name and occupation for the court?" Maeve asked.

"My name is Beck Mallory, and I work for an energy plant in the Outer Ring. During the Oxbrow Incident, I was trafficked by Mr. Zeman's company for the use of poachers."

A roar of voices filled the courtroom, the jury aghast in confusion and excitement. The Judge stood from his seat with a roar, "I will have order in this court! For this city's sake *and* my own, we *will* end this ordeal today."

Reynolds rose from his seat, "Objection! This is obviously some ploy. How can such a transaction occur in the middle of town, in the day, with ample security and witnesses? I'm sorry, it just does not seem remotely possible!"

"We will hear what Mr. Mallory has to offer," The Judge said.

Maeve tried not to smile. This testimony could very well turn the jury in her favor.

"The world outside Saint Evedis works differently, sir. Any kind of transaction is possible anywhere, with the right coin." Mr. Mallory said, "I was in the wrong place at the wrong time. I was taught to be on guard because of my gift, but after work one night, I suppose I was not paying enough attention to my surroundings. I was abducted and next thing I know, I'm going Saints-know-where on a caravan."

"Allow me to backtrack; how did these 'abductors' know of your aura?" Maeve asked.

"I work at an energy plant. Not many non-magic folk work those kinds of jobs. I assume they connected the dots from there."

"I feel like we are missing one crucial piece of information. How do you *know* that your kidnapping was conducted my Mr. Zeman?" Reynolds asked, "And how do we know any of these claims are credible? It's not like the last testimony came from a credible background…"

Scrutiny of Maeve's work, her witnesses, struck a nerve in her. The voice in her to remain calm was not enough.

"The audacity of you lot absolutely sicken me. These are citizens of *our* nation, and they deserve to be heard just as much as much as any of you—!"

Maeve caught the leering eye of Judge Hornik. To her surprise, Mr. Mallory spoke up.

"Queen Maeve— err, Your Majesty? It's quite alright, you needn't defend me." He turned his attention to the prosecutors. "The truth is, good sir, that I didn't know my attacker. It wasn't until I was rescued by Alice's crew and let go that I hear word of Zeman & Company being robbed in Oxbrow by members of the *Coral Fang*. Wasn't hard to piece it together from there. I will also prove to you my experience." Mallory paused to roll up his sleeve. He revealed a distinct mark in the middle of his forearm. "This is the mark poachers leave when they test for aura," He explained.

This was news to even Maeve. She had seen the mark the Guard uses to test initiates, but the mark fades over time. The gnarled one before her seemed cruel and intentional.

"May I have a medic observe the witness' mark?" Maeve asked.

"I deem this worth further exploration. I'll allow it," The Judge said.

The Chief Crown Medic was summoned. She approached silently from the margin of the courtroom. Maeve gained a moment to gather herself in this unofficial break from testifying. She scanned the room. The conversations between the jury hummed through the court. Reynold's men remained silent, not with newfound uncertainty in their case but rather in anticipation, like waiting for the right time to strike. With what, who could say.

Her eyes laid on Mr. Zeman. The slight change in the his stance, the altered quickness in his actions—all without a change of face—seemed so minuscule. But to her it spoke a weakness. Whatever were the results of the medical exam, she prayed it would be enough to crack him.

To Maeve, Alice was always easy to read. But as the Princess watched the examination on Mr. Mallory, Maeve was at a loss. Alice did not falter in any way physically, yet her confidence did not shine as bright as it usually did. Maeve hypothesized she was simply mulling things over. With what, she did not know.

The Chief Medic set aside her gear, "… Based on the healing process, the laceration is aged approximately three months. In Saint Evedis medical records, some magic-wielding immigrants were also found with this mark."

"It seems that Mallory acquired this mark during the same time as the Oxbrow Incident," Maeve said, "Does the prosecution have any objections to this?"

"No," Reynolds said, monotone.

"So, Mr. Zeman, I will ask again. Exactly what 'wares' were you selling at Oxbrow?"

—

Zeman did not admit anything. As frustrating as it was, Maeve knew it was well within his right, and smart to do so. He was retained for later questioning, and the Court reconvened after a brief recess.

"Mr. Mallory, if I may ask about one more detail of your experience with Miss Alice Irving, what happened aboard the *Coral Fang*?" Maeve asked.

"I was brought into a room to speak privately with the Captain. She asked me about information of my previous captors, which at the time I didn't know anything about. She then asked me about knowing anything about a few other names—I apologize, but those names have escaped me. I could not answer. Finally, she asked me what port I wanted to leave on."

Maeve turned to the prosecution. "I happen to hold record of *Coral Fang* sightings off the coast that back this claim. Even with proof literally *in the flesh* of my witness' testimony… would the prosecution care to object?"

"… The prosecution has no objections at this time," Reynolds said.

The Judge nodded, "It seems we have enough information to move on towards a verdict."

Alice flagged the attention of the Judge. "Excuse me, but it 'seems' like we are forgetting the testimony from the defendant…?"

"I will allow it."

Maeve watched her sister warily when she passed by. The Queen swallowed her doubt and her pride, and Alice gave a rare smile.

"It's no news I left the Crown as a child. I left, taking Viviane LeClair with me in hopes to find the family the Crown separated her from. I also committed piracy. I may have gone overboard here and there, no pun intended. But when I found out about the trade in people— and for *parts*, I couldn't stand idly by. And my sister was right; I returned to Saint Evedis because it was absolutely necessary to do so. So, if I can be convicted of whatever it is I need to be convicted of, can we get through with it so I can actually tell the nation what I needed to say?"

"And what might that be, Princess?" Reynolds asked.

"It's that a group of power-hungry men are trying to infiltrate Saint Evedis with powerful weapons. Whether you believe me or not is on you."

Silence filled the room. Finally, the Judge struck his gavel.

"Court adjourned. We will come to a final decision after a final recess."

58

Chapter 58

Maeve found herself in a room with the prosecution, the Judge, and the representatives of Parliament who Maeve couldn't recall seeing before. Maeve refrained from showing her frustration. *When did Reynolds have the time to remove the old Parliament...?* Maeve wondered. She was certain that, despite the change, it wasn't going to be good for her case.

"Seems to me you've grown close once again to your sister. Why is this?" Reynolds asked.

"That is irrelevant to the case," Maeve said, "Do I need a reason to converse with the defendant like a human being?"

"I've seen how you talk to her, it is different. Why would a *Queen* even waste her time with an ex-royal and high-class thief? My theory is this: perhaps Miss Irving sowed some problematic ideas in you. Perhaps she convinced you of the 'wicked ways' of our system, and convinced you to try to overthrow everything we worked so hard for to maintain peace."

"What—what are you even getting at?"

"I'm saying that, with such aggression towards your *advisors,* of all people, it suggests you are trying to shift Saint Evedis into a dictatorship."

"That's absurd!"

"… And to think, after everything we had done to keep your reputation safe."

"Do I dare ask what that is supposed to mean…?"

"You don't remember? Or are you feigning ignorance before your peers?"

"No. *Enlighten* me, on what I could have possibly forgotten."

"I was sure you would remember the night we lost our late King and Queen."

Maeve's eyes widened. Despite how much he loathed the man, Reynolds knew everything about her. He *knew* bringing up the subject would be treading on thin ice with Maeve. But just what was he playing at?

Reynolds continued, "I found you that night, did I not?"

"Watch yourself, Reynolds." Maeve felt her disposition begin to fade, as her words sounded less like an order, but rather a suggestion.

"I found you that night, cowering. You must recall the cause of their—"

"Food poisoning. It was deemed to be an accident."

"That is what you would like to think. This is what we would *all* like to think. But we found was poison of aural origin. We also know that our Queen Maeve holds the ability, even proficiency, of poison aura."

"You are insinuating that I killed my parents."

"I am claiming for a *fact* that you did. Now, clearly you were a child, and therefore cannot be held accountable for such a disaster," Reynolds said, "But what *can* be held accountable is trying to silence the only ones who knew, and to rule on your own."

"Are you accusing me of manslaughter and being a bleeding dictator? How dare you?!" Maeve stood from her chair. "You're wrong. I *don't* want to rule alone—if I had the choice, I wouldn't rule at *all!* But rest assured if I had total authority, you'd all be gone—You hear me?! *GONE.*"

Wreaths of vines shot out from under Maeve. But not from her. She reflexively coiled, but nothing struck her. She opened her eyes, finding that it lashed out instead at Reynolds.

"Y-Your Majesty! Unhand me—PLEASE!"

Maeve froze, realizing what happened. *I'm being set up.*

It was no use battling any longer with words. Bailiffs were already at her neck with halberds and magic. For the briefest moment the air stood still, everyone frozen in place, and Reynolds pinned to the wall with wooden coils and dagger-like thorns. Maeve breathed, and then she fell.

The Queen hit the floor with full force, surprising even herself when her body made impact. With an arm draped over her face from her 'fall,' she peered beneath the table. She followed the source of the vines to Ali, his clenched fists producing the aura. The bailiffs scrambled to reach for Maeve. She had to act fast. She grasped at the vines, shifting to her feet to pull them with her full power.

She released the vines. The sudden surge of aura she used made her feel like she might actually black out. She leaned against a wall, struggling to regulate her breathing. She opened her eyes, bringing into focus the disaster she brought to the room.

The table collapsed with two of its legs swept out from under it and shattered. Attendants stood back in shock. Reynolds, no longer shackled with vines, looked unscathed from his 'attack.' He looked *through* Maeve with a bitter, almost predatory gaze. Ali, on the other hand, laid limp against the wall, unresponsive. A bold crack in the wall revealed the brick foundation beneath. Ali's breathing was labored as his aura siphoned back into his body.

Maeve scanned the room. Pairs of eyes shifted from Ali, to Maeve.
Did... did I *do all this?*
Feeling her strength return, she broadened her stance as she carefully chose her words. "... Reynolds," His gaze was unshaken. "Members of the Court, observe how there are no vines attached to my person. Pay *close* attention to the fact that Ali, Reynold's colleague, is the caster. Note Reynold's lack of injuries, and how the evidence is literally *etched in stone*," Maeve gestured to the vines embedded in the marble floor, "that this is clearly a frame-up."

Maeve swayed, and grabbed a chair for herself to fall into. She was sure to keep watch Reynolds, unsure of his next move. Regardless, she took a deep breath.

"I now, *finally,* rest my case. Members of the Court, make your judgment."

What ensued came to Maeve in bits and pieces. It occurred to her how much power she used to uproot Ali's attack—no staff, just with her hands. She saw her advisors apprehended by bailiffs as Parliament argued overhead.

It did not take long for medics to come amongst the chaos. They escorted Ali away, and took Maeve to a quiet room to revive and treat her. As she recuperated, it occurred to her the reason of her blackout. She *fought* with her aura—no staff, or even a wand. She reflected on her power, tamed for all these years to tend to gardens and entertain parties.

Is this what Alice has been doing all these years? Is this what our militia feels?

Judge Hornik entered the room. The medic was not done but he excused himself.

The Judge exhaled, "… Never in my decades of service have I reviewed a case this divisive and fraudulent… Given the unique circumstances of the case, we need to discuss what comes next."

—

After the final findings were delivered and deliberated by the jury, the Court reconvened. Reynolds reappeared to serve as the face for the prosecution, but notably he was alone and flanked by bailiffs. Entering the courtroom, The Queen met the gaze of Viviane. Admittedly she tried to ignore her presence throughout the trial so she could focus.

Despite their mutual animosity, Viviane still looked worried as Maeve sauntered in, fetching her staff and putting her weight on it. Viviane had yet to go through her own trial. At the very least, it would not be anywhere as much of a spectacle. But Maeve figured whatever Alice was convicted of, Viviane would be served the same.

Judge Hornik made his closing statements. Then he delivered the verdict.

"The Court declares Her Highness Princess Alice Marja Irving, not guilty of treasonous intent or kidnapping. She is, however, found guilty of all other charges. To pay for her crimes, Alice Irving is to admit all possessions within and including the *Coral Fang.* She is to be stripped of her title and place in Saint Evedis nobility, and she is to be banished from Saint Evedis as of sunrise tomorrow. Court dismissed."

The gavel dropped. Like that, nearly everyone left the courtroom. The air buzzed with chaos, and Maeve knew the press would be outside the palace gates. Surely the whole city would know of the outcome by tomorrow. With

Alice being exiled tomorrow, Maeve figured Viviane's trial was occurring post haste. Which meant she had somewhere else to be.

"... Well played, Your Majesty," Maeve heard Reynold approach from behind, "It's an honor to finally match you in court, despite the circumstances."

"Likewise."

It was not a lie. Despite the man's despicable actions, Reynolds still taught and, in a sense, raised her. In another life, Maeve wondered is a path in law would have called to her.

59

Chapter 59

Viviane's trial followed the same outcome as Alice's. Maeve chose to sit in her case as well, just in case something went awry. Of course, Alice, Ber, and Nora were required attendance.

After the trial officially dismissed, Alice approached her sister cautiously. She found relief in Viviane at her side. The two stepped forward.

"I guess we're both finally getting our wish. I'll be out of your hair for good…" Alice said, "… All that aside, I wanted to thank you for defending me today."

"I should be thanking you, actually. If you didn't force yourself into the palace, I would have never known about—well, everything threatening us."

"So it's agreed, you're in the wrong. How about in exchange, you lend me back my ship?"

"I've no control in the matter, Alice. Count yourself lucky you left the courtroom free of shackles."

Alice shrugged, "Worth a shot."

"What happens now…?" Viviane asked.

"I reckon you'll be escorted out of the city tomorrow. I suggest you two figure out a plan," Maeve said.

"Nora and Ber must still be nearby. I'll see if I can flag them down to consult with them," Viviane planted a kiss on Alice before excusing herself from the room.

Alice and Maeve were alone.

"... I expect you and Miss LeClair will be searching for her family. While researching the scope of the city's civil unrest, I found some migration records of refugees from our adjacent nations."

From her coat pocket Maeve retrieved a small map, delicately cut from a larger parchment, and crisp markings around the archipelago south of Stromshire, including Rinesant.

"There's record of Rinesant citizens seeking refuge along the belt of Kifitar Province. I suggest you continue your search there."

Something in Alice took hold of her. She found herself in embrace with her sister. "... I was hoping there was still some good in you."

"The feeling is mutual..." Maeve said. She did not remember the last time she cried like this, "... As nice as this is, my internal bleeding is making this unbearable."

Alice released her grip, and smiled. "Well," She paused, realizing she was out of breath from her own sobbing, "... If I don't see you later, then—eh..."

Maeve smiled, "I will see you later."

—

"... So, we will be here a few more weeks at the very least. We need to brief the Queen on further details, loop Lieutenant Amund in, and hope that whatever support she sends our way will be enough," Ber explained.

He, Nora, Alice, and Viviane regrouped in Maeve's garden, away from any watchful eyes as they discussed their plans— They were no longer being heavily surveilled, but the habit remained. Despite their convictions, the guards laid off of Alice and Viviane for the evening. A final mercy from the Queen, they figured.

"We're one step closer to finding my parents..." Viviane mused.

"Yeah, but we have no way of getting over there." Alice said.

"For now, we could steal a horse... What are they going to do? We're already banished."

"Ed and Arvo might be able to help," Nora suggested.

"Are those the secret society fellows you mentioned?"

Nora nodded, "They might be able to set you up with transportation.

Hell, Ed could probably find more information for you."

A quiet beat passed among the four.

"When do you think we'll all be together like this again?" Alice asked.

"Soon enough, I'm sure. Just, eh, send us a message when you get there, yeah?" Nora asked.

"You got it!"

They turned to find Viviane with her arms wide open for hugs. Her eyes were already flooded with tears.

"Such a sap…" Nora said as she piled into the hug with Alice and Ber, but she was also crying.

60

Chapter 60

Nora and Ber were kept on palace duty during Alice and Viviane's exile. Nora understood, but it still hurt not to say goodbye. Despite her best efforts to be away from Lieutenant Amund that day, the woman still found her. As it turned out, the sky bridge between the palace's Post and roost was a favored spot between the two.

"Lieutenant," Nora nodded to her.

"It's General, as of this morning," Amund said, "Reynolds held the position 'temporarily' until he could find a good candidate… Apparently twenty-odd years of service wasn't enough from me."

Nora turned, "*He* was the General!?"

Amund nodded, "I've got a lot of work ahead of me to reverse what he's done. But first, I wanted to run something by you. Actually, two things."

Oh Saints, what now.

"I was going through some neglected paperwork and decided to be nosy… I'm surprised no one caught this— Are you and Ber actually married?"

Nora choked. For a split second, she considered leaping off the bridge.

"Oh my fucking god— If I tell you the truth, will you not arrest us?"

"I'm not arresting you. And if I did anything to our 'golden boy,' the whole city would be out for my head."

"No. We fudged the papers to get him in."

"Smart," Amund said, "Embarrassing for *you*, but smart."

"What else did you want to ask me?" Nora asked, desperately trying to change the subject.

"Your dragon you spoke of. I could grant her access to the city. It would really be no problem, as she would be a useful asset to the Guard," She said, "Hell, we could start training her today, if you wanted."

"I'd… I'd really like that, Lieu—eh, General. Thank you."

Nora figured this to be a peace offering between her and her mother. Still, it was one she would happily accept to see her dragon again.

"It's a commute to the Outer Ring from here. Let's get going, shall we?"

Before Nora could respond she caught a familiar face. Standing proper on the stone railing was one of Arvo's hawks. The bird grew impatient as she approached, preening and ruffling its tawny feathers.

"Aren't you a sight for sore eyes, sweet thing," She said to the bird. "But… Why are you here?"

Hearth's most recent message came a week before Alice's court date, in the middle of Queen Maeve and Amund's research. The last memo she received gave some beyond concerning findings in the field. Nora prayed this one would be better.

She unraveled the envelope and read the note. Her face sunk as she finished. She read the note again. Amund drew in close as she read aloud:

"'Dense fog was spotted rapidly encroaching on Saint Evedis territory. Large beast spotted emerging from the fog. Safety precautions are no longer needed, as total, immediate evacuation of the city is a must. Signed, Arvo Kava.'"

It was dated for that day.

"Surely this must be a fluke," Amund said.

Little shadows briefly blotted the sun, as birds fled from the roost in a V-formation out of the city.

"It's not a fluke."

—

They hurried to Central Tower where they found Queen Maeve, alone. They approached her and spoke.

"Pardon the intrusion, your Majesty, but this is urgent."

The Queen faced them, her face sullen. "I know." She showed them her own note. Nora was surprised she retrieved Hearth's note so quick. "This just dropped in. Tell me. Can we trust this alert?"

"Yes," Nora said.

The Queen went silent. "… Very well. Bring back *exact* details of this threat. General Amund, I assume you can handle the preparations. I will grant authorization once I deem we are ready to evacuate."

"Yes, your Majesty," Nora and Amund said at once.

With her nod, they were dismissed. They rushed down from Central Tower, grabbing Ber in the process. Amund briefed them on what had to be done. She tore a note from inside her coat and handed it to Nora.

"Get your beast. The gates will not give you any trouble with this. Scout the barrier and find where the threat is coming from."

Nora and Ber obeyed.

Like the General said, no one questioned Amund's note. If only Nora had this magical paper sooner. Her and Ber summoned Lotte, and they got to work.

Even for such a massive city, a dragon's wings made quick work of the perimeter. Before they could finish their loop Lotte perched on the south end of the outer wall. Before Ber could ask why, Nora signaled him to watch and listen. In the horizon there stood their ever-present threat, creeping alarmingly quick into the valley below.

Despite the distance, Nora noticed something stirring under the fog's cover. She thought the movement could have been a rock slide, until the 'rocks' began to shift upwards. It shifted into a fully formed figure, of what she could not tell, but it was *massive.* Lotte noticed this too, and darted back into the city before given any direction.

"What… was that…?" Ber asked.

"I was hoping *you* would know! Let's get the Queen, Amund— Whoever we find first."

—

General Amund made her rounds throughout her stations. With decades of training and numerous emergencies she lived through, she moved every station expertly at her hand. Half of the forces moved through all areas of the city in preparation to evacuate. The second half moved around Central, in preparation for the attack.

Alongside her strode her own beast, one that rarely saw action. His talons clacked against the stone while dish-like ears swiveled atop his head. Amund paced up and down the courtyards, checking if everything was in order when Nora and Ber returned.

The two saluted, "The fog is impeding from the south," Nora said.

"How much time do we have?" Amund asked, "I need numbers."

"Two hours, three at most. Something *big* is in there, and it's moving fast." Amund's face soured. She continued, "It's some form of beast, I think. Neither of us have seen anything like it."

General Amund turned at her heel towards her troops. Nora and Ber trailed behind her, trying to catch up and retrieve their next order. Instead Amund spoke, partly to herself, "We'll treat this like any other attack: When something threatens us, we will fight back."

"What about the city? There's so many people..." Ber hesitantly asked.

"I sent troops already to prepare. As for if—or when we move citizens, we will cross that bridge when we get to it. I cannot authorize a mass evacuation until the Queen says so." She pulled out a notebook and swiftly scrawled on the paper. "We need to pull from Central's troops. This is my emergency code. Tell the Officers I need at least four troops, and give them this. We'll meet back here and move out."

Nora and Ber held many more questions, but now was not the time. The two saluted and left, and they prayed that four troops would be enough.

—

Alice and Viviane set forth on their journey southward. Equipped only with a piece of intel a handful of smuggled daggers, what lay before her was an utter mystery.

Viviane felt it, too, though she had faced uncertainty for years now. She wrapped her hand around Alice's. For that moment, their worries, how they were to get to Kifitar province, how they were to survive with no money (other than what Alice managed to smuggle), slipped away.

From the brush came rhythmic steps or something large. Their horse (that they stole promptly after being kicked out of the city) heard it first, nervously pacing backwards. Viviane and Alice turned to the source as a man on horseback leapt out of the woods and onto the road.

The man pulled back on the reins upon nearly running Alice and Viviane off the road. His eyes met with theirs. He seemed out of sorts, his mind somewhere else entirely.

He spent a moment to wipe the sweat from his face before speaking, "Get as far away from Saint Evedis as possible—" He said, "Something— something *awful* is heading that way."

Before the man could sprint off, Alice turned her horse to block him. "What's this 'something?' We have friends there."

"Me too. There's no time for this—just go!"

Something felt too familiar to Viviane about the man. From head to toe the stranger was equipped like he was ready for battle. Atop his shoulder sat a large hawk, peering down at her. One she had seen Nora with before at the Post.

A few more people rushed in the man's direction, none of them bothering to stop. Directly behind everyone else rode a man atop a massive whalehound.

"Arvo, let's go!" shouted the man from afar.

Before the man could obey, Viviane stopped him again, "You're Arvo… Arvo from Hearth?" The man froze, and nodded. "You're friends with Nora and Ber, yes?"

"Yes—Saints, are they still in the city?!" Alice and Viviane nodded. Arvo cursed, spurring his horse towards the city.

Alice and Viviane were left in the dust. They looked at each other. Kifitar would have to wait.

61

Chapter 61

Ber and Nora lost count of how many Officers they encountered. They rushed through Central on a whirlwind tour, trying to flag down troops. They rallied up what they needed and hurried back to the courtyard.

Amund gave a briefing to her guards. Tension in the crowd grew as she explained their new role amongst the threat. Beasts, fog, evacuation— These words were close to foreign for them. Hardly any guards faced serious action during their time on reserve.

"… And I want to make something *very* clear." General Amund said, "Even *I* have no idea what we are up against. Blødeks and Dyr here are the only ones with experience with the fog. If they tell you to do something, I expect you to do it. Do I make myself clear?"

"Yes, madam!" The guards bellowed.

Amund pulled Nora away from earshot of Ber and the guards. Her brows furrowed as she looked down to her daughter.

"I want you back alive. Don't do anything I would do. *That*, is an order."

"Isn't the saying 'don't do anything I wouldn't do?'"

Amund held a toothy grin, "Eh, I'll be sure to show you what I mean sometime! Take care of my troops, alright?"

—

Nora and Ber led the team on horseback, weaving through the city as their beasts soared above. They passed the city wall and paused atop the valley. They set eyes on the colossus; it was more massive than they could have ever perceived. As it encroached on the city, its figure became clear. To Nora it resembled an ox, but built grey, necrotic, *wrong*. It feigned a sense of elegance as it sauntered down the valley, despite its devastating nature crushing the earth and leaving only rot. Its shadow eclipsed the face of the hills.

"It's… unbelievable," Ber said, "It'll get to the city within the hour at this rate."

"What do we do…?" Nora's cohort, Arc asked.

Nora dwelled on the question.

"… I have an idea. I cannot promise we will all leave unscathed, but we may have a chance of stopping it if we strategize," Nora continued, "That thing's reaching a valley. All of you need to scale down the valley on its path. Follow beside it and keep a distance. I will need you to surround it and try to find some weak points. Ber and I will do the same from above."

Ber spoke up, "I want to stress how important it is that *none* of you even go near the fog. Focus on applying force to the front and sides of the beast for now. If, gods forbid, we must attack near the fog, leave it to me and Nora."

Nora and Ber led the charge as they soared above the others on earthbound beasts and steeds. They scoped the monster below them. The guards were so small compared to the creature, it did not seem to acknowledge their presence. Nora hoped it stayed that way.

Descending even lower, Nora got a better view of it. The bovine was coated in grey, mossy fur that dangled at its legs and chest. It swayed with each slow step it took. Even at the bovine's shoulder height, Nora and Ber were still dizzily far from the earth.

She had to get moving. She dipped down to signal the guards to ready their attack.

Nora took a chance and flew towards the face of the bovine. She made sure to steer clear of its horns. The broad span of its horns could sweep out all of the soldiers at once, it they were not careful. Its eyes were glazed over and fixed on its target. Ber looked below, observing the soldiers as they shot arrows and fits of aura. It didn't have much effect on the bovine, as it shook it all off like flies.

"That's hardly doing anything… You and me will have to find a weakness, or something to slow it down."

"Then we'll make this thing notice us."

Lotte fell behind the bovine while Nora prepared an attack. Her magic could hardly reach the beast. But it sparked an idea from Ber.

"Pardon my reach—!"

He pulled her outstretched arm to his. From the withers to its flank, the two released a devastating attack of shadows carried by Ber's wind. Shards of shade struck the hide but it appeared to still have no effect. They dove down beneath the belly of the beast, dodging towering legs and hooves. Ber tried his ice this time. Nora joined in, creating a black ice that shattered on impact. Nora admired their work. She did not know aura could work in tandem like that.

As they rose from the belly, Nora felt the beast's eyes on her. It looked far from finished.

"At least we got its attention." She glanced at the soldiers below, who were preparing to trip its legs with a metal cable. She tried to think of more tactics to distract the monster so their plan on the ground could work.

Nora's dragon, she knew, was terrified. Her scales and horns were pressed flat against her body, her pupils thin slits. The fog dwelled on both sides of the valley. Alongside the monster, Nora feared she might go rogue.

Instead, Lotte's head turned, putting her eyes on Nora's. It was like she was waiting for an answer.

"… Do you have an idea?" After a beat, Nora raised her hands from her back. A (hopefully) universal sign for 'you're in charge.'

Ber's jaw dropped. "A-are you letting the dragon drive? *Seriously?!*"

Fortunately, Lotte understood the assignment. Nora felt beneath her as the dragon began taking in deep breaths. Nora had only ever seen her act defensively with physical attacks, and her own aura was still a mystery on what all it could do. Hell, she did not even know if she could "breathe fire" like they did in old children's stories.

But Lotte did not breathe fire. Instead, her shadowy aura emanated from the tips of her wings. Then she dove. From the withers to the flank, Lotte slashed at the bovine with her magic. It branded a deep, black scar down the body of the beast, causing it to bellow a haunting cry.

Lotte's magic petered out, but she was not done yet. She flew around its face like a pestering fly, its milky eyes following her now.

The monster was quicker than they thought. They were blindsided by the beast's horns. Lotte avoided it but Nora was thrown off. Ber grabbed her arm but she slipped from his grasp. Nora fought to remain conscious as she plummeted.

She hit the side of the beast's neck before continuing to fall. Arms outstretched, she clawed into fur and flesh, gaining any leverage to stop her fall. She allowed her beast form to transform har hands into claws. She took advantage and scaled the beast up its withers before collapsing on a somewhat-stable surface.

Adrenaline was dulling out from the fall. Nora clenched her abdomen, praying for the wave of pain to cease. When the pain dulled, her eyes came into focus. She found herself in one piece atop the bovine's neck in a bed of waist-high, rotting fur.

The colossus did not seem to notice her at the base of its neck. She took the advantage to unsheathe her sword and finish it off. She found a spot between two vertebrae. She wanted it done quick, for a soft spot in her knew whatever this thing once was, it deserved mercy.

Her legs quivered and her breath grew shaky. She focused, and with every ounce of power left in her, she stabbed the ox's spine, injecting as much of her magic as possible. The ox's cry rattled the air. It began to shake and buck, but fell short. Nora wondered if it was the guards' work keeping it still. She looked down at the deep wound she inflicted. The flesh and fur all around her turned ashen, and beyond ice cold. Regardless, the beast did not seem weakened, but enraged.

Nora growled. Both scaled hands gripped the hilt of her sword. She stabbed the beast, and stabbed again. She dug her blade down until the handle was the only piece not submerged. Still, nothing happened. Exerted of all her energy, Nora struggled to stand. It did not matter, as she plunged and grasped its fur when the beast shook once more.

Ber scooped Nora back up. Nora climbed onto Lotte's neck and slumped over. She gazed below at the beast, still going strong. She weakly checked her dragon over. Lotte's breaths grew labored, but otherwise seemed alright. Below them, the soldiers lost all progress they had for making it fall. If anything, the bovine looked like it was treading ground quicker than before.

"Nora, are you okay? Please be okay…!"

I stabbed that thing in the neck, how is it still walking? Nora peered at the horizon, Saint Evedis drawing awfully near.

Given Ber's expression, Nora figured she spoke the thought aloud. He was quiet. He stared at the beast's dark marks, then at the rest of its virtually untouched body.

"Nora", He began, "Serkan's men have done this countless times to so many other beasts. This thing's already dead."

"So you're saying we can't stop it."

"No. Maybe we're going at this all wrong. What I'm trying to say is that it maybe has a weak point, but it'd be in a place you wouldn't expect."

From below, she heard a *snap.* The cable was torn through by the hoof like it was nothing. Now the guards scrambled to find a way to support. Nora returned to her troops, signaling them to retreat. Nora counted them all from above, sighing in relief everyone was accounted for.

Before Nora could say anything to Ber about following the guards, he spoke up.

"You know already I'm not leaving you alone with a big, dead cow."

Nora mustered a laugh that hurt her chest, "I figured you'd say that. Let's try this again."

Nora scanned the beast for some form of oddity, or anything to give her the upper hand. In the distance, a small patch of skin between the ox's shoulders seemed off color. She must have missed it while scrambling to get to its neck. Nora strained her eyes to focus on the spot underneath the area of thinned fur.

Once more, she met again with the beast's pair of horns as it turned to ram into Lotte. Its attacks now were relentless. They had to keep moving to avoid getting gored. Nora had an idea, and Ber knew it.

Nora position herself to sidesaddle. "I need you to catch me if I drop further. Lotte will know what to do."

"Nora, please don't do this," Ber begged.

"If I don't stop it, no one will, Ber."

Ber hesitated.

"… I know." He drew in close, holding her hand before letting her go.

She clenched her jaw, unsheathed her blade, and leapt towards the colossus.

62

Chapter 62

In the years of seemingly pointless royal education, Alice counted herself lucky that at least one noble pastime came in handy. Gripping her horse's reins, she raced back to Saint Evedis. She skillfully directed the animal onto the quickest path, careful not to lose sight of Arvo.

Poor Viviane, unaccustomed to horses, held onto Alice for dear life. With every leap and turn she clutched tighter to Alice's waist.

"What kind of trouble do you think we're dealing with?" Viviane asked.

"Knowing Nora and Ber, I'm sure it's something weird. But with the whole city being in danger…" Alice refused to finish the thought. She forced herself to focus on the road ahead.

—

To the team's surprise, no guards stood between them and the city at the wall. Wherever the guards were taken meant an emergency was deemed much more important. Alice and Viviane swallowed, preparing for the worst.

Arvo and Edvard went straight to work leading anyone they could find out of the city. They ushered the citizens street by street, making quick work to direct the people while dodging the chaos and crowds. Upon reaching the first river, Arvo's heart sunk. He overlooked the rest of Saint Evedis, its labyrinth of roads, the zigzag of bridges atop of streets, the series of large towers to get through—how could he do all this in time?

Alice. Viviane, and the rest of his team came not long after.

"We haven't come across a single guard. We're going about this all wrong," Alice said.

"She's right. We need to start at the palace. Chances are Nora and Ber are still there, we can find a better plan of action there."

Arvo turned to Alice, "Alice, is it? I need you to lead me there. Please."

Alice nodded. With reins in one hand and Viviane's arm in the other, she dashed down the web of streets towards the palace.

The palace air was eerily silent. Alice found it more haunting than when she left, something she did not think was possible. Way down the courtyard she and Arvo spotted troop movement. Before they could flag them down, the hawk atop Arvo's shoulder made a shrill cry, batting its powerful wings at his expense. Arvo craned his neck to find a large beast descending on them. The beast landed beside them in the courtyard. A tall woman descended from its back, jogging towards them.

Alice blinked. "… Lieutenant Amund?"

Amund laid her icy eyes on Alice, then on the rest of the group. "You're back—and with more kids?! You are putting you and your friend's lives in danger. *Leave!*"

Arvo's bird shrieked once more. It seemed to want to challenge Amund's beast, despite the creature's utter disinterest as it loomed over the horses. Amund focused on the bird for a moment. Upon recognizing the hawk, a red strip of leather attached to its leg, her eyes widened.

"You," Amund said, approaching Arvo, "Did you send those warnings to us?"

Arvo looked down to her from his horse. From his position, she still looked quite intimidating to him. "Y-yes, Madam…?"

"You have my deepest thanks. This city is greatly indebted to you for your service. Those early warnings bought us a great deal of time to evacuate," She paused, "You can call me General Amund."

They rushed the group to a small annex, pushing the door open to a planning room. She swept the leftover items from an earlier meeting aside. She retrieved a large map and sprawled it over the table.

"I have here a map reflecting Saint Evedis evacuation protocol. Due to legislation beyond my control, many safety protocols such as this were deemed to be not useful, insisting our defense could handle any threat," Amund's hand ran down the canvas, "It's for this reason that our protocol is outdated. Population booms, changed layouts, faulty exit routes—all of these are going to prove huge setbacks in getting everybody out in time…"

Arvo scanned the map from where he entered. His guild rounded up every person they could find up until the southern branch of the river. He took in the few rows of streets they managed to help, before looking at the sea of streets forming the rest of the city. Edvard came up beside him. With his finger he traced up from the entrance to the palace courtyard.

"What are these circles?" He asked.

"Public transit trains. They only move around the inner circles. I'm certain they are deactivated by now." Amund moved to the lines jutting out from the circles. "Exports from freight trains are transferred in the stockyard here to external rail systems. These have been deactivated because of the civil unrest."

"If we start back up the trains, it's possible we could move hundreds of people at once to the exits," Edvard said.

"Even if we *do* manage herd people onto the trains, it won't be much use. The rails are locked to only move within the circle."

"Not if we force the track onto the freight route."

Edvard placed a fountain pen on the diverging routes of the map. He clenched his fist, willing the metal pen to curve perfectly in line with the freight route. Amund read Edvard's face. Golden eyes glinting up at her, he wore his confidence well. She leaned over the table to meet his gaze.

"I'll be blunt with you. At this rate, there is no feasible way to move all these people quick enough by our current means…" Amund said, "…Which is why I'm willing to rely on you for this absurd plan. But I need proof you can shift those rails without killing everyone."

Whines and screeches rang out from the wall behind her. Mounted spears gave into Edvard's command, shaping into two miniature rails. He pulled his fist back slowly, and the model rail path shifted.

Dyr observed his creation. If they weren't pressed for time, she would have spent more time admiring the craftsmanship.

"I spent my youth as an engineer on a whaler ship. I can't imagine starting up those trains could be much harder to maneuver."

A quiet air filled the room. In a moment of solidarity, they all understood what had to be done. A little voice spoke out.

"Saints… We're really doing this, aren't we?" Viviane asked, "Can it be done?"

Amund nodded, "There's only one way to find out."

From there Amund mapped out a plan. Edvard, Hel, and Amund were to head straight to the transit's center station to prepare the trains for loading. After, Amund was to meet up with the rest of her troops alongside Alice, Viviane, and Arvo to redirect inner city movement to the station. They set off on horseback, carrying on the plan from there.

"What about the outer parts of the city?" Arvo called out, "Surely you're not suggesting they fend for themselves!"

"I won't let that happen," Amund assured, "All our trains combined can't load every citizen. After I make sure Edvard's team has everything covered, I'm helping my troops escort everyone else out. What you do from there is up to you and your desire to live."

"Alright, but what about Nora and Ber? I thought they would be with you." Alice said. *And what about Maeve?*, she wanted to add, but she knew the answer to that already. She considered the Queen was likely escorted all the way to Mill Town by now. Still, she found a part of herself still worried.

Amund frowned, "They went to buy the city time. The fog had a package deal with a huge beast coming to wreck the city… All we can do is wait for their return."

"Saints, they're alone with that thing?!" Arvo asked.

"They have backup. Between their skills, I trust that they will return… And I trust they know when to quit."

"Let's—let's just focus on evacuating everyone. We just need to pray they are here before we leave," Viviane said.

They split ways for Amund to help Edvard start the trains. Though she had only basic knowledge on anything involving trains, Amund grew an aching suspicion that something would go terribly wrong if she weren't there to lead this absurd mission.

Her suspicions proved to be true when she arrived at the station. Only a few train cars were connected, while the others were cast aside for maintenance. Other cars sat on the opposite side of the boarding platform.

She cursed herself for already dismissing her beast. She rushed out briefly to call for her return. "Moving these things back on the train is going to take manpower we just don't have… let's do what we can for now."

Edvard nodded. He could manipulate weapons and rails, but an entire car was another story. He eagerly climbed inside the engine room of the train. He marveled at the advanced mechanisms inside, wishing he had time to study the board.

"Do you think you can maneuver this thing, Edvard?" Amund asked.

"*Absolutely,*" He answered, attempting to curb his enthusiasm, "I'll need a few minutes to boot up the engine."

"Meet back up with us when you do."

Amund proceeded to the first lone car alongside a woman with their guild, a masked blonde. The woman toggled the manual switches near the rails, changing direction to line it up to the rest of the train. With a confirmation from Amund, she rushed back to help push the car. Unlatching the brakes in tandem, they attempted to push the car.

"I have to ask, how are you related to this lost, Miss…?" Amund asked.

"Call me Hel. I'm their guild's seamster and shaman."

"That's… an odd combination of skills," Amund forced her whole body against the car to urge it to budge, "you wouldn't happen to have metal aura on your list of skills, would you?"

"Nope—!" Hel grunted between pushes, "I'm here in case we need another power supply! I wouldn't be much help out there with Arvo anyway—The mask scares people."

"Fair enough."

After a minute or two of force, the car had barely moved. Hel called over Ed's steed Magnus. She recruited the massive dog to pull from the other side. His paddle-like tail could be seen from the opposite end of the car, swishing wildly. After a few more tugs, the car lined up with the others.

Dyr's beast swooped in from the arched entryway, awaiting instruction. She directed Boadicea to help in pushing the next car alongside them. She felt quite foolish as she charaded with the beast to place its taloned wings on the roof of the car and begin pushing.

"Seems like between us, the dog, and the bat, we'd make a fine circus!" Hel laughed.

"I don't disagree," Amund said, "Edvard, whatever you're doing, wrap it up! We need your help down here!"

Edvard did not answer. In a field of polished steel machinery, he took a moment to acquaint himself with his surroundings. At least it seemed to work much like his old ship. Edvard methodically went down the line of valves and levers, activating the power and setting gear to drive. He smiled to himself, satisfied that his old muscle memory was useful for something after all these years. All that needed to be done now was to wait for the engine to warm up.

With a long whine and a creak, Amund heard the engine roar to a start. It echoed down the empty station, spouting clouds of pearly steam. Edvard hopped out from the engine room and ran towards Amund and Hel. He rolled up his sleeves and began helping with their car. Edvard focused himself on the car and began to will it forward. It gave way much easier than before, but still proved to be dreadfully heavy and slow to move. He went down the train line, securing each link with a flick of his wrist.

"It almost looks like you're enjoying this, Ed!" Hel said.

"This isn't *entirely* awful, I suppose," Ed said, looking away, "Amund, how many more cars do you reckon we need?"

Dyr assessed the cars they aligned so far. Despite its ornamental exterior, the cabins held plenty of seats, rows of polished wooden benches.

"All of them."

—

Alongside Arvo, Alice and Viviane scouted the streets, escorting citizens towards the central station. People of all walks of life were herded to their best ability—children, adults, and elders alike hurried along in fear of the unknown coming their way. Forcing their way against the crowd came guards and their Officer. The man practically barreled into Arvo.

"What is the meaning of this?! We have orders for escorts towards the gates!"

"We have word from Amund to redirect the inner city to the center station for transport."

"Says the lowlife," The man chided.

Slowly, Arvo dipped his hand into his shirt pocket. He unraveled the note and read it verbatim. "Code 513 from Amund: Movement within inner sectors must move to the Saint Evedis Centre Transit, effective immediately."

The Officer snatched up the note. He scanned the message, his brows threading together as he read. "But the transit's deactivated...?"

Arvo removed the note from the man's harsh grip. "We've a team working on that now. We don't have much time—just tell your troop and get it done."

With one more incredulous glance over the shoulder, the Officer marched off with his men. Looking back at the now crumpled note, Arvo frowned.

"Seems like even with an officiated note, people still don't believe me."

Alice peeked out of her hood once the guards were out of sight. "You might want to memorize that code. I've an aching suspicion were going to run into more like him."

Arvo looked around. Their street had traffic towards the station. Looking over to the next street over, people headed in the opposite direction.

"This is chaos," He said, "We need to alert as many guards as we can before we start escorting. I wish we could work on both but there's just not enough of us for that."

Viviane solemnly nodded, "I pray Nora and Ber make it out of—well, whatever they are fighting."

"They've mopped the floor with hellspawn before, I'm sure they'll be fine," Alice assured.

"I saw the fog, and that thing. Whatever else is in that fog, Alice... it's too much for anyone to handle. I hope the General's right. I hope they know when to quit."

63

Chapter 63

To Nora, the fight ended in an instant. Her blade struck into the beast a final time. Shadows surged into the mark, and she saw a flash of bright, white light. When she came to, she found herself in Ber's arms. He smiled weakly, tears streaking his face.

"What happened…?" Nora asked.

"You gave us more time," Ber hugged her, "Thank you."

Nora hissed in pain. She felt a sharp pain in her torso when she moved. Ber apologized profusely, to which she dismissed.

"I know you had to do it, but I—" Ber's tried, "I was s-so scared that…"

"Near-death experiences tend to be an occupational hazard among both of us at this point…" Nora said. Ber laughed weakly through his tears. "… But I'm sorry to make you worry."

—

They returned to an entirely changed Saint Evedis. People scrambled the streets, flooding every path to evacuate. Even with the wind's howls flooding her ears, Nora could hear Lotte's labored breathing. Ber filled her in that after leaping off, Lotte was struck by the ox's horn. The dragon's breath grew heavy as they traveled back, struggling to keep her neck upright as she flew. They descended onto a store roof with a clumsy landing. Nora winced as she slid down from her dragon. The sudden pressure as she dropped down ran a shock through her abdomen. She shook it off the best she could and checked over Lotte. Patches of scales on her drooped neck and tail were disheveled, and her wings were spread wide open.

"Lotte, can you still fly?"

Lotte looked to Nora, pupils blown wide. She nudged herself onto Nora for comfort. She took that as a no, and gently held her dragon.

"We're going to find help, alright?" Nora said.

Ber glanced over the streets below, trying to trace out a route to Central, or a plan of action in general. He pushed himself to ignore the fog, it's veil now visible from the city. The hawks delivering warnings had long since left, all except one.

"That hawk… Do you think Hearth might be here?"

"There's only one way to find out… and we're certainly of no use unless we know what's happening."

They made their way towards the hawk, praying for any signs of Amund, or Arvo, or anyone they recognized. Nora and Ber weaved through the crowds. The flow became so thick, Ber had to force bodies out of the way. Finally, the smallest break in the crowd appeared as people weaved around a set of folk on horseback.

"Nora!"

Alice saw her first. She threw herself from her horse and into a bear hug with her. Tailing behind came Viviane and Arvo. Nora did not recognize Arvo for a moment, as weariness turned his face sunken.

"Ribs're bruised, Alice," Nora choked, and Alice muttered an apology, "Please, take us to General Amund."

"You got it," Arvo said.

To relieve Lotte of some weight Ber opted to ride with Arvo, after Nora promised she was fine enough to hold onto Lotte. Together they took off, riding toward central station. Nora cursed how rough land travel was on dragons. Each bound shot bursts of pressure and pain through her abdomen.

Once they arrived at the station's platform, Nora practically fell from the saddle. Ber managed to catch most of her fall.

"Thank you,—I'm fine." Nora managed.

Nora rose slowly and met the eyes of Amund rushing over.

"Are you right? Come, sit down," They ushered Nora to a station bench. She moved to check her bruised face, to check for other wounds, but restrained herself, "... Tell me what happened."

"We... we killed the beast. It's gone."

"And your wounds...?"

"Lotte was struck, and I fell. I'm fine, but Lotte needs attention."

Amund watched her as she spoke, her face unreadable. "...You and Ber, and Lotte too, might have given us enough time. I can't thank you enough... And I'm relieved you made it back."

Nora ignored the pang in her chest. "What did we miss when we were away?"

Amund explained everything. She told them about the desperate movement to get everyone out of the city. She told her about Arvo's team rushing in alongside Alice and Viviane. After negotiation, the team earned her trust to help in the emergency. Amund explained the new plan, to gather the centralized citizens onto the train and escape to the cargo yards outside the city. "... I wish I could have had a more solid plan for this. But I'm fortunate that your guild here made the ideas we had possible."

Nora took a moment to take in her environment. On the opposite platform laid the passenger train, with linked cars shooting all the way to the outside of the station. She was relieved to see Lotte in a safe space for now. Along with the Amund's bat, Edvard's whalehound, and several horses, even the central station was beginning to feel like a full house. Nora figured that Edvard and Hel were working in the engine room. Herds of people already crowded the platform to board. Weighing the size of the crowd, Nora knew much more work needed to be done.

"General, where do you need me next?" Nora saw concern rise in Amund's face. Before she could speak, Nora cut in, "I can still work. I can still fight. Give me something, give me anything so I can help."

"You can't sit still, can you?" *Some things don't change.* "You can Arvo's team to shepherd people here, but I'm going to count on you to keep an eye on that fog. Come to me when we're running close on time, or something changes."

Nora forced her unsteady feet together to solute Amund, accepting the mission. With Lotte's poor condition, Nora coaxed the beast into staying put while she saddled up a horse. Amund watched Nora leave once again, and into the city with her team.

Before they could hop on the horse upon leaving the station, Viviane threw her arms up to embrace Nora and Ber. They squeezed around Nora's frame, shooting pain through her ribs. She hissed in pain, and she fell back.

"S-sorry, I forgot," Viviane said, "But I'm so happy you're okay!"

Nora mustered a smile. "Why did you come back? Did something happen?"

"We ran into your friends here on the road." Arvo looked down to Nora and Ber, "I'm not sure if I'm pissed or impressed that you took on the bull by yourselves… Either way you have my thanks. You gave us a fighting chance."

"What needs to be done, Arvo?" Nora asked.

"We made progress reversing traffic to go towards the station, but there's just so many streets. And so many… unyielding guards. I want as much street coverage as possible, yet I don't want us spread too thin with those damn mutts around…" He glanced down at Nora and Ber, clad in their filthy uniforms, "… Right, you're with them. Sorry."

Ber shrugged, "Don't apologize, they *are* mutts. And for the time being, so are we."

"You can leave the guards to us. Cutting the negotiations will give you more time to help everyone," Nora said.

Arvo nodded, "Alright. We'll have you work from here and clockwise around the Middle Ring… If we have time, we can check to make sure the Outer Ring has been fully evacuated."

With that, they set off to enable their new plan. Arvo, Alice, and Viviane followed behind Nora and Ber as they approached the guards. Nora barked new orders to anyone in uniform she could find. After the fifth street, she recited her codes from memory.

"… You doing alright?" Ber asked.

"Just fine," Nora rasped.

"Let's take a break on this."

Nora nodded, signaling to Arvo to focus on the streets they received clearance on. Ber spotted one of the city's many suspension bridges held a recently abandoned service lift. He took Nora and activated the pulley system to the top. They could peek just over the outer wall. They did not need much more leverage, as the fog was already brimming at the southern gates. Floods of cityfolk changed direction accordingly. Even from afar, Nora and Ber watched as the adjacent streets packed in with bodies. Nora felt a twinge inside her, and a haunting sense as she witnessed the panic and pleas for help among the crowd. It grew apparent to her.

"We can't save them all," She thought aloud.

Ber's hand laid on her shoulder, "... I know. Let's... we need the focus on the Middle Ring for now."

Nora fell silent. They dropped back into the city again.

—

Together, Nora and Ber paved what was left of the Middle Ring for Arvo's forces. Nora's voice went from hoarse to weak, so Ber took over alerting the guards.

Coming across their last street, hope for reaching the rest of the city dimmed as the sky was drained of all color. Hope died altogether upon their view of the fog. Its contents spilled far into the city, its opaque nature obscuring everything inside.

From the fog fled little pale creatures. Nora froze as they spread from the streets and sky. Like the abominations she faced before, their movement was unnatural.

Ber's color drained from his face. "I-I've *never* seen so many of those rotten things. Nora, we need to cut our losses— *Now.*"

Upon returning to the station, the group was swept up in more chaos. From what Nora could see, the train was already packed, with only a few more train cars on the end to be boarded. The massive domed station, vacant just an hour before, was rampant with panicked citizens and shouting guards. Amund was among them, pacing up and down the platform and screaming orders. She could recognize Nora's face in the crowd and strode over, cutting through crowd like air.

"Middle Ring's evacuated, but I have doubts they will all fit here," Arvo said.

"They won't. What is left of my guards will escort whomever remains." Amund said.

"You can't do that," Ber managed, "There's—we saw monsters leaving the fog."

"Is it something the Guard can handle?" Amund asked.

"… I don't know."

Amund looked to Ber, her gaze shooting through him. Her face remained unreadable as she weighed her options. "Well, it seems we don't have much of a choice. Tell the guards right away."

He did as she said, excusing himself. Before he left, Ber looked to Nora. "You need to rest."

Reluctantly, she nodded. Both her torso and her throat felt like they were in a vise. "… to Lotte…" She managed to say.

Alice and Viviane waited beside her, helping her into a shoddily connected freight car. Among hefty crates and several other large beasts laid Lotte. In a time of crisis, the beasts settled beside each other with no fret. They knew to weather the storm. *If only humans were the same.*

Lotte's breathing still was strained, but the dragon seemed to ease up upon seeing Nora. Viviane and Alice helped her down slowly to the floor beside Lotte. Viviane held her hand a moment longer.

"We'll be back soon, alright?"

"And save me a spot in the barn," Alice winked.

Nora mustered a smile and nodded. Left alone with her dragon, she pet the side of her face. All she could do now is what she hated most. Do nothing and wait. She tried to prove to herself she could keep helping by standing up, but her head swirled, and she felt uneasy. Her torso rang out again in pain as she sat back down, defeated.

Nora waited for what seemed like hours. It gave her a familiar feeling when she used to watch the days pass in the pasture. She grew accustomed, even skilled at watching and listening during those times, so it at least gave her something to do.

Crowds seemed to blur by—large and small, lively and weak. All were all crammed into the station, herded with little order into what was left of the cars. A guard closed their door. Nora tried to pick out individual voices in the crowd. Lost children screaming, confused folks searching for answers, and shouting guards flooded her ears.

"Our final car is now boarding! Please, give your seat to those that need it!" As soon as the voice rang out, another called, "We are asking for no further boarding! I said *no further boarding!* Everyone else will come with us— You'll escorted out of the city!"

Roars in anger and panic echoed through the station, as countless bodies tried to push through.

Violent clamor broke out on the boarding docks near Ber. He spotted guards and citizens alike forcing themselves into the already crammed cars. At first the families and guards pleaded with one another to get in. Patience broke when a guard pushed a passenger out and onto the station floor.

Other guards flanked their comrade's side, blindly joining in to take action. Ber could not tell exactly when it started, but when he saw a wave of passengers fall as guards forced them out of the car, he was already running. Without thinking, he forced his body between the guards and the passengers. The guards halted a moment upon recognizing him, before pushing him aside.

"Stand by or stand down, Blødeks."

"No. Let them board."

They shoved him again. And again. One guard bound his hands as the others forced him to the ground. Under the weight of so many people, and the yelling, the uniformed bodies pressing him further and further down, Ber felt the urge again. He was trained to fight dirty, to fight like a beast. He wanted to hear them cry under his boot. Not only did he want to, he *could* do it. *They were trained weak. I could take them all. Only then will I be safe.*

Then Ber remembered Nora. He remembered when they first entered the academy, she held his hand as they drowned in a crowd of other soldiers. She did the same when he broke after a especially rough day and a sparring session gone wrong. He swore he still felt her warmth around his hand.

Ber held onto the feeling. He pushed his urges back, settling to lash out with a sweep of the leg. Enough guards went tumbling down for Ber to get back on his feet, as well as the passengers. For a moment he turned to meet their gazes on him, and back at his fellow guards before rushing out of the station altogether. Guilt stung him as the image burnt into his memory. They weren't just running from the other guards, they were running from *him. A guard is a guard, after all.*

Ber did not dwell on it long, as the commanding officer pulled him up by the lapels. He recognized the jowly man immediately as Officer Doubek. Judging by the squint in his eyes, he recognized Ber as well.

"You were instructed to *stand down,* Private."

"Does it look like I care?" Ber said, "They need *our* protection, and your guards started shoving them aside to help themselves!"

The Officer threw the first fist at Ber. Ber swiftly dodged only to have another fist strike his stomach, and another to his eye. He doubled over, spending all his focus to stay on his feet.

"Listen here, you little punk," Doubek began, "I don't see what Hare sees in you. You've no right to call yourself a guard. If I had it my way, I would have let you suffer with the rest of the dogs like you under infantry."

"That's enough, Doubek." Amund said as she marched towards them.

"General Amund," He saluted. Reluctantly, he took his hands off Ber. "Thank the Saints. I need reinforcement on Blødeks, he's interfering in operations and challenging authority."

"Be as it may, I saw enough to know that your 'operations' were not what I assigned."

"General, If I may—"

"What made you think that endangering the civilians, the one you *swore* to protect, was part of the evacuation?"

"Surely you're joking…!" Doubek retorted. His steely stature began to visibly waiver, as he fumbled for the right words.

"I know what I saw, Doubek. I saw my men shoving people to the ground. Now, unless you want to be prosecuted to the full extent of the law, and try to have your words heard against mine in court, I suggest you do as you were told."

Amund and Doubek fell silent. To Ber, it looked like some kind of wordless standoff. He and the other guards looked on, anticipating what might happen next. After a long moment, Doubek stepped aside.

"... Yes, General Amund." Crestfallen, Doubek struggled to save his own dignity with a straight posture as he paced off, his guards in tow.

Amund remained still for a moment more, her eyes trained on the Officer. She spared a reassuring glance to Ber as he composed himself.

"Thank you, General," Ber said. He gingerly touched the tender flesh that began to swell around his eye.

"It's my job to keep hooligans like Doubek in check," Amund began, "I've worried so much about our external affairs, I've grown lax in the wrongdoings in my own city."

"Would you have really taken that to court?" Ber asked.

"I don't think there will be a court to take this to once this is all over," Amund cracked into a small smile, "I'm just glad he took the bluff."

64

Chapter 64

Soon after, the train began to move at a crawling pace through the city. Ber watched off the side of the train, as the Central Station shrunk away. Even still, he saw those who began to evacuate on foot, looking back to their train. Their faces have long since blurred from distance, but Ber could still feel their sense of dread on him.

The fog lurked even closer towards the center of the city. More swarms of pale creatures began to emerge, unmistakable to Ber that they were the same kind that terrorized him in the fog only months before. His small team stood beside him, Alice, Viviane, Arvo, and Amund. They overlooked the same sight.

"Do you think we did the right thing?" Ber asked, hoping someone would answer.

"Whether or not it's 'right' doesn't matter. What matters is that we did *something*. Otherwise, none of these people would be alive," Amund said.

At the railing of their car Alice and Viviane held onto each other. Looking back at the palace, they watched as it drew further away until it shrunk to a set of little spires, both of them certain that they would never see it again.

Even as an outsider, the sight took its toll on Arvo. Even within the chaos, Saint Evedis was the largest, most beautiful city he had ever seen. It was held as the not only the stronghold of the entire nation, but a shelter to all wielders, an offering of a second chance. To see it now, under siege by forces he and everyone else could hardly understand, made his spirit sink.

He sneaked a glance at Amund, standing beside him by the railing. Arvo found it difficult to nail down what she was feeling; instead of being in shock or disheartened, she seemed tired more than anything else.

At the Middle Ring's border, the train slowed to a crawl.

"Is this supposed to happen...?" Arvo asked.

"No. Something's wrong." Amund took initiative, turning at her heel and pacing towards Edvard at the head of the train. As exhausted as she looked, Arvo could not help but be impressed how quickly she got to work. Her steely attitude to just about everything seemed awfully familiar.

A few, quiet minutes passed between them all. Looking at the streets below, Alice spotted the same pale creatures, closing the space between them and the train. With lightning speed, myrtle vines struck the monsters. They were sideswiped and pierced with woody tendrils. Alice wondered if this was another divine intervention, or a very powerful mage. The vines looked familiar.

As she turned to alert Arvo and Ber, screeching metal pierced their ears. They followed the sounds to the left side of the train. Surviving pale beasts began to cluster, recklessly damaging the windows to get inside.

Alice found herself on her feet. Viviane linked their fingers together a half second more to flag her attention.

"The passengers—"

"Go. Make sure no one's hurt." She gave Satya to Viviane and dashed off.

Alice effortlessly scaled to the top of the train, sprinting towards the threat. Ber stayed in tow, with Arvo close behind. Pale bodies drew close, gathering from the rails and scaling up to the car roofs. They wasted no time sprinting forwards to attack. Arvo breathed out, stepping in front of his party as he aimed his bow at the maw of the first lunging beast.

—

Amund marched down lanes of each car to the engine room. She ignored the looks and hushed tones of why the city's General seemed ready to crack a skull. She decided to stay satisfied in the fact that they stayed out of her way.

"What is the meaning of this, Edvard? Are your plans to evacuate by next month?" She asked, unbothered to make an introduction before barreling through the door.

Edvard's eyes stayed threaded to the rails ahead. He remained vigilant that all the levers and switches were in order. "I'm in charge of conducting the train, remember? I don't know what's happening with the power, and I can't exactly leave my post."

Amund cursed under her breath. She had a feeling her normal sling of threats would not work on a vigilante, let alone Edvard's attitude.

"Then where's the engine room? Where's Hel?"

"Downstairs."

Amund's coat billowed behind her as she rushed down the stairs. Before she could speak, Hel turned.

"General Amund! Glad you're here."

"What is the meaning of this? Why're we slowing down?"

"Well… I can lay on a case of good news and bad news."

"I don't have time for these games, Hel."

Hel ignored her. "Bad news is our power supply can't carry this much weight onboard, so we're stalling. The good news is I know how to fix it! …But, the additional bad news is if I try it, I might blow up the train." Hel gestured to her hands. Even while idle, Dyr could feel the immense amount of power coming from her hands.

"I don't exactly have time to find anyone else on board for this job… Should I get Arvo?"

"No. I adore him, but his aura… It doesn't get much warmer than body heat. And before you ask the others, I'm pretty sure adding wind and rain to an engine will be counterproductive to say the least."

A long, shrill screech of metal tore through the side of the engine room. From the other cars Amund heard panicked cries of the passengers.

"… What—In all Saints, was that?!"

"General Amund, you need to get up here…!" Edvard called.

Amund cursed again. *If I make it out alive, I'm taking a vacation from people.* She stepped back up into the control room to see the front window infested with beasts from the fog. They scraped at the window, recklessly wearing away their claws on the glass.

Edvard scoured the control panels for some method of defense. He set off the horn, exhaust valves, and even the windshield wipers, but to no avail. The wiper prodded the back end of an especially enraged beast, its blue eyes peering right through Edvard. Moments later the glass fractured, replacing the view with a blurred mosaic of little shards.

"... Damn it," Edvard muttered.

With a swipe of his hand, he severed a long piece of metal from the train's outer gilding. With another swipe, the metal ran through the beasts. They stumbled into the city below. What was left of the window formed webs of fractures, significantly obscuring the rails ahead.

From below Hel called out. "Is anybody going to tell me what that was just now?"

Amund stepped back downstairs. "Beasts. Lots of them. We need to get this train going now before any more show up." She cuffed her sleeves, revealing the dark marks up her arms. "Have you ever been channeled before?"

Hel barked in laughter to the point where Amund stepped back and narrowed her eyes. Maybe she chose a mad crew.

"Last time I was 'channeled' I almost died! But being as you're not an eldritch horror, I'm willing to give it another try."

—

Nora perked up at the sound of scraping metal. Jolting up from her resting spot, she spooked the beasts that meandered over to her lap. One horse, Edvard's whalehound, and a rather hefty lizard-like beast all managed to find peace and rested by her legs. She muttered an apology to the animals, spending a moment to stroke the horse's velvety nose, before investigating the noise.

She pressed an ear to the metal wall as the sound dulled back into the rhythmic lugging of the engine. Then it returned in full force. Thuds and scratches rattled through the metal, its echoes running over the car and worrying the beasts. Nora cursed. *Whatever that was, it wasn't good.*

"Wait here," She told Lotte. She pushed down the pain in her chest as she made her way to the door and headed outside.

Investigating the source of the sound was cut short, as shadows of beasts flashed over her. She heard the telltale sound of Alice's anguished groans, a sound forever burned in her from that night at the lake. She raced up one of the train's ladders as fast as her strained chest would allow. She paused for a moment to gasp for air in shallow, painful breaths.

Alice stole a glance before tossing a pale beast—some skittering monster larger than a cat—off her face and overboard. "Nora, what are you doing here?!"

Ber turned around, taking out a swine-like creature with his axe blade in the process. "You're hurt, get inside!"

It was too late to leave the fight. Nora was met with a swarm of incoming beasts. They began to encase her, pinpointing her in jabs and bites. *Just how smart are these things to gang up like this?* Overwhelmed in weight and pain, Nora knelt on the car roof.

A particular beast pricked Nora at her ribs. The sharp, excruciating pain jolted through her core. It hurt to stand back up, but it certainly hurt more to lay there and take it. She coiled back like a spring and shot a punch though the cluster, sending several beasts flying. She took a step. Then another.

"I—am going—nowhere!"

Ber rushed in to swing at the horde but fell back. From where Nora stood was her beast form. She stood on hind legs as she bit through the now-fleeing beasts, eclipsing Ber in a large shadow.

This form was different. Arvo and Alice stepped back, wary of the new beast. Before them stood an even larger, black animal meshed with fur and feathers. Long talons clacked against metal as Nora began to charge. Ber saw her look at him. He prayed that it meant Nora was in control behind those glowing eyes.

Together they ran towards the beasts, teeth and blades bared.

—

Amund breathed out as she took hold of Hel's wrist. Hel did the same, hoping to gain focus. Calamity tended to follow Hel wherever she went. She grew used to it at this point. But now, Hel could not help but feel vulnerable as the woman firmly wrapped her scarred fingers around her.

Amund lent her an inkling of her own energy, only for it to be converted into wild, sporadic branches of lightning. Hel mimicked a hyena with her cackles as light shot through the room.

Sheepishly, Hel cleared her throat. "Sorry, it just tickles."

Amund did not reply. She took in a deep breath and refocused. Nothing happened, but Hel swore she could hear a faint humming.

"Place your hand here on the engine," Amund said.

Reluctantly, Hel obeyed. She wrapped a gentle hand around a set of coils, and the engine burst back to life. Mechanical humming crescendoed as the wheels went from a soft lug to whirring with speed. The two almost lost their footing from the force.

"Thank the Saints, it worked!" Hel shouted.

"Let's not thank them just yet. Those hell spawns are still outside." As Amund removed her hand from Hel's, electric arcs shot in all directions. Before the engine room could explode, Amund slapped her hand back on Hel's and the aura stabilized. "Well, I hope you don't mind the company, Hel. Let's just hope the speed knocks those beasts off."

—

Nora tore through beasts alongside Ber, Arvo, and Alice. Her altered form seemed to dull the pain in her torso, so she relished in the ability to ward off the beasts, to be useful. Creatures lashed out with their varied bodies—wide mouths and plump bodies, large, scaled tails and snapping beaks, slender limbs and sharp spines. They served little use when matched with Alice and Ber's blades, Arvo's bolts, and Nora's sheer force.

They all crouched as the train hurtled from a trot to a sprint. What was left of the pale beasts skittered off, or tumbled down to the city below.

Alice whooped in rejoice, flaunting her lent blades at the beasts, while the rest of her party searched for the best way down from the roof of a speeding train.

Before Arvo could descend the ladder, a pair of bloodied jaws launched at him. He hurtled back, missing the brunt of the attack, but was knocked prone by the beast's force. The beast thudded down on the roof as its limbless form slithered towards Arvo, its center width rivaling that of a grown oak.

The beast was a form of serpent, adorned in glossy white scales and icy, featureless orbs for eyes. The only imperfection on the monster was its recent injury, a massive welt on the side of its face where a blunt object must have struck it.

Alice whipped the beast with water as a distraction, for a moment losing her nerve as the beast's head reared towards her. Its nostrils flared as it prowled along the roof. It feigned a strike at Alice only to instead go for Ber. Ber rolled out of the way but caught the wind as he bridled the edge of the car. Alice pulled him back before gravity could claim him. The beast lunged at her, grabbing at her waist with its translucent, needle teeth. As Alice let out a grunting scream, Nora retaliated, sinking her fangs deep into the beast's belly.

Nora took no questions and no pleas from the beast. Even if she wanted to, everything she attempted to understand coming from the serpent, and all the other pale beasts, was a garbled mess, merely with an intent to kill.

She sank her teeth down harder until her senses were drenched in the metallic scent of blood. The serpent unlatched from Alice's abdomen and lashed out at Nora.

From afar, Arvo shakily rose to a kneel as he wielded his bow. Between all the movement, he did not trust himself to make a shot to the beast's head at the risk of shooting the others. Instead, he launched numerous shots to its swollen belly, praying it would be distracted once more.

Between the eighth and ninth shot he succeeded. The beast's eyes were back on him, hissing in rage. Nora took the advantage as its head was turned.

Nora leapt, her jaws clenched tight to the beast's neck. The beast's mouth hung wide, trying to snap back at her but to no avail. Its long body writhed wildly trying to break free, nearly knocking everyone else clear off the train. Nora struggled to stay on. All she could do was dig her claws and teeth in and clench tighter. Her effort paid off with a crisp *snap,* and its massive, coiling body went limp. With the last of her power, Nora hurled the serpent overboard. She heaved and panted heavily, blood dripping from her maw, as she watched the serpent's lifeless body plummet down to the abandoned streets below.

—

From the engine room, both Amund and Hel heard heavy thunks echoing through the train. Amund pressed down the urge back to investigate. It was not like she had a choice in the matter, anyway. Moments later, Edvard called out.

"Ease up on the speed!"

"What in hell for?!" Amund yelled.

"Just do it!"

The General huffed and obeyed. She began to plan how to chastise the man if they made it out of the city alive.

Upstairs Edvard stood at the helm, onlooking the blurred mess before him on the rails. He did not wait for the engine to slow as he kicked down the splintered glass. He stepped just outside of the control room to the nose of the train.

Before him laid what remained of the beast swarm. Branches of overlapping railways drew closer. He pushed himself to remember the rail maps Amund showed him hours before, but he was running out of time. He carefully inched out of the speeding train, sensing the steel tracks ahead. He reached out his tightened fist, willing the steel to shift to the rail he hoped led to a way out.

Little footsteps sounded off again from above. White blurs crawled closer from the corner of his vision. Another fork in the road came. A white blur leapt at him. He used one fist to turn the train left, and the other to shoot shrapnel at the blur. More of them crept into view.

Edvard sighed. He reached for any metal he could use; sheets, loose screws, control panel sidings. He took another left, then another swing at the monsters. Amund and Hel were stuck downstairs. Nora was down for the count. Arvo, Ber, and their two new friends were likely off fighting the same monsters elsewhere, he reckoned. He took another slash and another turn, and prayed for rest.

—

Nora felt a gentle tug at her shoulder as she was met with Ber's weary face. He leaned into her transformed body, loosely holding the side of her bloodied face. In an odd moment of peace, Nora closed her eyes.

A black cloud encased Nora. Her body shifted to her human form. The transformation proved especially painful, as flesh, bones, and tendons shifted back around her old injuries. As the black cloud dissipated, so did Nora's vision, falling into blackness once again.

Ber felt her body go limp. He caught her before she fully collapsed.

"Gods, Nora!" Ber said, "Please be alright…!"

Ber knelt over her. He struggled to block out the whipping wind as he tried to listen for a heartbeat. He felt her chest rise after a moment of silence. He sighed, gently lifting her into his arms.

Together Arvo, Alice, and Ber carrying Nora limped their way through the train to find Viviane. Most of the train cars were laid to waste by the beast swarm. Shattered glass from the ruined windows covered the cabin floors. Passengers crammed into the center as far away from the windows as possible, horrified as they anticipated another attack. The crowds of wary faces parted for the group, caught in shock from the trail of blood they left in their wake.

They met Viviane a few cars down while she tended to injured passengers alongside a couple onboard nurses and healers. She muttered something to one of the medics before turning her attention to them, eyeing their injuries.

"What happened?"

"Eh, big snake," Alice simply replied, "I should be asking you the same thing."

Viviane clutched her other arm. The knit shirt she wore hung low as it was heavily torn and frayed. "What I hope was the same snake wreaked havoc in here, too. No one here is severely hurt, thank the Saints, but it took everything in me to drive it off."

"You *drove it off?*" Alice remembered the fresh, violet bruises blossoming on the serpent's face. "How?"

"Cast-iron skillets are quite versatile," Viviane said, "Surely I've told you this before, Alice."

Alice beamed at Viviane. She did not know whether or not to shower her in compliments or to just pick her up and kiss her.

"Let me help you all with your wounds—and *why* is Nora covered in blood!? I thought she was resting!"

"She was, but she got out." Arvo replied.

"We'll get patched up. I promise, Viv. But right now, we need to find Amund."

"I heard she was rushing to the head of the train not too long ago," Viviane said, "But *please* come right back, I don't want that going septic," she gestured to the gash on Alice's waist.

"Of course," Alice said, sealing her promise with a kiss before heading on.

The group hurried their pace as the clanging sound of metal boomed through the train from the engine room. Upon their arrival, they found Edvard, fighting off remnants of the swarm they encountered. He and Arvo exchanged a look. Arvo knew Edvard never asked for help in anything, but he knew that look meant the same.

Ber and Alice took on the swarm head on, going on the offensive to whip the monsters back out of the gaping window. Alice weakened the faster beasts with quick cuts of her blades, while Ber swung heavy blows. Arvo stayed beside Edvard as he conducted the train, slicing away at any stragglers that drew near him.

They made quick work of what was left of the swarms. What remained of the pale beasts back out the window they came. A scant few fled down the stairs to the engine room.

Alice chased the beasts down. Ber followed hot on her heels, leaving Edvard and Arvo in the control room.

Arvo took a moment to breathe, assessing the situation, and what remained of the room. Wind whipped through the room, further scattering the shards of metal and glass left from the fight. Most control panels were stripped bare, yet still proved technically functional, if he did not touch the wiring. Without a word, he joined Edvard in helping control the train.

"Did you ever think we'd be back to playing with engines like when we were kids?" Arvo asked.

"I'd hardly call this 'playing,' But I'd always hoped…" Edvard said. He grunted, pulling a heavy level to switch gears. "But I must say, the runaway train is a surprise."

Edvard was rewarded with Arvo's laughter. He found himself chuckling as well, as the two grown kids worked together.

Downstairs, Ber and Alice found the monsters in a last-ditch effort for blood. They bounded, scuttled, and soared towards Amund and Hel. Amund did all she could with one free hand, attempting to ward the beasts off with daunting storms of shadow, but to no avail. Ber was not used to seeing the two as defenseless targets, as they stood at the center of the room, their bodies stuck to the engine.

Alice changed pace, sheathing her blades in exchange for her shards of ice. Ber instead opted to protect Hel and the from both monsters and possible rogue shards. Despite this, Alice struck every last monster down with pinpoint accuracy, before dissipating her daggers back into water.

Amund composed herself, turning her attention to Ber. "Where is my daughter?"

"Nora's being seen by a healer. She looks rough, but I think she should be fine."

Hel whipped her head up to Ber, and then Dyr. "You're a mother?! You're the mother to *Nora?!*"

"Focus, Hel," Amund reminded her. Her warning proved unhelpful, as Hel was beaming, continuing to beg for details.

"We can tell you everything later, I promise. For now, let's just focus on leaving the city."

"You got it!"

From above, the group heard a clunk, and a series of whirs. Edvard called out from the mechanical harmony.

"Ease off the engine! General Amund, we need your assistance!"

"Needy for such a proud man…" Amund complained.

"Tell me about it," Hel chimed, as the two carefully removed their hands from the engine.

Hel stayed behind as Amund, Ber, and Alice scaled up to the control room, now more of an observation deck as a third of the room was blown open. The whipping wind fell to a soft howl as the train slowed. The train coasted through a small portal in the once-thought impenetrable wall, out of the doomed city and into the countryside.

—

Viviane took her time patching up Nora.

"I know you did what you needed to but…" Viviane struggled to find the right words, "… But with what happened to Alice, and then Ber entering that tournament… I didn't want to see you, or anyone else hurt."

Nora looked away. Even if she could speak to defend her case, she knew she could not justify her actions. She could handle the guilt of worrying the others (hardly), but it stung when she worried Viviane.

Viviane dabbed the few abrasions around her chin and neck.

"Are you able to speak?"

"I think—so. Getting—better."

"Stay quiet for now. Let's get that voice soothed, at least a little."

"I wish I could re—pay you, for everything you've done— for me."

"You already have so many times, dear."

65

Chapter 65

Queen Maeve refused to rest before each ring began to evacuate. As expected, she was met with much confusion. But since the results of Alice's trial and the upheaval of her counsel, no one dared question her commands.

Among her commands, of course, was a mass exodus of the palace itself. Only bare essential staff stayed behind for a while longer, the Lieutenants commanding from Central, medics, and a determined archivist. Even her wolverine she requested to be taken out of the city. Though it was a war beast in times past, the thing was more docile than most lap dogs and needed protection. With everyone gone and all her commands put into order, Maeve finally had time to breathe.

She watched as beasts and man fled the city. The air grew colder. Saint Evedis was running out of time. With a city so expansive, Maeve figured it to be impossible to get everyone out.

Maeve paused, gazing down from the railing of a bridge. The Evedis River rushed silently downstream. *Perhaps I can buy some time.*

Maeve rushed through the palace gardens. She carried a key to an unassuming grotto, protected by rusted gates and overgrown weeping willows. She was pulled from her path by a pull to the shoulder.

"… Maeve… Maeve!"

"Jamesson," Maeve said, "*why* are you still here?"

"I was looking for you. I figured you'd be too stoic to evacuate with the others."

"Saints, you piss me off. But it's nice to see you."

"What do you need?" Jamesson asked, "Better make it count– you might not have a city to govern after all this."

"I need to access the Evedis Headwaters. I could use the extra hands while I do what I need to do."

"Vague, but alright."

Maeve and Jamesson entered the nearby grotto that held the Headwaters. It welled from an underground river, and its mouth laid within the grotto.

It was considered a most sacred place, as only the royal family was allowed access to its waters. Maeve, along with most of her family, hardly stepped foot here. The tradition was nearly forgotten with the turn of modernity.

One of the few royals that embraced the old traditions was Maeve and Alice's mother, the last true Queen of Saint Evedis. It was for that reason she and the King were buried here. Their funeral was the last time Maeve stepped foot in this place.

Maeve figured Alice was too young to remember any of it. But for Maeve, it was more than her parents' deaths. It was the turn of a nation, she told herself. But selfishly, she regarded it as the day she had to grow up.

Jamesson watched as Maeve sunk her hands into the water. He stood at attention– the waters here ran especially swift and deep.

Maeve tried to tune into the river's latent power. Well versed in history and tradition, Maeve knew how to request power. But in practice it was a much more difficult feat.

Saint Evedis himself asked for power at the Headwaters many centuries ago. Even Alice awakened her aura not far downstream. But when Maeve focused, she felt nothing.

She made a prayer.

Saint Evedis... ancient waters, I request your aid... Please we are in dire need of your power. Your city is in danger. Please lend me your strength so I may protect her.

Still, nothing.

For the first time in a long time, Maeve experienced self doubt. There was talk of Maeve's legitimacy. Looking through old diaries, it was clear her mother had her own vices.

But Maeve looked enough like her father, right? *Alice certainly does...*

The static silence began to speak volumes. No one would help her.

Maeve considered maybe it was not about bloodline. *Perhaps I'm not worthy.* She carried herself like the epitome of perfection. The truth was she made many, many mistakes.

She made the mistake of trusting her advisors. She made the mistake of not questioning their methods sooner. She made the mistake of letting fear take over, of poisoning her sister.

The most sobering mistake of all was that she refused to listen to the warnings of the fog before it was too late.

Whether or not Maeve held the Evedis bloodline, she was certain of one thing; she was not worthy of any blessings.

Maeve sunk her arms deeper into the rushing waters, her long braids grazing its surface. She prayed once more.

Please, I beg of you. Allow me to protect this city in the one way I can. I understand now I was never meant to rule. Let my protection be the one feat I will not fail.

Maeve felt something on the air she was familiar with– she sensed hesitation.

A quiet moment passed. The river stopped flowing. What Maeve did not know was that its waters retained memory. The Evedis River held generations of knowledge, of decisions made. Beneath the icy waters a hand reached for Maeve's. The waters listened.

Jamesson by as Maeve did– whatever it was she was doing. At any other time, he would challenge Maeve's decisions, but now he hoped whatever she was accomplishing would be enough.

She's been still for a while...

He looked to the rusted gates he locked behind them. Yellow-grey clouds loomed overhead. Throughout the palace he heard news of the invasion in passing. It started with jokes; surely nothing would get past the walls. Save, of course, for the weather. When the fog began to descend, the panic set in.

Palace attendants began to set forth their escape. But Jamesson stayed for Maeve. He wondered how helpful he really was to her. He certainly was not built to guard.

Jamesson looked back to Maeve. She knelt beside the Headwaters, deathly still. He did not pretend to know what magical ritual she might be performing, but worry began to set in. *Should it be taking this long?*

The monsters could come any minute. Jamesson approached to check on Maeve, but what he saw, he was at a loss to understand. She appeared to be in a wakeless trance. Her face was expressionless, save for tear stains along her cheeks. Her eyes were wide, glowing a brilliant green.

Before Jamesson could do anything, vines rose around her. These were not the same she would typically summon.

The vines towered over Jamesson, as grand and tall as the oldest elms in the garden. They took root, their mass shifting the ground like an earthquake, spreading out of the Headwaters, out of the garden, and throughout Saint Evedis.

Maeve was no longer in the Headwaters, not mentally. She had never experienced her aura in this way, as she 'saw' through the vines she grew. But something, someone else was guiding her.

Maeve witnessed the city in chaos. Pale beasts of all kinds clambered up the walls and towers in search for fresh blood. Though most folk had already fled, the beasts aimed to snuff any stragglers out.

Maeve swiped at the beasts. One after another, the beasts were slashed and tangled in her tendrils. Her aura branched throughout Saint Evedis like lightning and nearly as fast.

—

When Maeve came to, she found Jamesson holding her beside the river, its flow returned. The whites of his eyes were stained red.

"Thank the Saints. I thought I was going to lose you," He sobbed, "Are- are you hurt? What happened?"

Maeve was unsure how to answer. Every muscle felt a sort of weariness she had never experienced before.

"I wiped out so many monsters… but not all of them. We need shelter."

"Is… it too late to leave?" He asked, hardly above a whisper.

"There's an old escape tunnel. Deep underground. We can try it."

Jamesson swallowed. "Can you stand?"

Maeve willed herself to stand. She felt her legs buckling beneath her, but forced herself to be stable. She and Jamesson hurried through the gardens and courtyards. It was silent, void of life. It haunted Maeve.

The two entered the west wing of the palace. They went down, down deep into what was once the palace catacombs. As they fled deeper, the passageways appeared noticeably older. Their presence made here made Maeve uneasy. She and Alice never dared to explore this far down, even as adults.

Maeve and Jamesson made their way down the final passageway. They reached a set of mechanisms that stuck out against the ancient walls.

"What is this place…?" Jamesson asked.

"These tunnels were part of the original temple here. A few decades ago it was repurposed as an emergency evacuation route."

They reached the end of the long hall, coming to a single lift. Maeve flipped the switch. Mechanical clunks echoed down the hall, and the cables in the lift shaft whirred to life.

The dusty meter illuminated. Its flickering light showed its hand on the base floor. Slowly, the hand trudged to their level.

"At least the others evacuated," Maeve said.

Another clunk echoed down the chamber, then another.

"Any chance those noises were from the lift?" Jamesson asked.

"I don't think so."

The sound of unearthly shrieks and howls drew closer. The two watched as the hand ticked tediously to the surface.

Maeve got into position to summon her aura, to form some kind of barrier between them and the beasts. When she called to her power, she was not just tapped. She could not feel *anything*. It felt like the connection to her power was cut.

The sounds grew louder. The beasts must have picked up on their scent, The two were silent. Maeve looked again at the meter. It crept closer to the surface, but not fast enough.

From the dim light of the hall, Jamesson and Maeve were met with glowing white eyes, like a sinister constellation of stars. Jamesson was not a guard, but he figured he might as well try. He stepped in front of Maeve, a desperate attempt of protection for what was to come.

"Robin," Maeve said, "I love you."

"Let's not say things we don't mean… fuck it, I love you, too."

The beasts stampeded at breakneck speed. The two only had seconds to see what came for them. The first thing coming into light were the teeth. Shaggy manes and blood-stained tusks and mandibles followed.

The lead of the pack pursued them, its fangs bared. A melodic bell chimed from behind the two.

Jamesson had a split second to react. The lift arrived, its doors opening slowly. They could pile in , but there was no guarantee the monsters could not rip them back out. Worse still, Maeve stood petrified.

He knew what he had to do. He shoved Maeve into the lift. She stumbled back and off her feet.

Jamesson reeled back. He struck the pack lead in the jaw. It bought enough time for Maeve, but not for him. The rest of the pack surrounded him. The lift door shut with a heavy *thud.*

Jamesson steeled himself, not daring to look back.

"No– *NO*," Maeve screamed out.

She reached out again in a desperate attempt for her aura, but the tie remained cut. The lift descended. Its mechanisms rattled loudly, but not enough to drown the sound of monsters tearing into Jamesson.

Maeve collapsed, crying out for Robin. The Queen sunk lower, lower. The lift cables rattled louder. For the first time, she was helpless, and utterly alone.

She clung to the lift's fencing in front of her. Through heavy tears she screamed out, her hoarse voice echoing down the lift shaft. She caught her breath, cursing the sound and thought of her own breathing. Robin deserved to live. *I do not deserve to escape after what I have done.*

Maeve was too lost in her own mind to acknowledge the sound when the cables snapped. But for Robin, amongst the cacophony of shredded flesh and rancid maws, that cable snap was the last thing he ever heard.

66

Chapter 66

Nora did not remember falling asleep. Ber was beside her, looking at the moving scenery out the train car. She did not remember the car looking like this.

"Where are we?" Nora asked.

"On another train. You've been out for a while. We managed to get out of Saint Evedis and to some kind of stockyard."

"Where are the others?"

"They're here, and a few townsfolk, too. We moved the rest of the people to freight trains to other cities. We're headed east… I think."

"I'm sorry for putting myself in danger. Sorry again for making everyone worry. For making you worry."

Ber teased, "Yeah it was kind of stupid, but I'm just glad you're alright… You hurled a snake off a train, so I can't be all that mad. You turned into a new beast, by the way."

"I did?"

Ber nodded. "Were you… Were you in control? Honestly, sometimes it's hard to tell."

Nora dwelled back on her transformation. Unlike before, she remembered everything clearly while in her state. "I think—I think I had more control than ever before."

Ber laughed. It felt out of place, but Nora appreciated the gesture. Ber let her rest for a while longer after that. He left to meet with the others.

Nora admitted to enjoying her rest in the freight car. To say the least, it was unpleasant—the fresh musk of combined animal scents hung stagnant in the air. Her sore body, and the various beasts struggled to find stillness as the car jumbled along uneven terrain. Despite all this, she appreciated the familiarity of being bundled up alongside the animals, even if they were war beasts instead of mostly-docile livestock. She considered the ride may have been more daunting if Lotte was not beside her.

In protest of her sore body, Nora stood up, hobbling over to the next train to get an update on the situation. Ber requested her to rest, but really the man should have known better by now.

—

Amund briefed the situation to Nora. While she was unconscious, they managed to arrive at the shipyard in one piece. From there, the citizens of Saint Evedis were loosely organized. Most boarded different trains— some heading the next big cities of Warcove and Felbury, others planning from there to return to their homelands, and others taking their chances towards the commonwealth islands (What was left of them, anyway). A few stragglers remained in the shipyard, anxiously awaiting their separated parties. The train she boarded now held just a few families. Together they were headed east, towards the Province of Kifitar.

"… What then?" Nora asked.

"I don't know. I believe Arvo will be addressing their intelligence later this evening."

When evening came, they all gathered in the control room. Edvard sat at the helm, listening in on the meeting while watching the terrain. Amund barred the door– the folk on board did not need any more reasons to worry.

Arvo stood at the center– at first. As he went along, the man began to pace.

"This is what we know," He began, "The nation— world I mean, that Ber, Amund, and I suppose Nora are from, plans to overthrow the political and natural order of this world. Political leader Serkan began to make connections to this world about twenty years prior, and has reached out again, now with substantial force. He's working with powerful people, likely a close knit group, as well as supernatural forces. We can infer this based on the scale of his attacks and movements… Also based on the fogs barricading and isolating the continent. We know only a handful of his team, based on our previous encounters:"

Arvo continued, "The Bachelor, Suryc Harland, political puppet and bounty hunter for Serkan. There has been no trace of him since his attack on Alice. We received far less missing persons reports, so it is our hope that his threat has been neutralized. Next there is the 'Heir', Arel Haidar. This is Serkan's right-hand man. In a way, it's a miracle we know he's involved. It gives us a gauge as to what exactly we're dealing with… which, to no one's surprise, is a lot. The Heir's intentions and whereabouts, other than to serve Serkan, are unknown."

Nora stole a glimpse at Ber. She hoped he would add some kind of information, but he stayed silent, eyes trained to the freight door. Maybe there was nothing else to add.

"The next threat we know of is the 'Collector'. The Bachelor was kind enough to let some confidential information slip, so we are hypothesizing that this Collector is the one harboring magical people and beasts… What we still don't know is how Serkan is manipulating the spiritual world, as well as how people and creatures are turning into monsters. We infer there are at least two more to Serkan's main force: For now, we've dubbed them the Disciple and the Scholar. And of course, we are also dealing with Serkan himself."

"The Light," Ber said, "This is what they call him."

Arvo nodded solemnly, "This list, of course, excludes whatever external or supernatural forces we may have to deal with. So… now would be a good time as any to open the floor for ideas, information, or anything that might help us."

Edvard was first to speak up, "The guild's received word of spiritual disturbances just east of Stromshire Province. There's reports of missing people, too. I suspect our 'Disciple' is behind this."

"Are you serious?!" Alice exclaimed, "I thought Arvo said *less* people were going missing!"

"Here in Stromshire, yes... If we exclude the thousands we just lost in Saint Evedis." The comment made a visceral response in Alice. Edvard wanted to mutter an apology, but he continued on. "Those in the cities east of Stromshire are beginning to go missing. Difference is, those that are coming back, they return changed. That's all the information we've received, but it's the best lead we've got."

"'Changed' in what way? More monsters?" Nora asked.

Edvard shook his head. "It seems people are seeing their loved ones undergo erratic behavior."

"If I can err on the side of macabre, the magic folk and beasts have to be going somewhere. *Someone* must be responsible for processing their blood," Viviane said.

"That brings me to my next point. The 'Scholar,' or Scholars. Wherever their facilities are being kept, they must be massive. With luck, our research and surveys can lead us right to them," Arvo said.

"General Amund," Edvard said, "You have the most experience of everyone here. You witnessed the start of this battle. Would you have any information on how we can end it?"

"For the record, I'm not the General of anything anymore. Just call me Hilda," She said, "There is not much I can tell you that would not be outdated information. Most of these names and concepts are new to me."

"But the Light, you know of him, yes?"

"Yes."

"If you could, write down any and all pertinent information from your time. Even if it's outdated we need any information we can get."

The conversation lasted late into the night. They solidified the plan, to head to Kifitar, and begin their research at the Hearth base from there.

—

Nora spent the night curled up, struggling for sleep. Giving up her endeavor, she gazed longingly at the rising sun. Nora laid by the corner, with turmoil and despair rampaging through her mind.

Ber knelt beside Nora, but gave her some space. "Couldn't sleep either?

You want to talk?"

She looked at him and asked, "What is there to talk about?" Nora had noticed by the red and tenderness of his face that he had broken down too. His soft voice contradicted his obvious pain.

He sat beside her, releasing a silent exhale. "I love this time of day. Did I ever tell you that? Your sunrises remind me of home. Sunsets, too."

"It must be beautiful. Maybe someday you can show me."

"I'd love to."

The sound of the rattling wheels filled the silence.

"… We saved as many people as we could, Nor."

"I know."

Together, Nora and Ber watched the sun rise. No one knew what tomorrow would bring. Ber only had some clue of what they were up against. All he knew was that it was not going to be pretty.

Then, Nora rested her head on his shoulder. A small gesture. But to Ber, it meant the world to have his closest friend at his side. For now, everything was okay. For now, it would be enough.

Acknowledgments

I'd like to give a very special thank you for the friends I made along the way— Tacky, I know. Thank you, Kaela, my bestie of twenty years, for becoming the little sister I did NOT ask for, but by God did you weasel your way into my heart. To Jeremy for being such a kind soul and utterly chaotic DM. To Alyssa, Katie, Lillie, Julianna, Brooke, Courtney, Mykal, Danny, Michelle, Teddy, and everyone else who makes my weekend a delight at book club, thank you. To the old house mates and work besties, we might not talk every day but I wanted to also thank you for your kindness and laughs when I desperately needed it. In short, friends you make in your mid-to-late twenties are built different!

About the Author

Marcel Holt (she/her/he/him) is the final boss of side hustles and hobbies. While writing this story is her main focus, she can also be found making art, cooking, working out, and cosplaying. He grew up a latchkey kid with an obscene amount of access to the internet, 90's and early 2000's anime, and video games. This love of fantasy and sick fighting sequences formed eventually into the book you are holding now. At the time of publishing, Marcel is attempting an escape from the confines of Florida.

You can connect with me on:

- https://www.instagram.com/authormarcelholt